THE LAST CONCLAVE

GLENN COOPER

Copyright © 2025 by Lascaux Media

All rights reserved.

No part of this book may be reproduced in any form or by any electronic or mechanical means, including information storage and retrieval systems, without written permission from the author, except for the use of brief quotations in a book review.

Published by Lascaux Media

Cover design by JD Smith

Title Production by The Bookwhisperer

Author Photo by Giliola Chistè.

ISBN(eBook): 979-8-9925745-2-4
ISBN(Paperback): 979-8-9925745-3-1

CHAPTER ONE

Rodrigo Da Silva had discovered that a pope is rarely alone. At his first stirrings, the nuns entered his bedroom with orange juice, tea, and his favorite biscuits. Before breakfast, he celebrated Mass in the private chapel atop the Apostolic Palace with a select few Vatican employees. He took his breakfast in his apartment in the company of Mario Santovito, his stern, black-suited valet, and the cheerful Azorean nuns of his household who wore the white habits and black veils of their order, Sisters of Mary Immaculate. The family-style meal was catered by the affable papal chef, Eduardo Antelao, who flitted in and out of the kitchen, making sure the pope, a serious gourmand, was satisfied with the hot dishes. Once settled in his library office, his private secretary, Mario Finale, walked him through the choreography of the day's meetings, audiences, and meals with the myriad clerics and laypeople vying for slices of his attention before finally, in the evening, he could retire in solitude.

Pope John XXIV rested his small feet on an ottoman, watching a British detective series on Sky Italia, and sipping an amaretto. Some popes never wore anything less casual than the trousers and collared shirt of a simple priest, but inside his living room, John enjoyed the comfort of civilian clothes, preferably one of his oversized tracksuits. On this evening, he chose the one gifted by the Boston Red Sox during his tenure as Archbishop of Boston. *Cardinal Da Silva* was stitched onto the back of the jacket in bold white script. He proudly wore it the day he threw out the ceremonial first pitch at a game at Fenway Park. His weak effort bounced twice in the grass before bisecting the diamond on a roll, whereupon the catcher, a Catholic, raised the baseball into the air and shouted, "It's a miracle!"

At eight o'clock, the pope found himself doing battle with his old adversary, hunger pangs. He had been on the losing end of this conflict all his life. After his last physical, the papal physician, an esteemed professor at the Gemelli Hospital, was blunt. "Holy Father," he had said, "everything is higher than last year. Your blood pressure, your sugar, your weight. Everything must go down. I know how you enjoy a good meal, but please, show some moderation."

"Overindulgence in food—specifically, beautifully prepared food—is my only sin," the pope had cheerfully deflected.

"Think of me, Your Holiness," the doctor had replied in a mock-pleading tone. "What will happen to my reputation if, on my watch, the pope has a heart attack or a stroke?"

With the doctor's admonitions playing in his head, the pope padded on stockinged feet into the kitchen and peered into the refrigerator. The youngest of the household nuns, Sister Maria, on duty to attend to his evening needs, heard the door open, came in, and in Portuguese, asked if he needed anything.

The pope was born in the Azores. In boyhood, he emigrated with his family to New Bedford, a fishing community in Massachusetts, a destination favored by Portuguese islanders ever since Azorean whalers flocked there in the nineteenth century. When he was elected pontiff following the death of Celestine VI, he became only the second Portuguese pope in history and the first American pope. He had lived most of his seventy years as an American, but his Portuguese heritage meant a great deal to him, and he enjoyed the attentions of the Azorean sisters.

"Ah, Maria," he said. "You're still up and about. I'm sure I can find something myself."

"But Holy Father," Maria said, "Eduardo left your favorite with instructions how to serve it."

"Really? What is it?"

"Chocolate lava cake with cream," she said with a beaming smile.

The pope patted his enormous waist and said, "Oh, my. That *is* my favorite. Don't tell Doctor Bellisario."

"It will be our secret, Holy Father."

He watched appreciatively as she warmed the small molten cake in the microwave. He made childlike sounds as she poured heavy cream over it, and accepted the plate with a heartfelt "Obrigado." He urged her to retire for the night, but she demurred and said she would wait until he went to bed.

"I know better than to argue with you, dear Maria," he said. "I'll just have this delicious treat and watch a little more TV. I think I know who the killer is."

"Holy Father?"

"On the TV show."

∽

ALONE AT NIGHT, Monsignor Mario Finale would sometimes take a moment from whatever he was doing and think about his old apartment in Rome's Balduina neighborhood. It was modest—a small studio in a post-war block of flats accessible by three flights of steeply pitched stairs that left him with heaving chest and aching haunches, but it was cozy, and it sated his material needs. He dearly missed his overstuffed couch, the bathtub, wide enough to accommodate his girth, and his well-stocked refrigerator and pantry. On days when the weather was fine, he used to give himself enough time to walk to work through the eucalyptus-lined paths of Monte Ciocci Park, and on inclement days, he would deploy his umbrella and take a quicker, more direct route that skirted the park and led to an employee gate near the Vatican museums. The portly forty-eight-year-old cleric, who wags in the Curia called Mini-Me because of his resemblance to his taller boss, reckoned that his commute of five kilometers per day had kept his weight in check. In the two years since giving up his apartment and shortening his perambulation to a mere hundred meters, he had been obliged to let out the waist of his clerical trousers, not once but twice.

Finale had been private secretary to Cardinal Da Silva at the Secretariat of State. When Da Silva was elevated at conclave, the new pope asked him to become his papal private secretary. Serving as the pope's gatekeeper, timekeeper, and constant companion was his life's honor. The career-long denizen of the Curia burst with pride every time he stepped into the Apostolic Palace. However, he needed to be immediately available to the pontiff, so Vatican residency was a necessity. And so, he moved into a room at the Domus Sanctae Marthae guesthouse until a permanent living space became available. Vatican apartments were not plentiful, and he was still waiting for one—the death and demotion watch as one of his friends described his plight. Besides, they told him, John will elevate you to bishop before long, and they'll have to find something nice for you. In the interim, it wouldn't do to complain about the modest guesthouse accommodations. After all, Pope Celestine, who had famously eschewed the finery of the Apostolic Palace, had lived just a few doors down the corridor from Finale's room. Lacking a kitchen, he took his meals in the guesthouse cafeteria, but it closed after supper, so he was obliged to keep a small store of microwaveable convenience foods in a dresser drawer and drinks in a mini-fridge. He was bent over, reaching for an orange soda, when shortly after eleven, his phone rang.

"Finale," he said gruffly.

He heard the distressed voice of one of the pope's Portuguese housekeepers, first in Italian, her third language, then in English, her second. "Monsignor, it's Sister Maria. You must come! You must come right away."

"What's the matter, Sister?"

"It's the Holy Father!"

Sweating from his dash across Saint Peter's Square, the priest arrived at the papal apartment to a chaotic scene. The front door was propped open by a first aid chest, and the reception room was filled with uniformed Vatican gendarmes and paramedics from the Vatican Corps of Firefighters. Finale pushed past them into the lounge, where he saw weeping nuns, the valet, Mario Santovito, his head bowed, and the pope's physician, Massimiliano Bellisario, still as a statue, arms folded.

"Doctor, how is the Holy Father?" Finale demanded.

The physician was not a large man, but his erect posture and sonorous voice gave him a commanding presence. "It was sheer coincidence. I was in the Vatican tonight visiting Archbishop Detratti at the Palazzo San Carlo when I got the call," Bellisario said somberly. "I came immediately. The paramedics had arrived. They were in his bedroom working on him."

"Working on him?" Finale croaked. "What happened?"

"A coronary event, more than likely," the doctor said in a faraway voice. "I tried to get him to take better care of himself."

"But it's good you were here to help him, no? How is he?"

Bellisario was staring at the rug as he spoke, but at the secretary's last question, he lifted his head and said, "He's past help. I'm afraid he's gone."

"No, no, it can't be. He can't be gone," Finale said in confusion, awkwardly shuffling toward the bedroom. "I saw the Holy Father only a few hours ago. He was perfect—full of energy, as usual." He had almost reached the threshold when a woman appeared at the door, clutching a dressing gown to her chest. It took the monsignor a blinking moment to recognize Sister Elisabetta Celestino, whom he had never seen without habit and veil. He was drawn to her moist eyes and stricken face, always pale but now completely without color. Someone knowing nothing about the Vatican might have jumped to salacious conclusions about a beautiful middle-aged woman in night clothes emerging from the bedroom of a fallen pope, but Finale understood that the nun had been hastily summoned from her nearby apartment on the third floor of the Apostolic Palace.

"Madam Secretary," Finale gasped. "It's true?"

"The pope is dead," she said. "It's a terrible shock, Mario, but we must do what is demanded of us. There will be time enough for grieving. Please summon the Cardinal Camerlengo. I'll try to reach Silvio Licheri."

Finale nodded and worked on composing himself. "Yes, of course, I'll call Cardinal Sauseda. After the camerlengo has done his duty, we need to summon the Vicar of Rome. But why Silvio? Isn't that premature? Many others must be informed first."

"There will be leaks. The Press Office must prepare a statement."

"Who else knows?"

"Only my brother, Emilio, and Commandant Studer."

Finale nodded a few times. "Yes, Studer. The Swiss Guards must protect the apartment once it is sealed." The priest seemed to remember something important. "The viaticum," he said. "Was it given?"

"According to the paramedics, he was dead when they arrived," she said. "They did their usual procedures although they knew it was hopeless. There was no opportunity to administer last rites. Besides, you're the first priest to arrive."

The Vatican Secretary of State and the pope's private secretary withdrew to separate corners of Pope John's lounge, and amidst the artifacts of a man's life— reading glasses, books, pens, personal photos, and the like—they reached for their mobile phones and began making calls.

∼

BEFORE HIS ELEVATION to cardinal by Pope Celestine, Hilario Sauseda, the Cardinal Camerlengo, had been Archbishop of Pamplona and Tudela. It was John who made Sauseda camerlengo, and when the Spanish prelate saw his body, he almost lost his balance. On most days, the lugubrious Sauseda seemed to cast a pall on even the lightest of conversations, but on this night, his dark countenance matched the mood inside the papal apartment. The principal duties of the camerlengo were pedestrian. A combination of property manager and accountant, he oversaw the department that administered the Holy See's real estate portfolio. Yet, upon the death of a pope, the camerlengo's role shifted, and for a few weeks, he became a critical figure within the Holy See. Until a successor was chosen, the Cardinal Camerlengo became the Vatican's acting sovereign, a ceremonial but visible duty, and a key participant in preparations for the coming conclave.

But the first responsibility of a camerlengo in an interregnum was to verify the pontiff's death, not from a medical standpoint but an ecclesiastical one, and those present in the apartment crowded into the bedroom to watch him perform the rite. The nuns had carefully pulled the sheets and bedclothes over the pope's body. His closed eyelids and curiously pleasant expression made it seem he was enjoying a deep slumber. And so, it seemed rather benign when Sauseda leaned over the bed and, invoking the dead man's baptismal name, asked three times in Latin whether he was sleeping. "*Rodrigo, dormisne?*"

The camerlengo dolefully proclaimed, "The pope is truly dead," and attempted to remove the Ring of the Fisherman. Despite his best efforts, the ring wouldn't budge from the pudgy finger. Elisabetta turned away at the Spaniard's exertions, weeping for the man who had chosen her to become the highest-ranking woman in the history of the Vatican.

"Doctor," Sauseda said, "I have the ceremonial shears with me, but I don't wish to tear the flesh. My eyesight isn't the best. Could you—"

Bellisario stepped forward, took the small shears, made a neat snip, and wriggled the silver ring free.

"Give it to me," Sauseda said. "In the presence of other members of the College of Cardinals, I will crush it with the hammer of my office."

It was done. The brief reign of Pope John XXIV was over. Per tradition, the camerlengo began to recite Psalm 130.

Out of the depths, I cry to you, Lord.

∼

Elisabetta and her top aides worked the phones at the Secretariat of State until four in the morning, informing apostolic nuncios, ambassadors to the Vatican, and heads of state of the death of John. Only then did she return to her apartment to catch a couple of hours of sleep before the Press Office would release the news to the general public. Seated on the edge of her bed, she pulled her mobile phone from its charger to make one last call.

It was ten o'clock in Boston. Cal Donovan had been searching for a way to extricate himself from the tail end of a blind date. It arrived in the form of his phone lighting up with *Sister Elisabetta* on the caller ID. The dinner had been arranged by one of Cal's fellow professors at the Harvard Divinity School, a self-described yenta, who felt he needed help finding a good match. The famously eligible bachelor hadn't dated for an uncharacteristically long spell, a drought completely of his own making. It had been, he thought, a breather from his torrid and exhausting history. He agreed to the date because Ruth Steinberg, Professor of Hebrew Bible, was such a dear friend.

"Ruth," he had said. "I'm not looking for love."

"Who's talking about love?" she had replied. "I'm talking about having a nice dinner."

"Who is she?"

"A friend of my sister's. She's an associate professor of biochemistry at MIT. She's smart, and she's a knockout."

"I'll bet."

"Google her, you'll see. She's divorced, no kids, age-appropriate. She's Jewish, you're Jewish."

"I'm half Jewish."

"No one's perfect. She Googled you. She told my sister she thinks you're extremely handsome. Call her."

Cal had to admit that his date was indeed smart and attractive, but he found her creepy. She had clearly done a deep dive into

Calvin Donovan, renowned Professor of History of Religion, and seemed pleased to let him know how much she knew about him. He learned from her that his father was the late great Harvard Professor of Archaeology, Hiram Donovan, that his mother had been a philanthropist who had given heavily to Jewish causes, that Cal had chosen to become a practicing Catholic like his father, that he had been the youngest full professor in Harvard's history, and that the press called him the pope whisperer because of his friendships with Popes Celestine and John. The cherry on the Cal sundae was her revelation that she knew his former girlfriend, Jessica, the CEO of a biotech company in town, and had called her to get the scoop on him.

"You spoke to Jessica?" he said with widening eyes.

"I mean, I understood you hadn't seen her for a couple of years. You don't mind, do you?"

Cal would have taken a call from Elisabetta under any circumstance, but the fact that it was four in the morning in Italy sent him up from the table. He excused himself and, on the way to the front of the restaurant, slipped a credit card to their waiter.

He answered in Italian. "Eli, hi. Is everything all right?"

"Oh, Cal, I hope I'm not disturbing you," she said. "It's just that—"

Her long pause alarmed him. "What is it? What's the matter?"

"It's the Holy Father."

He heard her choking back tears, and immediately, he knew what had happened.

CHAPTER TWO

By tradition, a pope is buried between four and six days after death. Considering various logistical issues and meteorological reports, the College of Cardinals set the funeral for the twentieth of May, initiating a mad scramble among clerics, dignitaries, and the lay public to book flights and hotel accommodations in Rome. One call from Monsignor Finale was all it took to secure Cal Donovan a suite at his preferred hotel, the Grand Hotel de la Minerve, adjacent to the Pantheon. When he arrived midday on the nineteenth, the hotel reception desk was crowded with people awaiting check-in. The hotel's general manager was on VIP alert and spotted Cal, warmly greeting him as he entered the lobby.

"I'm so glad to see you again, Professor. Welcome back to the Minerve."

"I wish the circumstances were happier, Michele."

"Indeed. Such a shock." The manager lowered his voice so that other guests could not hear him." Come with me. I can personally register you in your suite. And I have a letter for you."

Cal glanced at the envelope—it bore the seal of the Secretariat of State.

When alone, Cal parted the curtains of the Melville Suite. Herman Melville stayed in this room in 1857 and likewise had gazed down on the Piazza della Minerve. The great novelist seemed to have lost his power of exposition when he wrote too plainly about the Bernini masterpiece below his window. *In the square there is an obelisk that arises above an elephant.* Cal thought Bernini's description did the statue a profound injustice because the elephant, with its animated, tilted head, was so artfully sculpted that you could almost hear the roar trumpeting from its outstretched trunk.

He opened Elisabetta's letter expectantly. He liked its informality. To Cal from Eli. Was he free to come to her father's apartment for dinner that night? Her brother and sister would be there. He smiled and replied by text. *Yes*

⁓

THE CELESTINO SIBLINGS, Elisabetta, Emilio, and Micaela, used a WhatsApp group to coordinate the care and feeding of their father, Carlo. The retired mathematics professor was in his eighties, and while his mind was sharp as ever, his body was beginning to fail. For many of his former colleagues at the Department of Theoretical Mathematics at the Sapienza University of Rome, their physiques seemed almost an afterthought, mere superstructures for finely tuned minds. Carlo was the outlier—a bruiser of a man who happened to be a genius. He grew up the child of dairy farmers in the wild countryside of Abruzzo and, until recent years, he would return to his ancestral farm several times a year to lay dry-stone walls and mend fences. Hard labor had taken a toll on his hips and knees, and his lifelong pipe-smoking had left him with bad lungs. Now he rarely ventured from his flat on a narrow sloping street in Rome's Trastevere neighborhood. It fell to his children to ensure he was well-supped and keeping up with his ablutions. They received reports from his housekeeper, but nothing replaced hands-on visits. So, they periodically compared calendars. Each visited one evening a week, and all came for Sunday dinner. It was no small feat for three busy people to carve out the hours. Elisabetta had a vast portfolio of domestic and international affairs at the Vatican Secretariat, Emilio shouldered critical duties as the Inspector General of the Vatican City Corps of Gendarmerie, and Micaela was an overworked physician at the Gemelli Hospital.

Micaela arrived before the others, sniffed the air, and went ballistic. With her fire-engine red hair, when angry, she resembled a lit firecracker.

"Papa, where is it?"

The old man looked up from his favorite chair and put down the pencil he'd been using to jot equations. "Where's what?"

"The tobacco. Who bought it for you? Was it Valeria? I swear I'll fire her."

"Leave Valeria alone," he sputtered. "She's a good girl."

"She's forty. She's not a girl."

Through a spasm of coughing, he said. "I'm too old for a feminist reeducation. At my age, she's a girl. When is Cal coming?" He leaned forward, hacking away.

His coughing fits paralyzed Elisabetta and Emilio with fear, but Micaela was too hard-boiled for that. "What do you expect when you keep smoking?"

He managed a dismissive wave.

"He's coming in an hour."

"Good. I like him."

Cal had met Elisabetta years earlier when Pope Celestine asked for help investigating an ancient Vatican debt. Back then, the nun, an archaeologist by training, was the president of the Pontifical Commission for Sacred Archaeology, the first woman to hold the position. As Cal assisted Pope Celestine and later Pope John in various delicate matters, he came to know the nun better. Celestine made the controversial decision of making Elisabetta his papal secretary—another first for a woman—and John had gone considerably further by appointing her secretary of state, a post that had always gone to a cardinal. And as the years passed, Cal Donovan, perennial bachelor and commitment-phobe, fell in love with this unobtainable woman who was fully aware of his intentions but never wavered from her devotions. And so, he settled for friendship. He made frequent research trips to Rome, and each time he was in town, Elisabetta invited him for a family dinner. Cal had worked with Emilio on several investigations, and he liked the affable policeman a great deal. He was always entertained by Micaela, whose personality was as incendiary as her hair. But, it was Elisabetta he came to see. It was always about her.

Emilio was next to arrive, hanging his suit jacket and shoulder holster on the coat tree. He helped himself to a beer from the fridge before wandering into the living room, where he remarked on his father's sourness.

"It's your sister's fault," Carlo said, pointing his pencil at his daughter. "She won't stop. Tell her to stop, will you?"

"Stop," Emilio said to Micaela before he added, "Stop what?"

Micaela was on the sofa with a glass of wine. "I'm only trying to prevent him from killing himself."

Emilio seemed to notice the tobacco haze. "Oh, that. Please don't kill yourself, papa. We'll miss you terribly."

"It's not funny," Micaela fumed. "Your boss, the pope, didn't take care of himself, and look what happened to him."

Emilio sighed and changed the subject, eyeing his sister in her yellow blouse, green miniskirt, and pink tights. "You look colorful today," he said. "Like a parrot."

"Someone's got to brighten the place up. Look at you in your boring blue suits, papa in his gray cardigan, and don't get me started on Eli, the penguin."

They heard the front door opening and a hello from down the hall.

"The penguin is here," Emilio said.

Elisabetta removed her veil in the kitchen. As she passed the living room on her way to her childhood bedroom, she said, "The food isn't here yet. Can someone call Tonnarello and see when they're coming?"

"I'll call," Micaela said. "Can you imagine what mama would have said about ordering takeaway for a guest?"

Carlo answered, "Your mother had a vocabulary that included every swear word."

Elisabetta reappeared, silencing conversation, for she had swapped her black habit for a pair of jeans and a high-necked, camel-colored cashmere sweater, her silky black hair spilling over her shoulders.

Micaela looked up from her phone and said, "Wow."

"What?" Elisabetta said. "You've never seen me in street clothes?"

Micaela said, "All the time, but has Cal?"

Elisabetta said, "I don't recall," but quickly added, "I suppose not."

"What's the big deal?" Emilio asked. "She's not dressed like *you*, Mic?"

"Men are so stupid," Micaela said. "She's sending a signal."

"No, I'm not," her sister insisted.

"If you're truly unaware, then it's a subconscious signal," Micaela said.

"Oh, yes, Dr. Freud?" Elisabetta said, flopping onto a chair.

"We all know Cal is in love with you," Micaela said. "We all know he invited you to join the faculty at Harvard. We all know you said no. We all know you've been doing great things at the Vatican despite all the asshole men trying to undermine you. We all know the pope is dead, and whoever becomes the next pope will want their own man in the Secretariat, and I stress the word man. We all know you use your nun outfit like a force field against Cal. And we know your ugly black habit is hanging in the closet. *QED*: a signal."

Carlo grinned at her use of the Latin abbreviation for proving a mathematical theorem.

Elisabetta laughed lightly. "You're insane. I just wanted to be comfortable tonight. How many times has Cal come to dinner? He's become a family friend. Wearing street clothes in a casual setting doesn't violate any rules of my institute. Anyway, you'd make a terrible psychiatrist. When is the food coming?"

"The delivery guy is on his way. Why don't you go a little further and throw on some makeup? You can use some of mine."

"I'm fine as is, thank you very much."

Cal would have agreed. He thought of her as a natural beauty. Painting her face would be like putting lipstick on the Mona Lisa.

Carlo shifted in his chair, reached for his pipe, and stared Micaela down. "I'm not going to light it! Listen to me, Eli. This is a good time to leave that den of vipers. You made history already. Your next step is a demotion. There's nowhere to go but down."

"You make it sound like a job at a company, papa."

"More like a cartel," Micaela said.

"Oh please, both of you!" she laughed. "Your opinions about the Vatican are rather well known. Come on, Emilio, defend your sister!"

Emilio instinctively began his answer with hand gestures, but he stopped because of the beer he was holding. "I have to be truthful. Other than the Holy Father, may he rest in peace, and maybe a dozen cardinals and bishops I can think of, you never got the support and respect you deserved at the Secretariat. Plus, you're talking to the guy who's had to deal with all your death threats. I think papa's right. Maybe this is a good time to do something else. We should ask Cal what he thinks."

"We know what Cal thinks," Micaela said wickedly.

The downstairs bell rang. Elisabetta said it must be the takeout and ran downstairs to collect it.

It wasn't the food delivery; it was Cal looking sporty in a button-down shirt, blazer, and khakis. He had recently turned fifty, but if he had any gray hairs, they were well hidden in a tussled sea of black.

"I'm sorry, I must have the wrong apartment," he said with delight. "I was supposed to be having dinner with a nun."

"Maybe she's upstairs," she said. Her smile faded as she said, "Come in, Cal. It's good to see you. I'm so very sorry about your friend."

"It's horrible, Eli. I still can't believe he's gone. It's more than a loss for his friends. It's a loss for humanity. He was just getting started."

As he followed her up the stairs, Cal couldn't help spying the shapely legs never-before seen. She picked up the pace, and he wondered if she sensed his gaze.

In the living room, she announced, "It wasn't the food."

Micaela ran for a hug, and Emilio warmly took his hand. Cal made the pilgrimage across the rug to the chair of the old academic. "Professor, you're looking well."

"There's only one professor in the room who looks well, and it's not me," Carlo said. "Someone get Cal a drink. Emilio, there's half a bottle of vodka in the freezer from Cal's last visit. I assume you still like your vodka."

"You assume correctly."

When everyone had a glass in hand, Elisabetta proposed a toast. "To the everlasting memory of our inspirational friend, His Holiness Pope John XXIV."

"To Rodrigo," Cal added, slamming his shot.

When the food arrived, they filled their plates and assembled in the dining room. Cal happily lost himself in the freewheeling and animated talk around Carlo's table, so different from the formality of the family meals of his childhood. His imperious father, the great Harvard professor and scion of a monied Boston Catholic clan, insisted on wearing a suit for dinner. His mother, too, came from privilege. Her father was a wealthy Jewish New York investment banker and philanthropist, and she was raised around servants and housekeepers. As an only child, Cal suffered through deadly dinners where his parents talked over him, and laughter was in short supply. He toed a strict line until his teenage years, at which point he discovered girls and alcohol and began crossing that line in one spectacular way after another.

Emilio poured wine and asked Cal how long he planned to stay in Rome after the funeral.

"It's open-ended," Cal said. "CNN contacted me and asked if I'd be their on-air commentator during the conclave. Our spring semester is over, I finished marking my papers and exams, so I said yes. If the conclave is fast, I'll go back soon. I'll be here for a while if it's drawn out."

Micaela seized on the news and bulled her way into the china shop by saying, "Good. You'll have plenty of time to persuade Eli."

"Persuade me to do what?" her sister asked.

"To take a job at Harvard," Micaela said.

"Oh, my God!" Eli snapped at her. "Do you ever stop?"

Cal searched his mound of pasta for the right thing to say, but Carlo, ever the academic, rescued him. "Would this be a tenured position?"

Cal couldn't ignore his host's question. He lubricated his palate with white wine and turned away from Elisabetta's frown. "Well, this is all hypothetical, Carlo. If this is something that Eli might want to do, she would likely be an adjunct professor at first. If it seemed like a good fit, there could be discussions on joining the faculty on a permanent basis."

"With tenure?" Carlo managed through a bout of coughing.

Cal was sitting beside him and hastened to fill his water tumbler.

"Water won't help him," Micaela said. "Stopping smoking will help."

Carlo managed to say, "Would you let Cal answer?"

"Some professors are hired directly into a tenure track," Cal said. "Others aren't."

Cal was grateful that Emilio was shielding his sister from even more scrutiny. "Cal, I don't think I ever heard how you and the Holy Father first met."

Cal put his utensils down, glad to get stuck into an anecdote. "I was a speaker at an academic conference in Boston organized by a Portuguese cultural society. The topics revolved around the history of the Church in Portugal. I remember being interested in meeting the new Bishop of Providence, Rodrigo Da Silva, and I wasn't disappointed. He filled the auditorium with his enormous personality and laugh. I quickly learned that besides being highly intelligent and well-spoken, he was also a huge foodie. After the conference, the speakers were taken to dinner at an excellent Portuguese restaurant. Rodrigo was holding court, extolling the excellence of Portuguese cuisine and ingredients. He launched into an extended monologue on Portuguese olive oil, which he insisted was the best olive oil on Earth. He was bragging that he was quite the student of the olive and that just like a wine expert can identify the vineyard in a blind tasting, he could identify Portuguese olive groves. Of course, someone challenged him, and he reached for the unlabeled bottle of olive oil on the table and put a drop on one of his palms. Then he performed this whole ritual. He rubbed his hands together to heat the oil and unleash its aromas, deeply sniffed his palms, furrowed his brow, talked about the notes of grass and tomatoes, and finally declared, 'These are cold-pressed cobrancosa olives from the Trás-os-Montes region of northern Portugal, almost certainly from a producer called Magna Olea.' Then he called over the maître de and asked him to bring out the can. To our astonishment, it was, in fact, Magna Olea olive oil. He let us marvel at his prowess for too long a time, before admitting with a belly laugh that he was a restaurant regular and knew their brand."

"I can hear that laugh," Elisabetta said. "My goodness, the pleasure he got from a good meal. He would have enjoyed this one. Tonnarello was one of his favorite restaurants."

Carlo nodded and said, "You all know I don't much like popes, but this one wasn't a bad guy."

Thankfully for Elisabetta, for the rest of the dinner, the conversation steered clear of her future, but over dessert, it was Emilio who got the treatment.

"So, brother of mine," Micaela said. "You going to work for another pope?"

"The next one will be my fourth. Honestly, I don't think so."

Elisabetta looked like an electric shock had passed through her. "You never told me. What would you do?"

"I get calls all the time from companies looking for security chiefs. You can't believe the money."

His father grunted and said, "You should do it. Then you should get married. Then you should have children."

"Thank you for the life plan, papa."

"You're welcome," Carlo said. "As always, my advice is free of charge."

"I can see you in a big, fancy company," Micaela said. "You already have the blue suits."

"Well, I can't see it," Elisabetta said. "You're a policeman at heart. You need the adrenaline. You'd be bored sitting at a desk all day."

"I do my fair share of sitting at this job. Besides, I'll be happy when I don't have to butt heads with Herr Studer and his Swiss Guards anymore."

"He'd be sad," Elisabetta laughed. "He enjoys butting heads with you. What do you think, Cal?"

Cal grinned. "About the job or the marriage and children?"

"Why not all of the above?" she said.

"Give Cal a break, Eli," Emilio said. "He's my hero: great job, no wife, no children."

"No children that we know of," Micaela sniggered.

"Mic!" Elisabetta exclaimed. "Don't say something like that!"

Cal leaned back in his chair. "But it's true. None that I know of."

Emilio reached over to pat Cal on the back, bro style.

Cal turned serious and said, "You want my opinion? I think the first obligation a person has to themselves is to do what brings the most joy. I can't answer for my friend, but I'm sure he'll make an excellent decision."

"Hear that, my lovely family?" Emilio crowed. "One person at this table gives me credit."

The funeral was the next day, and Emilio and Elisabetta had early obligations, so there would be no lingering after dinner. Elisabetta disappeared into her old bedroom and emerged in her black habit.

"Mustn't scandalize the Apostolic Palace," Carlo quipped.

"Indeed," Elisabetta said. "More importantly, I don't think the Swiss Guards would recognize me in blue jeans. I've got a driver if you'd like a lift to your hotel, Cal?"

"I can take you too," Emilio said.

Micaela looked like she wanted to clobber him. "Eli offered first, you idiot. If you want to drive someone, drive me."

Cal felt his face warm. "You heard your sister, Emilio. I'm going with Eli."

Elisabetta's limo was double-parked outside Carlo's building. From the back seat, Cal asked the driver in English whether he was having a good night. When the driver apologized for not speaking the language, Elisabetta shook her head and laughed.

"I know what you just did. Very clever, Professor Donovan," she said, also in English.

"What did I do?"

"You wanted to see if he could understand before you spoke to me."

"I'm fairly transparent, aren't I?"

She told the driver to stop at Cal's hotel and, switching back to English, said, "Transparent, I don't know. I'd describe you as direct. But I like that. I spend most of my time communicating with people within the Curia and at foreign embassies who dance around and hide behind masks like Kabuki actors instead of plainly stating what they want to say."

The car made a sharp turn pressing her shoulder against his. The physical contact emboldened him. "Can I live up to my reputation and be direct with you?"

"Of course."

"Come to Cambridge. The new pope would be crazy if he didn't keep you at the Secretariat, but you know that's probably not going to happen. New broom and all that. Spend a year teaching at Harvard. See if you like it. See if you like America."

She didn't look at him. Her gaze was out the rain-streaked window. It had poured during dinner, and the dark streets of Rome were bathed in the golden reflection of the sodium street lights.

"I appreciate your thinking of me," she said.

"I think about you all the time. You know that, don't you?"

He wasn't expecting a direct answer and didn't get one.

"I wouldn't just be leaving the Vatican," she said. "I'd be abandoning my order and possibly my vows. I'd be leaving my family behind."

"I understand," he said. "It would be a big step."

"More like a great leap into the unknown."

"I'd be there to catch you."

He thought he heard a faint sigh as her small hand disappeared into the pocket of her habit.

"I have your ticket for the VIP stands at St. Peter's Square," she said. "The funeral starts at ten, but with all the security cordons, you'd do well to arrive at the Vatican by eight. It will be an unspeakably sad day."

Cal accepted the ticket and said, "Yes, it will."

CHAPTER THREE

CNN PAID THE CITY OF ROME A HEFTY FEE TO BE ONE OF THE broadcasters with access to a viewing stand on the Piazza Papa Pio XII. The media center, a two-story erection of ten scaffolded cubes, was on Italian territory just outside the main entrance to Vatican City. Through long camera lenses, the dome of St. Peter's Basilica loomed large over the shoulders of the on-air reporters.

The CNN team was led by their religious affairs correspondent Gloria Hernando, a veteran of two previous conclaves. Cal had gotten to know her during production meetings and didn't much care for her. He found her vain and more than a little vapid, but he had to admit, that when the camera light went green, she was a pro. From their first in-person meeting, it was apparent to him and her somewhat embarrassed producers that she had more than a collegial interest in her new colleague, and he spent the *novemdiales* between the funeral and the conclave, fending her off. "We really must have dinner," she would say, or, "I have some of your books in my suite. Why don't you swing by my hotel and sign them?" There was a sultriness to her. The old Cal would have shown up with bells on. But the Cal Donovan in love with a nun kept his animal spirits in check, a test of sorts to prove his worthiness.

The windless late-May afternoon was warm and bright. Cal got comfortable on his director's chair and waved off a last-minute dusting of makeup. Beside him, Gloria scrunched her eyes during her touchup and said, "Ready to go, superstar?"

Cal let out a fake chuckle and told her he was born ready, a cringe-worthy response he instantly regretted.

Their director was in the production truck parked on a side street. He notified them through their earpieces that they were about to go on air and counted them down.

"This is Gloria Hernando reporting live from the Vatican. We are less than an hour from the start of the conclave, the ancient and mysterious rite in which the Catholic Church chooses its next pope. I'm joined by the eminent Harvard professor of theology, Calvin Donovan, an expert in the history of Catholicism and a personal friend of the last man to lead the Church, Pope John. Professor Donovan, let me start by offering our condolences. This must be a sad time for you."

Cal didn't have to feign a sorrowful expression. "Thank you for that. I'd say that it's a bittersweet moment. It's terribly sad that I've lost a friend, and the Church has lost a leader only two years after he became pope. Pope John was enormously talented and charismatic, and we'll never know what he might have accomplished at the Vatican and on the world stage had he lived. However, it's also a time of promise. The conclave is a vibrant and theatrical way to choose a new leader for the billion and a half Catholic faithful."

Gloria smiled at him, then reengaged with the lens. "We don't know how long the conclave will last. It could be over today—it could take several days, even a week, or more. But Professor Donovan will be with us every step of the way to explain all things conclave and tell us what is likely going on behind the closed doors of the Sistine Chapel. He will be right here, by my side, until we see white smoke rising from the Chapel and hear the words, *habemus papam*, we have a pope. So, Professor, here we are, fifteen days after the death of the pope and nine days after his funeral. You attended the funeral."

"I did. It was a somber, dignified ceremony, witnessed by

pilgrims who came to Rome from all corners of the globe and by millions on TV. Pope John is now interred in his final resting place in the crypt below St. Peter's Basilica alongside ninety-one other popes, and the eyes of the world turn toward the conclave to choose his successor."

Gloria leaned in and said, "But what about Pope John's legacy? By appointing a woman as his secretary of state, he was seen as a champion of women. Will this legacy live on?"

"That remains to be seen. It was a bold move and a controversial one. John's critics attacked him for it throughout his pontificate. I would say that all serious observers must acknowledge that the present secretary of state, Elisabetta Celestino, has done an excellent job. That bodes well for future appointments of women to important jobs within the Church hierarchy."

"Let's hope you're right," Gloria said. "The cardinal electors will soon depart from their hotel, the Domus Sanctae Marthae, located within the grounds of Vatican City. When they arrive at the Sistine Chapel, the conclave will begin. Our viewers will have many questions. Let's start with some of them. Tell us about the conclave, Professor. What will happen inside the Chapel? What does history tell us about how long it's likely to last? Which cardinals are considered the front-runners to be the next pope?"

Cal knew which topics were coming and eased into teaching mode. "The conclave we see today traces its origins to the thirteenth century, although the procedures have been periodically revised. All cardinals under eighty are eligible to attend and vote at conclave. Right now, one hundred eighteen so-called cardinal electors are participating in this conclave, and it will take a two-thirds majority of them to elect a new pope. It's impossible to predict how long it will take to get to that two-thirds majority. The longest conclave in history was in the thirteenth century. It lasted over two years if you can believe it."

"Oh no!" Gloria exclaimed. "My cat will be awfully angry at me for leaving her so long."

"I wouldn't worry," Cal said. "That one was an outlier. It took place in the Italian village of Viterbo. The prolonged deadlock between Italian and French factions so strained local resources that the villagers bolted the cardinals inside their palace and fed them a diet of bread and water. When that didn't end the proceedings, they tore off the roof to make it even more unpleasant. The tradition of speeding the plow by making conclaves uncomfortable has continued. Until recent decades, the cardinals were made to sleep on cots within the Sistine Chapel, and even now, the Vatican guesthouse provides relatively spartan accommodations.

"Since the late nineteenth century, conclaves have not gone longer than five days, so I think your cat will be fine. Under the dictates of the Apostolic Constitution, the electors take a single vote on the first day, then four votes per day—two in the morning, two in the evening—on each subsequent day, pausing for a day of prayer and reflection on the fourth day if no candidate has reached the threshold of two-thirds of ballots."

"So, take us inside the Sistine Chapel," she said, "and tell us what a fly on the wall would see during the conclave?"

"Sure. To take a step backward, the cardinal electors assembled this morning in Saint Paul's Basilica to celebrate Mass, then returned to the guesthouse for lunch and a brief rest. Shortly, they will travel, some on foot, some by minibuses, the short distance from the guesthouse to the Pauline Chapel in the Apostolic Palace. From there, in their red and white choir dress, they will form a processional to the Sistine Chapel, singing the Litany of the Saints. The chapel has five doors. Three are regularly used by tourists transiting between the Vatican Museums and Saint Peter's Basilica. During the conclave, they are sealed. The fourth door leads to the Sala del Pianto, the Room of Tears, where new popes contemplate their fate before facing the public. The procession of cardinal electors will cross the Sala Regia, the ceremonial Royal Hall, where they will enter the chapel through the fifth door. During voting, this door is locked and manned by Swiss Guards in their distinctive blue and gold Renaissance uniforms.

"Inside the chapel, the cardinals find their assigned places on double rows of tables draped in ermine cloth placed on each long-axis of the chapel under Michelangelo's painted ceiling. Three cardinals are chosen to be scrutineers, or vote counters. They sit at a small table on one end. To protect the marble tiles of the chapel, carpenters have constructed a raised floor covered in carpet. The under-floor space is put to good use. The Vatican police, or Carabinieri, place their electronic jamming equipment under the floor to counter any attempts to spy on the proceedings."

"Fascinating," Gloria said.

Cal continued, "Once seated, the cardinals will sing *Veni Creator Spiritus*, a hymn that invokes the Holy Spirit, the manifestation of the Christian God they believe will inform their decision-making during conclave. Then, one by one, by seniority, they swear to observe the Apostolic Constitution's procedures and to maintain secrecy. That means swearing off social media during the conclave and not talking to anyone about the proceedings, especially the media."

"Oh, darn!" Gloria said.

Cal thought he ought to chuckle and forced one out. "And, of course, no mobile phones are allowed," he said. "They leave them in the guesthouse. After all the cardinals have sworn the oath, the master of papal liturgical celebrations orders everyone to leave except for the Cardinal Electors and a conclave physician. At the door of the Sistine Chapel, he shouts, *extra omnes*. That's Latin for leave, all of you. Then he locks the door behind him, and the conclave gets underway."

"I am learning so much," she gushed. "What happens next?"

"A cardinal will have been selected in advance to deliver a brief sermon on the current state of the Church and the qualities that the new pope ought to possess to meet the current challenges. Then they vote. Each cardinal has the same items: a ballot card, a pen, and the *Ordo Rituum Conclavis*, the conclave prayer book. The ballots are pre-printed with the words, *Eligo in Summum Pontificem*, I Elect as Supreme Pontiff, with a space for a name.

"One by one, they will be called forward to present their anonymous ballots to the scrutineers, who will perform the count and certify the results. Each cardinal will hold his ballot paper over his head and recite in Latin, 'I call as my witness Christ the Lord, who will be my judge that my vote is given to the one who, before God, I think should be elected.' Then they will place their ballot on a plate atop an urn of silver and bronze made and tilt it so the paper falls inside."

"And that has to happen one hundred eighteen times!" Gloria exclaimed. "That must take a while."

"It can take a couple of hours," Cal said. "Some of these men don't move very fast."

"How are the ballots counted?"

"Once all votes have been cast, one scrutineer shakes the urn, and another removes and counts the ballots. Assuming the count is good, each ballot is unfolded by the first scrutineer, and all three scrutineers separately write down the name indicated on the ballot. The last scrutineer reads the name aloud. Then, the scrutineers add the votes and make the tally known to the assembly. If seventy-nine or more electors choose one cardinal, they're done. They have a pope. If this threshold hasn't been met, they will reassemble tomorrow morning and try again."

"Assuming they don't elect someone today, we'll see black smoke over the Sistine Chapel this evening," Gloria said. "How does that work?"

"Ballots are bundled together and burned at the end of every morning or afternoon session. Two iron stoves have been brought in for the conclave. They're attached to a long stovepipe that comes out through the chapel roof. One stove is for burning paper ballots after each electoral round. The other stove makes black or white smoke signals, depending on which chemicals are added. As you said, black smoke means they failed to reach a two-thirds majority, and white smoke means a new pope is about to be announced."

"And then we'll have the *habemus papa* moment on the Benediction Loggia of Saint Peter's," Gloria said.

"Exactly right," Cal said agreeably.

"Okay, we're about to take a break at the top of the hour. Before we go, who would you say are the most likely candidates to become the next pope?"

"The term heard a lot around the streets of Rome leading up to the conclave is papabile—who is in a position be the next pontiff. It's not just a matter of conversation. Betting companies lay odds on various candidates. The odds-on favorite is an Italian, the Bishop of Como, Cardinal Domenico Colpo. He's seventy-four, which is a little on the old side, but that's not necessarily bad. Many electors might be wary of signing up for a papacy that could last for three decades. Colpo was made a cardinal by Pope Celestine's predecessor, who was a conservative. Colpo is a conservative at heart and one of the most academically gifted theologians in the College of Cardinals. He holds a Ph.D. in theology from the University of Bologna. Usually, someone with this background would have been brought into the Curia to run a major congregation, but Colpo always resisted going to work at the home office, if you will. That outsider quality has made him acceptable and well-respected among many of his peers. There's an American moderate high on the list—Cardinal Macy of New York. I know Macy fairly well, and I like him. Even people who disagree with him find him likable. An African stands a good chance. Raymond Koffi of the Ivory Coast is very charismatic and an excellent orator. The African delegation tends to be on the conservative side, a disadvantage given that so many cardinal electors were appointed by the liberals, Celestine and John, but Koffi is somewhat to the left of most of his African colleagues. There are others, and you can never accurately predict how a conclave will turn out, but the oddsmakers rate these three as the favorites."

"Thank you, Professor. We're going to go to break now," Gloria said. "Stay with us here on CNN, and our coverage will continue shortly."

Gloria touched Cal's shoulder and said to her producer, "He was wonderful. Absolutely wonderful. I knew you'd be good, but this good? Oh. My. God. Cal, you are so natural in front of the camera. Please don't take my job!"

"Thank you, Gloria. You're too kind," he said. "You don't have to worry. Your job is safe."

~

As the cardinal electors congregated, the lobby of the Domus Sanctae Marthae became a sea of red and white. Two monsignors from the Office of the Camerlengo were cat-herding the cardinals to the buses with limited success.

"Right this way, Eminences," one of them called out from the door. "Please come. The first bus is here."

The lone Haitian, Cardinal Samuel Laguerre, sidled up to the lone Rwandan, Cardinal Gasore Bizimana.

"Are you walking or riding?"

"It's a nice afternoon," Bizimana said. "Come, walk with me."

They reached the entrance, where Emilio Celestino had stationed himself by the lead bus. Emilio prided himself on knowing every cardinal's name and key bits of information about their personal lives—hobbies, taste in movies, and the like. He greeted the pair, and after a brief exchange, they told him they would pass on the bus. Emilio waved them toward the cordon of gendarmes spaced every twenty meters, marking the route along the rear of the basilica.

The Spring sun blinded them, and as they began their ramble, both men fumbled for sunglasses. "Did Koffi speak with you last evening?" Laguerre asked, bending toward the shorter man. He spoke in a low voice. Electioneering, particularly on the day of conclave, was unseemly, and when horse-trading occurred, it was done with the utmost discretion. Electors, as theology dictated, were meant to dialogue, not with men, but with the Holy Spirit.

"He found me this morning before Mass," Bizimana said.

"And?"

"I imagine he told me what he told you and every other elector. That it is time for the continent of Africa to take its rightful place at the head of the table."

"And what did you say?"

"I said, 'Raymond, I do not want to be pope.'"

The Haitian laughed. "I love it. How did he react?"

"He smiled at me with his beautiful smile and said, 'Gasore, I think you would make a wonderful pope. I would be honored to cast my ballot for you.' Of course, I then told him what he wanted to hear."

"Which was?"

"That I would vote for him on the first scrutiny, then see how the landscape developed."

"And that pleased him?"

"Well enough. He left me for another ear. How are you leaning?"

"Koffi is soft on some of my core issues," My ancestors may have come from Africa," Laguerre said, "but having an African pope is less of a driver for me."

"Who do you like, then?"

"Montebourg."

"You're joking!"

"I am not. I see eye to eye with him on many things."

The African said, "Philosophy aside, it's said that Montebourg was one of the plotters who employed falsehoods and attempted to discredit Sister Elisabetta when she became secretary of state. Tosi's head rolled. Unlike his forebearers during the French revolution, this Frenchman kept his head."

Laguerre had a lilting laugh. "What do the Americans say—Cardinal Tosi took a hit for his team? Navarro may also have been one of the plotters, and he too is sitting high and dry."

"But surely, you would agree that Elisabetta Celestino has done an admirable job at the Secretariat," Koffi said.

"What I would say—" Laguerre's answer was interrupted by a cheer from the crowd in Saint Peter's Square. "What was that for, I wonder?" he said.

"They must have caught sight of our procession. The game is on."

"What I was about to say," Laguerre continued, "is that while I agree that one would be hard-pressed to find significant fault in her job performance, the fact is that this is, always was, and in the future should be a job for a cardinal. As a woman cannot become a cardinal or, for that matter, a parish priest, the job, *ipso facto*, should not be held by a woman. Tosi was wrong to invent accusations against her, but his heart—and perhaps Montebourg's heart was in the right place. Paul is a serious cleric with a correct doctrinal view of the world. Foundational theology comes first. Everything else comes second."

"Let's agree to disagree on that, my friend," Koffi said. "I would say that humanity comes first. But at least can we agree that Paul has no sense of humor."

Laguerre convulsed in laughter. "Yes, yes, on that, we can most certainly agree."

Cardinals Victor Macy and Domenico Colpo boarded the second minibus in lockstep, generating a wisecrack from Cardinal Bettencourt of Chicago, in the first row.

"All papabile to the back of the bus, please."

"That's precisely where my friend and I are heading, Louis," Macy said, laying a giant hand on Bettencourt's shoulder. Colpo might have preferred a seat closer to the front, but Macy's invitation was impossible to decline.

The last row spanned the aisle, allowing the towering American to stretch his long legs. Macy was not the only cardinal who had been athletic as a youth, but he was certainly the best. An all-star forward on the University of Notre Dame basketball team, he might have turned pro if two knee injuries had not put the kibosh on his plans. To this day, he displayed a framed copy of the front page of his hometown newspaper in his diocese office, bearing the headline:

Basketball God Decides To Become a Priest.

Macy, now in his mid-sixties, was a gregarious backslapper, equally comfortable lifting a beer with senators and bricklayers. His exuberant personality and moderate views made him popular among a large swath of his peers. Simply put, it was hard to be angry with the man.

If asked to name a member of the College of Cardinals more diametrically opposed to Macy, most would mention Colpo. Macy was a sequoia of a man who prided himself on maintaining his physique. The Italian was short and slight with slack musculature and a paunch like a kangaroo's pouch. Macy was a handsome devil with a theatrical shock of white hair who managed to stay tanned for much of the year. Colpo had only a narrow fringe of short hair on the back of his head, and he possessed one of those faces so ordinary, so utterly lacking in distinguishing characteristics, that it was hard to remember it. Macy had a perpetual smile and a booming laugh. Colpo's mouth was usually fixed in a straight line of equanimity. Macy's theological views demonstrated a tendency to flexibility and pragmatism. Colpo's were academic, doctrinaire, and rigid. It was an unfortunate byproduct of Pope John's polarizing tenure that both men were papabile.

"So, the hour is nigh," Macy told his seatmate.

"Indeed."

An awkward silence followed.

Beyond pleasantries, the two men had not conversed during the *novemdiales*, and they were probably thankful that the bus ride would take all of three minutes.

"Cardinal Sauseda did a nice job at Mass today, don't you think?" Macy said.

"A credible performance, yes."

Macy braced himself with his stuck-out heels as the bus began to roll. "Who are you sharing a room with?" he asked, finding another neutral topic.

"Cardinal Quang."

"Now that's somewhere I've always wanted to visit," Macy said. "Ever been to Vietnam?"

"I have not."

The bus rolled alongside Cardinals Koffi and Laguerre, and Macy gave them a passing wave.

"The two of them seem deep in conversation," he said.

"Do they?" Colpo said. Seemingly unimpressed by the small

talk, he muttered under his breath in Italian, "Perhaps I should have walked too."

"Sorry, Domenico, I didn't catch that," Macy said. "My hearing's not what it used to be."

"I said, it's a fair day. Perhaps we should have walked too."

∽

EMILIO CELESTINO POSITIONED himself in the Sala Regia, waiting for the last cardinals and the official Vatican photographer to file into the Sistine Chapel. It was 4:30 p.m., and everything was precisely on schedule. He peered through the doorway as the prelates found their seats. The photographer flitted around the ornate chapel, clicking his shutter, then beat a hasty retreat. The cardinals stood to invoke their oaths. After that, Bishop Antonio Antonelli, the master of papal liturgical celebrations, came to the doorway, bellowed *extra omnes* at those inside the Sistine Chapel, and stood aside as all the Curial functionaries scurried out. The only non-cardinal to remain was Doctor Bellisario, the pope's physician, who volunteered to attend the opening day. Other medics would assume the stand-by emergency duty on subsequent days.

Bishop Antonelli pushed the heavy doors closed and made way for two chiseled Swiss Guards who snapped to attention by the portal, clutching medieval long-handled halberds.

Emilio bowed his head and said, "Excellency," to Antonelli as the cleric passed him and then hailed his far-flung command officers via a cuff microphone. "The conclave has begun."

∽

THE CNN TRUCK was parked directly in front of a café, a block from the broadcast booth. The pod coffee inside the truck was free, but Cal preferred the atmosphere and the espresso at the café bar. The conversation among the regulars was lively, and a bottle of Grey Goose awaited when the broadcast was over for the day. Cal and Gloria had been off the air for about ninety minutes, biding time for live coverage to resume.

Cal heard, "There you are!" and turned to see Gloria, wearing her makeup shield around her neck.

"I wasn't hiding," Cal said, forcing a grin. "Want a decent coffee?"

"Oh, my goodness, I'm fully caffeinated," she said. "We go back on in ten. They want our keisters in our chairs."

At six-thirty, the sun began to dip behind the dome of the basilica, bathing the Vatican in a cinematic glow. When their coverage renewed, Gloria gave a spiel directed at new viewers, introduced Cal as the CNN expert, then asked, "Professor. They've been at it for two hours now. When can we expect to see smoke over the Sistine Chapel?"

"It shouldn't be long now," he said. "Generally, the electors would be able to cast their ballots and have them counted within two hours. So, all eyes are on the stovepipe on the chapel's roof."

"White smoke or black smoke?" she asked. "What do you think?"

"I'd be shocked if they arrived at a two-thirds majority on the first ballot. I mean, it's possible, but it would be remarkable, given the divisiveness of the past two years. Some electors will want the liberal, pro-women agenda of Pope John to continue. Others will want an anti-John to take over. So, black smoke, almost certainly."

With a camera trained on the barrel-tiled chapel roof, Gloria and Cal kept the conversation going through multiple station breaks. Half an hour passed, then an hour, and in his earpiece, Cal could hear a debate between the Rome-based CNN producer and a producer in Atlanta, trying to decide whether or not to remain live. During a break, the Atlanta producer asked Cal for his advice.

"Like I said on-air," he said, "three hours is a very long time. I can't imagine what's going on."

He was asked if one of the cardinals might have become ill.

"There's always that possibility, but there's a doctor on duty inside the chapel for that kind of emergency. If someone needed advanced care, the conclave would have been interrupted so that a cardinal could be taken to the hospital. The Press Office would have put out a statement."

The producers decided to stay live for another thirty-minute block and then reassess. The delay was becoming the story.

As sunset approached, the atmosphere within the Sala Regia grew tense, and the hall began to fill with conclave functionaries and various Curial officials. The commandant of the Swiss Guards, Eric Studer, joined Emilio. Neither of them could come up with a credible explanation. They drew in Bishop Antonelli to ask what he thought, but the master of papal liturgical celebrations was equally dumbfounded.

"What about Doctor Bellisario?" Studer asked. "Can we ring his phone?"

"Even he had to leave his mobile phone outside the chapel," the bishop said. "If there were a medical problem, he would have alerted the Swiss Guards by rapping on the door."

Emilio rubbed his face. It was late enough that a crop of dark stubble had formed. "They've been going for three hours and forty minutes. I think we are obliged to interrupt."

"That is expressly prohibited," Bishop Antonelli said. "I can't possibly violate the conclave."

"Who can?" Emilio asked.

"The Cardinal Camerlengo, I suppose, but he's in there."

"What about the secretary of state? She's the highest official, not inside. What if she authorized it?"

"At least it wouldn't be me," Antonelli sputtered.

Elisabetta was in her office, lost in work, and not paying attention to the hour. She answered her brother's phone call and came down the steps to the hall. After spending a few minutes querying Antonelli and other conclave officials and getting no satisfactory answers, she announced, "Bishop Antonelli, I order you to break the sanctity of the conclave and open the door."

The bishop nodded solemnly, withdrew a large brass key from his cassock, and turned the lock. The mechanism shifted with a loud clunk. He pushed the doors hesitantly and apologetically and prepared himself for reproach from within.

Emilio was only a meter behind Antonelli's shoulders. He watched him poke his head inside and reached for him reflexively at the sight of the cleric falling hard on his knees.

"What's happened?" Emilio cried, stepping around the kneeling man.

The Sistine Chapel was softly lit. From the frescoed ceiling, Michelangelo's God hovered over the chapel, surrounded by angels at the moment he created Adam. Emilio struggled to make his brain comprehend what he was seeing or not seeing.

The Sistine Chapel was empty.

CHAPTER FOUR

Emilio ran into the Sistine Chapel and stopped at its center, directly below Michelangelo's hand of God. In confusion, he spun in a full circle, then dashed around, trying the doors. All of them were locked except for the one leading to the Room of Tears. He entered that small chamber. It, too, was empty. Papal vestments—one small cassock, one medium, and one large—to accommodate the habitus of whoever was chosen to be the next pontiff hung forlornly on a rack. When he returned to the chapel, others were inside, doing what he had done, slowly spinning in confusion. Commander Studer had the presence to block the entry of additional conclave officials from the Sala Regia by barking an order to his Swiss Guards to reseal the door. Bishop Antonelli rubbed his hands in agitation while saying in a pitch considerably higher than his natural voice, "I don't understand. I simply don't understand." Elisabetta brushed against her brother and whispered, "What is happening, Emilio?" He had no answer. As a testament to his surreal mental state, he responded by lifting the skirting cloths on rows of tables on one side of the chapel to see if anyone was underneath. Elisabetta started checking the tables against the opposite wall, as absurd as the task seemed.

When they were done peeking, Emilio muttered weakly, "We had to look."

Elisabetta said, "You checked the doors?"

"It was the first thing I checked. Eric, can you confirm that your men are still behind these doors?"

Studer bristled, "I can assure you, they have remained at their posts."

"Please," Emilio said.

Studer got on his radio, demanded a roll call and status report from the chapel guards, and announced, "The doors have been and are secure."

"I feel I'm losing my mind," Elisabetta said. "There has to be an explanation."

"Of course, there's an explanation," Emilio said. "We just have to find it. One hundred eighteen cardinals don't just vanish."

"Did they vote yet?" Elisabetta said to no one in particular. She sought the answer at the scrutineers' table and inspected the ballot urn. It was empty.

Then, moving along the tables, she saw that none of the ballot papers had been marked.

"They never even started," she said, returning to the scrutineers' station.

Emilio began walking toward her. When he was about three meters away, he stumbled and fell on his side, yelling, "What the hell?"

"Are you okay? What happened?" Elisabetta said, rushing forward.

He got up and inspected the section of carpet nearest him. There was a shallow, square-shaped depression.

"It's been cut!" he shouted.

He bent over and lifted a two-by-two-meter rectangle of the carpet by its three cut edges. Underneath was the plywood platform built by Vatican carpenters to protect the ancient marble tiles. And there was something else, dark and sinister in the middle of the rectangle, a square-shaped black hole cut through the plywood.

Studer said, "My God. There's a hole through the marbles."

Emilio used the flashlight on his phone to look down, but it wasn't powerful enough.

"Who has a proper flashlight?" Emilio said. "Anyone?"

No one did. He got on his radio and called for any gendarmes near the chapel to bring one.

Elisabetta reached into her habit for her pen, and dropped it into the void. It clattered against something hard.

"It goes into the basement!" Bishop Antonelli said.

A gendarme came into the chapel with a flashlight, and Emilio trained the beam through the hole. A second hole, cut through terra cotta tiles of the basement floor, was visible, and next to it, an aluminum ladder.

"There's a hole cut through the basement floor," Emilio said. He removed his jacket and said, "I'm going down."

"We can go through the palace and take the stairs," Antonelli said.

"I'll meet you down there," Emilio said.

"You'll hurt yourself," Elisabetta said.

"I don't want to wait," he said. "It doesn't look like it's more than five meters. I'll be all right."

He lowered himself through the hole in the marble floor, dangled by his fingers for several seconds, then let go.

Peering down, Elisabetta heard a loud "Ooof" and a shout. "Get the medics down here! Hurry!"

The basement of the fifteenth-century Sistine Chapel, the lowest of its three levels, was vaulted to support the tremendous weight. Elisabetta, Studer, a contingent of Swiss Guards, and a team of Vatican paramedics ran down stone stairs and through a series of drab storerooms filled with centuries of old furniture and architectural materials.

Elisabetta knew these rooms. Years ago, at the Pontifical Commission for Sacred Archaeology, she had surveyed the basement, doing an inventory of potentially valuable artifacts. She led the way on flat shoes, her habit flowing behind.

"Almost there. A few more rooms," she called out.

Emilio had already found the light switch, and when the group entered, they found him on his knees beside two elderly cardinals lying on their sides. Near them was another hole piercing the basement floor.

"Someone," Emilio said. "Give me a knife or scissors."

A paramedic quickly produced a folding blade. Emilio used it to cut plastic ties from wrists and ankles.

Emilio said to the paramedics, "Cardinal Rotolo first. They had birettas stuffed in their mouths. He's not doing well."

Elisabetta knelt beside the other man, Cardinal Stocchi, the president of the Prefecture for the Economic Affairs of the Holy See.

"Eminence," she said. "Are you okay?"

He sat up and rubbed his wrists. "I'm all right. I'm concerned about Ennio. He was making gurgling noises."

"They're working on him," she said, touching the cleric's shoulder. "Where is everyone?"

"Down there," he said, gesturing toward the irregularly shaped hole. "Ennio and I told them we couldn't possibly climb another ladder. Ennio got terribly out of breath. My leg and arm are weak from my stroke. They had to help me down the first one."

"Who are they?" Studer demanded. "Tell us what happened here."

One of the paramedics interrupted to say that Cardinal Rotolo had likely suffered a heart attack and needed to be taken to the hospital immediately. The call went out for a stretcher and a wheelchair, and they proceeded to intubate the dusky-skinned cleric.

"Let me go to him," Cardinal Stocchi said.

"Please," Elisabetta said gently. "He's in good hands. You must tell us what happened here so we can help the others."

"There were six of them, I think. Yes, six. They appeared in our midst as Cardinal Sanz was delivering his sermon."

Emilio said, "Appeared from where, Eminence?"

"They came from underneath the platform at the western end of the chapel. I didn't see them until they were standing there. They must have crawled to that end, pushed through the carpet, or cut it.

They had weapons—military types of rifles and pistols. Their faces were covered by—what do you call these full-face masks?"

"Balaclavas," Emilio said.

"Yes, balaclavas. And they all had flashlights strapped to their foreheads. They addressed us in English and told us to be silent or they would cut the throat of Cardinal Fischer who was one of the scrutineers. We did as we were told."

"Then what happened?" Studer asked.

"One of the men took a knife and cut through the carpet at the center of the chapel, then used a small power saw to cut through the wooden platform. One of their compatriots pushed a ladder through the hole from below, and we were made to climb down. Cardinal Macy, who is a forceful man, as you know, objected and asked them what they wanted and what they hoped to achieve. He tried to start a negotiation, but that made them angry. One of them, their leader by my reckoning, told Macy they would achieve some of their objectives by detonating grenades and shooting us on the spot. If that was what he wanted to happen, then keep talking. Macy fell silent, and one by one, we climbed down. We are not people used to climbing down ladders. It was difficult for most of us, especially in choir dress, but even Rotolo and I were taken down. When we were told we had to go down an even taller ladder through that hole, I told them that I could not do it because of my infirmity. My arm was in spasm, you see. Rotolo was in worse shape than I was. Our captors conferred amongst themselves and decided to bind and gag us. The Holy Spirit protected us. It could have been worse."

"And the others went down," Emilio said, pointing at the hole through the cement floor.

"Yes, and from there, I do not know. Please, you must find them."

A stretcher arrived, and the stricken cardinal was lifted onto it. The paramedics turned their attention to Cardinal Stocchi, lifted him into the wheelchair, and took his vital signs.

"The men who captured you," Emilio said. "Could you tell

anything about them from their accents? Any distinguishing characteristics?"

"Their accents were French. I am sure of it."

"Anything else?"

"Two were women, the others, men."

"White? Black?"

"It wasn't so easy to tell. Their sleeves were long. They had gloves. The only skin showing was around the eyes. Maybe one of the women had dark skin. The others were fair, I think."

"And did they say anything—anything at all—about where they were taking everyone or their intentions?"

"Not a word. After their warning to Macy, no one dared ask questions."

A paramedic interrupted, placing an oxygen mask over the cleric's mouth. "His pressure is sky high. Please, we need to take his Eminence now."

Emilio shone his light through the hole in the floor. "What's down there?" he asked. "What's under the chapel?"

The question jolted Elisabetta out of a shock-induced stupor. "The ground beneath us is Imperial Roman," she said. "We stand on a city of the dead, built by the ancient Romans outside the boundary of the city walls. It's called the necropolis of the Via Triumphalis, named for the old road that bordered the Vatican Hill."

"This is what you used to do, is it not?" Studer said. "You were an archaeologist. Have you been down there?"

"Yes and no," she said. "There were a series of excavations done in the past that are now Vatican exhibits open to the public. I'm sure you've visited them yourself, Commandant. However, they are approximately one hundred meters west of here, under the museums and the autoparc. To my knowledge, the section of the necropolis beneath our feet has never been excavated."

"That's where they were taken," Emilio said. "We're going after them."

Emilio and Studer got on their radios, and soon, a contingent of heavily armed Swiss Guards and gendarmes were assembled.

As Emilio stepped onto the ladder, Elisabetta told him, "I'm going too."

"Absolutely not," he said. "It could be dangerous. The leadership of the Church is gone. You're needed above ground."

"And you need an archaeologist below ground," she insisted.

"I don't want to get between brother and sister," Studer said, "but she's right."

"Look how you're dressed!" Emilio said, exasperated.

"And look how you're dressed. At least I have sensible shoes."

Elisabetta agreed to let the military men descend first, and the soldiers disappeared down the hole. Emilio called up to Elisabetta with an all-clear, and with flashlights trained on her, she began her climb. The lower she got, the cooler the air. She estimated the depth every few steps, and when her feet touched the subterranean soil, she announced that they were six to seven meters below the basement of the Sistine Chapel.

"This isn't a conventional builder's ladder," she said, surveying the aluminum colossus.

"It's something a firefighter would use," Emilio said.

She asked for a flashlight, swung it in a slow arc, and murmured, "My God! Look at this!"

They were in an earthen chamber approximately five by five meters in size, soaring up to the Sistine Chapel's basement floor. The walls were reinforced against cave-in by a lattice of railway ties.

"Were you aware this cavern existed?" Studer asked.

"Absolutely not," she answered. "To my knowledge, there has never been an authorized excavation under the chapel. There's no archaeological purpose to it, and it undermines the structural integrity of the building. No, whoever did this, did it for the sole purpose of violating the conclave."

"But this must have taken weeks or months to dig this volume of dirt," Emilio said.

"Look, it extends through there," she said, pointing her beam at a passageway leading from the chamber. "And see there? Tire tracks."

"How the hell did someone get a vehicle down here?" Studer said.

"There's only one way to find out," Elisabetta said.

The soldiers led the way through a tunnel that was approximately three meters wide and three meters tall. Emilio stuck by Elisabetta's side to protect her and listen to her running commentary.

"This framing," she said, passing her fingers over rough timber. "It's been done by someone who knew what they're doing. A mining engineer, perhaps."

Emilio paused to drop down and inspect the tire tracks. "Look how deep the treads are," he said. "The vehicle was heavy."

"It had to shift tons of dirt and wooden supports," she said.

"Also, our cardinals," he said.

"Many are elderly," she said. "They must have been driven out."

They walked through the tunnel for a minute before Emilio complained that he didn't know the direction they were heading. That prompted Elisabetta to pull open a compass app on her phone.

"Northeast," she said. "We're heading under the Vatican Gardens toward a section of the necropolis that's never been excavated."

"Until now," he said.

"The people who did this weren't archaeologists," she said.

Hearing the excited voices of soldiers at the front of the column, Emilio and Elisabetta pushed forward until they reached the stalled vanguard at a spot where the tunnel widened and curved to the left.

Elisabetta examined the source of consternation and grew angry.

"This is a sin," she said.

They were standing at the façade of a barrel-vaulted brick tomb, its front wall crudely sheared off by the excavation. Inside, skeletons were visible, laid into nooks in the side and rear walls.

"What is this?" Emilio asked.

"A family mausoleum," she said. "Probably second century AD. The people who made this tunnel didn't care what they were destroying."

"We need to press on," Studer said testily. "Our problems are greater than the destruction of tombs."

As they progressed, they discovered scattered artifacts—broken Roman pottery and statues, human and animal bones, brickwork and masonry, oil lamps, and cremation urns. At one point, where the tunnel bored directly through a large mausoleum, the track was thick with crushed skeletal remains. Elisabetta said a silent prayer as she crunched over them. A Swiss guard suddenly shouted that he had found something. When everyone had gathered around, he held up a red biretta.

Emilio examined it and found a nametag stitched inside the hat. *Louis Mertens.*

He showed it to Elisabetta, who said, "Louis is the president of the Pontifical Commission for Sacred Archaeology. This is him telling us that he was here and that he saw this abomination."

"Let's keep moving," Emilio said.

The tunnel floor became knobby, and Elisabetta stooped to brush away dirt with her hand.

"Cobblestones," she said. "They're following the Roman street that ran through the necropolis. It will be straight as an arrow." She took another compass reading and said, "We're heading directly to where the ancient Via Triumphalis intersects with the modern Vatican perimeter road, the Viale Vaticano."

Emilio pointed out a section of tunnel walls and ceiling where the timber braces were few and far between and said he didn't like its look.

Elisabetta didn't either and encouraged the column to move faster.

She had been keeping track of the distance they had traveled by adjusting her stride length to a meter. When she hit a round number, she called out, "Two hundred fifty meters."

Emilio said, "What?"

"That's how far we've come from the chapel. We can't be more than fifty meters from the northeastern boundary of the Vatican Gardens."

Suddenly, she heard a rumbling noise from behind, and she shouted, "Run!"

The beams of a dozen flashlights bobbed wildly as the search party ran for their lives through the dark tunnel. The rumbling stopped, and the air grew heavy with fine debris.

"Keep going," she called out. "It could start again."

"There'd better be a way out of here," Emilio said, "because we're not going back the way we came."

Then, a gendarme called out, "Look here!"

Elisabetta kept running until she saw the rear end of some kind of vehicle. Studer had already made a cursory inspection and offered his breathless assessment.

"It's an electric tram, a people-mover like the ones used in theme parks. It's two cars coupled together. Each one can seat perhaps twenty. They must have made three trips from the chapel to transport all the cardinals. From here, there's an upwards incline. I've sent the men forward."

Above their heads, they could hear muffled noises and felt vibrations.

"We're directly under the Viale Vaticano," Elisabetta said.

She squeezed around the sides of the tram to reach the incline and saw earthen steps fortified by railway sleepers cut into the slope. Ahead of her, she heard a soldier say, "It's a house! We're inside the basement of a house!"

Emilio and Studer unholstered their pistols. Emilio told his sister to stay where she was.

"Enter the house," Studer said coolly to his Swiss Guards. "If you see our people, hold your fire and drop back while we call for reinforcements. We don't want casualties. Every cardinal must be returned safely to the bosom of the Church."

CHAPTER FIVE

Elisabetta did as she was told and waited on the last step of the earthen slope. She made out a few muffled words, footsteps, a door swinging shut, but no gunfire or shouts. After a short while, she ventured a couple of meters into the basement and stopped in amazement. It was impossible to tell how large the room was because much of it was packed to the ceiling with excavated dirt. In a corner, there was a hot-water heater, utility pipes, a fuse box, and directly in front of her, basement stairs leading to an open door.

As she got closer, Emilio appeared at the door and said, "They were here. They're gone now. You can come up."

The large villa on the Viale Vaticano was directly across the street from the fortress-like walls of the Vatican. It had an expansive back garden almost entirely concealed under a canvas tent that rose to the roofline. Inside it were tons of dirt piled high. A mini mechanical excavator sat idly on a mound of rubble. Inside the house, a grand, centuries-old abode, was a mess born of careless living. The tunnelers must have been there for some time. The kitchen was piled high with provisions and garbage, and the rooms were filled with sleeping bags and cots. There were boxes and boxes of disposable latex gloves, useless for digging, useful for avoiding fingerprints.

The villa had a high masonry wall with an iron gate leading to a driveway strewn with several red birettas.

Elisabetta saw Studer on the driveway, his head bowed, talking urgently on his mobile phone.

"He's speaking with the prime minister's office," Emilio said. "We're mobilizing the resources of the Italian state." He picked up a biretta. "Some of the cardinals left clues."

"Whoever did this worked for months," Elisabetta said. "Every cubic meter is filled with their excavations, but many more tons of earth were shifted to make a tunnel this length. Look, there. They removed part of the villa's back wall to make a ramp for the excavator to travel from the basement. They must have parked a lorry in the driveway, loaded it with dirt, and shuttled back and forth to a dumping site. What the hell did the neighbors think was going on?"

"I sent my men knocking on doors," Emilio said. "We'll know soon."

Studer took the phone from his ear and joined them. "Every organ of state security is responding," he said. "A great many experts will join us within the hour. The perpetrators have as much as a four-hour head start. Unfortunately, we don't know how they were transported from here or where they went."

"We have cameras on the Vatican City perimeter that will have captured the comings and goings from Viale Vaticano," Emilio said. "I'll have my people start pulling video."

"There will be leaks about this," Elisabetta said. "I've already gotten a dozen messages from the press office asking why the smoke signal has been greatly delayed. We'll have to make an announcement. But what will we say?"

~

FROM THEIR PERCH on the broadcasting stand in the fading light of the evening, Cal and Gloria heard the wail of sirens and saw the blue lights of emergency vehicles converging on the Vatican. They were on air, obligating them to a certain composure, but it took an effort. Something was wrong. Terribly wrong.

Gloria thrust her lower lip out and scrunched her chin. "So, here we are, still waiting for the smoke to rise from the Sistine Chapel to mark the conclusion of the first ballot of the conclave, and instead, we are seeing numerous police cars and vans heading to the northern border of Vatican City. Cal, what's over there?"

Their view was partially obstructed, but Cal had a mental image of the geography. "The authorities seem to be responding to some kind of emergency on the Viale Vaticano, a Vatican ring road on Italian territory. It's hard to see from here, but the arriving vehicles appear to be stopping across the street from the Vatican Museums. I don't know specifically what's there. Clearly, this is a potentially alarming development. It's speculation, of course, but we have to ask whether this is somehow related to this extraordinarily elongated initial voting session. As we've been saying, we are a good two hours beyond the usual time it takes to cast and count ballots."

Gloria's earpiece was feeding her instructions. "We're going to take a quick break," she said, "and when we return, we hope to have more information on this worrisome and breaking news story."

Off air, they stood and tried to make out what was happening a few hundred meters from their cameras.

"What the hell is going on?" Gloria barked at her producer.

She was told that the Vatican Press Office wasn't responding to their calls and texts. An assistant producer, dispatched on foot to the Viale Vaticano, reported that the police had blocked the road and sidewalks, and she couldn't get through.

"Cal, you've got all sorts of contacts around here," Gloria said. "Can you find out what this is all about?"

"I'll see what I can do," he said, pulling out his phone.

Elisabetta was in the rear of the villa, standing amongst mounds of dirt, waiting to hear back from Silvio Licheri on the status of a press statement. She quickly glanced at her phone and hesitated when she saw it was Cal calling.

"Cal. I—"

"Eli, where are you?"

"On the Viale Vaticano. Where are you?"

"On the broadcast stand. CNN is on commercial break."

"Are you calling as a commentator or a friend?" she asked.

The distress in her voice was palpable. "I can be whoever you need right now."

"I need a friend who can keep a confidence."

"Then that's who you're speaking to."

"They've been taken," she said.

He went to the platform's edge, turned his back on Gloria, and whispered, "The cardinals?"

"All except two who were left behind. There was a tunnel below the chapel. It goes under the gardens, through the necropolis to a private villa."

"Where are they?"

"We've no idea. Emilio and Commandant Studer have mobilized the army and the security services."

"What are you going to be saying publicly?"

"I don't know yet. Some version of the truth."

"What can I do?" he asked.

"Call me later. We'll talk later."

Cal turned back to his co-anchor, who shot him a quizzical look.

"What did you find out?" she asked.

"The official I spoke with knew nothing."

"That was a long enough conversation about nothing," she said.

"They thought maybe I knew something. CNN and all that. We'll have to wait for the Vatican or the Rome police to put out something."

"All right, we're back live in a minute," Gloria said. "We're going to have to keep saying a whole lot of nothing."

EMILIO'S MEN fed him reports from preliminary interviews with the occupants of neighboring villas. There was a sameness to them. The family who previously lived there had moved overseas and rented or sold the property. No one had met the new inhabitants or laid eyes on them. Shortly after someone took occupancy, a large tent was erected covering the entire back garden, and for the past several months, large trucks pulled through the gates, only to depart days later with tarps pulled over their loads. When asked whether there had been any unusual noise from the house, the abutters replied they only noticed the mechanical droning of some sort of vehicle. They were asked whether it was like a small tractor or a digger. Yes, exactly, that was the reply. They assumed that the new occupants were doing major renovations on the villa, and because the noise and disruptions were annoying at worst, it had been left at that.

Within the hour, the villa became a jurisdictional tangle of competing agencies. Emilio struggled to preserve the crime scene's integrity as every high-ranking official demanded to see the tunnel. Eventually, he persuaded all parties that the crime scene technicians needed to do their work and that the investigation would be best served by everyone convening inside Vatican City at the command center of the Vatican Gendarmerie.

The mood around the conference table could best be described as grimly urgent. Emilio felt that too much time was being devoted to how this could have happened. Both of the Italian security services were present. The Agenzia Informazioni e Sicurezza Interna, the internal security agency, was represented by its director, Carmelo Trombetta, a Carabinieri general who Emilio knew personally. Trombetta was cordial, but the director of the foreign intelligence service, the Agenzia Informazioni e Sicurezza Esterna, General Maurizio Cremonesi, was banging the drum of blame. The prime minister had insisted that AISE be involved at the outset in case the plot had arisen on foreign soil. Cremonesi was a pugnacious fellow who opened with the inflammatory comment that it was inconceivable a tunnel such as this could have been constructed right under the nose of the Vatican police and Swiss Guards.

Studer eventually rose from his chair in umbrage, declaring, "You have seen the depth of the tunnel with your own eyes, General. No reasonable person would believe that an excavation at this depth beneath the unoccupied Vatican gardens would have been detected. The final connection to the Sistine Chapel could have been accomplished in a single night, probably within the past few days, as the carpenters completed the platform and laid the carpet only this Thursday."

Cremonesi began to reply, but Emilio interrupted him. "I'm sorry, General. There will be a comprehensive review of our security procedures in due course. Our immediate concern must be our cardinal electors' location and safe return."

The colonel in charge of the Gruppo di Intervento Speciale, the Italian Carabinieri special operations group, vigorously nodded as Emilio spoke. Sergio Tavassi was relatively new to his post. Emilio had never met the barrel-chested officer with a neat black mustache and long thin nose.

"Colonel Celestino is, of course, completely correct," Tavassi said. "A question, please. I noticed several Vatican City cameras pointing toward the Viale Vaticano. May I ask whether you have begun to examine the recordings?"

Emilio seemed grateful for the man's support. "The review has begun," he said. "I've asked my people to prioritize the period beginning with the initiation of the conclave and ending an hour and fifteen minutes ago when we entered the villa. We should be getting a report any minute."

Tavassi asked whether there was a map of Italy, and Emilio had one projected on a central monitor. Tavassi asked to address the group and stood before the map.

"I've made some rough calculations," he said. "We have a statement from the two cardinals left behind that the abductors entered the chapel soon after the conclave began—approximately five hours ago. Let's assume it took thirty minutes to get about one hundred men of a certain age down two ladders. Let's further assume that the electric people-mover made three trips through the tunnel, each taking ten minutes. That's another thirty minutes. Assuming the electors were immediately transported away from the villa, they did so approximately four hours ago. Clearly, this transport must have occurred by road, as there are no other means of egress possible from the Viale Vaticano. Let us now assume that the average speed of the get-away vehicle or vehicles is eighty kilometers per hour—a blend of city and highway speeds." He took a pointer from the podium and moved it in a circular motion over the projected map. "Three hundred kilometers," he said as those in the room shifted in their chairs. "This is the hypothetical maximum distance of their travel to this point. It is as far north as Pisa. As far south as Naples. It includes hundreds of kilometers of coastline on both the Tyrrhenian and Adriatic Seas, several major and dozens of small general aviation airports."

General Trombetta piped up, "So, you're saying they could be quite far from Rome and potentially out of the country by now."

"That is precisely what I'm saying," Tavassi said.

All heads turned when Elisabetta swept in. The all-male group rose deferentially.

"Please, gentlemen, be seated," she said. "I'm sorry to interrupt. I've been working with my people on a press statement. Have there been any developments?"

Studer spoke for the group. "Unfortunately, none, Madame Secretary."

"We can presume this is a kidnapping scenario," Trombetta said. "When demands are made, to whom do you think these will be directed?"

"To me at the Secretariat, perhaps," she said. "Directly to the media. Who can say?"

"We must anticipate the kind of demands they will make," Trombetta said.

"Who are they?" Tavassi asked. "Who do we think has the motive and expertise to pull off an operation of this complexity? We need to anticipate the kinds of actors across from us in a negotiation."

Cremonesi spat out, "I will tell you, gentlemen—" After a hesitation, he added, "—and Madame Secretary, that the people who did this are terrorists—most likely Middle Eastern Islamists with an anti-Catholic agenda. Our task would be easier if this were the work of a criminal organization that only wanted a billion euros." He snorted in amusement at bandying about this kind of number. "But

I fear they will want things we cannot give. I fear that blood will spill before this affair is over."

"Cardinal Stocchi told us the men had French accents," Elisabetta said. Surely, this has some significance."

"Have you not heard of French Islamists?" Cremonesi said, oozing condescension. "Paris and Marseilles are thick with these vermin."

Elisabetta maintained her composure. "Indeed I have, General. If this affair, as you put it, was conceived on French soil, then I imagine you will have your work cut out for you. The prime minister and Senate will wish to know how the AISE missed the signals."

The general's face turned crimson, and Emilio stepped in to defuse the interchange. "When will the Vatican put out a statement?" he asked.

"We have a draft press release," Elisabetta said. "I didn't want to authorize its release until I spoke with this group."

"What will it say?" Tavassi asked.

"We have decided on transparency," she said.

"A novelty," Cremonesi grunted.

She opened a folder and glanced at the document. "It will state that before casting a ballot, the cardinal electors were abducted by persons unknown and taken via a tunnel under the Sistine Chapel to a place unknown. It will further state that there has been no communication with the abductors and that there will be further updates when warranted."

"There will be a firestorm," Trombetta said. "The world will erupt. The pressure on the police, the security services, and the government will be unimaginable."

"It's happening already," Elisabetta said. "It hasn't gone unnoticed that something is terribly wrong. People understand that the absence of a smoke signal after these many hours indicates that something unprecedented and extraordinary has happened. We must say something. In our opinion, any kind of non-statement will only cause more problems. Of course, we don't want to interfere with your investigations. Do any of you wish to express an alternative strategy?"

One of Emilio's lieutenants entered and whispered into his ear.

"Put it on the screen and walk us through it," Emilio told him.

The lieutenant opened his laptop, clicked on a file, and a video opened in place of the map of Italy. He addressed the group, saying, "This video was recorded by a security camera located on the perimeter wall of Vatican City looking more or less directly toward the villa in question on Viale Vaticano. The timestamp is 18:14. Here, you will see the gate of the villa opening. Here is the first vehicle to exit the villa. It is a white Iveco Furgonato transit van with two people visible in the cab—a driver and a passenger, wearing caps and sunglasses despite the late hour. The van turns left, heading east. Fifteen seconds later, a second van appears. It is an identical white Iveco Furgonato, with two people in the cab, and this one also turns left. Finally, a third identical van appears here, and this one makes a right-hand turn, heading west. The gate closes behind it."

"Where do they go from there?" Studer asked.

The officer replied that they were examining footage from other Vatican cameras, but they would need the cooperation of Roman authorities to search for video evidence beyond the immediate confines of Vatican City.

General Trombetta rose to hand the officer his card. "Send me the file immediately. My people will mobilize all relevant agencies."

"Does anyone know how many people each of these vans carry?" Tavassi asked.

Emilio said. "I've seen this type. Packed like sardines, three vans could probably hold all our people."

"We need to put all Italian airports and ports on high alert," Tavassi said. "We can't let the kidnappers take them out of the country."

"Consider it done," Trombetta said, placing a call.

Elisabetta got to her feet and said, "I believe it's time to release our statement." Hearing no objections, she rang the press office and told Silvio Licheri, "We can send it now. Answer all queries the same way until further notice: no comment."

~

Cal and Gloria were on the Piazza Papa Pio XII chatting with reporters from other media outlets when in their earpieces, they heard their producer yelling, "Jesus fucking Christ. I mean, what the actual fuck? Guys, the Vatican just put out a statement. Listen to this. 'The Vatican wishes to inform the public that a major incident occurred during the first day of the papal conclave. The Vatican police have discovered that all cardinal electors were forcibly removed from the Sistine Chapel through a tunnel under Vatican City. Their whereabouts are currently unknown, and there has been no contact from their abductors. Two cardinals were left behind. They are currently under medical observation and assisting the police. Vatican City and Italian state authorities have mobilized to investigate this heinous and brazen crime. The Vatican will provide further updates as appropriate.' I'll send you the press release. Get up to the booth. I want you to read the statement verbatim. We need to be the first broadcaster to go with this."

"Then what?" Gloria said, starting up the stairs to the platform.

"Then react and keep talking. Professor, if you have any historical parallels to this kind of thing, lob them in. We'll line up counterterrorism experts, state department officials, the US ambassadors to Vatican City and Italy, and whoever else I can think of and feed them to you when available."

Soon, they were in their seats, in a thirty-second countdown.

Gloria leaned toward Cal. He felt hot breath on his ear. "You didn't look shocked when you heard the news," she said. "You knew already, didn't you?"

"I heard something in confidence," he said.

"Don't forget which team you're on," she said coldly. "You get a scoop, we report the scoop. This is important shit, Cal. This is how careers are made—my career, specifically. When this is over, I don't get to trundle off to an ivy-covered campus."

He didn't spend a second thinking about his co-anchor. He handled Gloria with a non-committal grunt and turned his mind to Elisabetta. He wanted to be with her, not parked in front of a camera.

"How much can we speculate about the perpetrators?" Gloria asked their producer.

"Speculate all you want," the producer said, "but do it responsibly. Remember, this is CNN, not Fox."

~

AN HOUR LATER, the epicenter of police activity had shifted to a location seven kilometers from Vatican City. To combat municipal crime, the city of Rome opened a twenty-four-hour video surveillance monitoring center inside a converted cigarette factory on the Piazza Giovanni da Verrazzano. Rome lagged behind the surveillance capabilities of other major European cities. Paris had a network of over sixty thousand cameras. London had over one hundred thousand. Rome was in catch-up mode, with fewer than five thousand police and public transport cameras. The director of the Sala Sistema Roma, a major in the Rome Polizia Locale, positioned himself in front of a bank of thirteen wall monitors and began to brief the assembled brass that included Emilio, Studer, Colonel Tavassi, and Generals Cremonesi and Trombetta.

"All shifts of personnel have been ordered to report to the center. We are systemically reviewing CCTV footage from around the city," the major said in an officious tone. "Here is the procedure we are following: we begin the search at a timestamp of 18:14 when the first Iveco van leaves the villa on the Viale Vaticano. We organize our efforts in a hub and spoke pattern with the villa as the hub and divide the compass into a pie of eight equal slices with a team of monitors assigned to each slice. Some slices have more cameras than others. Because the three vans did not initially go in the same direction, it is necessary to cover all compass sectors."

After a brief discussion of methods, the director excused

himself, leaving one of his men behind in the control room to field additional questions.

General Cremonesi found the empty chair beside Emilio. "The nun knows to contact us immediately if the kidnappers contact her?"

"The secretary of state knows," Emilio answered without turning his head.

"As I understand it, the sister is also your sister," Cremonesi said.

"She is. Why do you bring it up?"

"I find it interesting, that's all. I've always found the Vatican to be an inscrutable institution—lack of transparency, financial wizardry, rampant homosexuality, nepotism."

Emilio swiveled his head to look at the general full on and, with a poker face, asked, "Whom do you accuse of benefitting from nepotism, General? Me or my sister?"

Cremonesi's mouth cracked open to a crooked smile. "My goodness, Colonel, do you think I was referring to you? Heavens, no. I read somewhere there were family dealings among Curial officials. That's all."

Emilio wasn't inclined to let the insult rest so easily, but General Trombetta piped up and loudly asked the officer on duty, "Is there anything to eat around here? All this talk about slices of the pie has made me hungry."

~

CAL WAS RELYING on his memory, something he was loathe to do on live television, but his co-anchor and producer kept egging him on to fill the dead air.

"Violence during conclaves," Gloria said. "Is this a first, or has something like this happened before, Professor?"

Cal crossed his legs and leaned against the canvas chairback. "Like this, no. What happened today is unprecedented in scope and audacity. But there have been violent incidents in the history of papal transitions. In the fourth century, upon the death of Pope Liberius, two clerics representing opposing factions of the young

Church were elected pope simultaneously. Armed men supporting Archdeacon Damasus attacked the church where supporters of his rival, Deacon Ursinus, had gathered, murdering scores of them. Damasus ruled as a bloodstained pope for about twenty years."

"What about kidnappings?" Gloria asked.

"I don't know of a kidnapping occurring during a conclave, but a famous kidnapping led to one. In 1798, during France's invasion of Italy by Napoleon Bonaparte, Pope Pius VI, the ruler of the papal states, was asked to renounce his leadership of the conquered territories. When he refused, he was kidnapped and taken to France as a prisoner, where he died in captivity. His successor, Pope Pius VII, also ran afoul of Napoleon, who had him kidnapped in 1809 and exiled to France, where he was held until Napoleon abdicated in 1814."

"Have cardinals been kidnapped before?"

Cal wrestled with the question for several moments, wondering how it would look if he pulled out his phone. Then, he heard the disembodied voice of the producer in his ear. "Googled it. Congo, 1977, Cardinal Biayenda, killed. Cameroon, 2020, Cardinal Tumi, released."

Cal was scrupulously honest. "Our amazingly talented producer has just jogged my memory. "In 1977, Cardinal Biayenda of the Congo was kidnapped and murdered by one of the country's political factions. More recently, in 2020 in Cameroon, Cardinal Tumi was kidnapped by a separatist faction, but he was released unharmed. Again, there has never been a mass kidnapping of cardinals during or outside a conclave."

Then, Gloria got a prompt from their talented producer and said, "We have a tweet from a CNN viewer who asks, 'With this ongoing crisis, who's in charge at the Vatican?"

Cal rubbed his chin professorially and said, "That's a fair question. We are in a *sede vacante*, so there's no pope now. Several of the kidnapped cardinal electors ran important departments within the Vatican bureaucracy. Of course, other cardinals aren't electors because of their age, and some remain in Vatican positions. In addition, a permanent staff of bishops and monsignors keeps the gears of the Curia and Vatican City moving. But if I were asked who is the single person in charge of the Vatican, I'd have to say the secretary of state, Elisabetta Celestino."

"A woman in charge of the Vatican," Gloria said. "Now we've seen everything."

※

IN THE ABSENCE of crisis updates, there was only so much airtime to fill with recaps and talking heads. After two hours, CNN in Atlanta pulled the plug on live coverage from Rome, and Cal was freed from his duties. After ten local time, he and Gloria climbed down from the booth.

"I guess this is it," he said.

"There's no way of knowing when the conclave is going to resume, is there?" she said. "You're a big hit with the audience. The producers say you're trending on Twitter. You going to stick around? I think the network will want you to keep going in some capacity."

He shrugged. "I think my pundit days are over," he said. "Time to trundle back to the ivy-covered campus."

She flicked her tongue like a viper. "Well, it was fun while it lasted."

Cal walked toward the dome of the basilica, glowing softly in the darkness. The square was crowded with news crews and pilgrims, continuing to look toward the night sky as if refusing to believe there would be no smoke billowing from the cold chapel stovepipe. The lights were on in the Apostolic Palace from the myriad offices of the Secretariat of State. He looked to Elisabetta's office windows and called her mobile, not expecting her to pick up.

She did, on the first ring. "Hello," she said. "How are you?"

"I'm done with television."

"For the night?"

"Forever."

It was good to hear her laugh.

"Do you want to come up?" she asked.

"If you're not too busy."

"I'll clear it with the Swiss Guards. They have the palace on strict lockdown."

The office suite of the Secretary of State was grand, designed to convey the power and majesty of the office. Her private secretary escorted Cal inside. The cavernous space and massive desk always made her appear small, but as he trod over the shiny parquet floor, she seemed even smaller. She was hunched over, on the phone, talking in English to someone speaking so loudly that he could hear an American voice spilling from the earpiece.

She smiled at him and held up a finger as he took one of the armchairs.

"I disagree, Bishop Fuller," she said. "I see no need for you to fly here from Texas. You have a diocese to run. The authorities are doing everything possible to find our people and bring them to safety."

Cal saw her clamp the phone more tightly to her ear and grimace. He could no longer hear the voice on the other end.

"I can assure you that you know everything we know," she said. "We are operating in full transparency. Believe me when I say you will be kept fully informed. Now, please forgive me. I have people waiting for me." She hung up and gave Cal a wan smile. "You are the people waiting for me. This bishop from Texas imagines he should ride in on his horse, like in a Western movie, to save the town and the damsel in distress. Me!"

"I'm getting a mental image of a priest drawing a Bible from his holster," Cal joked.

"Yes, exactly."

"It's been a rough day and a rough night," he said gently. "How are you holding up?"

"I have no reason to complain about myself," she said. "I have my freedom. My colleagues do not."

"Is there news? Any word from the kidnappers? You should know that I'm officially retired from CNN."

"My goodness, I trust you, Cal. There's been nothing. Emilio is working with the police on accessing security camera footage from around Rome. Vatican cameras showed that the cardinals were taken from the Viale Vaticano by transport vans of a particular model and make. Tracking the movement of these vans is of the highest urgency."

"Have you eaten?" he asked.

"No, have you?"

"Nope."

She leaned back. "I can order a pizza," she said.

"They deliver to the Vatican?"

"They surely do." She called her private secretary and asked him to place an order.

"The usual?" the monsignor asked.

She was about to ask Cal his preference when he preempted her by saying that anything was good. "You have a usual?" he said with a chuckle.

"Late nights are common here," she said. "Our nuncios span every time zone."

She joined him in the conversation area and smoothed the folds of her habit over her knees.

"The timing of this—" she said, her voice trailing.

"I think I know what you're going to say," he said. "The planning and execution have taken months. The only way the kidnappers could have known all the cardinals would be together inside the Sistine Chapel is for a conclave."

Elisabetta finished the thought. "And the only time a conclave happens is following the death of a pontiff. The Holy Father was relatively young. He wasn't ill."

Cal buried his forehead into his hand and said what he had been thinking. "The pope was murdered."

CHAPTER SIX

IT WAS AFTER MIDNIGHT AT THE SALA SISTEMA ROMA. INSIDE THE control center, the counters were littered with empty pizza boxes and paper coffee cups, and the senior officers were getting edgy, bickering over jurisdiction and operational tactics. Emilio had tried being a peacemaker, but he tired of it and let them argue. Suddenly, the room quieted as the central monitor on the green wall lit with a still image—a white Iveco transit van on a roadway.

The director of the center rushed in. "We have a significant discovery," he said excitedly. "This is a frame from a camera on the A90 ring road between junctions 23 and 24, taken at 19:03. This is approximately fifty minutes after the vans departed from the Viale Vaticano."

"A map, please," Studer called out.

The major called up a map of Rome on another screen, showing the Grande Raccordo Anulare, the orbital motorway that encircled Rome, in green. "Here is the location of the speed camera," he said, pointing to a spot where the highway passed through Torricola, a village south of Rome. "The van is heading westbound, obeying the speed limit," he said. "At this speed, we would expect to see it again within ten minutes at the next speed camera located between junctions 24 and 25. However, there is no sign of the van ten minutes later, twenty minutes later, sixty minutes later."

"So, they exited at junction 24," Colonel Tavassi said.

"We may presume so," the director said. "I have more." He pulled up another image that looked remarkably like the first—a white van on the motorway in the pale evening light. "This was captured eight minutes after the first image by the same speed camera located between junctions 23 and 24. And then, five minutes later, we have this—" Yet another image appeared. "—the third white Iveco van," he continued. "Again, neither of these vans appear between junctions 24 and 25."

"So, all of them got off at junction 24," Tavassi said.

"It seems so," the major said.

Emilio said, "If they took that exit, what road would they be on?"

The director switched the map to satellite view and pointed to a two-lane road leading north. "This is Via Adreatina," he said. "It goes through the village of Cecchignola. There's a camera here at this roundabout, one-point-five kilometers from the A90. We do not see the vans passing by it. So—"

Tavassi interrupted him by leaping to his feet and demanding a pointer. The major instantly complied and ceded his laser pointer to the superior officer. Tavassi swept the red beam between the highway and the roundabout and said, "So they are somewhere between here and here." He shone the red dot onto a cluster of large structures in an industrial park and asked what they were.

"This one is an Amazon hub," the director said. "And these are part of a logistics center for a supermarket chain."

"What about this?" Tavassi said, moving the pointer a little north and settling on a building with a red corrugated roof.

"It's a warehouse," the director said. "I don't have information about it, but we will make inquiries."

"There are no other buildings of interest between the two camera positions," Tavassi said. "We need to do more than make inquiries."

GENERAL TAVASSI HAD ALREADY PLACED his special interventions group on alert. A hostage rescue unit had been forward deployed from GIS headquarters in Livorno to an operations base in Rome. At two in the morning, almost ten hours after the first van departed from the Viale Vaticano, a heavily-armed squad of GIS officers drew up to the warehouse in Cecchignola and surrounded it. Emilio, Studer, and Tavassi observed from a nearby sand quarry as the Carabinieri colonel in charge of the operation hailed the dark building on a loudspeaker.

"To the unknown persons inside the building: we are the GIS of the Carabinieri. We have you surrounded. Release the hostages immediately, and you will not be harmed. I repeat, release the hostages immediately."

Over the next half hour, the colonel repeated the message without a response, then informed Tavassi that he would attempt to visualize the interior. An operative proceeded to creep up to the windowless structure, drill a hole through the aluminum skin, and insert a fiberoptic cable.

Tavassi and his colleagues watched a live feed on a tablet that revealed one of the white transit vans in the darkness.

"I don't see any people," Studer said.

"We don't have a full view," Tavassi said. "We need a second camera on the other side of the building."

The general instructed his colonel to deploy another fiber optic cable. Ten minutes later, new images appeared on their screen. This time, they could see the other two Iveco vans and no human activity.

"We're going to have to go in," Emilio said.

There were large overhead vehicle doors and smaller pedestrian doors on both sides of the warehouse. Explosives officers protected by snipers pressed plastic charges against the pedestrian doors and awaited orders to breach. On command, the two charges went off, and columns of armed men pushed into the dark building.

Tavassi's tablet showed point-of-view images from helmet

cameras. Beams of torchlight crisscrossed the interior. Emilio leaned over Tavassi's shoulder. GIS officers approached the vans, threw open the doors, and shouted, "Clear!"

At the final shout of "All clear," Emilio sprinted into the warehouse with the rest of the team, and someone found the light switches.

One of the GIS officers waved a red biretta at Tavassi, "They were here, General, but there's no sign of them now."

"This was a transit point," Emilio said. "They knew we'd be looking for the vans. The cardinals were transferred to one or more vehicles to take them on the next leg of their journey."

"At this point, they could be anywhere," Studer said.

Emilio chewed the inside of his lip, a habit he thought he had defeated years ago. "There are a great many things that need to happen," he said. "We need to review the footage from all the CCTV cameras in the area to see what vehicles left here and trace where they went. We have to track down the owners of this warehouse and the villa on Viale Vaticano. We must scrutinize all airports, train stations, and ports. We can't leave a stone unturned."

"Gentlemen," Tavassi said. "I suggest we set up a command center at GIS headquarters in Livorno. We have state-of-the-art communications infrastructure and the ability to deploy hostage rescue teams anywhere in the country. With your agreement, I'll get us a ride. We can be there by helicopter within the hour."

~

The port city of Livorno on the Tuscan coast was home to the command center of the Gruppo di Intervento Speciale. At 4 a.m., a Carabinieri Augusta Westland helicopter landed at the headquarters on the Viale Goffredo Mameli, a short distance from the Ligurian Sea. Generals Trombetta and Cremonesi opted to return to their respective agencies, and Commandant Studer decided to stay at the Vatican. There was no pope for the Swiss Guards to protect, but the Vatican had been attacked, and its defenses needed hardening. General Tavassi and Emilio hopped out of the chopper and fast-walked across the courtyard. Tavassi had organized a war room during the flight, and when the two men entered the HQ, a command staff of officers and technicians received them. Communication links were already in place with the Agenzia Informazioni e Sicurezza Interna, the Agenzia Informazioni e Sicurezza Esterna, and the CCTV monitoring center at the Sala Sistema Roma.

Tavassi introduced Emilio to his team, threw his hat on the table, and said, "All right, people, what do we have?"

Data began to flow. Emilio knew about the operational efficiency of the GIS and its track record in dealing with national and international crises, but he had never seen their teams in action. One of the assembled officers informed them that thirty minutes after the white Iveco vans were last seen between junctions 23 and 24 on the A90, a container lorry was identified on the speed camera between junctions 24 and 25. The officer projected a freeze-frame image of a lorry with a white cab hauling a pale yellow container.

Tavassi tutted his skepticism before his subordinate could carry on. "Why would you think that this is significant?" Tavassi asked. "How many container lorries use this road, say every hour?"

The officer, a lieutenant with a crisp uniform, answered, "During this very hour, we can count twenty-two lorries captured by the same speed camera."

"Again, why are you interested in this particular lorry?"

"General," the lieutenant said, "this is because the number plate on this Scania R 420 container lorry was reported stolen two weeks ago at a truck stop in Liguria. All other lorries passing this point within the same hour had legitimate plates."

Tavassi said, "You have my attention. Where does it go?"

"We see it again approximately four minutes later, heading west between junctions 25 and 26. In another five minutes, here is the lorry between junctions 26 and 27, traveling just below the speed limit. Here it is four minutes later, between junctions 27 and 28."

"Is it going to the airport?" Emilio asked.

"It seems not," the officer said. "Instead of exiting onto the A 91 to Fiumicino, we see it here, heading north on the E 80."

"And then where?" Tavassi said.

"That was the last camera on this route within the jurisdiction of the Rome monitoring center. We are liaising with the police in all jurisdictions along the E 80."

Tavassi shook his head in exasperation. "My God, this road hugs the coast all the way to France. We need to notify the French authorities."

Another officer at the table, a female captain, said, "General, we took the liberty of making the call to the DGSE. The French are on the lookout for the vehicle. At its rate of travel, it could have reached the French border two hours ago."

Emilio interjected, "If the intention was to take the cardinals out of the country, there are multiple airports and ports accessible from the coastal highway."

"That is true," the lieutenant said.

"I'm concerned about putting all our eggs in one basket," Emilio said. "This vehicle seems promising, but the theft of the license plate and its appearance on the highway at the right place and time could be a coincidence."

The captain replied, "We're not ruling out other lorries. We have technicians running down other leads, but it seemed prudent to prioritize the Scania."

Emilio grunted his agreement.

"Well, what about the airports and ports?" Tavassi said. "What do we know about them?"

The female captain raised her hand to signal she was the one to answer. "Based on the route of the target lorry, we feel we can deprioritize the Rome airports and Naples. We are investigating all major airports north of Rome, including Pisa, Florence, Bologna, and Genoa. We are focusing on cargo flights departing in the past few hours or those scheduled to depart this morning."

"Yes, yes," Tavassi nodded, "a hundred missing cardinals aren't going to check in for a commercial flight, are they? Ports?"

"The Port of Rome is a strong possibility," she said. "Our port in Livorno is also on the list, and Genoa too. We are making inquiries about cargo ship departures. Cruise ships seem unlikely.

Once we have more CCTV data on the destination of the lorry, we can rule in and rule out ports and airports."

Emilio opened a water bottle, had a sip, and then said, "The kidnappers could have arranged to hide our people somewhere in Italy."

"We'll have a better idea about this scenario once we have more CCTV data," the captain said.

The lieutenant cleared his throat and said, "And we have to consider the worst-case scenario."

"Which is?" Tavassi asked.

"That the lorry is hauling dead bodies," the officer said bluntly.

"There was no blood at the warehouse," Emilio said. "Could they have been loaded into the lorry and gassed? I don't think that happened."

"How can you be so confident?" Tavassi asked.

"Because they didn't kill Cardinals Rotolo and Stocchi. They took the time to bind them. No, they want our people alive, at least for now."

"Let's hope you're right," Tavassi said. "Now, tell me—who's been looking for the villa and warehouse owners?"

A female corporal waggled her pen in the air and said, "Me, General. The villa on the Viale Vaticano is owned by a Swiss family named the Baumgartners from Zurich. We reached them late last night. They informed us they were contacted a little under a year ago by a lawyer based in Lichtenstein inquiring about renting the property. They replied that it was not for rent. They were devout Catholics who enjoyed coming to Rome for several weeks a year. The lawyer indicated that his client greatly desired to rent the villa for one year and would be prepared to pay an over-market rate. They negotiated and agreed to eighty thousand euros per month."

To the sound of someone whistling, Tavassi said, "They'll need that and more to fill in the hole in their cellar."

"Who is the client?" Emilio asked.

"The Baumgartners emailed us a copy of their rental agreement," the corporal said, showing a document. "It's a limited liability company called Viale Vaticano Rentals based in the American state of Nevada. The Lichtenstein lawyer had power of attorney and signed the document. We asked the lawyer who he dealt with. He told us he only met the woman by telephone. Her name, he said, was Annette Marie Tremblay. She had a French accent. He received his fees from the limited liability corporation's Las Vegas, Nevada bank account."

"What do we know about Annette Tremblay?" Tavassi asked.

"Nothing yet," the corporal said. "This is likely an assumed name. After completing the transaction, the Lichtenstein lawyer discovered that her French tax ID number was fraudulent. As he had already received his fees, he made a non-urgent submission to the French authorities and has heard nothing more of the matter."

"What about the warehouse?" Emilio asked.

"A similar story," the corporal said. "The warehouse owner is an Italian company that has previously rented all or part of the facility to outside companies. A limited liability company called Cecchignola Warehouse Rentals, LLC rented the entire warehouse for May. It seems that it, too, is based in Nevada. The rent of twenty-five thousand euros was wired to the company from a Nevada bank. We don't have the contract yet, but the warehouse manager told us an Annette Marie Tremblay signed it."

At this point in the morning, General Tavassi was showing his fatigue. His shoulders were slumped, his facial muscles slack. "I want the Guardia di Finanza involved. We need to try and pierce the veil of these American corporations and find out who the actual owners are. They're in the best position to work with the FBI and Interpol."

The corporal took ownership of the assignment and said she would contact the financial police as soon as their offices opened for business. Emilio's muted phone was on the table, and it began buzzing like a dying winged insect.

He went to the back of the room to answer. "*Et tu*, Eli?"

She laughed and said, "Yes, I'm up too. I didn't know you remembered any of your Latin."

"Only that and *veni, vidi, vici*," he said. "Did you get any sleep?"

"Maybe an hour. I was up late talking to our overseas nuncios and various ambassadors to the Vatican. Their concerns are legion, as you can imagine. We've been offered the full support of the EU and member states, the United States, the UK, Canada, Japan, Mexico, and even China. I can put you in touch. The US offered the cooperation of the FBI and CIA. The UK offered up the MI5 and the SIS."

"I think the Italian authorities are already working with them. I'll know more in the morning."

"Have there been any developments?" she asked.

He ran through what he knew and heard heavy breaths of exasperation through the line.

"I saw Cal last night," she said. "He finished his TV work, at least until the conclave resumes."

"Is he going back to the States?"

"He says he's going to stay here."

"I'm not surprised."

She asked why.

"You know why."

She ignored him and said, "He and I were talking about the kind of planning that went into this crime. The complexity. The time it must have taken. Everything hinged on the need for a conclave. Nothing else would have gotten all the cardinal electors into the Chapel."

"I know where you're going with this," Emilio said. "I've been thinking about it too. Do you think it's possible?"

"There's only one way to find out," she said.

"Who could authorize the exhumation of Pope John?" he asked.

"I believe that would be me."

~

EMILIO WAS GIVEN a small office at the GIS headquarters with a comfortable desk chair that he used to nod off between the hours of seven and eight. When he awoke, he groggily tightened his loosened tie and stumbled into the hallway to look for coffee. General Tavassi found him trying to make the espresso machine work and took over the barista duties. As he tamped the coffee and pulled espresso shots, Emilio guessed he was in his sixties and that his black hair and mustache, unflecked by gray, were dyed. As he hunched over, Tavassi's belly spilled over his belt, but when he noticed he was being watched, he sucked it in. As far as Emilio was concerned, vanity and arrogance often traveled together, but Tavassi had the quiet confidence of a competent, experienced officer.

"Did you manage a cat nap?" Tavassi asked.

"A short one," Emilio said. "I'm probably worse for it."

"I wouldn't let myself succumb," Tavassi said, "for that precise reason. I don't know how long I'll last today. This is the first all-nighter I've pulled since becoming head of GIS. Have you heard?"

Emilio's pulse picked up a notch. "Heard what?"

"We could follow CCTV footage of the Scania lorry northbound on the E 80 until it exited the highway."

"Where did it get off?"

"Villaggio del Fanciullo. From there, it took the SS1 to—"

"Civitavecchia," Emilio said.

"That's correct. It went to the Port of Rome. Drink your coffee. We're taking another helicopter ride."

∼

Two thousand years ago, Emperor Trajan decided that the Mediterranean coast of Italy needed a second port to complement the one near Rome at Ostia. He chose Civitavecchia, and the port he built there has been in continuous operation since its completion. Three million passengers per year travel from the Port of Rome by cruise ship, and its commercial docks link central Italy to the important Mediterranean routes. The three helicopters carrying Tavassi, Emilio, and members of the GIS hostage rescue team hugged the coast from Livorno. Out the port side windows, the morning sunshine made the Mediterranean look like it was made of gemstones. Emilio spotted the port's massive cruise and cargo ships at dock from a few kilometers away.

Over the din of the rotors, Tavassi heard his mobile phone,

yelled into it, and pressed it hard against his ear before shouting that they'd be landing momentarily.

"The police found the Scania lorry," he told Emilio, "but not the container."

The choppers set down on the expanse of tarmac between piers twenty-five and twenty-six. The port's general manager, Rocco Galiotto, was there to meet them. Ducking under the rotors, the short, overweight man with a red tie tucked through the buttons of his short-sleeved white shirt rushed to shake hands.

"I'm Galiotto," he shouted. "You want to see the lorry?"

"Take us," Tavassi said. "This is Colonel Celestino, the head of the Vatican gendarmerie."

"A pleasure, gentlemen. Come, we can go on foot. It's at the parking lot over there."

Tavassi told an aide to have the hostage-rescue team assemble on the tarmac and check their gear. He and Emilio began jogging toward the parking lot, and Galiotto, wheezing through cigarette lungs, tried to keep up. The Scania was easy to spot. The police had it cordoned off, and several officers were milling around.

"Who's in charge?" Tavassi asked.

A sergeant stepped forward and saluted. "Me, sir."

"Has the vehicle been searched?"

"Yes, sir. There was nothing of interest. The glove box and console were empty. The storage compartment behind the seats was empty. The forensic unit is on its way."

"Galiotto, where would the container have been offloaded?" Tavassi asked the late-arriving, huffing man.

"By the docks. If it's parked here, it probably was offloaded at either pier twenty-five or twenty-six. You see the cranes?"

"I see cranes," Emilio said, "but no ships."

"We had several departures last night," Galiotto said.

"We'll need the details immediately," Tavassi said.

"Yes, of course. We should go to my office. I'll radio for a car. This is about the cardinals, isn't it?"

"It is," Tavassi said.

"You think they were in the container?" the manager asked.

"We don't know," Tavassi said. "It's a working assumption."

The administration building was a short ride away. By the time they arrived, Galiotto had explained how containers were tracked through offloading from lorries to onloading to ships. The tracking system was highly computerized, relying on GPS positioning devices attached magnetically to the sides of each container and scannable bar codes on the doors.

"We know the location of every box that enters and leaves our port," Galiotto said proudly. "And the shipping company knows the location of each box, anywhere on the planet while they're in transit."

"Is there any way to make a container anonymous?" Emilio asked.

"Only if there is some kind of fraudulent scheme," the manager said. "You'd need corrupt actions by shipping personnel and port employees. I've never seen it."

"And I've never seen one-hundred-sixteen cardinals disappear," Tavassi said.

Galiotto's office was shabby and retro, with cheap metal furniture, a threadbare sofa, and a scuffed wooden floor. Only his computers were modern. The two officers hovered as he accessed inventory files.

"So, we don't know the name of the transport company that delivered the box, and we don't know the ship it was destined for," Galiotto said. "We're a little bit in the dark."

"There was some kind of number on the side of the yellow container," Emilio said. "We have this from highway speed cameras."

He showed the manager a picture he had saved to his phone but was told the code was unrelated to their tracking system.

"Maybe we can narrow this down using the time the Scania lorry enters the crane yard," Galiotto said. "We have a camera at the gate where the driver has to show the shipping manifest to the guard to be allowed through for offloading. I can look for the yellow box on our CCTV feed if you give me the approximate time."

They told him the lorry was captured on video exiting the

highway at 8:51 p.m. Galiotto immediately pulled up the CCTV files starting at nine o'clock. Scanning the images at four times normal speed, they saw the Scania at the gate at a timestamp of 9:12.

Galiotto rubbed his hands gleefully. "We have it! We're not busy at this hour, so we can assume the crane operator could have it in the air within ten minutes. All we need to do is check to see which barcodes were scanned into our system at approximately this time and which ship received it."

Emilio watched the man's chubby fingers fly over the keyboard, anticipating a eureka moment. What he got was a low grunt.

"What's the matter?" Emilio asked.

"Nothing!" the manager exclaimed. "The last box loaded at piers twenty-five and twenty-six last night was at 8:25. The yellow container wasn't entered into our system. I fear this is the fraud scenario I told you about."

"Which of your employees would have been responsible for clearing the yellow container?" Tavassi asked.

"I can look it up, but the evening shift won't report until four."

"Tell us who it is, and we'll send the police to pick him up," Tavassi said.

"What about the ships?" Emilio said. "Which ones were docked at nine o'clock?"

Galiotto pulled up another screen. "There were two of them. The *Cyan Sea* departed at 9:22 for Tunis. The *Menelaus* departed at 9:45 for Marseille. The box must be on one of them."

"What time are they scheduled to arrive at port?" Emilio asked.

The manager glanced at his screen and said, "It's similar for both vessels. The distance from here to Marseille and Tunis is equivalent—about six hundred kilometers. The *Cyan Sea* should have landed about ten minutes ago. The *Menelaus* will land in half an hour or so.

"We need to contact the ship owners," Tavassi said.

Galiotto told them he'd have his people get the phone numbers and asked what else he could do. "I'm a strong Catholic," he said. "The scum who did this don't deserve to live."

Emilio wondered where in the Gospels Jesus had expressed this sentiment but said, "Take us to the crane yard. I want to have a look around."

The morning sun grew stronger, and the concrete apron around the towering cranes radiated waves of heat. While Tavassi and Galiotto talked, Emilio walked around the massive orange structures, looking for what he didn't know. But he was a policeman, and this was a crime scene, and he was doing what police officers do. He turned to the sea, bright and shimmering on the horizon but brown and murky near the pier. When he turned back to the hardscape, a bright spot of light caught his eye. The sun was glinting off something near the base of one of the massive towers. He removed his sunglasses, went toward it, and reached down. The reflective object was silver, the length of a pinky finger. He picked it up, rolled it in his fingers, and returned to the two men.

"They were here," Emilio said, opening his hand to reveal a finely crafted Christ figure splayed across a silver crucifix. "It's engraved on the back. It says, Cardinal Santagati."

"But the containers are never opened here!" Galiotto said.

"Air holes," Emilio said. "They must have drilled breathing holes for the people stuffed inside the box. Cardinal Santagati left us a breadcrumb."

CHAPTER SEVEN

When Emilio and Tavassi returned to the general manager's office, a member of Galiotto's staff gave them the contact numbers for the shipping lines. He also informed them that the security guard who would have allowed the Scania lorry into the crane yard wasn't answering his phone. Hearing this, Tavassi arranged for the Rome police to pick him up for questioning.

A stale odor wafted up from the cushions when Emilio sat on the battered sofa. He rang the offices of Hamouda Shipping in Tunis and asked for the owner. The call was passed to Mr. Hamouda, who listened in silence as Emilio identified himself and the nature of the crisis. When it was Hamouda's chance to respond, there were continued seconds of silence on his end, and Emilio wondered whether he was still on the line.

"Yes, we have been hearing nothing else on our news," Hamouda finally said. "You say a container with the cardinals could be on the *Cyan Sea*?"

"Yes, sir, it's possible."

"Do you have the bar code for the box? Or its GPS identifier?"

"We have neither," Emilio said, "but we have a photo of the container with a serial number printed on the side."

"Better than nothing," the owner said. "Here is my mobile number. Text it to me, please."

"This ship has twenty-four bays and carries eight thousand containers," Hamouda said. "Ordinarily, without computerized identifiers, it would take several hours to look for it. However, from what you tell me, this particular container would have been the last one loaded because the records I have indicate the loading of manifested cargo was completed ninety minutes before the ship departed the Port of Rome. Last in, first off. If it's on the *Cyan Sea*, your box will be easily spotted on the top of the pile. Ah, here is your text. I will personally check. Our offices are at the port. May I ring you back?"

Hamoud called a quarter of an hour later, sounding relieved that his company was off the hook. The yellow container was not on the *Cyan Sea*.

Emilio reported the news to Tavassi and called the next company, Morlet, SARL, the French owner of the *Menelaus*. He was informed that its CEO, Mademoiselle Morlet, was out and was transferred to Charles Morlet, the Vice President of Operations. He answered in French but switched to English at Emilio's request. As Emilio described the nature of his inquiry, the Frenchman was more expressive than the Tunisian, interjecting gasps and tongue clicks.

"My God! You are certain this suspect container is on the *Menelaus*?" he asked.

"It seems likely. Can you tell me the location of the ship?"

"One moment. I will check."

"Are you at the port in Marseilles?"

"No, no. Our offices are in Montpellier. One moment, please. Okay, I have it docking in ten minutes."

"When does unloading typically commence?" Emilio asked.

"Almost immediately. Time is money."

"The authorities will meet the ship," Emilio said. "Please inform your people not to touch the cargo until the police allow it."

"But, this is highly irregular."

"As is the kidnapping of cardinals during a conclave."

Tavassi had been listening in on speaker and was already

making his own call when Emilio hung up. Emilio was slightly surprised to hear the general launching into a heated conversation in perfect French, making his case to his counterparts at the French Commandement des Opérations Spéciales for the immediate interdiction of the *Menelaus*. General Bayssas, a three-star general who was his liaison, conferenced Tavassi with the base commander of the Force Scorpion division in Marseilles. Bayssas ordered a special forces mobilization pending the final authorization of an interdiction by the Élysée Palace. Tavassi transmitted the photo of the yellow container, and then, they waited. Thirty-minutes later, Tavassi received word that the French president had given his go-ahead for the operation.

Again, they waited. The two men prowled Galiotto's office like a couple of caged animals, breaking the tension with conversation.

"Your French is good," Emilio said.

"When I was younger, I was assigned to NATO headquarters. I took lessons with my wife for three years. I hated that fucking tutor."

"Why?"

"She had an affair with him. That did it for us. I only speak French when it's absolutely necessary. You married?"

"Me? Never," Emilio said.

"I knew you were smart," Tavassi said, finding a crushed pack of cigarettes in his pocket. "Want one?"

"I don't smoke."

"See? Smart. Even my doctor wouldn't begrudge me, given the circumstance." He lit up and said, "I'm sure smoking isn't allowed here, but Galiotto won't mind. If he does, screw him. God, I hope they're not dead. Can I ask you something, Colonel?"

"Go ahead."

"What's it like working for your sister?"

Emilio smiled. He had never been asked the question. Although many might have been curious, he never encountered someone blunt enough to ask.

"It's not a problem," he said. "I respect her, and she respects me. She knows precious little about police work, and I know precious little about Church work. And we try not to talk shop around the family dinner table. The respect ends with the rest of my family. My other sister, a medical doctor, and my father, a mathematician, give us a lot of shit for working at the Vatican."

"Not fans?" Tavassi asked.

"Not fans of our little city-state, no. If I could get away with it, I'd wear earplugs around them."

"Well, at least your family are all smart. My sister is an imbecile. Her husband is an imbecile. Their children are imbeciles. God, when are we going to hear something?"

―

THE TACTICAL-RESPONSE squad leader of Force Scorpion was a quick-talking lieutenant named Gautier. The order to mobilize reached him during a volleyball game with his men. Minutes later, they were suited up and airborne to the nearby Marseilles docks. Their Eurocopter Super Puma helicopter set down on the tarmac of Porte 2A beside the newly berthed *Menelaus*. Gautier ran toward the port director, nervously waving to the disembarking soldiers.

"Nothing has been removed?" Gautier asked.

"Nothing," the director said. "That was my instruction."

"You haven't notified the captain we're going to board, have you?"

"We've only informed the vessel that there was a technical delay, and they needed to stand by for unloading."

"What did the captain say?"

"These ships have masters, not captains."

Gautier got testy. "All right, what did the master say?"

"I communicated with the chief officer. He acknowledged our instructions."

"Where's the master?"

The director answered with a shrug of his narrow shoulders.

"Okay, keep them in the dark," Gautier said. "They've seen the helicopter, but we want some element of surprise." He showed the director the photo of the yellow container. "Do you know where this one is?"

"The company sent the picture. It's on top of the stack of Bay 7, the bay farthest to the starboard side of the stern. Follow my finger? Can you see it?"

Gautier squinted and called for binoculars.

"Okay, here's the plan," Gautier said. "Half my men are going to board the ship and secure it. As soon as you see a flare, I want you to move the container down to the tarmac. I want total control when we open it."

"You think the cardinals are inside?" the director asked.

"We'll know soon enough."

The director remembered something and said, "One of my men has to accompany your boarding party. The container is locked into the bay. A longshoreman has to unlock it."

"Fine. Get a volunteer immediately. We go in five minutes."

"Should I tell the man it's dangerous?"

"There's no way of knowing. Like I said, a volunteer."

A motorized gangway was driven into place, and a dozen special operators and one dock worker toting a heavy tool began climbing the ship's starboard side. The chief officer of the *Menelaus*, a Sikh in a blue turban, was at the rail. He didn't flinch at the sight of the heavily armed boarding party.

The sergeant on point yelled at the chief to raise his hands. Another soldier patted him down for weapons.

"Is this part of the special operation," the chief said in French.

"What are you talking about?" the sergeant demanded.

"Don't you know what happened last night?"

"You'd better start talking, right now," the sergeant said.

"We had just disembarked from Rome when Master Abadie informed me that the French government had commandeered the vessel for a special operation involving international terrorism. He said there was a container onboard with human cargo. More than that, he wasn't authorized to say. I was ordered to collect the mobile phones for all crew members, myself included, and deliver them to the master's cabin. Further, I was ordered to confine myself and all crewmembers to quarters until 6 a.m. The only exception was engine-room staff who were confined to station. The master would control the bridge."

"You obeyed these orders?"

"To the letter."

"But these were peculiar orders, no?"

"Highly peculiar," the chief said.

"Then what?"

"At six o'clock, I left my cabin and proceeded to the bridge. The bridge was empty. The vessel was running on autopilot. At my station, I found a note from the master instructing me release the crew from confinement and dock at Marseilles as usual. I was ordered not to use the radio until it was time to contact the tugboats at port. Master Abadie was nowhere to be found. His cabin was empty. I ordered the men to search the ship. There was still no sign of him."

"Your mobile phones?"

"We haven't found them yet. They might be locked in the master's desk. I should mention, we did find something unusual. The cargo holds for the Rome to Marseille passage were not used. We only loaded container cargo. One of the empty holds was littered with empty water bottles, banana skins, apple cores, and food wrappers. There must have been people down there."

"Did you leave it as you found it?" the sergeant asked.

"We didn't touch it."

"If the master isn't on the ship, how did he get off? Did another ship pull alongside?"

"I don't think so. The ship would have had to execute a full stop for a safe ship-to-ship transfer. From my cabin, I detected no change in cruising speed."

"Helicopter?"

"It's possible. From below decks, with engines running, we would not have heard anything."

"What do you know about the last container loaded at Rome? A yellow one."

"We had completed loading, but the master informed me that there was one late-arriving box. Because of it, we almost missed our departure window. I was thinking that maybe this was the one with human cargo."

"We need to unload it now," the sergeant said. "I have a dock worker who will unlock it."

The exasperated officer kneaded his beard and said, "Can you please tell me what in God's name is going on?"

"The police will want to talk to you. My men are going to search the ship now."

"What about the special operation?"

"It was special, all right," the sergeant said.

He instructed his men to search the ship and detain all crew members, and have the longshoreman unlock the yellow container from its rails. He called his lieutenant on the radio.

"It's weird shit up here, sir." He regurgitated the chief officer's account, then said, "We're doing a search. The container should be ready for the crane soon. Their guy will signal the crane operator."

Lieutenant Gautier radioed a brief report to his base commander and trained his binoculars on the crane as the operator moved the gantry toward the yellow container. The longshoreman stood on an adjacent box, waved his hands, and the gantry latched onto the target. Once airborne, the operator swung the gantry arm and gently lowered the container onto the tarmac.

Gautier deployed his men in an arc around the rear of the container. Two dock workers unlocked both halves of the door, swung them open, and ran for cover.

Gautier pointed the flashlight on his rifle rail into the black interior of the container and swore.

∼

When Tavassi's phone rang, Emilio sprang from the ratty sofa to take the news on his feet. Tavassi answered with a "Yes, General" frustrating Emilio by keeping the phone to his ear. All he could hear was Tavassi grunting and saying, "Yeses, okays, and I understand." Finally, Tavassi put the phone in his pocket and retrieved his jacket.

"The container was empty," Tavassi said. "Well, not

completely empty. There were ecclesiastical garments—rochets, mozzettas, birettas, and the like, and energy bar wrappers and empty water bottles. That was it. No people. And you were correct. There were air holes punched through the walls of the container. There's more. The ship's master is missing. Somehow, over a hundred people disappeared from the ship between Rome and Marseille."

"What does the remaining crew say?"

"It seems they know nothing. They'll be interviewed by the French."

As Emilio stared at the sea in despair.

Tavassi was at the door saying, "Let's get back to Livorno. We'll throw all our resources into figuring out what happened on that ship. Are you all right?"

"I failed them," Emilio mumbled. "This happened on my watch."

"Don't blame yourself," Tavassi said. "These terrorists are clever and resourceful. We're going to catch them on your watch."

As the helicopter pilots went through their pre-flight checklist, Emilio called Elisabetta to brief her. She took the news calmly.

"Now what?" she asked.

"We'll be engaging with the Italian and French militaries, NATO, and the United States to find out how they got off the ship. There's bound to be satellite and radar data. Once we know where they went, we can calculate next steps."

"Are you sure they got on the ship?" she asked. "What if the lorry was a decoy?"

"With all the ecclesiastical garments in the container, the food wrappers, the water, it's highly likely they were in there."

"It could have been staged, no?" she said.

Then he remembered he hadn't told her about Cardinal Santagati's silver crucifix.

"All right," she said. "I'm convinced."

"Was the pope exhumed?"

"It took place early this morning."

"When will we have an indication?" he asked.

"Maybe later today or tomorrow. The president of the Italian Society of Toxicology is personally overseeing the testing."

"Did you announce the exhumation?"

"We felt we had to be transparent. The press office is dealing with it, but many people are upset with me for ordering it. I didn't ask you the most important question."

"What's that?" he said.

"How are you doing?"

He forced a laugh. "And I didn't ask you the same. I'm okay. Didn't sleep last night, and I'm running on adrenaline, but okay. Better than our people, I'm sure."

"Micaela's been calling. Papa too. They're more worried about us than the cardinals," she said.

"No surprise there. Is Cal still around?"

"I think so. He texted me this morning, but I've been too busy to answer. I've been inundated by calls from bishops in Rome and out in the dioceses, non-elector cardinals who aren't too ill or senile to pick up a phone, seemingly every billionaire Catholic in the world, heads of state, and countless journalists. The job is usually a juggling act, but today it feels like I'm juggling on a tightrope suspended over a lion's den."

Emilio was about to tell her he had to go when he heard Elisabetta's private secretary shouting at her.

"Madame Secretary! There's a video!"

∽

The video posted to YouTube was shot with a high-resolution camera, but due to low ambient light, the images were fairly dark. Also, the camera operator didn't seem to possess a steady hand, and the result was slightly stomach-churning. In the background, the cardinal electors stood in three long rows, staring toward the lens with grim, resolute expressions. Some still wore the full choir dress from when they entered the Sistine Chapel. Others had shed their hats and top vestments and only had robes. It was possible to see what those in the front row did with their hands. Most clasped them in front. Two fingered their pectoral crosses. One engaged in kinetic hand-wringing. One man in the second row had no ecclesiastical garments. He wore a dark suit with a dark tie still tightly knotted to the collar. This was Doctor Bellisario.

Four individuals in the foreground were dressed militarily in black turtlenecks, trousers, and boots, their faces concealed behind balaclavas. They had tactical belts for holsters, extra magazines, and knife sheaths, but displayed no weapons. Form-fitting shirts revealed that two were men and two were women, their sleeves rolled up. One woman was black. The others were white.

They were assembled inside a cavernous chamber, and when a woman began to speak, her words echoed. The last row of cardinals stood against a dark, metallic wall that extended as high as the upper edge of the camera frame.

For the first several seconds of the video, the only thing that could be heard was a low sort of hollow groaning, an inanimate sound. Then, the camera zoomed on the kidnappers. The white woman clicked a flashlight and began to read from a note in her hand.

"The Catholic Church is a sinful Church," she said in English with a heavy French accent. "For centuries, our Church has been ruled by men who have trampled on women's rights in the name of God Almighty, his son, Jesus Christ, and the Blessed Virgin Mary. The men who stand behind us, the cardinals of this Church who gathered yesterday to choose another man as pope, are the ones responsible for the subjugation of Catholic women. It is time this male domination ends. We have two demands. One: the cardinal electors must collectively agree with immediate effect to allow for the ordination of women as priests. Two: the cardinal electors must continue their conclave and their voting until a two-thirds majority elect as the next pope of the Catholic Church, the newly ordained Elisabetta Celestino, the Vatican Secretary of State, who is the only person we can trust to be the next person to sit on the throne of St. Peter. There will be four ballots per day following normal conclave rules. Failing a two-thirds majority in favor of Elisabetta Celestino, the voting will continue. If she is elected, the conclave will end and the cardinals will be released. However, in five days commencing tomorrow, if she has not been elected, the cardinals will be executed."

The shot pulled back to show the cardinals' stunned faces, and seconds later, the video ended.

∼

Elisabetta, Emilio, and Cal were among the million people to view the video within the first ten minutes of its posting. Elisabetta watched it the first time in stunned disbelief, a second time in horror, and a third in anger. She was angry about the threats. She was angry at the appalling treatment of the clerics. And she was livid that the sordid kidnapping had been done as a twisted homage to her. Eerily, the phones within the Secretariat stopped ringing for most of these ten minutes, but when they began again, they didn't stop for the rest of the day. Silvio Licheri couldn't get through to her and had to run wildly from the Vatican Press Office to the Apostolic Palace.

He barged into Elisabetta's private office without knocking and, gasping for air, said, "We need to put out a statement."

"I agree," she said, "but what should it say?"

"That the Vatican rejects these vile blackmail threats and is working with the relevant authorities to secure the safe return of the cardinals."

"And what shall we say about the elephant in the room?" she asked, clear-eyed.

"Nothing," he almost yelled. "We don't give it oxygen. Without oxygen, things die."

"This will not die," she said. "This is all the press, the faithful, and the rest of the world will want to hear about. Do you intend to say no comment to the thousands of requests you'll get soliciting comments from me?"

"Believe me, I can say no comment in my sleep," he said.

"I can guarantee you, as we speak, there will be conspiracy theories sprouting online, accusing me of orchestrating the kidnapping to promulgate my vicious feminist agenda."

"You must ignore the crazies as you have done the last two years," he pleaded.

"Yes, yes, Silvio, I will do so, but you are like the Dutch boy with his finger in the dyke. The wall is going to crack, and the flood is coming. We can only pray that Emilio and the others find them soon."

Emilio watched the video with Tavassi on the way to Livorno. Like Silvio Licheri, he tried to ignore the elephant in the room and concentrate on the forensic value of the posting. Tavassi seemed to understand his colleague's discomfort, and he, too, didn't acknowledge the big beast.

The two men had to shout over the rotors as they analyzed three aspects of the video: the location, the kidnappers, and the condition of the cardinals. They immediately concluded that the video had been recorded on board the *Menelaus*. The size and the metallic look of the chamber suggested it was shot within a cargo hold. The undulation of the camera frame was likely the result of wave action against the hull. Tavassi relayed a message to the French soldiers on board the ship to try and match the video footage with one of the holds.

"What do you make of these kidnappers?" Emilio asked.

Tavassi shouted into Emilio's ear. "Only the white woman speaks. She sounds French or from a French-speaking country. We can get a linguist to narrow this down. She sounded resolute. It goes without saying that these are highly organized terrorists with vast resources at their disposal. What do *you* think?"

Emilio shouted, "It's beyond belief that Catholics have perpetrated this. We do contingency planning for all manner of terrorist attacks. We never contemplated an enemy within."

⁓

CAL WAS JOGGING through the Villa Borghese gardens when his phone rang. He preferred running earlier in the morning, but he had stayed up late, watching TV coverage of the crisis and raiding his minibar. He had thought repeatedly about calling Elisabetta, but he didn't. She had his number if she needed to talk. When he unzipped his fanny pack and had a look at his phone, he almost didn't answer. Gloria Hernando was nothing if not persistent. He knew if he didn't pick up, she'd just keep calling.

She didn't meet his greeting with banter. There was a percussive, "Have you seen it?"

"Seen what, Gloria?" he asked.

"The hostage video that just dropped. Watch it and call me right back. It's everywhere. We'd like to get you on air right away. Where are you?"

"I'm having a run in the park."

"Stop running. Watch the video. Call me."

He found it on Twitter, clicked through, and watched it standing in the shade of an umbrella pine. He found a bench and watched it again. On the first viewing, he paid attention to the alarming ultimatum and its twisted rationale. On the second, he searched the clergymen's haggard, stoical faces and gestures, looking for non-verbal signs of how they were enduring their ordeal, and tried to make out the eyes of the kidnappers through the openings in their masks. They seemed unblinking and determined. His mood darkened and blotted out the sunshine and greenery of a fine Spring morning. He didn't feel like running anymore, and he didn't feel like speaking to Gloria. He texted her that he wouldn't be able to join her broadcast and slowly walked back to the hotel.

※

THAT DAY, Cal received calls from friends and academic colleagues around the world, but for him, the two most consequential ones were from Rome. They came in the afternoon as the wind swept over the dome of the Pantheon and through the Piazza della Minerva, turning the long lace curtains of his room into sails. He eagerly took the call from Micaela Celestino, who, in her inimical manner, opened with what he too had been thinking.

"This is terrible for our girl," she said. "It plays into the hands of her critics."

"It's not good," he agreed. "Have you talked to her since it came out?"

"Only for a minute. She couldn't be busier, but she knew she'd be in my shit book if she didn't answer."

"How is she?"

"She says she's okay, but you can hear the contrary in her voice. The situation is bad. Very bad. We didn't discuss what the fuckers in the video said about her. We didn't have to. You know, the funny thing is, she'd be a great pope. Better than all these asshole men put together. But the whole affair is an abomination. Who are these kidnappers? I mean, the French have always been strange, but this?"

"Who knows who they are?" he said, "They're not amateurs. Can you imagine what went into pulling this off? Have you talked to Emilio?"

"Me? No. Eli says he doesn't know anything yet about who's behind this. Are you staying in Rome?"

"For now, yes."

"Good. Eli's going to need all the support she can get. Especially from you. She knows you care about her—as a person, as a woman—not as the fucking secretary of state."

"I'm glad she knows that," he said.

An hour later, he received a call from a man who, although well-known to him, was not a friend. To Cal's recollection, they had met only twice before, years ago, at gala charity dinners in Boston, the kind where Cal was obligated to dust off his tuxedo and open his checkbook. If it were not for Cardinal William Donahue, Cal's friend Rodrigo Da Silva might never have become a cardinal and pope. Donahue was Da Silva's predecessor as Cardinal of Boston. He was an Irish kid from Roslindale who became a priest and rose rapidly through the ranks with postings to Rome before becoming a bishop and, finally, a cardinal. He might have lived out his days as a quintessential Boston power broker had he not been exposed as covering up the sexual improprieties and predatory behavior of more than a dozen parish priests in the name of protecting the

Church's reputation. The pope at the time, eager to sweep the matter under the rugs at the cardinal's diocesan mansion in Brighton, accepted his resignation. The Vatican put the disgraced cleric ever-so-gently out to pasture, naming him archpriest of one of the Seven Pilgrim Churches of Rome, the Basilica Papale di Santa Maria Maggiore, where the eighty-four-year-old prelate, now lived in relative obscurity.

"Professor Donovan, William Donahue, here. I hope this isn't an imposition, calling on your cell phone. I got your number from—heck—I can't remember where I got it."

It took Cal a long second to place the name with the craggy voice. "Cardinal Donahue. It's no imposition. I'm glad to hear from you."

"I saw you on CNN yesterday when the news of the kidnapping broke. I wanted to tell you that I thought you did an admirable job. You're a credit to Boston and Harvard. I was class of 1959, you might recall."

Cal didn't recall. "Thank you."

"Terrible times we're living in," the cardinal said. "One of the worst crises in the history of the Vatican. You going to be around tonight? Thought we might have a spot of dinner at my place if you're free. My residence is across from the basilica. You know I'm at the Santa Maria Maggiore, right? It would be my pleasure to be your host."

Cal wasn't keen on the idea, but he couldn't say no. The man sounded like he had an agenda beyond commiserating with a fellow Harvardian.

~

THE BASILICA WAS near the central Rome train station, a half-hour walk from Cal's hotel. Donahue's apartment was what Cal had expected—a grandly proportioned suite of rooms in a venerable Church-owned palazzo. It was a gilded exile for a cleric reviled back in Boston for transferring pedophile priests from parish to parish, free to re-offend. Cal remembered discussing the handling of the

Donahue affair with Cardinal Da Silva, and he recalled what his friend had told him. "The Boston Diocese will have no more Donahues. Not on my watch. If I had been pope, a job I hasten to add I do not aspire to, I would not have provided him a cushy landing in a papal basilica. However, he can no longer harm young people, which is the most important outcome."

A nun at least as elderly as the cardinal served drinks and finger food in the book-lined reception room, while Cal and Donahue discussed the events of the past twenty-four hours. The cardinal, in country-club attire, seemed to have picked up the art of Italian hand gesticulation, for he flung his meaty paws around as he talked. Cal couldn't help noticing that his large knuckles were bright red, as if he had been punching sides of beef, Rocky-style.

"So, there've been no developments?" Donahue said. "The authorities have nothing?"

"You know what I know," Cal said, working through a glass of red wine so heavy, it was almost chewy.

"Do I?" the cardinal said. "You're with CNN. And the way I hear it, you're more plugged into the Vatican than I am."

"I'm afraid the pope's death pulled the plug."

"You and Rodrigo were great friends. I can't claim the same. He was distant with me. I get it. As my successor, he had to dissociate himself from what came before. At least he didn't dismiss me from my position here. He could have. I served at his pleasure. I wish I had thanked him for that, but beyond a few passing remarks, usually about the Red Sox, we seldom spoke."

Cal nodded at him uncomfortably.

"But you're not unplugged, are you?" Donahue continued. "It's said that you've got the ear of our secretary of state."

"We've known each other for several years—that's true."

"She's really on the hot seat now, isn't she?" the cardinal said after wolfing down a bruschetta. "It was bad enough for her in the immediate aftermath, with all the optics of a woman appearing to be singlehandedly in charge of the Roman Catholic Church, but after that batshit crazy diatribe by the kidnappers, she's in an untenable position, don't you think? I mean, really! A woman pope?"

The cardinal's hidden agenda was declaring itself earlier in the evening than Cal had expected. He supposed it wouldn't be revealed until dinner was served. The nun hobbled over to refill Cal's glass. He didn't like the wine, but he needed more alcohol on board to make it through the next couple of hours. Donahue would have known to break out the vodka if he had done some homework.

"Well, she's in a tough spot, I'll give you that," Cal said.

"You know, my phone's been ringing off the hook," Donahue said. "Do you want to know who's been calling me? Old cardinals and younger archbishops. We've got quite the WhatsApp group going. There's a consensus that it would have been easier to understand this abomination if the kidnappers had been radical Islamists. Coming from fellow Catholics is a tough pill to swallow."

Cal sighed at his newly filled glass. "I had the opposite reaction. I was relieved they weren't Islamists. The world doesn't need that kind of divisiveness. Innocent people would have been caught up in the violence."

The elderly cardinal fiddled with the buttons on his sweater and said, "Yes, well, you know what I meant. This group of ours—the conversation is veering in a very specific direction. We feel obligated to respond to this ongoing crisis with measures designed to protect the integrity of the Church. We propose that we adopt interim measures until the crisis has abated and, with the help of God Almighty, all of our brethren return safely and elect a new pope."

"Interim measures?" Cal said. "Such as?"

"Such as a council of elders assembled from energetic and *compos mentis* cardinals in their eighties to oversee Vatican affairs. As a student of the Church, you'll recall it was Pope Paul VI who decided in 1970 that participation in conclave would be limited to cardinals under eighty. Five decades ago, eighty was ancient indeed. With modern medicine, many of our older brethren, myself included, are more than capable in mind and body to fulfill any and all duties."

Cal felt no obligation to hide his irritation at this standard-bearer of everything wrong with the old guard. Cal always got his hackles up when someone started a sentence with "with all due respect," but that didn't stop him from using the phrase himself.

"With all due respect, Your Eminence, the kidnapping happened only yesterday. As far as I'm aware, under Sister Elisabetta's leadership and the direction of the professional staff of the Curia, the Vatican is functioning as normally as possible and satisfying its obligations to the diocese and its international partners."

Donahue's smile was patently forced. "We don't know how long this crisis will last, do we? What if it grinds on for an extended time? How long before the wheels come off the cart? And here's another thing, Cal. What happens if the worst-case scenario comes to pass? What if all the cardinal electors are assassinated? Who will elevate bishops and repopulate the college of cardinals without a sitting pope? For the sake of the Church, we must do contingency planning, and at the same time, send a signal that we will never consent to a woman as pope."

Cal put down his glass of syrupy wine. "I'm not sure what this has to do with me."

"The nun is your friend. We would be grateful if you could persuade her to appoint an interim council of cardinals to assist her in the difficult days ahead. Our flock is large—one-point-five-billion souls. They are worried and fearful. Surely, they will be comforted knowing that men of great experience and deep faith are willing to step up and steer our Church in its time of need." Donahue abruptly stood, flashing a two-thumb's-up sign. "Why don't you come through to the dining room, Cal. I see you like the red. I've got two more bottles of it. They'll go down a treat with the lamb."

∼

When Cal got back to his room, the first thing he did was purge the memory of the wine with a bracing shot of cold vodka. He stripped off, lay on the bed, turned on the TV, and scrolled Twitter to see if there was news. There wasn't. He had a mind to call or text Elisabetta. But he imagined the pressure she was under and didn't want to spoil whatever respite she might be having by informing her about some old men's plans to coopt her authority. That unpleasantry could wait until the morning. Unsurprisingly, RAI News was replaying the hostage video for the umpteenth time, and because he had only seen it on his phone, he got off the bed for a closer look.

At the point where the woman reading grievances and demands said, "It is time for the male domination of the Church to end," Cal spotted something and reached for his phone to take a picture of the screen. Her turtleneck sleeves were pulled to the elbow, exposing a tattoo on her left forearm. A small tattoo of a simple yellow cross.

Has anyone else noticed this?

He was dissatisfied with the quality of his photo, so he pulled up the video on his laptop, zoomed in on the tattoo, and took a screenshot. It was past eleven, early enough, he thought, to call Emilio, but it went to voice mail.

"Emilio, it's Cal. I picked up something tonight on the video. Maybe you saw it too. I'll text you a screenshot. The woman who's speaking has a yellow cross tattooed on her left arm. I've written about this kind of cross. I think it could be important."

CHAPTER EIGHT

Cardinal Hector Sanz, the Archbishop of Buenos Aires, was chosen by his fellow cardinals to deliver the sermon at the opening of the conclave, believing he would launch the proceedings on a tone of equanimity. He was well-respected, studiously moderate in his views, and genial. After each cardinal swore an oath to adhere to the rules of the conclave, Sanz rose from his seat directly below Michelangelo's fresco of God creating the sun and planets. He was not one for extemporaneous speech. His printed remarks were laid out on the altar at the eastern end of the chapel, and donning his glasses, he began to read in Italian. The message he wished to convey was that the papacy was like a necklace of precious pearls, each one unique. For two millennia, every pope has been distinct from one another but just as precious. Pope John had left them too soon, but if they opened their hearts and put aside temporal ideologies, the Holy Spirit would guide their hand as they marked their ballots and lead them to the next pearl.

"My brothers in Christ, we came together two short years ago to elect Rodrigo Da Silva to become the father of our Church. Two years is a speck of time, but our beloved Pope John used it well. Had he not been taken from us so soon, we would have undoubtedly witnessed a rich and full pontificate. To me, the Holy Father was a bright and lustrous pearl—'

Sanz stopped reading to peer over his spectacles at the commotion at the chapel's western end. Cardinals seated there began pushing their chairs back and standing, and soon, most of the clerics were on their feet.

No one cried out, but questions began to fill the chamber.

"What is the meaning of this?"

"Who are you?"

"What in God's name is happening?"

The cardinals had been seated at tables along the long walls of the chapel on a wooden platform elevated fifty centimeters above the chapel's marble floor. The plywood platform was covered in a simple beige carpet. As Sanz began his sermon, the cardinals closest to the western end of the chapel heard the curious sound of carpet being cut. When they looked to the spot, they saw a head shrouded in black appear, followed by a torso, also in black. The nearest cardinal shot to his feet, and a man dressed fully in black crawled from a gash in the carpet and sprang up, brandishing a short-barreled military-style rifle.

"Say nothing. Do nothing," the man said in French-accented English. The chapel's acoustics were such that he didn't need to shout to be heard throughout the conclave.

As the cardinals looked on with mouths agape, four other black-clad intruders in tight-fitting turtlenecks emerged from under the platform like a swarm of insects skittering from the darkness into a lighted room. Two women and two men, fanned out around the chapel, menacing the clerics with their weapons and demanding quiet.

One of the women, whose white skin was visible through the openings of her balaclava, made her way toward the altar and pulled a hunting knife from a sheath. "If anyone calls out," she said, "I will cut your throat. Do you understand?"

When she reached Cardinal Sanz, she shooed him toward the others at the point of her knife, glanced at his sermon, and then delivered her own remarks through a dry throat.

"Your lives and the lives of your colleagues will depend on what you do in the minutes that follow. We don't intend to harm you, but we will kill you if you shout for the Swiss Guards. Follow our instructions carefully, and do not speak unless we ask something of you. Is that understood?"

The woman gestured toward one of her compatriots, a man positioned at the center of the chapel. He dropped to his knees, removed a small power saw from his backpack, and cut a large square of carpet and plywood from the middle of the raised platform. The cardinals with a clear view began murmuring at the sight of a ladder being pushed by unseen hands through the new opening.

Cardinal George Fisher, the Archbishop of Westminster and one of the scrutineers, turned to the dark-suited Doctor Bellisario standing behind him and whispered, "Did they let you bring your mobile phone?"

"No," was the reply. "If I required assistance, I was to bang on the door."

The woman at the altar noticed the whispered exchange and said, "You, in the suit. Who are you?"

"I'm the doctor on call in case of a medical emergency," he replied.

The woman had intensely blue eyes that gleamed through her mask holes. "I can promise a medical emergency if you keep talking."

A sixth intruder, a man with an exceptionally lithe body, appeared at the top of the ladder and hopped onto the platform. He searched for their leader, the blue-eyed woman, and gave her a jaunty salute. Then, he craned his neck to the frescoed ceiling and did a pirouette, leaving the impression he was awestruck.

The other woman in the group, with skin as black as her balaclava, stepped to the center of the chapel and said in a steely, accented English, "I want everyone down this ladder. You must move fast. As soon as one head disappears, the next man will climb. Once you are down to the basement, you will await further instructions." She pointed to the cardinal closest to her, the Haitian Laguerre, and said, "You. Go first."

At that, the lithe admirer of Michelangelo had one more peek and then scurried down the ladder to receive the human chain.

Laguerre did as he was told and approached the ladder, but before he put a foot on the first rung, he addressed the black woman in French. "You speak French, yes? Where are you from? Why are you doing this?"

She answered in the same language with a tone demonstrating ice in her veins. "You are not entitled to ask me questions. You are my prisoner. Get down the ladder."

Laquerre looked toward his colleagues, turned his palms upward in a sign of resignation, and began his descent. The black woman signaled who was next, using the barrel of her rifle as a teacher would use a wooden pointer. A conga line of red-robed clerics soon formed, the men whispering furtive protestations to one another.

"I'm an old man. How can I do this?"

"My knees are bad."

"I fear heights."

"Do you think they will kill us once we go down?"

Others took to comforting distraught colleagues.

"Have faith, dear friend. The Lord will protect us."

"I'll go before you and help you get down."

"The police will learn of this. We will be saved."

Thirty cardinals went down the ladder before it was Cardinal Macy's turn. The big American balked and addressed the person he took to be the leader, the woman with blue eyes.

"Please tell me what you hope to gain from this."

She drew close and tilted her head upwards, aiming those blue eyes at the tall man's florid face.

"No talking."

"Let us find common ground," he continued. "Surely there's a way for you to achieve your goals peacefully, and let us carry on with our sacred conclave. There's always a solution among people of goodwill. You'll find me a good listener."

The woman pushed the barrel into the cardinal's taut belly and hissed, "You're Macy."

Macy held his nerve. "I am. What's your name?"

She shook her head. "Here you are, one of the papabile, so close to the prize you can probably taste it. But you don't know if you'll be elected. Perhaps it will be Colpo. Perhaps a dark horse. You imagine you can show your courage and persuade us to negotiate, and we will melt away. You imagine how grateful the cardinals will be and how they will make you pope by acclamation. These are fantasies playing in your head, Cardinal Macy. Get down the fucking ladder, or we will detonate grenades and end the matter here and now."

Macy wagged his finger at her and was about to say something when he seemed to think better of it and stepped onto the ladder.

As Cardinal Rotolo awaited his turn, he commiserated with Cardinals Paul Montebourg, a tall Frenchman with thick white hair and matching bushy eyebrows, and Manuel Navarro, an obese Spaniard. Both men had been instrumental in a conservative putsch to unseat Elisabetta Celestino after her appointment as Secretary of State. When their plot collapsed, Pope John fired Cardinal Tosi, their ringleader, removed Montebourg and Navarro from the leadership of their major prefectures, and further salted their wounds by forcing them from their lavish apartments by reducing their housing subsidies.

"I don't think my heart can withstand a climb," Rotolo told them. "I can already feel it fluttering like a hummingbird. I've had two heart attacks in five years."

"I'll summon the doctor," Montebourg said.

The French prelate looked around for Dr. Bellisario, spotting the black-suited physician as easily as one might find a crow among a flock of red birds.

Montebourg slowly glided over, leaned into the doctor's ear, and led him to Rotolo. Bellisario inquired about Rotolo's cardiac problems and current medications as he fingered the man's wrist.

"You have a tachycardia," the doctor said. "Let me speak with one of them."

Bellisario waved his hand to get attention. The black woman was closest and asked what he wanted.

"Cardinal Rotolo has heart problems. I don't think he can safely climb down a ladder."

"Well, he must," she replied.

"What if he falls?" the doctor said.

"If he falls, he falls. Get back in line."

When Rotolo's turn came, he crossed himself, stepped onto the first rung, and tightly held onto the rails. When he failed to move for several seconds, one of the male intruders said in French, "Allez, allez!" and pointed a pistol at his head until he began to move. Rotolo slowly began his descent, searching deliberately with a foot for each rung. He begged the Holy Spirit for help each time he changed a handhold. Halfway down, he looked toward the men who had already finished the climb and cried out, "I can't make it! Help me!"

Cardinal Macy heard his cry and started toward him. The lithe intruder at the foot of the ladder went to stop the hefty American, but Macy was already off the ground.

In a youthful, pleading voice, the man said, "Non, non, tu ne peux pas."

Macy's French was passable, but he answered defiantly in English, "Oh, yes, I can."

The American climbed as far as Rotolo's feet and asked him how he was doing.

"Not well, I'm afraid. My chest is pounding. I feel light in the head."

Come on, Ennio. You're almost there. One step at a time. It'll be harder going back up. Besides, there's a man above you."

With coaxing and encouragement, Macy got Rotolo down and helped him to the tiled floor of the chapel's basement.

"Here, let's loosen your collar. The good news is you made it. The bad news is they're going to make us go down another ladder to whatever's below us."

"I can't. I simply can't," the Italian gasped, his brow beaded with sweat. Suddenly, he went limp and mutely slumped onto his side.

Macy shouted to the cardinals making their descent, "Pass the word! We need the doctor down here. I think Rotolo's having a heart attack."

"S'il vous plaît soyez silencieux," the young captor said, with a finger to his lips.

The black woman looked down from the top of the ladder, and Macy begged the young man in his best French, "Look at him. Have mercy. Ask her to send the doctor down."

Following the young man's intercession, Dr. Bellisario was allowed to jump the queue. When he got to the basement, he began attending to the stricken cardinal. The physician soon got to his feet and began spouting at the young captor in Italian, then English.

Cardinal Montebourg was in the basement and told Bellisario that the fellow didn't understand him. "Allow me to translate," he said.

"Tell him that this man needs to go to the hospital for his heart. He needs medicine. He needs oxygen."

The request was understood, but it was met with a shrug. "Je suis désolé, mais ce n'est pas possible."

"But he might die," Macy said.

The youth had a few more words that Montebourg translated, shaking his head and raising his busy brows. "Old people die all the time."

Another fifty cardinals made it down, and the youth herded them into a corner of the basement room with his rifle. Cardinal Bizimana, the Rwandan, found himself pressed against Cardinal Koffi.

"Have you ever been down here to the chapel's basement, Raymond?" he whispered to the Ivorian.

"No, never. Have you?" Koffi said.

"Once, years ago, on a tour. The vaulted structure was designed to carry the weight of the chapel."

"Thank you for the architectural lesson, Gasore," Koffi said drily.

THE LAST CONCLAVE

"I bring it up because there are a series of storage rooms that connect with one another and lead to a staircase. See the door behind us?"

"I do," Koffi said.

The two men took little steps to the rear until they reached the wooden door. Satisfied they were well hidden behind other men, Bizimana grabbed the knob and tried to turn it.

"Locked," he whispered in disappointment.

"I don't suppose you learned to pick a lock in seminary school?" Koffi asked.

"I have many skills," the Rwandan said. "Unfortunately, that is not one of them."

During their meager escape attempt, another cardinal encountered difficulty on the ladder. Cardinal Stocchi suffered a stroke some years back that had weakened his right arm. Two-thirds of his way down, the exertion of using the withered limb caused it to go into spasm, and he could no longer use it. Stuck on a rung, he called for help, and once again, the former star athlete, Cardinal Macy, sprang into action. He climbed up and helped the man down by pushing his lower body against the ladder, allowing Stocchi to grab the remaining rungs with his left arm without falling.

When Stocchi reached the bottom, he nearly collapsed in exhaustion into Macy's arms. The American helped him to where Doctor Bellisario was caring for Rotolo, patted Stocchi's shoulder, and left him on the tiles.

When the remainder of the congregation reached the basement, the kidnappers followed and pulled the ladder down.

The black woman pointed at the large hole cut through the terra cotta tiles and told the cardinals to follow the lithe young man down the next ladder.

Pierre Quang, the Vietnamese Cardinal, peered into the hole and said, "Oh, my! This ladder is even longer!"

"Go on, hurry," the woman said, brandishing her rifle.

Word spread that their climbing ordeal was about to worsen, and the clerics exchanged panicky words. Soon, Dr. Bellisario heard the news and moved through the throng until he was beside the woman he took to be the leader.

"I'm sorry," he said, "but I have two men who cannot climb another ladder. Cardinal Rotolo has likely suffered a heart attack, and Cardinal Stocchi's left arm is useless from a stroke. He barely managed the shorter ladder. He will fall off a higher one."

"Let me see them," the blue-eyed woman replied.

She stood over Rotolo and Stocchi for a few moments, then went to talk to one of her male compatriots. Following her orders, they went to work on the stricken cardinals, binding their hands behind their backs with plastic zip ties and stuffing their birettas into their mouths.

Bellisario objected to gagging Rotolo, saying he needed to breathe as freely as possible. One of the men replied in broken English, "This or knife. You can make choose."

The rest of the cardinals and Dr. Bellisario were forced to descend deeper below the ground. Above them, the faithful were streaming into St. Peter's Square to witness the pageantry of the smoke signal that would mark the conclusion of the first day of the papal conclave.

∽

"Where are we?" Cardinal Macy asked, moving away from the ladder and trying to orient himself in the chilly darkness.

The Cardinal of Milan, Domenico Colpo, the odds-on favorite to become the next pope, was already acclimatized to the darkness.

"We're in the Roman necropolis," he said, moving dirt with the point of his loafer.

"Why would they bring us here?" the American asked.

"I believe they intend to take us on a ride," the Italian said. "Look there."

The kidnappers had turned on the miner's headlamps worn over their balaclavas, and Macy realized they were standing within a large earthen cavern below the chapel's basement, its walls reinforced by timbers. Several meters away, he picked up the glint of a red taillight.

"How in God's name did they get that down here?" he said.

"I believe we are about to find out," Colpo said.

When the last cardinal had finished the climb, they were herded down a short section of tunnel to a two-car tram—one car pointed forward, one backward. Anyone trying to make out what lay beyond the lead car could only see blackness.

One of the male kidnappers said, "Forty of you onto the tram now. You others, wait here and keep quiet."

Twenty clerics climbed onto the first car and another twenty onto the second. One of the kidnappers got behind the wheel of the lead car and switched on the headlights. Another stood on the bumper of the second car and called to the driver, "D'Accord, vasy." The electric motor hummed as the tram began to roll.

Cardinal Bizimana, who was crammed against the side of the seat by the expansive girth of Cardinal Navarro, tried to lighten the prevailing sense of desperation. "I rather feel like we're on the Universal Studios tour."

"I have no idea what you're talking about, Gasore," Navarro said.

The two female kidnappers kept to themselves by the ladder, watching the remaining eighty or so cardinals huddling in the dark.

The blue-eyed woman checked the illuminated face of her watch and said in French, "Six minutes there, six minuted back."

"You're sure Felix can handle the first group by himself?" the black woman said.

"They're old men," was the reply. "They're sheep. The only one I worry about is the American, Macy. He's strong. We'll keep him with us hold until the third trip."

"We didn't know they'd have a doctor with them," the black woman said.

"It's okay," the white woman said. "Maybe he'll be useful."

Suddenly, the black woman's chest heaved like a steam boiler venting pressure. "We're doing it. We're actually doing it," she said, reaching for the other woman's hand. Their fingers intertwined. "All our work—"

The blue-eyed woman pulled her hand away and gave an unemotional reply. "It's going to plan, but there's a long way to go. We can't get comfortable."

Precisely twelve minutes later, the tram returned, empty except for the driver, now behind the wheel of car two. He hopped out, gave the women a thumb's up, and returned to car one. Another forty cardinals were loaded, and two male kidnappers, including the lithe young man, jumped onto the bumper of car two. Once again, the tram slowly disappeared into the void.

Like clockwork, the empty tram reappeared twelve minutes later. Cardinal Macy took a seat near the front of the first car. Dr. Bellisario chose to sit beside him. Just behind them were Cardinals Sanz and Louis Mertens of Belgium. The last male kidnapper crouched in the aisle, and the two women jumped onto the bumper of car two and held onto the frame.

"Cardinal Macy, I don't believe we've formally met," Bellisario said in English.

"Under the circumstances, please call me Victor," the American said.

"Then, you must call me Max."

"All right, Max. I'm sorry you got caught up in this mess."

"It's not exactly how I had pictured the day would go."

"No, I expect not. You have a family?"

"Yes, a wife and two children."

"Any pictures on you?"

"Only on my phone, which, unfortunately, isn't here."

"You were the Holy Father's physician."

"I was."

"It was your opinion he had a heart attack."

"It was. But now—" The physician's voice faded.

"You're thinking what I'm thinking," Macy said. "A lot of planning went into this attack. It didn't come together in the two weeks since his death. How'd they know there would be a conclave?"

"Indeed," Bellisario said. "How did they know?"

The tram's motor hummed, and the journey began.

"Do you think Cardinal Rotolo will make it?"

"It depends on how long until he's found."

Macy said, "I don't think that's going to happen for hours. The fastest we could cast ballots and have them tabulated is a couple of hours. They'll be reluctant to violate the sanctity of the conclave, so they'll probably give us another hour or more before they barge in. Are you saying he'll be gone by then?"

"Gone, or quite possibly beyond salvage."

Macy tried to examine the tunnel walls to his left and right, but the darkness obscured details. However, the track ahead was illuminated by the headlights.

He whispered in the doctor's ear. "Maybe I should try to get away. I could slip off. Maybe they wouldn't notice. I could go back and raise the alarm."

The doctor checked the rear of the car.

"It will never work, Victor. One of them is just there. Two more are riding at the back. They'll see you, and they'll shoot you. Whatever awaits us, I believe we'll be safer if you are there."

Macy nodded and touched the doctor's sleeve. "You're probably right. I think the Lord sent you to be with us, Max. It's all part of His plan."

CHAPTER NINE

As the tram moved through the tunnel, Cardinal Sanz noticed his seatmate, Cardinal Mertens, growing agitated.

"What is it, Louis?"

Mertens was the president of the Pontifical Commission for Sacred Archaeology. Unlike his predecessor, Sister Elisabetta, Mertens had no training in archaeology. Yet, he was a scholarly man who had studied his brief and had become knowledgeable about the catacombs and necropoli of Rome.

Mertens threw his hands toward the track illuminated by the headlights and said, "Look what they've done. They've brutally cut through the Necropolis of Triumphalis. Look at this tomb. It's been destroyed. We are driving over the bones of ancient Romans. It's heartbreaking."

Mertens mouthed a prayer, removed his biretta from his bald head, and dropped it over the railing onto a pile of crushed bones as a benediction.

"But where are we?" Sanz asked.

"Under the Vatican gardens."

"Where will we emerge?"

"Somewhere outside the Vatican walls, I imagine," the Belgian said. "We will know soon."

Mertens was correct. The tramcars snaked through the tunnel and, within minutes, came to an abrupt halt. The driver killed the motor and told everyone to exit to the right and follow him.

Cardinal Macy's instinct was to fall behind and help the older and less capable, but he was shooed along at rifle point up a slope toward a dim light.

Macy and Dr. Bellisario were the first in their group to grasp their location when they climbed a series of dirt steps reinforced by railway sleepers.

"We're in a house," the doctor said. "The basement of a house."

"So, we are," Macy said, looking around at the light of a dangling bulb. "They tunneled right into a basement. Would you look at all the dirt they've piled in here?"

They were ordered up a staircase, through a hallway, and out a kitchen side door. Rather than the afternoon sky, they saw brown canvas. The back garden and driveway were covered by a tent that concealed mounds of excavated dirt. The first two tram-loads of cardinals were seated on a dirt slope, passing around water, looking dazed and confused. Macy made a beeline to a palette of water bottles, and he and the doctor began giving them to the newly arriving men.

The black woman pushed her way forward and told the first group who arrived to climb into one of the three white transit vans parked along the side of the house.

"Where are you taking us?" Cardinal Colpo said. "We have a right to know."

The woman said, "You lost your rights the minute we entered the conclave. Get into the van."

The cardinals were herded unceremoniously and packed like livestock into the windowless, seatless cargo areas. With about forty men per van, most had to stand. A few of the older and weaker clerics were helped to the bare-metal floor by their colleagues. The cargo spaces were unventilated; had it not been for a cool evening, the suffering would have been greater. Cardinals Colpo and Koffi, who hours earlier had been enmeshed in soft politicking, found themselves pressed together as their van sped off. Koffi was several years younger, and he treated his colleague with respectful care.

"Are you all right, Domenico?" he asked. "I have water. Would you like a drink?"

"Thank you, I would," the Italian said, drinking thirstily.

"They'll be looking for us soon," Koffi said. "I am sure we will be found and rescued."

"I'm sure you're right," Colpo said, trying to hand back the water.

"No, you keep it. I've had enough. I don't want to have to pee and splash all these fine gowns of ours."

They heard one of their colleagues complaining about car sickness, followed by retching.

"Oh, well," Koffi said. "So much for clean clothes."

Cardinal Macy was in the last van to depart. He was the tallest man in the College of Cardinals and the only one who had to stoop to prevent banging his head against the ceiling. Bellisario was beside him, both of them near the door.

"I hope you're not still thinking about escaping," the doctor said to the American. "I saw them padlocking the doors of the other vans. I'm afraid we're as helpless as lambs for the slaughterhouse."

Macy managed a laugh. "Got to love your bedside manner, Doc."

∽

AFTER A JOURNEY OF ALMOST AN HOUR, green with carsickness from the swaying of the boxy vans, and exhausted by the effort of keeping upright, the cardinals climbed out and found themselves inside a poorly lit industrial space.

Macy's van was the last to arrive. He wandered over to one of his American colleagues, the cardinal of Chicago, John Rowekamp, a rail-thin Midwesterner with wire-rim glasses and a neat goatee.

"How're you holding up, John?" he asked.

"I used to answer that question with, 'can't complain,'"

Rowekamp said with a grin. "I'm never going to say that again. I can and will complain."

"Please don't lose your sense of humor."

"Any idea what this place is?"

"Looks like a warehouse. There's a tractor-trailer truck over there. I certainly hope it's not meant for us."

Cardinal Bizimana joined them and relayed that one of the Italian cardinals, cognizant of the local geography, estimated that based on their time on the road, they were still in greater Rome, or at most, the outskirts. North, south, east, west—he couldn't say.

One of the older cardinals, only a year shy of ineligibility to vote at conclave, raised his hand and asked if he could use the toilet. The black woman peeled away from a conversation she was having with the blue-eyed woman and loudly announced there was a lavatory behind her. Anyone who needed it had better go now.

"Speak now or forever hold your piss," she quipped, then went quiet when no one found it amusing. "There are water and energy bars over there," she added. "Hurry and get some. We won't be here long."

Macy and a few more able-bodied clerics circulated among the cardinals resting on the hard floor, handing out meager rations of food and water. Half an hour after arriving at the warehouse, there was another announcement: the time was up. Everyone needed to make their way onto the yellow lorry.

"My prayers were not answered," Rowekamp groaned to Macy.

One-hundred-sixteen cardinals, one doctor, and three male kidnappers climbed the ramp and crowded inside the yellow container. The three remaining kidnappers rode in the cab. The container was large enough that some of the weakest had room to sit on its steel floor. As the Scania lorry left the warehouse, some cardinals openly fretted about not having enough air to breathe. Dr. Bellisario pointed out the air holes drilled through the skin of the lorry at regular intervals and reassured everyone that they need not worry about asphyxiation.

This leg of their unfortunate journey took somewhat longer

than the last. The cardinals, out of earshot of their captors, whispered among themselves in the dark.

"I think we're on a highway," one said, commenting on the steady speed and lack of braking.

"We're probably going to someplace remote. The countryside, perhaps," another said.

When the lorry slowed and took a curve, someone said, "I think we've left the highway now."

When the lorry came to a stop, they all strained to hear the faint conversation between the driver and the Port of Rome security guard. One of the captors, worried that someone might shout for help, pushed his way through them, making shushing noises.

The lorry traveled another short distance before coming to a halt again. One of the cardinals, Riccardo Santagati, was finely tuned to certain smells and sounds. He was the cardinal of Palermo, a seaside city, and he stood, sniffing at the breeze coming through the airhole over his head.

He was a head taller than Cardinal Fischer, and he bent to say to him, "Do you hear the gulls? Do you smell the sea? I think I know what is about to happen to us."

"What?" Fischer asked.

"I think we're going to go on a short ride before we go on a longer one."

"Whatever do you mean, Riccardo?"

"You will see."

Santagati reached behind his neck and unclasped the silver chain holding the small silver crucifix that the diocese of Palermo had given him upon his elevation to cardinal. He slipped the crucifix from the chain, kissed it, and when he was certain the guards were looking elsewhere, he reached up and pushed the sacred icon through an air hole.

Minutes later, Santagati's prediction came true. The container lifted into the air and made the shortest of trips from terra firma to the sea.

"Good lord!"

"What now?"

"Where are they taking us?"

Exhortations and prayers rippled through the congregation. The darkness of their metal box fed a mounting sense of panic.

Cardinal Macy tried to calm people down. "Everyone, take heart. I don't believe we are in imminent danger. Our captors are locked in here with us."

One of the kidnappers heard Macy and called out in poor English, "Listen to him. Don't to worry. All is okay. Just to wait."

The container came to rest on the deck of the *Menelaus*, and soon, everyone heard loud clunks as it was locked into place. The cardinals stopped talking, and the cry of seagulls filled their ears.

∽

THE CAVERNOUS CARGO hold gave everyone ample room to stretch out, but that was the only comfort afforded the captives. The gunmetal floors were barren. There were no cushions or blankets. A small lavatory down a narrow corridor attracted a line. There was enough bottled water to go around, but the food was paltry, consisting of a few hundred bananas, a hundred or so apples, and energy bars. To preempt complaints, their captors informed them that their journey would not be long. The cardinals arranged themselves on the rolling floor in small groupings, mainly sorted by nationality. The Italian contingent was the largest. The men engaged in an animated discussion with a lot of hand-waving. The Latin American delegation was quieter and more contemplative. The Peruvian Cardinal Jaime Mamami, a small round man with cheeks like the apple he was eating, presided, leading them in prayer and discussing what the reactions were likely to be at home. The eleven American cardinals were, on the whole, indignant and angry. They focused on the political orientation of their kidnappers and the US government's response.

"What are they, French?" Cardinal Palmer of San Diego asked.

"Sounds like French to me," Cardinal Deetz of Galveston-Houston said.

Cardinal Emory of Washington said, "When you think of

groups who might be behind something as outrageous as this, you don't think of the French."

"The women are definitely the ringleaders," Cardinal Rowekamp said. "They've gone missing. They've left the men with guard duty."

"Speaking of women," Deetz said, "the secretary of state would have authorized breaking the conclave by now. They know we've been taken. The president and the State Department will be all over this. The CIA and Department of Defense—you name it—they're all mobilizing."

"How will they find us on a cargo ship on the high seas?" Emory said.

"Gentlemen, have faith in God and faith in the CIA," Cardinal Macy said.

As the clerics talked, Dr. Bellisario made his rounds, dropping in on the groups, encouraging the seasick hugging plastic buckets to keep hydrated, and asking about medical problems and medication needs.

Cardinal Sauseda, the camerlengo, told the physician he had insulin-requiring diabetes, but before Bellisario could red-line with concern, the Spaniard pulled a vial of insulin, a syringe, and an alcohol swab from his cassock.

"This was in case the conclave went long. If I reuse the syringe, I should be fine for a few days."

Bellisario made a list of medication requirements in the small notebook he had brought into the conclave. After he spoke to all the cardinals, he approached the lithe young man sitting on a metal stool, his rifle resting on his lap.

"Excuse me," the doctor said. "Can you speak English? Should I find someone who speaks French?"

"It's okay. I speak a little."

"Good. I have a list of the medicines these men must take. How can we get these medicines?"

Eyes stared out from mask holes.

"I don't know nothing about this," the young man said.

"I'm telling you about it," the doctor said testily. "We need to find these medicines."

"When she come, I tell her."

"When who comes? Your leader?"

"Yes, I'll tell her when she come." He put a finger in the air. "She's up there."

"You promise?"

"Yes. I promise. I am very rely—no, reliable."

∼

Hours later, the two women returned to the cargo hold. Some cardinals were curled on their sides, sleeping on the hard floor. Others were propped against the metal walls, dozing off or staring blankly. Some continued talking throughout the night.

The blue-eyed leader clapped her hands for attention and said, "I need you all to stand now. We need to make a video to show the world you are unharmed."

An Italian's voice rang out, "Where are you taking us?"

"You will see," she said. "Come now. Please stand. One row against that wall. Another row in front of them. A third, closest to me."

Those with creaking bones had others with fluid joints help them off the floor, and they lined up as instructed. The lithe young man set up a tripod and camera. The two women, flanked by two of the men, stood at the front and waited for the young cameraman to signal his readiness.

"D'accord, nous sommes prêts aussi," the blue-eyed woman said. She waited a few seconds, then began her monologue. "The Catholic Church is a sinful Church. For centuries, our Church has been ruled by men who have trampled on women's rights in the name of God Almighty, his son, Jesus Christ, and the Blessed Virgin Mary. The men who stand behind us, the cardinals of this Church who gathered yesterday to choose another man as pope, are the ones responsible for the subjugation of Catholic women. It is time this male domination ends. We have two demands. One: the cardinal electors must collectively agree with immediate effect to allow for the ordination of women as priests. Two: the cardinal electors must continue their conclave and their voting until a two-thirds majority elect as the next pope of the Catholic Church, the newly ordained Elisabetta Celestino, the Vatican Secretary of State, who is the only person we can trust to be the next person to sit on the throne of St. Peter. There will be four ballots per day following normal conclave rules. Failing a two-thirds majority in favor of Elisabetta Celestino, the voting will continue. If she is elected, the conclave will end, and the cardinals will be released. However, in five days commencing tomorrow, if she has not been elected, the cardinals will be executed."

The two women quickly departed through a bulkhead door before any cardinals could react or hurl questions.

Stunned silence gave way to an eruption.

"Outrageous!"

"Is she mad?"

"She thinks she can threaten us? Bend us to her will?"

"A woman as pope? Is that what I heard?"

"This abomination will not stand."

Dr. Bellisario was concerned with a more immediate problem. He approached the young kidnapper and said, "What about my medicines? Did you speak to her?"

"We leave here soon," the young man said. "We get you medicine when we go other place."

"What other place? Where are we going?"

"Wait, doctor. You will see."

⁓

Another two hours passed. The food and water had been consumed, and the men sat uncomfortably with listless expressions. Conversations dwindled, then ceased entirely. The ship's engine rumbled, and the vessel rolled in the chop. The seasick grew accustomed to their misery. And then, inactivity turned to urgent bustle when one of the male kidnappers loudly ordered them to stand and follow him. He led them, like a column of army ants, through long corridors and metal stairways until they emerged on a windswept foredeck.

It was before dawn. The gray sky glowed pink at the horizon, and a perfect new moon robbed attention from the planets and stars. But the cardinals did not engage in sky gazing because all eyes were riveted on a behemoth that none in the ship's bowels heard landing. The Russian-built Mi-26 Halo was the world's largest helicopter. Designed for heavy lifting, it could carry sixty tons of equipment, eighty fully-loaded soldiers, or, this morning, all the captives and their kidnappers.

Stiff waves were making the *Menelaus* sway. There was a seventh man in a balaclava and a blue uniform they hadn't seen before. He was bow-legged with a hefty build, confidently standing by the chopper's open door, unaffected by the swells. "Get in," he shouted. "Find a place on the floor. Squeeze yourselves."

The tired and scared cardinals boarded the giant bird and crammed together on yet another metal floor. When all were in, they were joined by the six kidnappers in black and the new man in blue.

The Halo lifted off and moved away from the ship. Some of the cardinals prayed in voices drowned out by the roar of the twin rotors. The rest prayed silently. The helicopter was not built for tourism. There were only a few small windows, but their shades were taped shut. As they flew into the dawn, light leaked around the window shades and the cabin brightened a bit. The Frenchman, Cardinal Montebourg, sat underneath one of the porthole-shaped windows. About thirty minutes into their noisy journey, he half-rose, and checked to see if any of the kidnappers had eyes on him. He peeled back a piece of tape, lifted the shade a little, and peeked out. In the sharp sunlight of a May morning, he could see sharp triangular fingers of brown land protruding into deep-blue waters.

"I know where we are," he whispered to the men nearest him. "As a boy, I went sailing here. This is France."

CHAPTER TEN

When Emilio checked his phone messages, it was well past midnight. He would have waited until the morning to respond if Cal's "call me" hadn't sounded so insistent.

Cal pounced on his phone. "Emilio, you got my voicemail."

"Sounds like you're awake," Emilio said.

"Couldn't sleep. Did you see it too? The yellow cross?"

"We noticed her tattoo," Emilio said. "But with everything going on, it hasn't received much attention. One intelligence officer said, 'That rules out Islamists. What kind of jihadi has a tattoo of a cross?' Another guy said, 'The kind that wants to throw off our investigation.'"

"No one talked about the cross's color?"

"No. What's the significance?"

"Ever hear of the Cathars?"

"Who?"

"The Cathars. They were a Christian sect that sprung up in southern France in the twelfth century. Their beliefs were unorthodox, to put it mildly. The Catholic Church declared them heretics, launched an inquisition, and began exterminating them. By the end of the thirteenth century, they'd been wiped off the face of the earth."

"And this yellow cross?" Emilio said.

"The Catholic inquisitors forced them to wear a yellow cross on their clothes to identify and stigmatize them. In modern times, the good people of the Languedoc region of France promote their Cathar roots and drum up tourism by selling bric-a-brac with yellow crosses."

With undisguised weariness, Emilio said, "Tell me what this has to do with my cardinals."

Cal was also dog-tired, but since spotting the tattoo, he'd been on a manic tear. "I don't know. Maybe nothing. Maybe something. Catharism was mostly a French movement. They were anti-Catholics. The kidnappers had French accents. One of them has a Cathar cross. That's it. That's all I have for you."

Cal thought he heard a breathy rush on the line. "Okay, my friend. All tips are appreciated. I'll feed it to the intelligence guys, and we'll see if anything comes of it. It's been a shitty day. I'm going to try and get a few hours of sleep. Hopefully, tomorrow will be better."

⁂

ELISABETTA TOOK her first call of the day while making tea in her Apostolic Palace apartment. Ordinarily, she wouldn't have responded to an unknown cell phone caller, but these were not ordinary times.

"Please excuse me," came the formal voice. "Have I reached Elisabetta Celestino?"

"Yes, who is it?"

"Ah, Madam Secretary, this is Professor Guido Lo Presti, the president of SITOX, the Society of Italian Toxicology."

She began vigorously dunking her Auchan tea bag. "Oh, yes, Professor. How are you?"

"I'm well, thank you, Sister. Is there any news on the cardinals?"

"Unfortunately, no."

"Such a tragedy. I'm calling about the toxicology results on the Holy Father."

"Of course," she said. "Please tell me."

"I wonder if I might come by the Vatican this morning and deliver them in person?"

She pulled the tea bag from the cup and dropped it in the sink. "In person? Is that necessary?"

"It would be preferable."

᠆

Professor Lo Presti was middle-aged, but he walked with a cane because of a congenital hip defect. Given the attack on the Vatican, his stick attracted a fair amount of scrutiny from the Swiss Guards. Its dapper silver handle set off the magnetometer, and while they debated having it x-rayed at the Vatican Museum's laboratory, Lo Presti tried to make them comfortable.

"I assure you, it's merely a cane."

"Do you require it?" a guard asked.

"I need it to stay upright if that's what you're asking."

Elisabetta's private secretary, informed of the issue, solved the matter by borrowing a cane from an elderly priest for the professor to use during his visit.

Lo Presti was good enough, not to mention the snafu with Elisabetta. He sat across from her eighteenth-century desk and produced a sealed envelope.

"The results of the testing we performed at SITOX," he proclaimed. "Would you like to read it?"

She left the envelope lying on the burled walnut. "I wouldn't know how to interpret a toxicology report, Professor."

"Why would you?" he said, trying her patience. "Do you know what digitalis is?"

She was tapping her foot under her desk. There were dozens of issues awaiting her attention, and this toxicologist was hell-bent on playing twenty questions.

"I do not," she said.

"It is a useful medication for people with heart failure."

He stopped talking, waiting for her to ask the obvious question, which she did.

"According to the records from the Gemelli Hospital, the Holy Father was not taking digitalis," he said.

Elisabetta opened her arms in exasperation. "And—"

"Digitalis is derived from the foxglove plant. It is an effective medicine but also toxic when given in excess. The toxicity of foxglove has been known for centuries. Very high doses will predictably cause heart arrhythmias and death. The Holy Father had the highest concentration of digitalis in his blood and tissues we have ever seen."

Elisabetta had been steeling herself for something like this, but the news was still shocking. "Is it your opinion that the pope was poisoned?"

"It is not my opinion, Madame Secretary. It is a medical fact. We calculate that the quantity of digitalis the Holy Father ingested is approximately one thousand times the usual therapeutic dose. The source of the poisoning is not something SITOX can determine. That is for the police. However, there are only three possibilities: an accidental overdose as might occur in the case of a patient to whom the drug is prescribed, a deliberate overdose by a patient as a suicide attempt, or deliberate poisoning by someone intent on harming."

Elisabetta eyed her phone. Emilio needed to hear this. "Is there a way of knowing when this poisoning took place?"

"There is. We estimate that no more than three hours would have elapsed between ingesting this massive dose of digitalis and death. According to the information provided to SITOX, the Holy Father was found unresponsive in his bedroom by the nuns at eleven o'clock. Therefore, I would say that he was administered the fatal dose at approximately eight o'clock that same night."

"You said he ingested one thousand times the usual dose. How much powder would that be?"

"Not very much. About a teaspoon. The amount of sugar I take in my coffee."

∼

Emilio left a morning briefing to take the call from Elisabetta. The confirmation that Pope John had been murdered was a body blow.

"With you in Livorno, who can lead the investigation at the Vatican?" she asked.

"I'll have Andrea Gambino start immediately. He has my full confidence. Have you spoken to Cal today?"

"No, why?"

"We talked late last night. He noticed that the woman in the hostage video had a wrist tattoo of a cross. A yellow cross."

"I didn't notice."

"If you have a chance, look at the video again. The people in Livorno also spotted it," Emilio said, "but Cal is more excited about it than we were."

"What does he think it is?" she asked.

"He says it's a Cathar cross. I never heard of Cathars. Have you?"

"Only that they were a persecuted Christian sect in the Middle Ages," she said. "Nothing more."

"Next time you speak with him, he'll tell you about them."

She heard a voice calling for Emilio.

"I've got to go," he said. "They're looking for me. I'll let you know if anything new develops."

∼

Lieutenant Andrea Gambino was Emilio's right-hand man at the Vatican Carabinieri. Like his boss, Gambino had been a policeman in Rome. He was a bright young officer with a charismatic streak who Emilio had been grooming as his successor. Minutes after receiving his assignment, Gambino charted the outline of an investigation plan and began scheduling interviews at the shuttered papal apartment.

His began with the pope's valet, Mario Santovito. Gambino had never visited the apartment, and when he walked through the space, he had to shake off twin emotions of awe and sadness. He chose the kitchen table for his interrogations and sat across from the valet. Both men were in uniform—Gambino in his blue tunic and trousers, Santovito in his impeccable black suit. Both avoided the pope's chair.

"I want to get a picture of his last day, particularly his last evening," Gambino said. "Who was in the residence? Did he dine in that night or elsewhere? Did he have visitors? Who was the last person to see him alive?"

Santovito moistened his lips with a dart of his tongue and said lugubriously, "May I know why you're asking these questions, Lieutenant? I am aware of the rumor that the Holy Father's body was removed from his crypt. There is talk of a connection between this and the kidnappings."

"As you can imagine, Signor, I can't talk about our investigations," Gambino answered impassively. "If you could address my questions."

"Very well. The household staff was not a large one. Five Portuguese nuns who assumed domestic duties—mainly cleaning, washing, and tending to the needs of the Holy Father, Eduardo Antelao, who served as the chef, and myself."

"What were your duties as valet?"

"I saw to the Holy Father's wardrobe, assisting him in dressing and undressing. I ran his baths, helped with morning ablutions, worked with Eduardo when the Holy Father had guests for supper, supervised the work of the nuns, ordered the household supplies, and served as the liaison between the Holy Father and Monsignor Finale, the pope's private secretary. The Monsignor was frequently summoned to the residence on Curial matters."

"How frequently?" Gambino asked.

"On most days, at least once."

"And on the day of his death?"

"He stopped by briefly after morning Mass. The next time I saw him was late at night when Sister Maria summoned him."

"All right, we'll get to her," the officer said. "Start with the morning."

"Sister Rosa brought him his morning juice, tea, and biscuits. I drew his bath and laid out his garments. Then he went upstairs to the chapel and celebrated Mass with the assistance of Father Monroe, who was often tapped for liturgical duties. If I recall, the pope invited a group from the Vatican post office to attend that morning. When the Holy Father returned to the residence, Monsignor Finale came by to review the day's schedule, and then breakfast was served here in the kitchen."

"Who was there for breakfast?"

"The nuns, myself, and Eduardo. Once Eduardo served the food, the Holy Father always insisted that we all take the meal together."

"Do you remember what was served?"

"Poached eggs with sausages, American-style banana pancakes, toast, jam, sliced fruit, yogurt."

"Was it the same every morning?"

"Oh, no; always different. I remember this day for obvious reasons and because the Holy Father was especially delighted with the pancakes."

"And after breakfast?"

"He spent a few minutes alone in his bedroom, then took the lift to his office. I didn't see him again until supper."

Gambino looked up from his notebook. "Tell me about supper."

"It was an early supper, per the usual. The Holy Father again dined with the nuns and me—he called us his little family." At this, the stoic valet was forced to take a white pocket handkerchief to his eyes. "Eduardo served us a simple pasta dish, roasted lamb with vegetables and tiramisu. The conversation was light and satisfying. Then the Holy Father changed into comfortable clothes and watched television in his lounge."

"What time did you leave?"

"Shortly after seven."

"And how was he?"

"He was perfect. Completely well."

"Who was with him that evening?"

"Only the nuns. Eduardo went home after supper, shortly before me. The nuns stayed to clean the kitchen and prepare his bedroom. Sister Maria stayed the latest to attend to any last requirements before the Holy Father retired. She is the one who found him."

∼

Monsignor Finale was next to arrive. When he crossed the threshold, he was overcome with emotion. Gambino offered a glass of water and gave him time to compose himself.

"Coming back here——" Finale said. "It's quite difficult. His life force was so strong. I still can't believe he's gone. And then the conclave. It's too much. Too much."

"I understand," the policeman said. "We won't begin until you're ready."

"I know why you're doing these interviews," Finale said.

"Why?"

"You think his death was not from natural causes. That is why his body was exhumed."

"I know there's been talk," Gambino said, "but I can't comment on speculations. I do want to understand the events of the Holy Father's last day. Can you take me through his schedule?"

Finale was precise in his detailed account, complete with start and stop times for all the papal meetings, telephone calls, and the individuals he met on the day. Pope John spent the morning in his office library in a series of one-on-one meetings on Curial business, interspersed with phone calls with overseas bishops. At midday, the prefect, the secretary, and two staff members of the Segretaria per L'Economia came to the office for a working lunch on the annual Vatican budget. The Vatican cafeteria provided paninis, beverages, and fruit. If Finale recalled properly, the Holy Father had a porchetta panini and a Pellegrino water. The afternoon was mainly given to correspondence and reading, although Sister Elisabetta stopped by to discuss growing threats to mission schools in Nigeria. The Pope finished his work at half-past five and left his office for the last time. The next time the priest saw him, he was dead.

Gambino concluded the interview and waited for Eduardo

Antelao. When ten minutes passed, he rang Eduardo's mobile, left a voice mail, and tried his home number. Eduardo's wife answered and said her husband was out. Did she know if he was on his way to the Vatican for his appointment? She had no idea, but her rushed and throaty response left Gambino wondering. He bided his time by reviewing the notes he had taken during the earlier interviews. He was pacing the apartment when Sister Maria arrived for her slot.

She was tiny with large brown eyes and sunken, acne-scarred cheeks. Gambino had expected a show of emotion akin to the valet and priest, but she betrayed none. She briefly looked around the kitchen as if considering what, if anything, needed doing domestically, then took a seat and folded her hands.

"I will help you in any way I can," she said in a small voice. "I loved the Holy Father. It is good you asked to speak with the sisters now. We are returning to our convent in Ponta Delgada this weekend. We have no reason to remain in Rome."

"That's in the Azores?"

"Yes. The Holy Father's people were from there. There is much mourning on our island."

"Sister, I am trying to understand the details of his last day, particularly his last hours. I understand you were the last remaining domestic staff member at the residence that night."

"Yes, that is so," she said. "Mario and Eduardo left after supper. The other nuns finished their work and left for our residence at seven-thirty. I wouldn't want to say this in front of the other sisters, but I think the Holy Father liked it when I had the nighttime duties. He was always so playful with me. He said I reminded him of a great-niece. So, I was with him at the end. If he hadn't passed away, I would have stayed until midnight. He was always asleep by then."

"Did anyone come to the apartment that night?"

"No one."

"Were there any telephone calls?"

"No."

"What did the Holy Father do after supper?"

"He stayed in his lounge, on his favorite chair, watching a television show."

"And that's it? Nothing else?"

"Nothing out of the ordinary. It was about eight o'clock when I heard him in the kitchen, and I asked if he wanted anything. I knew he did. He always went looking for a snack at this time of night."

Gambino sat a little straighter. "Always? Like clockwork?"

She gave out a childlike laugh. "Always. Every night he said he shouldn't, and every night he always had a sweet. The Holy Father had a sweet tooth."

"What did he have that night?"

"It was a chocolate lava cake with cream."

"From a bakery? A store?"

"Oh, no. Eduardo always provided the nighttime treat. The lava cake was the Holy Father's favorite. He loved it very much. I would heat it in the microwave and pour cream on top. He ate it with great pleasure."

Gambino circled the words lava cake twice. "He took it back to the lounge?"

"No, he couldn't even wait that long. He sat down in that chair and ate it in the kitchen."

"And you cleaned the plate?"

"The bowl, yes."

"Were there any other cakes?"

"Eduardo left just the one."

"And the cream?"

"Eduardo left a beaker in the refrigerator."

"Then what happened?"

"The Holy Father finished his show and retired to his bedroom at ten. Everything was quiet until I heard a strange noise, like a thud, coming from his bedroom at approximately eleven thirty. I knocked on his door several times, and when I heard no reply, I opened it. I found the Holy Father lying by the bed. He was not moving or responding to my calls. There was a panic button on the bedside table. The Swiss Guards came quickly. One of them pushed on his chest until the medics arrived. They worked ever so hard, but there was nothing they could do. It was a dream to have a Portuguese pope. The dream has died."

~

When Sister Maria left, Gambino called Eduardo again, and this time left a more urgent message. He followed with a second call to Eduardo's wife to ask if she'd spoken with him. She hadn't and sounded terrified. An infant cried out, and she seized on maternal obligations as a reason to hang up.

Emilio was between meetings in Livorno when Gambino called and got straight to the point.

"I believe the chef, Eduardo Antelao, had the opportunity to poison the pope with a nighttime snack. He was the only domestic staff member who failed to present himself for an interview, and his whereabouts are presently unknown. His wife sounded scared. I believe she knows something. I would like to request that the Polizia Municipale and the Carabinieri look for Eduardo's car in Rome. He had a parking pass in the Vatican, so we know the make, model, and number plate."

Motive," Emilio said. "What possible motive would this man have to harm the pontiff?"

"I don't know," Gambino said. "With your permission, I would like to begin an immediate investigation into Eduardo's actions on the day the pope died and explore any political associations he might have with terrorist groups."

"Do whatever it takes," Emilio said. "Find him."

~

Elisabetta had meant to ring Cal about the yellow cross, but it seemed that every Curial department head, every papal nuncio, prominent bishop, and octogenarian cardinal demanded her attention. She desperately wanted to steal a sliver of time to get a little fresh air and afternoon sunshine in the Vatican gardens, but when she was about to capitalize on a gap between scheduled meetings, her private secretary entered, shaking his head.

"I'm sorry, Madame Secretary. I tried to tell Cardinal Donahue that we couldn't accommodate an unplanned visit, but he won't leave. He's insisting on seeing you."

"Demanding?" she said.

"I'm afraid there's no other way to put it," the priest said apologetically.

"Fine," she sighed, glancing out the window. "Tell him he can have ten minutes."

Elisabetta offered Donahue her hand, but before she could free herself, he cupped it with his other hand and held it in an overly long, avuncular clasp. What followed was the type of charm and empathy offensive that had made him a popular figure in Boston political and social circles until scandals made him radioactive.

"How are you holding up?" he asked. "Everyone I speak with is impressed with how you've been steering the ship of state through these turbulent waters."

"It's difficult for everyone," she said. She tried not to wrinkle her nose at his spicy cloud of aftershave. "How can I help you, Eminence?"

"Oh, no. I need nothing from you, Madame Secretary. I'm here to see how I and others can help you." Before she could turn her quizzical expression into a question, he added, "I saw Professor Donovan last night. Have the two of you spoken since then?"

"We haven't, no."

"He said he'd call. I'm sure he will. I know that Cal was a great friend of the Holy Father's and if I'm not mistaken, a friend of yours too. He's such a well-respected scholar. A credit to Harvard. You probably don't know because it's ancient history, but I'm also a Harvard man. The Vatican has been fortunate to have his counsel over the years. He knows this place like an insider. That's why I wanted to run an idea by him."

She knew everything about Donahue's checkered past and, like Cal, was not an admirer. "What idea was that, Eminence?"

The cardinal tented ten fingertips across his chest. "I'm sure you'd agree that this nightmare we are living through has left an immense void in the governance of Church affairs. Everyone knows you and the Curial staff are doing a heroic job filling that void. Your efforts are accruing universal admiration."

Elisabetta's grip tightened on a fold of her cotton habit. She waited for the compliments to turn into something altogether different.

"Thank you," she said coldly.

"There's an American sports term I'd like to invoke. When a team has abundant talent beyond the starting players, we say that the team has a deep bench. I believe this also applies to our Church. Our first team, the cardinal electors, has been taken from the playing field. God willing, they will soon return to active service. However, in the interim, I and others within the ranks of our senior clergy believe that it would steady the nerves of the faithful if we utilized our deep bench."

She loosened her clenched jaw to say, "And what would that look like?"

"It would be a council of elders composed of non-elector cardinals, healthy in mind and body, who would oversee Vatican affairs during this unprecedented interregnum. We believe that eight of us would suffice. Think of it as an office of the papacy. To be sure, we wouldn't have papal authority. For example, we couldn't call ecumenical councils or appoint bishops or cardinals, but we would fulfill the *sede vacante* duties many of our missing colleagues have undertaken since Pope John's death. The lawyers tell me such an arrangement would be permissible under existing canon law."

"You've spoken to canon lawyers," she said, staring.

"We didn't want to approach you unless we fully understood the legality of our position."

"Well, Eminence, this is certainly an interesting suggestion. However, fewer than forty-eight hours have passed since the kidnapping. The authorities are working feverishly to find our people. Hopefully, the crisis will resolve swiftly and safely. Don't you think your proposal is premature?"

"Hardly," Donahue said, straining to maintain a benevolent expression. "If we were to announce the formation of this advisory council today, and the cardinals returned tomorrow, nothing would have been lost. We will all be applauded for responding to the crisis in a timely fashion, and the council will become a footnote to history. On the other hand, consider the ultimate disaster. The terrorists kill them all. Who could appoint new bishops and cardinals to the ranks in the absence of a new pope? I'm sure you don't believe you would have that authority as secretary of state."

She relaxed her right hand from its clench and absently plucked a pen from her blotter. "And I'm certain you don't believe your council of elders would have that authority either. I pray your hypothetical scenario never comes to pass. If it did, that is when our esteemed colleagues, the canon lawyers, would have to perform their magic and figure out a mechanism for the appointment of new bishops."

The cardinal's face hardened as he dropped all pretense of comity. He produced a folded paper and placed it on her desk. "These are the men who, along with me, have agreed to serve in this office of the papacy. Although you would answer directly to us, we would prefer it if you announced its formation. You can even take the credit for it if that makes it easier. If you aren't prepared to do this, we will have to make the announcement on our own behalf."

"I hear this as an ultimatum."

"That word is too strong, Madame Secretary. Take it as an urgent proposal from men who care deeply for our Church and over a billion of its faithful."

"I wonder, Eminence if the issue of preeminent concern is that I am a woman?"

He rose and placed both hands on the opposite side of her desk. "What concerns me the most is that a radical feminist terrorist organization has the gall to demand that you be ordained and made pope. Do you know what kind of firestorm is raging beyond the walls of the Vatican? Prominent Catholics, influential lay organizations, and important publications are lined up in outrage and solidarity against these demands. My council will calm the waters and send a powerful message."

She rose and faced him off across her antique desk. "Your council," she said. "I wonder what these prominent Catholics, influential organizations, and publications will think of a cardinal leading this office of the papacy who was removed from his position for protecting pedophile priests who destroyed hundreds of lives and cost the diocese over one-hundred-million dollars in settlements?"

Sufferers of tetanus develop a spasm of the face, the *risus sardonicus*, that fixes the mouth into a contorted, stony smile. Cardinal Donahue had such a grin.

"We'll be expecting your answer at the soonest convenience."

∼

IN LIVORNO, the inter-agency task force worked desperately to solve how the cardinals left the *Menelaus*, the key to discovering where they had been taken. Emilio and Tavassi sat beside each other in the war room as the videoconference screen lit up with personnel joining from Italian and international agencies. It was Tavassi's meeting, and he opened it succinctly.

"All right, people, let's have everyone's best assessment on the two modes of escape from the *Menelaus*: sea and air. Who wants to make a case for the sea?"

When no one spoke, Tavassi called on an Italian admiral at La Spezia Naval Base.

"I didn't volunteer because we cannot support the premise of egress by sea," the admiral said. "The *Menelaus* was not designed for ship-to-ship transfer of personnel. The only way to get leave the cargo ship would be over the side by rope ladders or netting. A company of trained soldiers or sailors could accomplish the task in meter-high waves, but it's unthinkable that a hundred elderly men could. No, I'm sorry, they didn't leave the ship that way."

A French admiral leaned into his camera and said, "I concur."

Tavassi whispered to Emilio that he agreed too, but wanted to be thorough. "Admirals, let me play devil's advocate," Tavassi said. "If, by some small chance your assessment is wrong, do the French or Italian navies have the capability of knowing whether any vessels approached the *Menelaus*?"

The French admiral responded. "The cargo ship had a transponder that had not been disabled. We have its full course from the Port of Rome to the Port of Marseilles. No other vessels with transponders came within two nautical miles of the *Menelaus* until it entered French territorial waters, and the first to do so, was a tug boat near the port."

The Italian admiral said, "I agree with my colleague. We also have a plot of the ship's course. Could a large vessel have disabled its transponder, or could multiple smaller vessels not equipped with transponders come alongside the *Menelaus* without our knowledge? Yes, it's possible, but I stand by my opinion that old men could not have gone ship-to-ship."

"All right," Tavassi said, "I'm convinced. That leaves the air. I assume we are talking about helicopters. Let's hear from the Air Force."

An Italian General at the Aviano Air Base in northeastern Italy responded, "It would have been multiple medium-sized helicopters or a single heavy-lift aircraft. Operationally, it is easier to contemplate a single transfer. That would be our best assessment."

"Why is that, General?" Tavassi asked.

"Most medium-sized helicopters can transport eight, perhaps ten passengers. There were over one hundred cardinals and an unknown number of kidnappers. That would have necessitated a dozen or more landings and takeoffs from a cargo ship that was not designed for helicopter landings. I happen to think that even if highly skillful pilots were landing on the foredeck of the *Menelaus* in a one-meter chop, there would have been one or more accidents that would have been detected when the ship came to port in Marseilles. No, I think it is more likely that a single heavy-lift helicopter with a highly experienced pilot would have been the safest and most efficient way to move the prisoners."

"And what kinds of helicopters can accomplish such a thing?" Tavassi asked.

"A few come to mind," the general said. "The American Sikorsky CH-53 Super Stallion, V-22 Osprey, CH-47 Chinook, the Russian Mi-26 Halo and Mi-28, and the Chinese Avicopter AC313. All of them can transport more than one-hundred souls, tightly packed together."

"What type of pilot flies these helicopters?" Tavassi asked.

"They could be military or civilian-trained."

"And who operates them?"

"Outside of the military, any number of private companies that move heavy equipment payloads."

"Now, tell me, general, if one of these heavy-lift helicopters had landed and taken off from the *Menelaus*, would it have been detected on radar?"

"If a pilot were to keep his altitude below one hundred meters, he could be confident that the aircraft would not be detected by radar."

A French colonel representing the French Air and Space Force interjected, "We can confirm that there were no aircraft detected in the vicinity of the *Menelaus* during the relevant period. I agree with my Italian colleague that a heavy-lift helicopter flying at a low altitude could have accomplished this mission without radar detection."

Tavassi searched the large video screen for the face of Maurizio Cremonesi, the Italian foreign intelligence service director. "General Cremonesi, what can the AISE tell us about other mechanisms for detecting a low-flying helicopter? Mechanisms such as satellite tracking. Surveillance drones."

Cremonesi thrust out his chin. "This is a non-secure channel, and I doubt many participants have the required security clearance to hear about this matter. I can say, as a generality, that many state actors have satellite and drone tracking capabilities that may or may not have been operational in the Mediterranean on the night in question. All I can tell you is that our American, British, and EU partners report no reconnaissance data of marine vessels or aircraft within the immediate vicinity of the *Menelaus* that night."

Tavassi sat back and looked toward the ceiling before saying, "So, people, beyond a consensus that a single large helicopter removed the cardinals from the ship where the hostage video was recorded, we know little more. Who cares to summarize the status of our investigation?"

Emilio took it upon himself to respond. "I would say that we have no earthly idea where our cardinals are."

CHAPTER ELEVEN

When these kinds of raids occurred, the attackers usually struck in the small hours of the night. The security at the Pope Celestine School for Girls in Bauchi, Nigeria, was lighter at suppertime than it would have been after midnight. Only two guards were on duty at the gate of the walled compound off the Bauchi-Gombe Road, when four olive-green trucks bearing the red, yellow, and black insignia of the Nigerian Army arrived. Men in fatigues jumped down through canvas flaps.

"Open the gate," one of them demanded.

The older security guard, all of twenty, seemed confused by the demand but wished to be helpful.

"Yes, yes, we can do this, sir. The headmistress didn't inform us. I will call her."

The last words he heard were, "There's no need," before his throat was cut by a machete.

The heavy trucks lumbered through the gate, past the dormitories and scrubby playing fields. They stopped at the main building where the children were having their evening meal.

The leader of the party, a compact, bearded man with aviator glasses and an AK-47 slung across his chest, assembled his men.

"Remember. No bullets. People will hear. The police will come. Only these," he said, nonchalantly waving his machete.

The girls, aged eight to eighteen, sat at long communal tables wearing school uniforms of blue pleated skirts and white collared shirts. When the men entered, they stopped tucking into their rice and chicken stew. No one talked, and no one cried. The only sounds in the dining hall came from boots stomping on the floor and wooden chairs creaking as the girls shifted positions to see what was happening.

Fear can create the illusion that time has slowed, and two hundred girls witnessed the following events in slow motion: their headmistress, Sister Chioma, a name that meant good luck, approached the men and was met with a killing machete blow to her head. The school porter, a young priest, six teachers, and two cafeteria ladies were hacked in a frenzy of blood-letting. With the adults dead and dying, time sped up again, and the girls heard themselves screaming.

The leader's eyes were invisible through his aviator glasses as he sharply clapped his hands three times. "Stop this at once! Stop crying! They were bad people who were poisoning your minds. You are better off without them. We are the ISWAP. We are the true voice of Islam in West Africa. You are coming with us. We have trucks outside. If any of you don't want to come, you can join the pile of bodies. It doesn't matter to me."

∼

IN THE EARLY EVENING, Lieutenant Gambino got a call from the Rome Carabinieri headquarters from a Captain Marone informing him that a patrol car had spotted Eduardo Antelao's Fiat Panda in the Torre Angela neighborhood.

"Any sign of him?" Gambino asked.

"At this time, all we know is someone is inside the Fiat. Officers are approaching the vehicle. I'm heading there now. Do you want the address?"

Gambino fixed a blue light to the roof of his vehicle and sped away from the Vatican. When he arrived at Via Prosperina half an hour later, a dozen Carabinieri cars were blocking the narrow street, and residents were leaning over balcony railings. He showed his credentials and asked a corporal where to find Captain Marone. He was near the blue Fiat, engaged in an animated phone call, and when Marone saw him approaching, he held his hand over the phone's microphone and said, "Are you, Gambino?"

"Yes. What's going on?"

"Let me get rid of this call."

The captain ended his call and told Gambino to duck under the red-and-white police tape. The Fiat's driver's side door was open. Gambino had never met Eduardo but instantly recognized the chef from his Vatican employee photo. His neck was arched toward the headrest, face tilted upwards, mouth half open, his arms at his side. A paring knife rested on the crotch of his blood-soaked denim jeans.

"He's been dead for a few hours, in my opinion," Marone said. "He was a chef, right? He used his knife skills on both wrists. You see? He would have bled out fast."

"Any signs of a struggle?" Gambino asked.

"A physical struggle, no. One has a harder time detecting mental struggles. You never said why you were looking for this guy."

"We think he might have poisoned the pope."

"Holy Mother of God," the captain said, putting on Latex gloves and extracting a plastic evidence bag from his tunic. "You're probably going to want to read this immediately. It was in the glove box. It's sealed. We haven't opened it."

Gambino put on gloves and slit the envelope with his pocket knife. The folded piece of paper inside was filled with neat handwriting.

~

To the police:

My people no longer live here, but I choose to end my life on the street where I was born. How can I go on? Since the death of the Holy Father, my life has been a living Hell. I cannot look at my reflection in the mirror. I cannot bear to see the way my wife looks at me. I realized my part in the tragedy when the cardinals were taken from the Sistine Chapel. I know you are looking for me. I am a coward and too ashamed to face your interrogations. The answers you seek are here.

In the early morning of the day the pope died, before the sun came up, there was a knocking on our apartment door. I got out of bed and was confronted by two men in ski masks who pushed me back and entered the hall. They had guns. They forced me into the bedroom and told my wife to be quiet, or they would hurt her. They knew what my job was. They knew I would leave for the Vatican in one hour to prepare breakfast for the Holy Father. They knew I stayed at the Vatican until seven at night. They asked if the Holy Father usually had food late at night. I asked why they wanted to know, and they punched me in the stomach. I said he did. They asked what his favorite was. I said chocolate molten lava cake with cream. They told me to make it for him. They gave me a vial of white powder and told me to mix it into the cream. I asked what it was, and they punched me again. My son woke up and came to the bedroom. They had him lie beside my wife and told me they would stay all day in my apartment, holding my wife and son hostage. If I didn't do what they said or if I sent the police to the apartment, they would kill them. I was in turmoil. I didn't know what to do. I didn't know what was in the powder. I thought surely it was meant to harm the Holy Father, but I couldn't risk having my wife and little boy murdered. Finally, I did what they asked. I made the small cake and added the powder to a beaker of cream. I told Sister Maria I had made it. The dear woman seemed pleased because she knew it was his favorite. When I returned to my apartment, the men asked if I had done what they had asked. I told them to please leave, but they insisted on staying until very late. They had a radio to listen to the transmissions of the emergency services. When they learned the Holy Father could not be saved, they were happy and said they would go. If my wife or I told anyone about what I had done, they promised they would come back and kill the three of us. I cried all night and into the following morning. I have not stopped crying. I poisoned a man I truly loved and admired. He discovered me working in the Vatican cafeteria and gave me the job of a lifetime. Now all the cardinals are missing, and I fear this, too, is my fault. I cannot continue to live. I know suicide is a mortal sin, but I feel I have no choice. Please tell my wife I love her very much.

Eduardo Antelao

⁓

During a lull in her schedule, Elisabetta texted Cal to see if he could join her for dinner. The Swiss guards were not letting her leave the protective cocoon of the Vatican, so she arranged for the employee cafeteria to prepare a simple meal. She was getting ready for dinner when Emilio called.

"Our fears are confirmed," he said. "Eduardo committed suicide after we asked him to appear for an interview today. He left a note saying that masked men held his wife and son hostage and threatened to kill them if he didn't put poison in pope's food. Eduardo chose their lives over the Holy Father's."

"The poor man," Elisabetta said. "He had a terrible dilemma."

"Andrea Gambino met with his wife. You can imagine how she is. One of the men who held her spoke a little Italian, but he communicated with the other man in French."

She held a hand to her head and said, "They dug a tunnel. They poisoned the Holy Father. Then they waited for the conclave to begin. It's diabolical."

"That's the word for it."

"Do you have any leads?"

"We have nothing."

"I know you're working hard. Cal is coming for dinner. He wants to tell me about this yellow cross."

"You need a little break," Emilio said. "Let me know if he tells you anything I should hear."

⁓

The Swiss Guards at the Apostolic Palace recognized Cal, but that didn't stop them from subjecting him to a vigorous search. Elisabetta met him at the door of her apartment in her habit and veil. He had never been inside the secretary of state's apartment, but wasn't surprised that it was grander than the papal apartment a floor above. Throughout the past and into the present era, several cardinal secretaries had not been shy about allocating funds to redecorate the Renaissance rooms and upgrade features.

Cal noticed her private secretary at work in a small office as she took him through to the dining room. If the priest had work keeping him late, Cal thought he would probably perform it at his own office inside the Secretariat suite. No, his presence was strategic. If Cal Donovan was seen having dinner alone with her, tongues might start wagging, which was the last thing she needed.

Elisabetta insisted that the cafeteria staff need not stay late, so they left chafing dishes with pasta and meat courses on a sideboard. She and Cal divided the domestic duties. He opened and poured the wine. She filled salad bowls and cut the bread. As they sat across from one another at one end of the banqueting-size table, Cal proposed a toast to the memory of Pope John and a prayer for the missing cardinals.

"How bad has it been for you?" he asked.

"I won't lie to you," she said. "These have been among my most agonizing days in this job, and you know—"

Her voice faded. He knew what she was thinking. Two years earlier, her mentor and Cal's friend, Pope Celestine, had died a short distance from where they were dining.

"I know," he said.

She smiled in gratitude for not having to finish her thought.

"You were already in the hot seat," he said. "The hostage video made it hotter."

"Fortunately, I haven't had the time to read the barbs aimed at me. My secretary is keeping a folder of articles and social media posts to read in the future in case I'm ever feeling too good about myself. I understand that many believe I've been working with the kidnappers to force the Church to ordain women and seize control of the Vatican."

"The world is full of crazies," he said. "Always has been, always will be."

"Please, start," she said, breaking a piece of bread in half and dipping it in olive oil. "So, I can tell you: our suspicions were born out. We have a toxicology report showing the pope was poisoned by a fatal dose of digitalis and we have a confession from the pope's chef. French-speaking men held Eduardo's wife and child hostage and forced him to introduce the poison. The poison was in the cream the Holy Father poured over a late-night favorite, a chocolate cake."

"It's terrible to say," Cal said, "but Rodrigo always said that food would be the death of him. The scope of the plot is staggering. Think about the planning, the funding, the logistics."

"It's difficult to take in," she said. "Emilio told me about the tattoo. Do you think it's important?"

"The yellow cross," he said. "Last night I whipped myself into a frenzy about its significance. Today, I've convinced myself it was all in my head."

"This cross—it's associated with the Cathars?" she said. "Perhaps I should know more about them, but I don't."

"Do you want the short story, the long story, or the very long story, otherwise known by my students as the version where Professor Donovan doesn't know when to stop talking?"

She laughed. "Maybe the short one to start."

"Short one it is. The Cathars were a religious sect that arose in Southern France in the twelfth century. It was so popular that by the early thirteenth century, Catharism was probably the majority religion in the Languedoc area. It was a dualist religion, centered on Christ, so in that sense, you can say it was a Christian religion, although it was markedly different from the Christianity of its day."

"Dualist?"

"Its foundations rested on the twin pillars of good and evil. It likely arose from the far more ancient Persian religion of Manichaeism, later reimagined by the Bogomils of Bulgaria, who blended it with Christianity, and that form begat Catharism. In the Middle Ages, some Catholic theologians called them Christian heretics. Others said they weren't Christian at all, and to this day, that's the current position of the Vatican. It's still called the Great Heresy."

Elisabetta was picking at her salad. "I must say, in ignorance, I have no position."

"Yeah, it's hardly a burning topic these days. I mean, there aren't any Cathars left. How they were wiped out belongs in the long version."

"What were their beliefs?" she asked.

"They venerated Christ and followed what they considered to be his true teachings. They called themselves Good Christians. They believed in the dual principles of good and evil embodied by a good god and his evil adversary—think God and Satan. The good Christian god created the immaterial, spiritual realm. The evil entity created everything material—the world we live in. The two powerful deities in the universe, one good and one evil were in constant war. The purpose of life was to serve the good by serving others and escape from the cycle of rebirth and death and return home to the Christian god."

Elisabetta sounded surprised. "They believed in reincarnation?"

"They did. They thought a soul would be reborn again and again until it renounced the physical world and escaped incarnation. They also believed that God was dual, both male and female. This belief informed the equality of the sexes, a hallmark of Catharism. They believed in absolute celibacy for the priest class, those who had withdrawn from and renounced the world—those they called perfecti, or perfects. They also encouraged celibacy for the masses of followers, known as credentes, because they thought that every person born was just another poor creature trapped by the devil into an evil, material body."

"How does a religion that discourages sex and procreation grow and flourish?" she asked.

He flashed a smile. "An excellent question. One presumes that many credentes played fast and loose with that prohibition. They also believed eating meat or any animal products was evil because animals were the vessels of reincarnated souls. The perfecti were strict vegans. The credentes were allowed to add fish to their diets because they thought fish reproduced by spontaneous generation. They believed in the dignity of manual labor. Even priests and bishops worked manual jobs. They didn't regard suicide as a sin. In essence, they had a ritual called Endura, end-of-life euthanasia to let the fallen soul return to heaven. They considered death no more than taking off a dirty tunic."

Elisabetta hated interrupting him, but she said that the cafeteria staff would be chagrined if they didn't make a dent in the meal. They filled their plates at the sideboard.

Cal said some nice things about the food and added, "You're probably wondering. If this is the short version, what must the long version be like, let alone the very long version?"

"Not at all," she said. "You're being marvelously succinct."

"I swear, I'm almost finished," he said at the table. "So, a couple of things got me thinking last night. The first was the yellow cross. During the inquisition that preceded their annihilation, the Church forced repentant Cathars to wear yellow crosses on their clothes for identification. So, why does this kidnapper have this tattoo? Is it because of Cathar beliefs, or was it something she got from a tattoo parlor in the Languedoc region after a drunken night out? Then there was her accent. The Cathars hardly existed outside of France. The other thing was her insistence that the Church ordain women and elect a female pope. The Cathars treated men and women as equals. Many women became perfectae. I don't know if there was equal representation of the sexes within the priesthood, but there was no barrier to that. I tend to think that the presence of women within the hierarchy accounted for Catharism achieving a measure of culture, tolerance, and liberalism otherwise unseen during the twelfth and thirteenth centuries."

Elisabetta reached over to clink glasses. "What became of them?"

"The Cathars railed against the Catholic Church for being immoral and insisted that most of the books of the Bible were inspired by Satan. Centuries before Martin Luther, they denounced the Church for acquiring land and wealth and the greed and lechery of its priesthood. It won't shock you to know that the Church didn't take kindly to Cathars. They condemned them as heretics and began a crusade of purges and wholesale massacres. Crusaders devastated towns and entire Cathar regions of Southern France, killing locals indiscriminately. As many as half a million men, women, and children were murdered. The purge wiped out Catharism, root, and branch. A few people nowadays claim to be Cathars, but they're probably neo-Cathars, not from a direct lineage. And that's it. That was the end of the Cathars and the end of my short story."

After some desultory pushing of food around her plate, she had already put down her knife and fork. "It's quite the story," she said. "I can see why you were in a frenzy about the tattoo. What changed your mind?"

He was chewing and pointed to his mouth. She apologized and told him to take his time.

He took her advice, swallowed, and smiled. "You know, I woke up this morning and said to myself, Cal, maybe you're guilty of confirmation bias. I saw the yellow cross, jumped to a conclusion, and emphasized the facts that supported my theory. In the cold light of day, I've calmed down. There'd need to be more evidence than a woman with a tattoo. Many residents and visitors to the Languedoc region of France are proud of their Cathar heritage or intrigued about Catharism. You pop into a tattoo parlor and walk out an hour later with a bandage. I guess I'm accusing myself of a rush to judgment."

"Well, I think it's intriguing," she said, "even if Catharism has nothing to do with this. If nothing else, you've taught me things I should have—"

Elisabetta's private secretary entered the dining room, bent over her, and whispered. She rose from the table and said, "Cal, will you excuse me for a few minutes? I've got to take an urgent call."

Alone, he had a few more bites, then got up to roam the large room and admire paintings of past cardinal secretaries staring down from the walls. He was wondering if Elisabetta would be asked to sit for a portrait one day, when she returned with flushed cheeks.

"I'm sorry, Cal. I've had a call from our nuncio in Nigeria. This evening, two hundred girls were abducted by Islamist gunmen from our mission school in Bauchi. Staff members were murdered. A note was left on one of the bodies telling us to expect their demands tomorrow. I'm going to have to leave you now."

If her secretary hadn't been hovering, Cal would have said more than he did. He might have reached for her hands and held them while he commiserated. When he left Vatican City, he headed to the café he frequented while he worked for CNN. They kept a cold bottle of Grey Goose for him in case he returned.

CHAPTER TWELVE

Kayode Nwogu, the vice president of Nigeria, a lawyer with a degree from the London School of Economics, spoke excellent English. He was delighted that Elisabetta was also fluent. Early into their phone call, he dismissed his Italian translator.

"Our communication issue is solved, " he said. "Would that our other problems be so easy."

"Please tell me the situation, Mr. Vice President," she said.

"The group that took the girls calls themselves ISWAP, the Islamic State in West Africa Province. It's a splinter group of Boko Haram that has gained power by being more clever than Boko Haram. They have the same hard-core jihadi ideology, but they treat local Muslim civilians better than their rival. In their areas of influence, they dig wells, provide a modicum of healthcare, and discipline their soldiers if they abuse the locals. Today, a video was uploaded to their website. It's in Hausa, one of the languages of the north. I've just spoken to your nuncio in Abuja and informed him I would give you a courtesy call."

"What does the video show?"

"The leader of ISWAP is a ruthless character named

Mohammed Nur. In the video, he is with the girls gathered in a forested area."

"How do the girls look?"

"As you might expect. Tired and fearful. We count one-hundred-ninety-four. Do you have an accurate headcount on your end?"

"We don't," Elisabetta said. "Nor does our nuncio. He tells me the records are at the school. His understanding is that the total student body was approximately two hundred. What does this Nur say?"

"There is rhetoric and there are demands. He rails against modern Christian crusaders who wish to harm Muslims around the world and in western Africa. He specifically targets Catholics for your missionary work in Nigeria and Chad. Then he speaks about the abduction of your cardinals. He says you are feeling the wrath of Allah for your sins against Islam. I am afraid he specifically mentions you, Madame Secretary."

"Oh yes? What does he say?"

"He asks what kind of religion is led by a woman."

"I see. And their demands?"

"They want to see the Catholic Church immediately withdraw from all your education and missionary activities in West Africa, or they will kill the girls."

Elisabetta took the phone to one of the windows overlooking St. Peter's Square. Since the kidnapping, groups of faithful had been meeting on the cobblestones for prayer and vigil. Some brought children, and Elisabetta watched two young girls skipping around the circle of adults.

"Do they give any kind of deadline."

"Indeed they do. They say you have three days to make your decision. Then they will begin the executions."

"You know these people and these groups, Mr. Vice President. What do you advise?"

"Nur is nothing if not opportunistic. He sees the problems you have in Rome, and he capitalizes on these. He sees that your institution has weakened. This school in Bauchi and its children are the weakest link in a weakened chain. My advice to you is not to negotiate. It will not get the girls back. It will only embolden them. We in Nigeria will be left with the aftermath of a strengthened terrorist group. So, no, Madame Secretary. You must have a strong stomach and a strong mind and refuse to engage with these animals."

∼

Cal was having coffee near his hotel at his favorite coffee shop, Sant'Eustachio il Caffè when he got a call from Emilio.

"Any chance you could come up to Livorno?"

"Why Livorno?"

"The special operation group of the Carabinieri is up here. I've been with them the past few days."

"Tell me what you need?"

"Your brain. I want you to talk to the group about the yellow cross."

Cal slurped his coffee before it could get cold. "I'm regretting sounding the alarm on this yesterday. I think I got carried away."

"I really would like you to come if you're able."

Cal hesitated before agreeing. The Nigerian schoolgirl kidnapping had made the news, and he wanted to stay in Rome if Eli needed his support.

"What is it, around two to three hours by train? I can probably be there by mid-afternoon."

"We need you earlier I'm sending a helicopter. And, Cal, pack a bag."

∼

The Carabinieri helicopter picked Cal up from the heliport in Vatican City and deposited him in the courtyard of the GIS headquarters in Livorno. Emilio was waiting and ushered him to General Tavassi's office. The officer was shoeless on his sofa, his tunic unbuttoned. He got to his feet and began putting his uniform back together. Emilio told him Professor Donovan didn't require formality.

"Cal is a friend of mine and of the Carabinieri," Emilio said. "There's no need for ceremony."

"That's very true, General," Cal said, smiling. "As you were."

"Ah, you were in the military, Professor?"

"If two years in the army as a private and getting booted out for punching my sergeant counts, then yes."

"May I ask why you punched your superior officer?"

"The son-of-a-bitch deserved it, and I deserved what happened to me."

Tavassi wagged a finger at Emilio and said, "You were right. I do like him. Thank you for coming on short notice, Professor."

"I'm happy to help any way I can, but I don't know what I can do."

Tavassi finished buttoning up and fixing his hair with his fingers. "Emilio, could you see if Francesco Di Marino can come in? We're going to show you what you can do, Professor."

Di Marino was a pimply civilian in his thirties who wore his long hair in a top bun to fit in better with the spit-and-polish officers at GIS. Emilio introduced Cal as an American professor assisting the Carabinieri, and Di Marino as a civilian employee of GIS with a psychology degree and expertise in profiling and social media research.

They gathered at Tavassi's conference table, and the General said, "Explain to the professor what you've been working on and what you found."

Di Marino opened his laptop and turned the screen toward Cal. The photo was of a fleshy-faced man with close-cropped gray hair and trimmed beard.

Di Marino talked in a monotone. "I was tasked with researching the background of the master of the *Menelaus*, Pierre Abadie, looking for clues about his affiliations, motivations, and social attitudes. He is a French citizen, and therefore, we secured the cooperation of the French police. I began with available public records, reviewed pending or past criminal cases, and financial information. Next, I reviewed the case files of the French police who interviewed his family. Finally, I scoured his social media accounts looking for anything that might shed light."

"I assume you found something," Cal said. "Otherwise, I wouldn't be here."

"Certainly," the man said with an air of superiority. "Abadie is sixty-four years old. He had no evidence of financial stress, and no past or pending criminal offenses. After graduating from school, he attended the naval academy at Brest and became an officer assigned to amphibious assault ships, rising to become a frigate captain. He took his retirement at age forty-five and since then, has been employed as a ship's master for Morlet, SARL, the company that owns the *Menelaus*. Abadie has been divorced for many years and lives alone. He has two adult sons. The police interviewed the family. They say he has been treated for prostate cancer. The police are getting a judicial order to compel his doctor to divulge medical details. His family claims to be baffled by his involvement."

"Where is he from," Cal asked. "Where does he live."

The researcher checked his notes. "Narbonne. He was born there and currently has a flat there."

"The heart of the Languedoc," Cal said.

Di Marino frowned. "That's the historical name for the region. I believe it's called the province of Occitanie now."

"Forgive me," Cal said with a small smile, "but I'm a history professor."

"I see," the young man said humorously. "May I continue?"

Cal told him it was his presentation.

"I looked into Abadie's social media presence. He doesn't maintain any personal accounts, but his sons do. I found these pictures of interest posted by his youngest son six years ago from a birthday party for Abadie's grandson."

In the pictures, Abadie was grilling steaks in shorts and T-shirt over a backyard barbecue. Di Marino had added red circles to the area he wanted to highlight. Cal saw it before he noticed they were circled.

"A yellow cross," he said.

Abadie's tattoo on his bulging left upper arm.

Emilio said, "A second person with the yellow cross. The ship's master and a female kidnapper. When we talked this morning, your opinion was softening. Do you still think you overreacted?"

Cal shook his head. "I guess I should trust my first instincts."

Tavassi said, "Okay, thank you, Francesco. You may go."

As the young man collected his laptop and left, he looked doleful, as if wounded he wasn't allowed to participate in discussions above his pay grade.

"Emilio has to leave us for a meeting," Tavassi said, "but we would greatly appreciate it, Professor, if you could give a lecture to our working group on the Cathars. We need to understand what and who we are dealing with. Everyone needs to be on the same page."

"I'm flying to Montpellier to interview the owners of the *Menelaus*," Emilio said. We'll record your talk and I'll watch it later tonight. Can you stay a day or two in case new information comes our way?"

"Of course."

"Do you have a problem making a talk without notice?" Tavassi asked.

Cal pointed to his bag. "My academic life is on my hard drive. All I need to do is decide which talk on Catharism to give."

※

THE OFFICES OF MORLET, SARL were located on an old piece of farmland close to Montpellier's airport. Unlike the drab, utilitarian buildings in the nearby industrial estate, the Morlet headquarters was an architectural prize-winner, an angular masterpiece of tinted glass and steel. Emilio arrived early and was told the Morlets were in a meeting. He bided his time examining the wall of photographs in the lobby. There were ships and more ships, pictures of ports, and portraits of four generations of the controlling family. Emilio wasn't interested in the dour-looking founding patriarch, Laurence Morlet, his portly son, Henri Morlet, or his balding grandson, Claude Morlet. He focused on the present generation—the founder's great-grandchildren, Charles and Sabine Morlet, both expensively tailored with movie-star smiles. The researchers at GIS had given him background information on the company. It was founded after the first world war and steadily grew until the second world war when the Germans seized it and turned it to their military needs. Post-war, the Morlets regained control and resurrected it. By the time Sabine and Charles took the reins, it was a thriving regional player. The siblings received their education at the finest French schools universities. Sabine, the CEO was forty-five. Charles, the vice president for operations, was thirty-eight. The two of them modernized the company and turned it into a global enterprise serving the shipping requirements of Europe, Africa, the Middle East, and Asia. The siblings were the sole shareholders of the company. According to *Forbes* magazine, Sabine was presently the eighty-second wealthiest European with a net worth of 4.2 billion euros, and Charles was one-hundred-fortieth on the list at 1.8 billion.

Emilio was escorted to the executive suite, where he was obliged to wait some more, watching takeoffs and landings at the airport. When it was finally time for his meeting, he was taken to Sabine Morlet's corner office, where she and her brother were waiting. It was as if the photographs in the lobby had become animated, and Sabine and Charles had sprung from their frames. Their suits were nearly identical to those in their portraits. Sabine's blonde hair was straight-cut at the collar and severe. Charles's dark hair was stylishly long in the back, rising to a tall construction at the front. They had the same eyes, the same dimpled chins, and the same Gallic noses of their forbearers. Neither was exceptionally good-looking, but they exuded confidence and wealth. If they had been ordinary office workers, no one would have given them a second glance.

Charles approached with an extended arm and his best Italian. "Welcome. We are sorry to keep you waiting. We had a meeting with—" He asked his sister in French how to say lawyers in Italian.

Emilio tried English. "I don't speak French. Does English work for you?"

Charles beamed. "Yes, perfect. Sorry to keep you waiting. We were tied up with our lawyers. You can only imagine. I am Charles Morlet. This is my sister and my boss, Sabine Morlet."

Emilio gave them business cards and shook hands with Sabine. In the lobby photos, she was a little taller than her brother, but in person, she was shorter—a bit of Photoshop magic to elevate the CEO.

Sabine read Emilio's card. "You have the same surname as your secretary of state."

"She's my sister."

"We know a few things here about brothers and sisters working together," she said.

"How is she doing?" Sabine asked.

"This is a difficult time for everyone at the Vatican and Catholics worldwide."

Sabine steered Emilio to a low-slung white leather chair with long views of verdant farmland. They sat across from him on a matching modernist sofa.

"Thank you for seeing me today," Emilio said.

From this point forward, Sabine took control of the Morlet side of the conversation. "You said it was urgent," she said. "May you tell us if there have been developments to which we are unaware?"

"I don't have to remind you that your ship's master is missing. We believe the most likely scenario is that Pierre Abadie left the ship by helicopter with the cardinals."

"We have spent hours with the French police," she said. "We are aware of Pierre's apparent involvement. It's shocking. We have no explanation. We know him intimately. He has worked for us for over twenty years. We have been in touch with his family. They are grieved and baffled. We initially thought that the kidnappers must have taken him hostage, we must conclude that the facts point to a different scenario—that he was a willing participant in this crime. Do you have any idea where they are?"

"Not at this time," Emilio said, looking out the windows at land as far as the eye could see. Land, but no water. "May I ask why your company is based in Montpellier when the bulk of your trade, as I understand it, goes through the Port of Marseilles?"

"This is where our great grandfather, Laurence, established the company," she said. "Laurence built his business around the inland port of Marseilles, a Mediterranean trading terminal on the River Lez since the twelfth century. After the second world war, our father, Claude, expanded our operations to Marseilles, and our company grew significantly. Our operations manager is based there, but we are not Marseilles people. This is our place. When we outgrew our old building by the river, we decided to build here, by the airport. Air freight is a growing component of our business."

"I know you have been cooperating with the French authorities. I'm here because we have photographic evidence directly linking Master Abadie with the female spokesperson on the hostage video."

"May we see this evidence?" Sabine said.

Emilio had the photos. Sabine looked first, then passed them to her brother, who glanced and returned them to Emilio.

"The Cathar cross," she said. "Here in Occitanie, it is everywhere."

"Have you ever talked with Abadie about the Cathars or Cathar beliefs?" Emilio said.

"I haven't," Charles said.

"Same for me," Sabine said. "I'm not sure I understand the connection between tattoos and the kidnapping."

"That is what we are trying to understand," Emilio said. "Are you aware if Abadie had any affiliations with extremist or terrorist organizations?"

"Of course not," Sabine exclaimed. "If we ever had such an indication, we would terminate an employee immediately. But let me ask you, Colonel Celestino, are you suggesting that a terroristic group exists based on Cathar ideology? We are well-versed in Cathar history in the Languedoc. Tourism based on our Cathar past is a large economic driver in our region. The Cathars had a peaceful ideology. Besides, the last of the Cathars died in the fourteenth century."

"We are obligated to pursue all leads," Emilio said forcefully. "Here are the facts. Your ship was used to transport one hundred seventeen hostages and their kidnappers. One of your employees appears to be complicit and has an identical tattoos to one of the kidnappers. The Morlet shipping company is central to one of the greatest crimes in history."

Sabine thrust out her dimpled chin. "We, at Morlet, are distraught. We cannot believe that any of our employees would be involved in this barbaric act, yet, we have to accept the facts. We have reviewed the personnel records for Pierre Abadie and found nothing unusual. We immediately turned over copies of his files to the French police, and if you wish, you may have copies. Our lawyers object to our approach as French privacy laws are very strict, but we will deal with any consequences. This affair has severely damaged the reputation of the Morlet company. We know and admire one of the hostages, Cardinal Montebourg, from his years as Archbishop of Toulouse. We will do anything required and more to help the French authorities, the Italian authorities, and any authority to find the cardinals and bring the perpetrators of the crime to justice. Charles, please give the Colonel the files and assist him with other inquiries. You must excuse me now. I have meetings in Toulouse and Paris with our lawyers, insurers, and bankers. When there's blood in the water, the sharks begin to circle."

∼

THE WAR ROOM in Livorno was packed to the gills with military and civilian employees of GIS. It was an unusual audience for one of Cal's lectures, but an audience was an audience, and Cal was in his element as he paced before the screen, gesticulating and engaging in rhetorical flourishes. He had lectured on the Cathars on multiple occasions, and he selected a presentation from his files that best fit the needs of the GIS. His PowerPoint slides were replete with medieval paintings and lithographs of Languedoc towns and castles, Cathar and French personages of the day, present-day scenes of the region, and the yellow Cathar cross. The slide text was in English, and he translated them into Italian on the fly. The first part of his talk covered much of the same ground as his discussion with Elisabetta. Having established why the Catholic Church vilified the Cathars, he turned to what the Church did about it.

"I can't stand here today and tell you that the kidnappings are related to the Cathars and their beliefs. That's not why I was asked to come today. Finding the perpetrators and establishing motives is your job, not mine. But if the kidnappers *were* Cathar sympathizers, let me tell you what their motives *could* be. And I stress the word *could*. I can almost hear what some of you are thinking. Tell me, Professor Donovan, how could events that happened eight hundred years ago possibly motivate violence today? I need only remind you that the Catholic Church's crusades to conquer Jerusalem and the Holy Lands from Muslim rule commenced almost one thousand years ago. And I think you'll agree that some extremist groups have used the historical memory of the crusades to justify their actions.

"So, what became of the Cathars? Talk turned to violence in January 1208," Cal said. "A papal legate, Pierre de Castelnau, was negotiating with the Cathar nobleman, Raymond VI, the Count of Toulouse, to resolve differences. Things got heated, and threats were exchanged. After de Castelnau left Toulouse, he excommunicated Raymond. On his way back to Rome, he was murdered, allegedly by one of Raymond's men. At this point, you know what hit the fan. Pope Innocent III declared a crusade against the Cathars. He enlisted the Catholic nobles of France, led by Baron Simon de Montfort, to wage what would become a twenty-year war against the people of Languedoc. To the French, this wasn't a civil war, because they didn't consider the people of Languedoc to be French. The first significant event in the crusade was in 1209. It was the siege of the town of Béziers. What followed was the massacre of over seven thousand men, women, and children by Catholic forces. Béziers was a Cathar stronghold, but Catholics had lived peacefully among them without persecution. The commander of the Catholic forces that finally broke through the town's gates was a Cistercian abbot. When his men asked how they could distinguish the Cathars from the Catholics, the abbot told them: kill them all—the Lord will recognize his own. Ladies and gentlemen, keep that in your heads. That was the mindset of the crusaders. The Inquisition that followed lasted through the thirteenth and a good part of the fourteenth century. Cathar heretics were interrogated and tortured. More massacres followed. In Champagne, one-hundred-eighty-three were burned at the stake in a series of executions. In Montségur, over two hundred Cathar perfects were burnt together in an enormous pyre at what came to be known as the prat dels cremats—the field of the burned.

"The Cathars who escaped the Inquisition scattered and went into hiding. It took a century for the Inquisitors to finish the job. The last known Cathar perfect was executed in 1321. After that, the trail runs cold, and any remaining Cathars were probably assimilated into Catholic France. Today, there is a celebration of Cathar culture in the Pays Cathare—that's French for Cathar country. The stimulus is almost certainly tourist revenue, not a revival of the Cathar religion. As far as I know—and I've done the research—there are no modern practitioners of Catharism in its original form. Could the conclave kidnappers have been motivated by an ancient hatred of the Church? Could Cathar philosophy about the equality of men and women have permeated into their demands? Could I be making a mountain out of a molehill? Maybe some of the kidnappers had tattoos of the yellow cross because they lived in Languedoc or were tourists passing through Pays Cathare. Maybe they are red herrings. I was asked to pose questions and give you background data. It's up to you to find the answers."

As Cal lingered in the war room, answering questions, Francesco Di Marino, the civilian who had unearthed the photos of the tattooed ship master and chief steward, was outside, walking off his irritation. It was drizzling, and the courtyard was empty, giving him leeway to talk loudly on his phone.

"No one is giving me any credit," he vented. "I was the one who found the crucial evidence. Do you think my department head praised me?"

The woman on the other end of the line said, "Poor baby. What evidence?"

"I shouldn't say. General Tavassi kicked me out of his office the second I delivered my findings."

"He's a bastard. But here you are, talking about evidence and findings. What's going on?"

He ignored the question. "This American professor is getting all the credit, and I had to sit like a lump through his lecture."

"Oh yes?" she asked. "What's this professor's name?"

"Cal Donovan."

"I've heard of him," she said. "Tell me what you found, baby. Tell me what Cal Donovan talked about. When I see you this weekend, I'll find a way to thank you."

∽

Di Marino's girlfriend was a producer on a Milan-based live TV news show called *La Guardia Notturna*—the Night Watch. Their *modus operandi* was to move fast and hit hard; if they got something wrong, they would deal with it later. Since the kidnappings, the show had covered nothing else, but the same set of facts and speculations was getting stale. The information that Di Marino's girlfriend pitched to the production team that afternoon drove everyone to a frenzy of activity.

The veteran newscaster, Alessandra Giannattasio, nervously twirled some of her platinum hair around a finger and said, "Keep your eyes on the prize, people. We're going to blow our competition out of the water tonight."

CHAPTER THIRTEEN

The castle was massive, one of the largest in the region. The men who built it in the twelfth century would recognize only the Romanesque church at the heart of the original construction. In the eighteenth century, the medieval structure was swallowed whole by an architectural design that saw the castle transformed into an abbey palace of yellow limestone—its conceit was that of a mini Versailles. In its current form, it was over sixty-thousand square feet of living and utility space set on two hundred acres of vineyards, meadows, and woodlands.

The castle's house staff, the groundskeepers, and agricultural workers had been furloughed for a fortnight. When the giant helicopter settled onto its grounds before dawn, only a handful of men with balaclavas and weapons were there to see it. The two women got off first and embraced them. These men took charge of the hostages, high-fiving their four male comrades when they climbed off the chopper.

Months of planning had preceded their arrival, but nothing fully prepared the kidnappers for the care and feeding of over one-hundred elderly men. The kidnappers had assigned duties. The first order of business was taking the hostages to the ancient vaulted church they had converted into a dormitory. Rows of cots sat on the stone floor—each with a sheet, a blanket, a pillow, a towel, a medium-sized red tracksuit sealed in plastic, and a sanitary kit with soap, toothpaste, and a toothbrush. There was a single toilet in the corridor that connected the church to the main house, but that would only suffice for nocturnal emergencies. A bank of portable toilets was deployed in the church courtyard alongside a long metal sink trough with spigots fed by hoses. The courtyard was tented to block views of the countryside.

The kidnappers pulling guard duty were obliged to keep their faces covered at all times. Henri Vaux, the lithe young man, watched in amusement as the cardinals tried to decide who they wanted to be near.

"This reminds me of my first sleepaway night in the Scouts," he told Felix Bain, the kidnapper closest to his age. "The cool kids wanted to bunk together."

Half the cardinals needed to use the toilets right away, and a traffic jam ensued. Complaints about the stiffness of the thin mattresses began. They were hungry. The doctor wanted to know about the medications he wanted.

Six kidnappers were assigned to food preparation. The first lunch served was convenience food—each cardinal received a military-style ready-to-eat meal, a piece of fruit, and a bottle of orange juice. In anticipation of the evening meal, institutional-sized pots were set to boil, vegetables were chopped, rice was cooked, and chickens were roasted in the ovens.

In the evening, the blue-eyed leader, the black woman, and Pierre Abadie slouched on overstuffed furniture in a lounge reception, allowing themselves a glass of wine. The women called themselves by their childhood nicknames from *Bouli*, their favorite cartoon series from the nineteen-nineties. The blue-eyed woman was Bouli, the leader of the snowmen. The black woman was Bear.

"So, Bouli. You did it," Bear said.

"*We* did it," Bouli said, raising her glass. "But it's just the first step."

"To us," Pierre said, yawning. "There were many days I didn't think we could pull this off."

"You should get some sleep, Pierre," Bouli said.

"Just because I'm twenty years older than you ladies doesn't mean I need a nap."

Bouli looked as if she remembered a detail. "You got rid of your mobile phone?"

"It's at the bottom of the sea," he said. "None of my men have phones with them. I double-checked. What about the landlines? Discipline and willpower only go so far."

"I cut the main phone line," Bear said. "There's a computer in the office, but I disconnected the router. We're cut off."

Bouli pointed to her mobile phone. "Only this one."

"When are you going to talk to them?" Pierre asked.

The two women looked at each other. After all their years together, they could sometimes communicate without words.

"Bear and I agree that we should let them settle in, have a decent meal, and talk among themselves," Bouli said, her speech thickened by fatigue. "They heard our manifesto. They know what we're asking of them. I'll see them later tonight. They can start their conclave in the morning."

"You two look worse than I do. Get some sleep," Pierre said.

Bear got up, leaving a half-full glass. "I'll check on our guys in the church. Then Bouli and I are going take your advice and head upstairs for a lie-down."

∼

THE CARDINALS SAT on their mattresses, eating their first meal in captivity with plastic utensils. Many had changed into tracksuits, putting their folded ecclesiastical garments under their beds.

"Red tracksuits," Cardinal Bizimana said. "Either they have a sense of humor or no sense of irony."

Cardinal Macy was two cots over. His tracksuit trousers ended halfway to the knees, and he couldn't zip the jacket.

"Anyone have a large or extra-large?" His question echoed off the limestone vault.

Macy peeled back the foil on his meal and pushed some dehydrated potatoes and mystery meat around. "Oh well. It's not our only indignity."

Cardinal Quang's tracksuit hung loosely on his frame. "Does anyone have any idea where we are?"

Cardinal Montebourg cast his meal aside, uneaten, and bit into an apple. "We are in the south of France."

"How can you be sure?" Cardinal Sanz asked.

"I looked out the helicopter window and recognized the coast near Marseilles. We didn't fly very long after that."

Cardinal Rowekamp had wolfed his food down hungrily, and only when he was done did he complain to Cardinal Fisher that it was inedible. He asked the men around him if anyone recognized the church.

Montebourg heard him and said, "France has many such medieval churches that were originally built near a nobleman's castle or inside its keep. Some, like this one, became part of a more recent grand house. You can be sure we're on private property."

Cardinals Colpo, Sauseda, and Navarro had been speaking at the end of the church where the altar would have been. When they concluded, Colpo clapped his hands to get everyone's attention, prompting their guards to raise weapons in a knee-jerk response.

"My friends," Colpo said. "We believe we should celebrate Mass this morning. It is right and proper that we do so, and it will surely lift our spirits. I have conferred with my learned friends, and we agree that liturgical objects are unnecessary for a Mass to have validity. All we require are bread and wine. Save a piece of your bread roll. We will request wine from our captors. Choir dress is preferable to these horrid tracksuits."

"We should discuss this ersatz conclave they're demanding," Cardinal Deetz called out.

"I have some choice words for them," Macy said.

After a series of small-group discussions, Cardinal Mamami

called to everyone, "I think, perhaps, we should believe them when they say they'll execute us if we don't elect the nun."

"I was with Rotolo and Stocchi when they could not climb down the second ladder," Cardinal Mertens said. "They could have killed them, but they did not. They may not be as bloodthirsty as they might wish us to believe."

"Let us discuss what must be done after we celebrate Mass," Colpo said.

They turned at the sound of footsteps on the ancient stone floor. Henri, the youngest kidnapper, came running, waving a bottle.

"I have some wine for you," he said. "They told me it was a good vintage, better than the cheap wine you usually get at Mass."

∼

Cardinal Reginald Archer of Boston, was a fitness buff who exercised daily. Not content with stretching and calisthenics, he organized a circuit of brisk walking around the church's perimeter and the tented outdoor space beside the toilets and sink trough. Following Mass, about thirty of his comrades followed his lead. Twenty minutes into the routine, Bouli and Bear, both masked, came in and had them assemble.

The acoustics of the ancient church carried Bouli's voice without having to shout.

"I wanted to see if you had the essentials for your time here," she said. "Tell me if you require anything."

Dr. Bellisario immediately spoke up. "When we were on the ship, I gave you a list of needed medications. Please tell me when you will provide these."

Bouli whispered to Bear, who answered, "I looked at your list. We are unable to satisfy your request. I am not a doctor, but I recognize that most medicines on the list are for conditions that are not immediately life-threatening. We intend to release you once the new conclave has ended. It should be a matter of a few days at most. Therefore, I must ask you which ones are absolutely necessary to sustain life?"

Bellisario had not changed out of his suit. He rubbed at his dark stubble and said, "Insulin. We must have the insulin and syringes."

"By when?"

The doctor went to Sauseda and asked to see his vial.

"Three days," Bellisario said. "We must have it in three days, or his Eminence will have difficulty."

Bouli said, "Any other needs?" Hearing nothing, she quickly moved on. "Tomorrow morning, you will reconvene your conclave. You all heard what I said on the ship. The video was released, and now the world knows too. You will say, 'How can we vote under duress?'" she said mockingly. "'The Holy Spirit informs our choice for the new pope, not some kidnappers with guns.' And my answer to you is simple. The Roman Church, for centuries, has coerced people to bend to its doctrines. In past eras, it was by torture, Holy Wars, or the threat of excommunication. In our more genteel present day, your coercion takes more subtle forms. Your missionaries proselytize, harangue, and bribe people to convert to Catholicism and follow your narrow path. We intend to use threats to bend you to our will. You will vote to ordain women as priests. Then you will vote to make Elisabetta Celestino the next pope. After that, you will be set free. You have five days, starting tomorrow. If you cannot meet our demands, we will have no choice but to end your lives. We don't wish to do it, but we will do it if we must."

Cardinal Macy shouted at her. "Tell us why you are doing this. We deserve to know."

"Who here knows about the Cathars?" she said.

Several cardinals whispered to one another, but no one raised a hand.

"Come now," Bouli exclaimed. "Some of you are scholars of church history. I know for sure that one of you knows. Where is Cardinal Montebourg?"

The courtly Frenchman, who had refused his red tracksuit, stepped forward in his wrinkled and stained robes.

"I am from the Languedoc," he said. "I was ordained in the Languedoc. My ministry was in the Languedoc. Although I have spent many years at the Vatican, my heart is in the Languedoc. We know full well about our Cathar past. I have always found it a curious reflection on human nature that a heretical sect could be recast as something other than a heretical sect and embraced and romanticized by modern society. I suspect that the root cause is tourism revenue. The mayors are addicted to the money that flows like water to the local businesses. Are you going to tell us that this outrage you have perpetrated is about this perverted sect?"

Bouli rolled up her sleeve and held her arm high so everyone could see her tattoo.

"The persecuted members of the Cathar faith were forced to wear the yellow cross, much like the Jews in Nazi Germany were forced to wear the yellow star," she said. "I wear it out of pride and remembrance. What am I proud of? I am proud that this perverted sect, as you call it, achieved a perfection not seen in Christendom until the nineteenth century when Protestant sects began the practice of ordaining women as priests. From the first days of Catharism, women were equal to men. And here we are, well into the twenty-first century, and still, the Church of Rome clings to its discrimination of half the Catholics on the planet. What is it I remember? I remember that the Church waged a Holy War that burned, beat, hung, slashed, and raped Cathars until these good and gentle people ceased to exist. If the Church had not done this, Catharism would be a thriving religion today, embodying the true message of our Savior, Jesus Christ. We did not take you from your conclave for revenge. We seek a remedy. To honor our Cathar fathers and mothers, sisters and brothers, we demand that the Church elevate women to the ranks of men. We want to see women become priests. We want to see women as bishops. We want to see women as popes. You will call it coercion. We call it justice."

~

WHEN THE ROMANESQUE church was deconsecrated centuries earlier, its windows were bricked, so now, the morning brought no natural light. The clergymen had to settle for the small doses of sunlight that permeated the courtyard's canvas tent while they performed morning ablutions. Their captors, Henri and Felix, served them a breakfast of rolls, jam, and coffee from a five-liter beverage dispenser. The cardinals made their beds and discussed a seemingly mundane issue. Should they dignify this bastardized conclave by changing out of their tracksuits? The consensus answer was no. However, some traditionalists who had used them as pajamas, refused to wear tracksuits during the day. They were in some approximation of choir dress when Bear pulled on her balaclava and entered.

"It's nine o'clock. Please begin your conclave. We have ballot papers and pencils. There will be two ballots in the morning, and two in the afternoon, separated by lunch. Knock on the door to communicate your results. Your white smoke will be the helicopter's exhaust fumes when it comes to collect you after you have done what is required."

For the first hour of this conclave, no one rose from their cots to speak. It was tacitly understood that silence was a form of protest. It was an uncomfortably long interlude for men whose tools of the trade were disputation, teaching, and prayer. It fell to Hilaria Sauseda, the camerlengo, to break free.

He stood and wobbled, prompting Dr. Bellisario to ask if he needed a piece of fruit for low sugar.

"No, Doctor, I'm fine. It's only my neuropathy," he said. "My friends, we have a choice to make. We can refuse to bend to their will. We can remain silent, or we can have a principled discussion about the ordination of women. I, for one, have no problem with the latter. The Congregation for the Doctrine of Faith has thoroughly considered the ordination question. Apostolic letters have been written. Nevertheless, there is nothing wrong with engaging in further theological discourse on the matter."

Domenico Colpo got to his feet and stamped one of them. "The matter of female ordination is settled. It was not what Christ willed and runs counter to apostolic teachings."

"I agree with Domenico," Samuel Laguerre said. "Our position on ordination has nothing to do with gender equality and everything to do with Jesus Christ and the history of the Church. By his choice of twelve male apostles, the Church has reserved the priesthood for men since its earliest days. We shall not be moved because medieval heretics or our Protestant brothers thought otherwise."

Manuel Navarro, one of the plotters who had tried and failed to undermine Elisabetta Celestino's appointment as secretary of state, said, "I have had it up to here with this feminist nonsense. Who do they think we are? We are the Holy Roman Church!"

Wilford Emory of Washington, DC, evoked chuckles when he said, "I've heard it said that I'm the most liberal member of the College of Cardinals. Does anyone care to challenge me for the honor? No, thought not. I am one hundred percent for gender equality. I am an enthusiastic supporter of our secretary of state. I believe Pope John did something of historic importance by elevating her to the position. I believe she has done an admirable job. If she were a man, if she were a cardinal, I would have no issue casting my vote for her to become pope. However, she is not a man, so I cannot. We often hide behind tradition as a reason to make poor choices. However, if we change our doctrine on the bedrock tradition of ordination, the church will lose its identity. And if we lose our identity, we will lose our way."

Victor Macy began to clap, and applause echoed through the chamber.

"I believe we've come to a decision on their first demand," Macy said. "I say we take a vote on their second demand. I also believe that Elisabetta Celestino is a fine secretary of state, but I will be marking my ballot—*I Refuse*."

∽

CAL'S HOTEL in Livorno wasn't up to his usual standard, but he was not inclined to complain or upgrade hotels on his own purse lest he embarrass his host, General Tavassi. However, the restaurant Tavassi chose that night, Osteria del Mare, made up for the small hardship. The food was excellent, and Emilio made sure the waiter attentively replenished Cal's glass of vodka.

"Well, Professor," Tavassi said, "in the absence of a better lead, you certainly have the team-oriented to the Languedoc area and this Cathar angle. We need the help of the French, but they're pushing back—as the French do. Would you be able to give your lecture to the French intelligence people tomorrow?"

"Of course. I'm at your disposal," Cal said. "I'd like to know if you were convinced by what you heard?"

The general dipped his bread in sauce. "In our intelligence world, we deal in probabilities. Certainties for or against a proposition are often elusive. Your thesis is based on circumstantial evidence. Now, it's a very nice collection of circumstantial elements —the tattoos, the French accents, the feminist demands—but it's not conclusive. When we reported to the prime minister this afternoon, we gave your hypothesis a fifty-percent chance of being correct."

"A coin toss," Cal said.

"Each new piece of evidence will tilt the balance," Emilio said. "We're trying to find companies that may have rented a heavy-lift helicopter. We're looking deeper into the financial records of Pierre Abadie. I got his personnel files from his employer this afternoon and there was nothing helpful. They were aware of his cancer diagnosis, but it didn't seem to impact his work history."

"People with cancer sometimes change their behavior," Tavassi said.

"For sure," Emilio said. "We need to keep that in mind. Lawyers are trying to pierce the veil and find the owners of the Nevada LLCs that rented the villa on Viale Vaticano and the warehouse in Cecchignola, although we're being told that the Nevada jurisdiction was probably chosen because of its strong anonymity. We're searching social media channels for Cathar mentions. The British government has asked their GCHQ to scour the mass of data collected from intercepted phone calls, emails, texts, and the like for Cathar sympathy groups. Something will come up. It always does."

Cal lifted his glass. "I'll drink to that."

"How much does Elisabetta know about your hypothesis?" Emilio asked.

"You mean my coin toss? She knows the essentials of the argument. Have you talked with her today? This Nigerian situation looks bad."

"I haven't had the chance," Emilio said.

"Your sister is up to her rosary beads in alligators," Tavassi said. He was chuckling at his own joke when his phone rang. "When?—Now?—What channel?—He what?—Call me back when you've interrogated him." He hung up, rose from the table, and swore. "Come with me. There's a TV at the bar."

Cal took his vodka with him. "I don't think I like the sound of this," he said.

"You definitely won't," Tavassi said.

There was a singing contest on the TV, and Tavassi barked at the bartender to switch to *La Guardia Notturna*. The journalist, Alessandra Giannattasio, was prancing before a giant screen filled with Cal's face.

"Again, dear viewer. Tonight we're presenting to you a *Guardia Notturna* exclusive," she purred. "The famous American Professor, Cal Donovan, friend and confidant to Pope Celestine and Pope John, believes the Vatican kidnappers were motivated by admiration of an ancient Christian cult. These cultists were called Cathars. They wore yellow crosses to show their faith."

"What the actual fuck!" Cal said.

Giannattasio gestured at Cal's photo with her clipboard. "They call him the pope whisperer. Professor Donovan, has discovered that cultists, who tattoo themselves with a yellow crucifix, are the group who violated the sacred conclave and took the cardinals. Here is the hostage video we have seen again and again. Listen again to their demands, but this time, look closely at the spokeswoman's forearm."

"How?" Cal asked helplessly.

"We have a leaker," Tavassi said gravely. "It's the civilian, Francesco Di Marino. He turned himself in when the show was about to start. He admitted he talked to his girlfriend about the case. She's a producer at *La Guardia Notturna*."

"Total shitshow," Emilio said.

Cal flagged the bartender. "Would you get me another vodka?"

"Make it two," Emilio said.

Tavassi shook his head and said, "No, three."

∼

BOULI WAS HAVING a late dinner in the castle's dining hall with Bear and Pierre. Rene Chaput, one of their men, had cooked them a mushroom risotto, and they were heaping praise on his shoulders.

"I think we're eating better than the red hats tonight," Bear said.

"So, we need to talk about today's result," Pierre said. "What are we to do?"

The cardinals had procedurally done what had been demanded of them but failed to deliver the desired results. Their decision on female ordination was a unanimous no. And the outcome of all four papal ballots was identical: one-hundred-seventeen papers were marked, *I Refuse.*

"I say we shoot one," Bear said matter-of-factly. "That will get them focused on the only outcome to save the rest of them."

Bouli put her fork down and wiped her mouth. "We're not going to shoot anyone," she said. "It's only the first day."

Rene came running into the hall, words spilling from his mouth. They followed him to the kitchen, where a small TV was playing a French news channel.

"—unable to confirm the report of the Italian TV magazine, *La Guardia Notturna.* They claim that a Harvard University academic named Calvin Donovan has identified the Vatican kidnappers as members of an obscure Christian sect called the Cathars who flourished eight-hundred years ago in the Languedoc region. A professor from the Sorbonne who is an expert on the Cathars has dismissed the claim as nonsense. Our religion correspondent, Nicole—"

Bear turned the sound down. "Has anyone heard of this guy, Donovan?"

"I have," Bouli said. "Stay here. I'll be back."

Bouli pulled her mask from her back pocket and burst into the church.

"Who is the cardinal from Boston?" she shouted.

Reginald Archer's blood drained from his face. "I am Cardinal Archer," he said.

"Do you know Professor Cal Donovan from Harvard?"

"I do," Archer said. "Boston is a relatively small community. I've heard him lecture. We've dined on occasion. We are acquaintances. Why do you ask?"

Bouli let his question slide. "Come with me," she said. "I want you to tell me everything you know about him."

CHAPTER FOURTEEN

1194
Lavaur, Languedoc

THE NINE-YEAR-OLD'S CURIOSITY AND EAGERNESS TO LEARN ABOUT the world was boundless. Her favorite word was why. Some children repeated the single-worded question over and over to be annoying, but Geralda sincerely wished to learn new things. Why did the crops begin to grow in the Spring? Why did the river flow in one direction and not the other? When her grandfather died, where did he go? Why did that Catholic boy spit on her and call her names? Why did the sky blacken at night? Her father and brothers tired of her questions and walked away in exasperation, but her mother, Esclarmonda, had infinite patience and tried to give her true answers.

By age seven, she had learned to read Latin, and by age eight, she had read all the Gospels from the Bible owned by Monsieur Bayard, a wealthy man who lived in one of the grandest houses in Lavaur. "Why don't we have a Bible?" she had asked her mother. She understood the answer, but it left her wanting to be rich enough to own her own holy book one day. So, Geralda did the next best thing—she memorized long passages and spouted the Gospels while fetching water from the river or chopping vegetables.

On a fine morning in April, she was working beside her mother outside their timber cottage. Her father was plowing his stony plot of land with her older brother, and Geralda could just make out the two of them laboring in the distance.

"Stop looking to the field," her mother said. "Your gaze should be upon the wheat. Grind every kernel, child. After this lot, there are only three more bags of grain from last year's poor harvest. Pray that this year's harvest comes early and is plentiful."

"Yes, mama."

"You're a good girl. Have I ever told you that?"

"Every day, mama, and twice on Sundays."

Esclarmonda smoothed her apron and looked lovingly upon Geralda's fair face. "I think you are ready."

"Ready for what?" Geralda asked.

"To learn certain things about our faith."

Geralda stopped working her pestle and said, "I already know things."

"Do you? Tell me what you know."

"We call ourselves Cathars. Do you know why?"

"Do you?"

"I do, mama! It comes from the Latin word Cathari. That means the Pure. Do you know what else we are called? Good Christians. You and I, mama, are Good Women, and Papa and Jean are Good Men."

"That is very good, Geralda. What else do you know?"

"The Catholics do not like us, and we do not like them."

"And what else?"

"That is all I know. Please tell me more."

"To begin with, there are two Gods," her mother said. "There is a good God, the God of light. He created the spirit world. Jesus Christ, our Lord, was the son of the good God. Then, there is an evil God, the God of darkness, who created the physical world. Some call him Satan. Everything in the physical world is filled with sin. A very long time ago, we humans were angels. The evil God forced humans to spend an eternity trapped here on Earth in his wicked material world. We Good Christians strive to become angels again by rejecting the material world and returning to Heaven. If we do not, we will be reborn again and again, trapped in this corrupt Earth, suffering endless human or animal lives."

"But, I am not suffering, mama," Geralda said, squinting at the sky. "Look at the warm sun in the sky. Listen to the sweet sound of the lambs."

"You are but a child," her mother said. "Your suffering will come."

"Did I suffer before?"

"You did, child. If you are on the Earth, you had a past life. We do not know who you were or how many times you were reborn." Esclarmonda feigned an angry face and said, "Keep grinding, child."

"But I want to be an angel, mama. How can I become an angel?"

"By taking the Consolamentum. This is our most important rite. When you take the Consolamentum, you immerse yourself in the Holy Spirit of the good God. You are absolved of all sin, and upon death, you will become an angel, dwelling forever in Heaven in a state of perfection."

Geralda pouted and said, "Why have you not given me the Consolamentum, mama?"

"You are a child. Children cannot take the rite. There are two times when a Good Christian can receive the Consolamentum. The first is if one becomes a perfect. Only a very few of us become perfect. The second is on our deathbed."

"What is a perfect?" Geralda asked.

"Monsieur Autier is a perfect," her mother said before naming three other villagers known to Geralda. "Perfects are the purest Cathars. They live strict lives of prayer and hard work. Those among us who are not perfecti are called credentes. Your father and brother, you and I, are credentes. We live our lives as Good Christians. We venerate Jesus Christ. We do not kill any creatures. We only eat that which can be grown. We do not eat animals or their milk or their eggs because animals carry reincarnated souls."

"But we eat fish from the river. Why?" Geralda asked.

"Fish are not born as animals are. They form from the bodies of other fish, free of fornication."

"That is good," Geralda said. "Fish is my favorite."

"Perfects are purer than we are," her mother said. "They are the ones who preach to us about Jesus Christ and administer the consolamentum. To be a perfect means that you must abstain from acts of the flesh."

"What are acts of the flesh?"

"They do not make babies."

"Oh. Can I be a perfect?"

"Yes. Cathar women are the equal to Cathar men. You may become a perfect when you are a grown woman. You may choose to do so. You may choose to remain a credentes."

"I choose to be a perfect," Geralda said.

"There is time. We shall see."

"Why do the Catholics and the Cathars hate each other, mama?"

"We hate the Roman Catholic Church because it is full of evil. They claim to be the true Church, but that is untrue. We are the true Christians. But remember, Geralda. We do not hate Catholic people. We have many Catholic neighbors in Lavaur. Some of them are very nice. The Catholic Church is corrupt. Their priests grow rich, fat, and lazy. They sell pieces of paper to poor people who believe they will never get to Heaven if they do not possess them. Perfects are incorruptible. They earn their own keep through manual labor and pay their way in the world. Their priests preach in Latin, the language few people can understand."

"I understand Latin, mama," Geralda cried.

"Yes, but you are more clever than most people. Catholics need their priests to tell them about Christianity, and so these priests are filled with arrogance. Perfects preach in our Languedoc language so that all the credentes can understand the word of Jesus Christ."

"Tell me more, mama."

Esclarmonda got to her feet and with a grunt, lifted the heavy grinding bowl. "That is quite enough for today. It is time to make the bread. What will you tell your father and brother if they return from the field and there is nothing to put in their bellies?"

Geralda sprang up and skipped toward the house. "I will tell them I was too busy learning about becoming a perfect."

CHAPTER FIFTEEN

It seemed as if fires were burning everywhere. The cardinals were missing. There was no pope. The prolonged *sede vacante* had left the Church adrift in uncharted territory, not seen for centuries. Schoolchildren were held hostage. As if these crises were not enough, there were other urgent Curia and Secretariat issues crowding Elisabetta's plate.

Perhaps it was her way of coping, but Elisabetta decided to throw virtually all her time and energy into the Nigerian emergency. She delegated administrative problems to deputies and Curia officials. Emilio and countless Italian and international personnel were dealing with the cardinals. There was nothing she could add to their efforts. But as she stared at pictures of the Bauchi girls on the school's website, she convinced herself that their safe return rested squarely on her shoulders.

The papal nuncio in Abuja was a Nigerian monsignor named Adeboyo Olubukola. The previous nuncio, a bishop, groomed the priest for career advancement and recommended Olubukola for a Vatican posting within the Section for Diplomatic Affairs. There, the young man caught Elisabetta's eye. When the old nuncio retired, Elisabetta sent Olubukola back to Nigeria as his replacement. She was fond of the affable and capable priest who had a knack for lifting spirits with his bright smile and expressive eyes.

Olubukola understood his boss's need for timely information and he had been updating Elisabetta frequently. She was gazing at a picture of Sophie, a schoolgirl with huge brown eyes, when her secretary announced an incoming call from the nuncio.

"Adeboyo," she said. "What news do you have?"

"I continue to press the government that it would be in everyone's best interest to negotiate with ISWAP. Unfortunately, their position is inflexible. They insist that they will not negotiate with terrorists. They say that doing so is politically untenable and would only encourage more outrages in the future. Of course, their position is not without merit."

Elisabetta controlled her breathing. She had learned that a man could explode volcanically and command respect, but if a woman did the same, she would be called an hysteric.

"The specter of future events is an abstraction," she said in a measured tone. "These girls are real, and they are in deep trouble. Their lives are more important than the government's political difficulties."

"Nevertheless, Madam Secretary, this is where we find ourselves."

"And this will be the situation when they kill the first girl. And the second. And the third."

"Your empathy and suffering are palpable, Madame Secretary. I have read the hurtful articles written by those within the Church who have criticized you for being more communicative with the media about the plight of the girls than about the cardinals. I wish I could give these people a piece of my mind or the back of my hand, especially those who say you secretly want to be the next pope." She heard the Nigerian sharply inhaling through his nostrils. "I'm sorry. I shouldn't have dignified what they write by uttering it out loud."

"I don't care what they write, Adeboyo. This isn't about me. I've been thinking—" She paused as if unsure about giving voice to her thoughts.

"What would you have me do?" the nuncio asked.

"What do you know about Mohammed Nur?"

"He is one of these men who took a path in life that was not foreseen. He comes from a good, Muslim family in Abuja. His father was a doctor who, poor man, had a heart attack when his son became a jihadi. Nur was a brilliant engineering student at university when he became radicalized. He became obsessed with jihad and direct action, dropped out of school, and declared his allegiance with Boko Haram. However, he became disillusioned with their scorched-earth tactics and fell in with ISWAP where he is, perhaps, their most important fighter in Nigeria. He is a very clever fellow, but I believe he will be as intractable as the government ministers."

"Is there a way to deal with him directly?" she asked.

"Without the involvement of the Nigerian government?"

"Yes, without the government," she said. "A direct backchannel with the Vatican."

"I don't have to tell you the dangers with this approach, Madame Secretary. Nur could exploit this to his advantage. The government would be furious. I would not be surprised if they expelled me from the country and shut down our embassy in protest. And at the end of the rainbow, you may not find a pot of gold, but instead, the bodies of dead girls."

"I understand your concerns, Adeboyo, but I want you to find a way. I want to talk with Mohammed Nur."

∽

Cardinal Macy took his plate of chicken and rice over to Cardinal Koffi's cot and asked if he could join him.

Koffi chose to respond in Italian. "La mia casa è la tua casa."

"That's funny," Macy said. "Your house is exactly like my house. How are you holding up, Raymond?"

"As I look around this room, better than some, worse than others. You seem strong and resilient, Victor. I've been watching you."

"I was an athlete as a young man," Macy said. "We were taught to have our game faces on in front of the opposition. I've got my game face on with our captors. Inside, I'm churning."

"If we ever get out of here, I'm going to vote for you," Koffi said.

"And I'll vote for you. We'll cancel each other out and leave the field open for Colpo."

Koffi laughed quietly. "Surely, the Holy Spirit would not let that happen."

"What do you think about tomorrow?" Macy asked. "Should we continue with this charade?"

"I see no harm in it," Koffi said. "It passes the time and sends a clear message to the kidnappers that we will not submit to their will."

"That's exactly how I look at it, too," Macy said. He forked a piece of chicken into his mouth. "This isn't half bad. Maybe they got a new chef."

∽

BOULI AND BEAR shared the primary bedroom in the castle, a splendid chamber with large windows overlooking endless meadows. By the light of a nearly full moon, the meadows glowed in ghostly monochrome. Bear was already under the covers when Bouli came from the bathroom, brushing her hair.

"Do you want to make a bet?" Bear asked.

"About what they'll do tomorrow?" Bouli said.

"Yeah."

"I think it will be a repeat of today. Four rounds of, I refuse."

"Then why are we bothering?"

Bouli slid in beside her and turned on her side to face her. "Because it will only be the second day of voting. They will continue to hold out. The third and fourth days will be the same. The last day will be the interesting one. That's when, God willing, they crack. Maybe not on the first three ballots. The last ballot of the last day will tell the story. They need to believe that they will die if they don't comply. We need to remind them every morning and every night.

They enjoy their existences. They live well. They eat well. They have power that most only dream of. They command respect from bishops and priests and countless Catholics. They're not fanatics. They don't want to be martyred."

Bear placed a hand on Bouli's waist. "My question to you is the same I've been asking for months. Are you prepared to kill them? To march them into the woods and rake them with automatic fire."

Bouli rolled onto her back. "My answer is always the same. Yes. No. Maybe."

"You know what I think," Bear said. "We should kill one or two to persuade the rest to vote for the nun. That way, we guarantee that we'll be able to spare the others."

"I don't want to kill any of them," Bouli said. "I still believe they will vote for Elisabetta Celestino on the last ballot of the last day. But whatever they do and whatever we do, our time will end."

"I know that," Bear said. "I accept it. Pierre too."

"We'll go together," Bouli said. "We'll be together forever."

Bouli's mobile phone rang, and she snatched it from the night table.

"Who is it?" Bear asked.

Bouli showed her the caller ID. "He keeps calling, and I keep ignoring him."

"It's for the best," Bear said. "He shouldn't get mixed up in this. He needs clean hands."

"Did he reply to your message?" Bear asked.

Bouli pulled Bear toward her. "Not yet, but he will."

∽

When Cal's phone chimed with a text notification, his first thought was that Eli was reaching out. The hotel room was the proverbial postage stamp, so he got it in two strides. His first reaction was disappointment because the text wasn't from her. His second was irritation. After glancing at the first line, he thought some troll had gotten his mobile number.

> To Prof. Donovan, the man they call the
> pope whisperer

He was about to hit delete when he read the rest of the message.

> Cardinal Archer sends his regards. He
> enjoyed dinner your last dinner at Mistral

> If you would like to see him and the others
> reply yes to this message and open an
> encrypted account on Telegram under your
> real name

∼

DESPITE THE LATE HOUR, General Tavassi rushed to the GIS war room to meet with Emilio and Cal. It was the first time Emilio had seen him without his uniform.

"What do we have?" he asked.

"They're working on the sender's number," Emilio said.

"Who can tell me about it?" Tavassi shouted to the crowded room.

A military analyst, glued to his screen, held up a hand and said, "The number is French with a Paris area code. We've been running our database of issued phone numbers and registered SIM cards. We didn't find it, but we thought our database might not be as complete as the French agencies. We asked the DGSE for help, but they couldn't find it either."

"And yet, this number was used. What's the explanation?" Tavassi asked.

The analyst said, "The kidnappers likely used an app like Burnrr. It generates temporary phone numbers that can be used for calls and texts without revealing the user's real number."

"Then contact the maker of this app to get information on who requested it," Tavassi said. "If we need a subpoena, get the lawyers involved."

"It's not as simple as that," the analyst said. "At least a dozen apps do the same thing as Burnrr. We would need to subpoena all of them. The process can take several days until a company complies. And then we might find that the app was installed on a prepaid phone. If we're lucky, we might find out where and when the phone was sold, but if it were a cash buyer, we would have to rely on surveillance videos inside the store for visual identification."

"My head is hurting," Tavassi said. "What's the solution?"

Cal had been half-listening and half-fiddling with his phone.

He looked up and said, "I just opened a Telegram account."

The room got quiet, and everyone stared at the professor.

"I don't think it's wise to engage with the terrorists," Tavassi said. "No. Let's find another way."

"Too late," Cal said. "I told them I'd come."

CHAPTER SIXTEEN

1208
Lavaur, Languedoc

It was a time of trouble and turbulence. There was violence in the air, so palpable that Geralda could almost see it, taste it, smell it.

Catharism was a young religion. Its elders hinted at ancient roots in the exotic lands of the east, but it had been entrenched in the Languedoc for less than a century. The mighty Church of Rome might have shrugged off this Christian sect and left them to their odd beliefs and practices if Catharism had not proved so popular. Sects came and went with the wind, but Catharism thrived because it resonated with peasants repulsed by the wealth and corruption of the Holy Roman Church. It especially struck a responsive chord among women who found the Cathar religion uncommonly welcoming. Much of the Catholic nobility of Languedoc protected their Cathar subjects and lent their support. To their minds, these were hard-working, non-bellicose folk who paid their taxes without undue complaint.

From his perch in Rome, Pope Innocent III watched with

mounting alarm as Catharism spread through southern France like a pestilence. What would prevent it from infecting all of France? All of Europe? His predecessor, Pope Eugene III, had sent envoys and small parties of soldiers to the Languedoc, tasked with curing the plague, but they had failed. Innocent, too, tried his hand at negotiation and peaceful conversion with the same lack of success. In the frigid winter of 1208, Innocent made one last peaceful effort, employing the formidable skills of Pierre de Castlenau, a Cistercian monk, theologian, and canon lawyer. Surely, Raymond VI, the Count of Toulouse, one of the Catholic noblemen who treated Cathars with benign tolerance, would be no match against Pierre's brilliant mind and acid tongue.

They parlayed at Raymond's gloomy castle. The strong-willed Frenchmen took an instant dislike to one another. Rather than negotiating their differences in the painstaking, courtly fashion of the day, they fought like Tom cats. Late in the day, before a roaring fire, Raymond asked how much Rome would pay to end his protection of the Cathars. The answer was not a single pound. Pierre's proposition was simple: help the Church stamp out this heresy or face excommunication. Raymond took great umbrage to a threat to his mortal soul and countered with a threat to Pierre's mortal life. In a rage, Pierre quit Toulouse for Rome to confer with the pope. He did not get far. A knight in Raymond's service rode him down and slayed the monk with a single axe blow to the neck.

The news of the monk's murder quickly reached Lavaur and the other towns and villages of Languedoc. No one understood the implications of the killing better than Geralda, a credentes woman of the highest intellect. She was twenty-three, tall and fair, with a bearing so regal, she might have passed for a noblewoman. There were many perfects in the village, but none had her facility with Latin, and no one else could recite from memory long passages from Bible and the other canonical Cathar texts, *The Gospel of the Secret Supper* and the *Book of the Two Principles*. She lived with her husband, Hugh, and her daughter, Fabrissa, in a large house on the square, and her neighbors stopped by her gate to converse with her as she fed dough into her bread oven.

"What will the pope do?" a man asked her.

"He will not let this pass," Geralda said.

"Bernard Belots told me the pope would threaten Count Raymond with seizure of his land holdings and force him to receive another envoy."

"Bernard is a wise perfect," Geralda said, "but he is wrong. Pierre Castlenau is the last envoy we shall see in our land."

"What then?"

"Innocent will send soldiers. I pray I am wrong, but I fear blood and fire will come our way. There is nothing to stop it."

A villager launched into a story about when she was a girl, and Pope Eugene sent soldiers to occupy Lavaur.

"They stayed for but a single season," the woman said. "Only one Cathar was killed. He was a demon-plagued youth who spit in a garrison commander's face. They were almost apologetic about hanging him."

"This time will be different," Geralda said. "There will make a crusade against us. More than demon-plagued youths will perish."

"Your words shoot fear into my loins," a man said. "When will your husband return? If you are right, you will be wanting his protection."

"Hugh is in Béziers. He will not return for at least a fortnight. I wish for his company, but I rely upon our Lord for protection."

On the day Geralda and Hugh first met, she was a girl of twelve; he was a man of seventeen. She had been wandering the hills above the village, the summer sun beating down on her kerchiefed head, when she heard a bleating from afar. She followed the plaintive sound and came upon a lamb wandering in tall grass.

"Where is your mother?" the girl asked. "Where is your father? Where are your brothers and sisters?"

There was a clap of thunder in the distance. Geralda pictured the poor lost lamb being lashed by rain in the darkness and took pity on the sweet thing. She had a belt of hemp that cinched her smock at her waist, and she looped it around the lamb's neck.

"Now, which farm did you stray from?" she asked. "The one

with a brook running through it, or the one on the road to Fiac? The one with a brook is closer. Let us pray it is that one."

The brook was a tributary of the mighty River Agout, where the net fishermen of Lavaur plied their trade. The muddy brook was muddy meandered lazily toward the sheep farm of family Clergue. Geralda followed it, leading the lamb by the rope. At first, the lamb resisted her tugs but soon, perhaps sensing it was heading home, it merrily trotted behind her. Beyond a stand of trees, she laid eyes on the lad who would become her husband. Hugh Clergue spotted her at the same instant. In the years to come, when they recounted the day to family and friends, they would tell the story from each one's remembrance.

Geralda would say: it was raining to the east. To the west, it was sunny, although it would not remain so for long. I saw Hugh running toward me, waving his arms. As he approached, I noticed his hair. It was long and fell in ringlets over his forehead and eyes. There was a dog in the village with hair that covered its eyes, and as with that dog, I wondered how this boy could see in front of him. The closer he got, the more fetching I found him. He was seventeen and had already reached his full height. His shoulders were broad, his eyes were dark, and his skin was baked brown by the sun. At the moment we met, a cloud passed before the sun, and a wall of rain reached us, drenching us to the skin. Hugh asked where I had found the lamb, and as I told him, he took off his shirt and gave it to me to drape over my head. I remember thinking, I am going to marry this boy. I am sure he was thinking the same.

Hugh would listen to her tale as he drank his wine, and when she was done, he would say: I had been looking for that lamb for hours. I knew my father would tan my hide if I lost the creature. The rain was coming, and I did not want to be out all afternoon if I could help it. I hoped the thirsty little lamb might stay close to the brook, and I followed the stream to the east. Before the rain arrived, I saw a small girl with yellow hair leading a lamb by a rope. I was relieved, of course, and grateful she was leading it to me. As Geralda said, the rain was suddenly upon us, and I did indeed remove my shirt. However, she is mistaken what I did with it. And he would roar with laughter and say, I draped it over that little lamb as I did not want it to be soaked to the bone! And I remember thinking, I hope this little girl does not intend to ask for a coin for her trouble.

Their courtship lasted three years. They might have been married in two, but the dowry negotiation between the families was protracted. Unlike their Catholic neighbors, the Cathars did not worship in churches and had no use for the priesthood and all its rituals. In the presence of their families, they had a ceremony of union before a notary, and on their wedding night, Geralda left her family home and moved to the sheep farm and into Hugh's small room.

Geralda always knew that Hugh had a good head on his shoulders and she encouraged him to aspire to greater things than shepherding the family flock. The sheep were not for eating. The Cathars did not eat meat, nor would they sell it to the Catholics. They were for shearing. The Clergues sold their wool to the villagers of Lavaur and a few hamlets within a day's horse-cart ride. Geralda saw how Hugh was able to keep accounts in his head. Hugh's father had always demanded payment in full on delivery. In 1202, the year of the great drought, crops failed, many weavers could not pay straight away. Hugh's father began to ail that year, and Hugh took charge of the selling. He would add a few pennies to a bill if the customer promised to pay in a month or a few more pennies if they needed longer. Hugh's father scolded his son for giving credit, but when he died, the farm passed to him, and he had license to be even more aggressive in his dealings. Before long, the wool trade became very profitable. Hugh was able to increase the size of his flock and broaden the geography to which he sold. The towns of Toulouse to the west and Narbonne and Béziers to the east had great appetites for wool. To serve them better, he began buying wool from other farmers and selling it to weavers as a middleman, accruing healthy profits. On the day after the Sabbath, he would leave Geralda and their young daughter, Fabrissa, his largest cart laden with bales of wool, and return a month later, tired but content, with an empty cart and a full purse.

Geralda, too had higher aspirations. Some days, when Hugh was away, she would finish her chores, bundle little Fabrissa in a basket, and drive the smallest horse cart from their farm to the village. There, she would meet with an aging perfect, Blanche Fayet, to read Cathar texts and do needlepoint while Fabrissa picked clover and chased squirrels. Their time together lasted an hour here, an hour there. When she had to leave, Fayet would place both hands on Geralda's head and tell her they both knew what she must do. She would say, "You are more clever than me and anyone I have ever met. The Cathar people need you."

Geralda would answer, "My husband needs me. What would I tell him?"

And Fayet would say, "Tell him you have the calling. Tell him that Jesus Christ cannot be denied the instruments he requires for his earthly work."

In the year 1204, Geralda found her courage and her voice. On the night Hugh returned from his month-long journey along the trade routes, he found his wife unusually quiet.

"What is the matter?" he asked as they lay in their cold bed under a mound of bedclothes.

"Do you love me?" she asked.

"Of course I do."

"I mean, truly love me."

He gave a tired sigh, meant to communicate how road-weary he was, and dutifully reached for her leg.

"Not that kind of love," she said.

"I love you this kind, that kind, and every-which-way kind," he said.

"If you truly love me, you will hear me out."

Hugh propped himself against the headboard and folded his arms. "I am listening."

She sat up and faced him. "I feel I have a calling. It is a calling beyond being a good Cathar wife and mother. When you are away, I often spend time with Blanche Fayet."

"What ideas is that old hag putting in your head?" he asked.

"She is not a hag. She is a perfect."

"A perfect hag," he said with a cackle.

"Stop saying that," she scolded. "She is a holy woman."

"Have you ever seen the way she looks at me?" Hugh complained. "I do not know what she has against me, but if looks could kill, I would be in the earth."

"Perhaps she knows what you say about her," Geralda said. "Now listen to me, husband. I have made my decision."

"Decision about what?"

She closed her eyes and said it. "I wish to become a perfect."

"Are you mad?" Hugh exclaimed. "You are but a young woman! You have a husband! This is the talk of a madwoman."

She knew he would be upset and determined to match his anger with equanimity. "Ever since I was a girl, I had the feeling from deep within my soul that I had reached the end of my cycle of incarnations. The Holy Spirit spoke to me. He told me I had reached the end. This will be my last spell on Earth, husband. My burden of reincarnation and worldly suffering will come to a close when I leave this body behind."

Hugh shifted away from her, leaving a gap between them.

"I am happy for you, wife. All good Cathars aim to receive the Consolamentum near the time of death and be free of the worldly cycle to dwell with Christ in Heaven for eternity. There is no need for you to take the Consolamentum in your youth. Wait, and take it near the time of death as most Cathars do. There is no need to become a perfect."

Geralda threw her covers off, grabbed her shawl from the floor, and sat on the wooden stool her husband used to pull up his boots.

"My calling is strong," she said. "I feel its tug every waking hour, even in my dreams. My calling is to help my fellow credentes in our journey through life and to be the one to imbue them with the Holy Spirit so that they, too, might return to God forever. We live in a time of danger. The Roman Church despises us. Their new pope loudly calls us heretics. Soon, he will be baying for our blood. We need the ranks of strong and faithful perfects to swell. To become a perfect—that is the ultimate good. Madame Fayet says that perfects are equal unto the angels because only a perfect can administer the Consolamentum. He or she who delivers the rite stands at the end of a chain of perfects who came before. Thus, they are a link to the apostles and Jesus Himself. How can I not wish to become one of the Elect? How can you not wish this for me?"

Hugh's only response was. "You are married."

"Marriage is no bar to becoming a perfect," she said. "You have heard of the famous perfecta Esclarmonde of Foix, have you not? She was a married woman."

"I am not learned like you," he said, "but I have a recollection she became a perfect late in her life after rearing eight children."

"That is so," Geralda said. "And her husband gave his consent, as I wish you will do. Perfects who have been married may remain married after the Consolamentum."

Hugh's fuse was lit, and he exploded like a cannon. "You refuse to say out loud what is most important to husband and wife. Perfects are not allowed to engage in sexual congress."

She hung her head and said, "That is so. I shall miss lying with you, and you shall miss lying with me. Madame Fayet says it will take three years of study to become a perfect. That is three years during which we might continue to enjoy the fruits of marriage and, God willing, have more children. In these uncertain times, three years is an eternity."

In time, Hugh consented, and Geralda threw herself into intensive study. Geralda knew the Bible and Cathar texts by rote, but through study and disputation with Madame Fayet, she began to understand the meaning of the sacred writings. Hugh's wool trade continued to prosper, and he came to believe that a successful merchant ought to live in a house in the village. He paid thirty pounds in silver to purchase a fine timber dwelling with a thatched roof on the village square. Geralda could not have been happier. It was just across the green from Madame Fayet's. Hugh's younger brother, Roger, was of an age where he could manage the day-to-day affairs of the sheep farm, and he was delighted to move into the main farmhouse on the property with his wife.

In 1207, Madame Fayet declared that Geralda was ready. The

night before her induction ceremony, she lay in bed with Hugh and wept.

"Are these tears of joy or sadness?" he asked.

"Both."

Try as they might, she had not conceived another child. No one complained more about her barrenness than Fabrissa. The eight-year-old desperately wanted a brother or sister, but it was not to be. As the little girl slept in the room next door, Geralda lifted her shift and climbed atop her husband.

"One last time?" he asked.

"One last time," she replied.

In the morning, villagers assembled in Geralda and Hugh's front garden, careful not to trample rows of vegetables. Geralda stood before Madame Fayet and three other village perfects, wearing her plain brown shift for the last time. Henceforth, she would wear the black dress of a perfect, and when she went out, she would don a dark-green tunic over it with a dark-blue hooded coat. Hugh stood behind his wife, holding Fabrissa's hand.

Geralda sucked in air as the ritual began with the bestowing of the

Melhoramentum, the formal acknowledgment to the gathering that Geralda had the Holy Spirit within her. Geralda knelt on the fertile ground she had sown by hand, bowed three times, and said, "Bless me, Lord. Pray for me and lead me to my rightful end."

Fayet answered her, "God bless you. In our prayers, we ask God to make a good Christian out of you and lead you to your rightful end." Then she held the Bible over Geralda's head and recited the Benedicite. When she was done, the old woman recited the Pater Noster, the Lord's Prayer, and Geralda called it back.

Geralda's knees dug into the soft earth as she solemnly renounced the rituals of the Roman Catholic Church that so persecuted the Cathars. She renounced their replicas of the cross, their sham baptisms, their Eucharist, and other magical rites.

Fayet and the other perfects then administered the only true baptism, the spiritual baptism, by laying on hands and touching the Gospel to Geralda's head. They reminded her of all that was forbidden—Hugh winced at the mention of celibacy—and all that was required of her. She must love her enemies, pray for those who malign and accuse, offer the other cheek to the smiter, and give the clothes upon her back to those who are naked. To each requirement, Geralda answered, "I have this will and determination. Pray God for me to give me his strength."

Fayet then adored the Father and Son and Holy Spirit three times and said a prayer asking God to welcome his servant, Geralda, and send down the Holy Spirit.

The last rite was the most sacred and solemn. Geralda recited the Pater Noster and the first seventeen verses of John the Gospel.

In the beginning was the Word, and the Word was with God, and the Word was God…

And when she was done, she was a perfect.

Geralda stood in the same garden a year later, speaking with her neighbors about the gathering storm. She was about to bid them a good day and take her freshly baked loaves inside for Fabrissa's supper, when the village carpenter stopped at her gate and climbed from his cart.

"Madame Perfect," he said. "Troubling times, are they not?"

"They are indeed," Geralda said.

"I have been in Toulouse, peddling my wares," he said. "A fellow Cathar gave me something and bade me spread the word about it."

"Pray tell; what is it?" Geralda asked.

He reached into his pocket and showed her a piece of cloth the size of two lengths of his palm. It was a yellow cross.

"The Catholic bishop is forcing our brethren in the city to wear these sewn to their garments, so they might be identified as Cathars."

"Oh, they mock us," Geralda said bitterly. "We despise their foul crosses. Yet, would that this sacrilege be the worst abomination coming our way. I fear for our children. I fear for our people. I fear for our faith."

CHAPTER SEVENTEEN

Mohammed Nur's temporary camp was in a densely wooded area of the Lame Burra Game Reserve, about one hundred kilometers north of Bauchi. He arrived with his convoy of vehicles before anyone knew the schoolgirls were missing. A wanted man of the highest order, he was a master of elusion who employed bribes and threats in equal measure to secure the silence of nearby villagers. As he set up camp, he realized he had not fully appreciated the challenges involved in taking care of this many hostages. There were tarps to hang from branches, latrine pits to dig, and rice and beans to cook on an institutional scale over fire pits. The sound of weeping drove him to distraction, prompting him to set up his tent at the camp's periphery. He was unconcerned about escape attempts. The girls were frightened by the isolation and soundscape of the forest and ill-prepared to deal with the elements. He was more worried about the young men under his command. They were religious boys, but he saw them leering at the cowering, nubile young girls.

Elisabetta's nuncio in Abuja, Monsignor Adeboyo Olubukola, had to employ detective rather than diplomatic skills to find someone who knew how to contact the rebel leader. An imam in Abuja knew an imam in Gombe who knew an imam in Bauchi, et cetera, until a courier was found who was known to hand-carry messages to a man who avoided using telephones, the Internet, and radios. That courier was persuaded to purchase a prepaid phone from a shop in Jimi, the closest town to Nur's camp, and deliver it to the hideaway with a personal message from the nuncio.

Nur read the hand-written message several times and discussed it with his second-in-command, Ibn Bako, an older jihadist who was missing an eye and two fingers from a bombing gone wrong in Chad.

"This is said to come from the Vatican, not the Nigerian government," Nur said.

"That surprises me," Bako said.

"Most unexpected," Nur said. "I wonder if the government even knows they have taken this action."

"What do you wish to do?"

Nur grimaced at the sound of a girl shrieking in alarm. He was about to investigate when the shrieking abruptly stopped. "She probably saw a spider," he said. "I believe I will make the call. We can get a better deal with the Christians. When have we ever been successful with the government?"

"We have successfully killed many of their soldiers," Bako said.

"You are correct, my friend, but I am after something different."

"Are you certain the phone is safe?"

"The courier is trustworthy," Nur said. "The phone and SIM card are in unopened packages. I think it is safe." He took a blade to the plastic, inserted the SIM card, and laughed. "They gave us two hours of talk time. They are tipping their hand. They expect a real negotiation."

Nuncio Olubukola refused to let his new phone out of his sight. He took it to bed with him. He took it to the bathroom. And he had it on his desk at the embassy when it went off, startling him into hanging up another call without warning. His message to Nur was in Hausa, and that was the language he used when he answered.

"Hello, this is Monsignor Olubukola." During the long few seconds before the caller spoke, the nuncio thought he heard birdsong.

"This is Mohammed Nur."

"I was hoping you would call."

"How old are you? You sound like a young man," Nur said.

"How old am I? What does that matter?"

"I hope you have not gone to all this trouble of arranging this call to have me negotiate with a boy."

"I believe I am the same age as you, but you misunderstand the situation," Olubukola said. "You are not going to negotiate with me. You are going to speak with the Vatican Secretary of State."

"Are you joking?" the rebel said. "You expect me to negotiate with a woman?"

"She is a woman who happens to be the highest-ranking official at the Vatican. Would you prefer to talk with someone of lesser authority?"

Nur had been chewing betel nuts, and he spat out a wad. "So, how is this supposed to work?"

"If you stay on the line, I will conference you with the Secretary. I hope I don't lose you. I've been studying the manual."

Nur chewed nervously and kept littering the undergrowth with brown saliva.

"Are you still there?" Olubukola asked.

"I am here."

"Good. You are on the line with the Vatican." The nuncio switched to English. "We understand your English is quite good. The Secretary is also fluent. Madame Secretary? Are you there?"

"Yes, hello," Elisabetta said evenly. "This is Elisabetta Celestino. Thank you for calling, Mr. Nur."

"I didn't expect direct talks with the Vatican," he said. "And I didn't expect to hold talks with a woman. In my culture, women do not hold such positions of power."

"Then your culture has some similarities with my culture," she said. "Many male clergymen had to get used to dealing with me. I must ask you, Mr. Nur, how are the girls?"

"I would say they are physically well. However, some of them are emotional about their circumstances."

"As they should be," she said. "I was told you slaughtered their teachers before their eyes."

"Who told you this?"

"One of the nuns who was hacked with a machete survived her injuries and gave a statement to the police."

Elisabetta heard what sounded like a spit.

"We did what needed to be done," he said.

"Taking innocent lives is something that must never be done," she said. "I believe that is a tenet of your faith as it is of mine."

"I see. This is how it is going to go," Nur said. "In school, I was studying to be an engineer. I am not an expert in the history of Roman Catholicism, but I am learned enough to know that in the name of your God, your Church has killed countless men, women, and children of many religions in many parts of the world."

"I believe we must learn from the past," she said evenly, "but we must not live in the past. We strive to live in a just world where violence is neither condoned nor tolerated."

"I am afraid that violence is my most potent currency. Without it, I cannot move the needle. Without it, the downtrodden of my faith will always be slaves to the depravity of the unclean and unfaithful."

Elisabetta sat forward and pushed the phone hard against her ear. "Tell me what you want," she said.

"Did you not see my video statement?"

"I saw it. Let me ask another way. What do you hope to achieve?"

"Precisely what I said in the video. I want the Catholic Church to withdraw from all of your education and missionary activities in West Africa. I want you to pull the plug and let the foul water drain from the tub."

"You must understand that the Catholic Church is not as monolithic and centralized as you might imagine," she said. "With few exceptions, the Vatican does not directly control or fund the educational and missionary programs you speak of. The local diocese within Nigeria and other West African countries are responsible for many of these activities. Many others are funded and staffed by international aid groups and charities. The Vatican cannot pull the plug, as you put it. There are dozens of aid organizations that make independent decisions on these matters."

She heard the same sound again and was certain her adversary was spitting in disgust or expelling something he was chewing.

"I expected to hear the bureaucracy argument. But it is nonsense. Your Vatican is decapitated. There is no pope. Your high men of the Church are held by some perverts who want you—*you*—to be pope! Maybe you want this too—I don't know. But here is the truth. You are the top person in the Vatican. At the moment, the decision is yours. With one statement, you can make all these so-called independent organizations leave West Africa."

"I assure you, it doesn't work like that."

"Then, let me tell you how things *will* work," he said. "The Nigerian government has no idea where we are, and even if they did, their soldiers do not like stepping into our territory. Thousands of school children are kidnapped every year in Nigeria, some by righteous fighters like us or Boko Haram, some by criminal gangs. When the ransom is paid, the children go home. When people don't want to pay, the children don't go home. If we are involved, we acquire a new generation of converts to the true faith. The boys make good soldiers. The girls make good wives. You should see the way my young men look at the girls. Believe me. They don't want them to leave."

Elisabetta felt rage twisting her guts. It took every bit of strength to keep her façade of dignity from crumbling.

"Mr. Nur, we both understand that this phone call is the beginning of a negotiation. In a successful negotiation, neither side gets exactly what they want, but both sides get enough to declare some measure of victory. We must try to find a way to get our girls safely back. You must find a way to tell your supporters you have achieved a good outcome. Can we strive to achieve that, Mr. Nur?"

He spat again and kicked a clod of dirt with his boot. "This can only work if the Nigerian government is not involved. It is not politically feasible for them to make any concessions to us. Do you truly intend to deal with us directly?"

"That is my intention. This will be between you and me."

He let out a sharp laugh. "It is not so easy for me to negotiate with a woman."

"I can assure you," she said without a trace of warmth, "it is not easy for me to negotiate with you either."

⁓

Since the day the cardinals were abducted, Elisabetta had not been permitted to take her usual solitary walks through the Vatican gardens. Commander Studer insisted on a protective squad of armed, plain-clothes Swiss Guards wherever she went. Three men walked ten meters ahead, three, ten meters behind, allowing her only a bubble of solitude. She had hoped that the warm Spring air, bright sunshine, and smell of freshly cut grass would be a balm for her soul, but when she returned to her office, she was still angry.

"Cardinal Donahue called again while you were out," her secretary said.

"How many times has he called?" she asked.

The priest used his fingers to help him remember. "Twice today, twice yesterday. What would you like me to do?"

She crumpled onto a side chair and poured herself a glass of water. "Today could hardly get worse. Get him for me, please."

Soon, Donahue's voice, laden with false bonhomie, came through her earpiece. "Madame Secretary, it is good to speak with you. I know how busy you must be dealing with the crisis. I was calling to get your decision on the matter which we discussed. My fellow cardinals and I are anxious to start assisting you with the weighty matters at hand."

She was grateful this wasn't a video call. "I'm sorry I didn't get back to you sooner. I have been busy with the schoolgirls."

"The schoolgirls? Oh, yes, I'd forgotten about them. I was referring to the cardinals."

"I have no involvement in the search for the cardinals, Eminence. That is for the police and security services. However, I am heavily involved with the schoolgirls."

"Should the Vatican be part of that?" he said. "Surely, this is a domestic matter for the Nigerian government. The Vatican can't be seen to be negotiating with terrorists."

"The Vatican has negotiated with terrorists before," she said briskly. "Every pope in recent memory has quietly paid ransoms for the return of kidnapped nuns and priests."

"Well, I didn't know that," he huffed. "I think that is a dangerous policy. A slippery slope."

"Yes, dealing with desperate human beings can often be slippery," she said. "I have made my decision, Eminence. I think forming a new advisory council now gives the wrong impression. The Curia is operating normally, and we have every expectation the cardinals will be returned soon."

The venom from his mouth dripped into her ear. "They'll be returned if they make the gutless decision to ordain you and elect you pope. What will you do then? Wear the ring? Sit on the throne of St. Peter? For God's sake, woman, stop this madness and publicly declare that you will never be a party to the demands of these Islamist kidnappers. Then step aside and let my council of elders lead the Vatican during the *sede vacante*."

"The security experts have advised me not to comment on the demands," she said. "If I were to do as you suggest, the kidnappers might feel their hand has been forced. They might resort to violence."

"I do not agree with that piece of advice. Perhaps they're telling you what you want to hear. Let's not prolong this further. I'm extending the courtesy of letting you know we will send a press release tomorrow. We will announce that a council of elders has been formed to make decisions on the governance of the Vatican during the *sede vacante*. Good day to you."

∼

CAL AND EMILIO were having lunch at a café near the GIS headquarters when Cal's phone awoke with an unfamiliar chime. Both men stared at it briefly before Cal picked it off the table.

"That's what a Telegram message sounds like," he said, opening it.

"What does it say?" Emilio asked, putting knife and fork down.

"They want me to come to Montpellier tonight, book into the hotel, Baudon de Mauny, and wait for further instructions. They said to come alone with no police, or they'd execute the cardinals."

"Now we know for sure they're in France," Emilio said.

"I've got to figure out how to get there," Cal said.

"Tavassi's on the record," Emilio said. He doesn't want you to go."

"I'm a private citizen. What's he going to do? Lock me up?"

"He knows you'll do what you want, but please understand where he's coming from. If this goes wrong—if you're taken hostage or worse, if the cardinals are killed on the heels of your mission—then it will fall on him."

"I guess that means I'm not getting a sweet ride on a GIS helicopter," Cal said. How about the Vatican one?"

Emilio grimaced. "I can't be seen to endorse this either—at least not officially."

"I understand. No worries. I'm happy to do this on my own. Just promise you're not going to follow me. That seems like a good way to put the hostages and me at risk."

"I'll be making that point quite strenuously," Emilio said.

"Well, I'd better find a travel agent," Cal said. "Do they even still exist?"

"You don't need one. You'll never get there in time by air. There are no direct flights from Pisa. The train will take forever. You've got to drive. You'll make it in seven, maybe eight hours with a heavy foot."

Cal got up and said, "Point me toward a car-rental place. Lunch was on you."

∽

THE MOTION DETECTOR on the castle's front-gate camera set off an alert on Bouli's mobile phone when she and Bear were in their bedroom, waiting for their evening meal. They had been having a repeat of the conversation they'd had a day earlier. The second day of the conclave was over. The cardinals had once again voted unanimously on four ballots.

I refuse

Bear wanted to make an example of one of them. Bouli preached patience.

Bouli looked at her phone and began to tremble.

"What?" Bear said.

Bouli showed her the image from the gate camera.

"Oh, fuck," Bear said. "Coincidence?"

"Not on your life."

"What should we do?" Bear asked

"What can we do?" Bouli said. "Tell the men not to shoot. Hurry."

A Mercedes sedan drove slowly down the gravel drive. The two women were waiting outside when it came to a halt at the front door. An elegantly-dressed man got out, sadly shaking his head.

"I knew it was you, and I knew you would be here," Charles Morlet said.

"Come in," Charles, Sabine said. "Bear, please join us."

"As you wish, Bouli."

Charles's demeanor flipped from sadness to rage. "You're no longer children," he said, "and still, you and Gaby call each other by these juvenile names."

"You're angry," Sabine said.

"I am beyond angry."

"I need to know if you came alone."

"I'm alone."

They went into the lounge off the kitchen, where, many years ago, the siblings laid on the rug and played board games after supper. Outside the windows, armed men crunched the gravel on patrol.

"Do you want something to drink?" Sabine said.

"Who are they?" Charles asked.

"Men I know," Sabine said.

"And Pierre? Is he here?"

"He's here."

"Jesus," he said, his thin chest deflating. "Get me a drink. Anything."

Sabine raised her chin, and Gaby went off.

"When did you know?" Sabine asked.

"When I saw your tattoo on the video."

"Why the delayed reaction?"

"Because I'm a coward. I couldn't face the truth."

"You could have said something yesterday to the Italian policeman. I thought you might."

"I could have, but I didn't."

"Here you are. You're facing the truth now."

He focused his watery eyes on the family photos in the bookcase.

"You brought them here. To our house."

"It's my house," she said. "Mother left it to me. You got the apartments in Paris and Monaco."

"It perverts their memories." His voice rose and transformed to a wail. "What have you done? It's more than ruining your own life. You used our ship. You destroyed our company. You destroyed me."

"This has nothing to do with you. Your hands are clean. You'll have the best lawyers."

"I'm sorry, you're wrong," he shouted loud enough that Gaby came running back with his drink. "It's the end of Morlet Shipping. It's the end of me and my family. My children. How could you do this to them?"

"It's okay, Bear," Sabine said. "He's allowed to be upset."

He took the drink and said, "Go fuck off, Gaby. I don't want you here when I'm talking to my sister."

Sabine gently asked Gaby to check on things, and she left them.

"Where are they?" he asked.

"In the church," she said. "They're unhurt. We're treating them well. They have a doctor who was inside the conclave."

"The church," he said morosely. "The three of us played football there on rainy days. Michel was unstoppable. Do you remember?"

At the mention of their older brother, Sabine's blue eyes clouded with tears.

"You have to tell me why you're doing this," he demanded. "Is this about Michel?"

"If course," she said, "but it's about more than him."

"Oh yes," he said, getting up to pace the room, drink in hand. "I know all your reasons. You're fixated on the past—Michel, a centuries-old vendetta, this make-belief religion of yours."

"You studied the Cathars in school," she said. "It's very real. You know how committed I've been."

"It's make-believe because it's been dead for seven-hundred years!"

"It's been kept alive in the hearts of the people of the Languedoc," she said.

"For God's sake, Sabine. Stop! Stop this insanity. I can't believe you used your fortune to bankroll this foul plot. You might despise the Church, but you've spit in the faces of a billion Catholics."

"A religion that treats half of them like garbage."

"Dear sister," he said, "I've always been fine having discussions, even arguments about your radicalism, but what you have done is monumentally wicked and stupid. How will this advance women?"

"Since its inception, one of the world's largest religions, has denied women. I'm forcing them to right two millennia of wrongs."

"And you think that under duress, in captivity, the cardinals will vote as you like? For a sophisticated person, your head is either in the clouds or up your ass."

"The cardinals hold their fate in their hands. They will make the correct decision."

"If they do as you hope, what will prevent them from reversing the vote once released?"

"People will see them as spineless liars and hypocrites. It will be the end of their credibility. The institution will crumble."

"And if they defy you? Will you kill these men?"

"I am a woman of my word."

He stopped moving and pointed a finger. "Then you will spend the rest of your life in prison, or you will die."

"Bear—Gaby and I don't expect to survive, but we are at peace. Pierre feels the same way. The end will have justified the means. We will have injected the Cathar ideals of the equality of women into the bloodstream of the Catholic Church. And we are optimistic that once people understand why we did this, and what Cathars believe in, that Christians of all denominations will consider conversion. Who knows? Maybe Catharism will be resurrected. If the Catholic Church had not wiped it out, it would have spread to all of France and Europe. It would have become the dominant form of Christianity. We hope it will have a fresh life."

Charles finished his drink in one gulp and said, "You've gone from zealous to irrational. My sister—my partner—my boss—has become a crazy woman who should be locked up for her own good and the good of others. I'm leaving. I'm going to the authorities. I love you, Sabine, but for the sake of the cardinals, I have to stop you."

His grip tightened around the crystal glass, and he cocked his arm. He glowered at her, threatening to throw it at her face, but instead sent it crashing into the fireplace.

She called after him. "Charles! Stop."

Gaby had been listening from the kitchen, and she followed him outside. He was standing by his car, punching a number into his mobile.

"Who are you calling?" Gaby shouted.

"Who do you think?" he said, reaching for the door handle.

"I won't let you," she said, firing a single shot into his back. He fell to the gravel, groaning, trying to crawl to the door.

She stood over him, and fired again into the back of his head.

Sabine flew through the front door and screamed, "No! What have you done?"

Gaby looked down at her handiwork and said, "I did what had to be done."

It was close to midnight, and Elisabetta was still at her office. Her secretary had stayed in solidarity, and he kept checking on her, trying to get her to eat something.

"Thank you, but I'm not hungry," she said.

"I'll stay," he said. "You go to bed. I'll wake you immediately if there's a call."

"I'm not leaving," she said.

The tall windows of her office suite weren't bulletproof, so the Swiss Guards insisted that her curtains remain closed at all times. Still, she parted the brocaded cloth to take in the lit dome of St. Peter's Basilica. She was looking at the loggia where new popes are introduced to the world when her secretary ran in, waving his phone.

"It's Monsignor Olubukola! He has Mohammed Nur on the line."

CHAPTER EIGHTEEN

Several cardinals were eager to lead morning Mass. Rather than haggle, the congregation agreed to have the camerlengo, Cardinal Sauseda, decide on the honor. Over breakfast of a roll and a cup of fruit yogurt, the Spaniard surveyed the rows of cots, then approached Cardinal Quang. The Vietnamese cleric eagerly accepted and set about choosing an assistant celebrant.

As the men changed from tracksuits to robes, they talked about the coming day of balloting.

Cardinal Mertens had kicked a shoe under his bed the night before and asked the more flexible Cardinal Palmer to help him retrieve it.

"There you go, Louis," the American said.

Mertens thanked Palmer and said, "What do you say? Do you think those were gunshots we heard last night?"

"I don't know, Louis. People assume that Americans know everything about guns. The only gunshots I've ever heard were on TV."

"Fair enough," the Belgian said. "Here's a better question. Are you in favor of spending a third day casting ballots again? I say it's a ridiculous sham. A waste of time."

Palmer turned his palms upwards. "If we had access to a library, cards, or chess boards, I'd tell our captors we would rather spend our time in recreation. Far more stimulating than marking one-hundred-sixteen ballots, *I Refuse*, four times a day. In the absence of diverting pastimes, I see no harm. It has the effect of paying lip service to their demands. I'm sure they're frustrated with us, but I doubt they will shoot us as long as we're somewhat compliant. The more time we string them along, the more time the authorities have to find us."

The Belgian nodded. "All good points, Mark. I applaud your pragmatism."

"When this is over, come visit me in San Diego. I'll take you for the best Mexican food you've ever had. If you don't like the spicy stuff, then the best cheeseburger."

"And you must come to Brussels. I'll treat you to the best mussels you've ever had."

"Moules et frite," Palmer said. "You're making my mouth water."

The two old men clapped each other on the shoulders and shook on it.

Dr. Bellisario was making his morning rounds, taking notes on the back of old ballot papers.

"How did you sleep, Eminence?"

"Your bowels. How are they functioning, Eminence?"

"You must take more exercise, Eminence. You might join Cardinal Archer on his walking circuit."

He stooped over Cardinal Sauseda's cot to inspect his vial of insulin.

"How many days do you think it will last?" Sauseda asked.

"Two at most," the doctor said.

"What have they said about getting more?" the cardinal asked.

"I have received repeated assurances we would receive another vial. I will keep pressing. It is a matter of life and death."

The Spaniard tutted and said, "You have a wonderful way with words, Doctor. I have to say. I would rather die from a bullet than diabetic ketoacidosis. I had the condition once. It was terribly unpleasant. Ah, help me up, would you? I see we are about to celebrate Mass."

~

Elisabetta searched the Internet for a photo of Kayode Nwogu to have a mental image of the man during a difficult phone call. Adeboyo Olubukola had arranged the call. The nuncio arrived early for the appointment and waited in a reception room of the Aso Rock Presidential Villa, where the vice president maintained an office. It was not particularly warm, but he was drenched in sweat. An aide who came to escort him to the meeting saw him blotting beads from his forehead and asked if he was well.

"Quite well, thank you," the priest said.

Elisabetta's secretary received confirmation that the nuncio was present in the vice presidential office and put the call through.

"Mr. Vice President," she began. "Thank you for accepting this meeting at such short notice."

"It is not a problem, Madame Secretary," Nwogu said. "However, if you were hoping for a meaningful update on the girls, I'm afraid I have nothing substantive for you."

"Actually, we wanted to update you on developments on our end," she said.

She heard a frostiness overtake the official. "Oh, yes? Whatever do you mean?"

She set her jaw, and said, "A short while ago, I was informed that the schoolgirls have been returned to their school's campus in Bauchi. They were driven there, not by the men who kidnapped them, but by lorry drivers pressed into service by the kidnappers. The girls are physically unharmed. They are being cared for by local aid workers until their parents are notified to come for them."

The vice president erupted in a volley of vitriol. "How is this possible? How did this happen without my knowledge? How do you know this, and I do not?"

"Monsignor Olubukola would like to share a press release with you," she said. "Go ahead, Monsignor."

The nuncio took a sheet from his portfolio and passed it over the vice president's desk. Elisabetta re-read her copy during the ensuing silence.

~

The Vatican is pleased to announce that it has secured the release of approximately two hundred children kidnapped from the Pope Celestine School for Girls in Bauchi, Nigeria. All the girls are unharmed. They are in the process of being reunited with their families. To secure their release, the Vatican agreed to a single demand of the kidnappers from the group known as Islamic State in West Africa Province. The Pope Celestine School for Girls in Bauchi will be closed permanently. The Vatican will make no further statements out of respect for the girls and their families

~

ELISABETTA HEARD heavy breathing over the line.

"My God! What have you done?" Nwogu cried. "You've gone behind our backs and negotiated with terrorists!"

"We did what we thought needed to be done to save the girls," Elisabetta said.

"By capitulating to these animals?"

"It was not capitulation," she said. "Their initial demands were for the wholesale removal of the Catholic Church from the fabric of Nigerian life. We pared down these demands to a single concession. Frankly, it would have been difficult to continue operating this school after the atrocities there."

"And a ransom? Did you also pay a ransom?"

Elisabetta asked the nuncio to respond.

"We did, Mr. Vice President. Time was of the essence. We asked a wealthy local businessman, a friend of the Church, to loan us the cash during the night. A courier delivered it to ISWAP, and the girls were released this morning. The Vatican will repay this gentleman."

"My God! How much did you pay?"

Hearing a pause, Elisabetta told the nuncio he could divulge the amount.

"Five million American dollars," Olubukola said.

"You know what you've done, don't you?" the vice president bellowed. "You've undermined this government's policy never to negotiate with terrorists or pay ransoms. Now, every group, from ISWAP to Boko Haram to criminal gangs, will feel emboldened to act against our citizens. It is open season against the rule of law."

"With respect," Elisabetta said, "in the past, the Nigerian government has quietly done what we have done. A few years ago, it was reported that you paid a large ransom to Boko Haram for the freedom of the schoolgirls from Dapchi in the Yobe State."

"That was a previous administration, not ours."

"Negotiating with this group was a bitter pill to swallow," Elisabetta said. "They butchered our teachers. They subjected the girls to a terrifying experience that will stay with them all their days. However, had we not acted swiftly, I was convinced we would begin losing girls to violence and disease. I was convinced that the kidnappers would have forced them to convert to Islam and subjected them to rape under the guise of marriage. And let me tell you about another bitter pill. I have learned that the school repeatedly asked the government and the army for enhanced protection against just such an event. Their pleas were met with silence."

She heard the sound of chair legs dragging on a hard floor and imagined the vice president was on his feet.

"Mark my words. My government will take strong actions against the Vatican," he seethed. "We will expel your nuncio immediately. We will recall our ambassador to the Vatican. We will condemn you for encouraging terrorist acts in our country."

Elisabetta had been up all night working on the details with Olubukola. They had choreographed the next moment.

"Or," she said, "we could send out this press release."

The nuncio handed over another version.

The Government of Nigeria is pleased to announce that it has secured the release of approximately two hundred children kidnapped from the Pope Celestine School for Girls in Bauchi, Nigeria. All the girls taken are unharmed. They are in the process of being reunited with their families. To secure their release, the Vatican agreed to a single demand of the kidnappers from the group known as Islamic State in West Africa Province. The Pope Celestine School for Girls in Bauchi will be closed permanently.

The Vice President of Nigeria, the honorable Kayode Nwogu, stated, "Our first priority has always been the security of the people of Nigeria. The kidnapping of these vulnerable schoolgirls and the murder of their teachers were intolerable acts of violence. We worked tirelessly to secure the timely and safe return of the girls in conjunction with the Vatican. The government has made no concessions to the ISWAP group and paid no ransom."

The Vatican Secretary of State, Elisabetta Celestino, stated, "We are grateful for the swift and decisive action of the Nigerian government. Without their leadership, these innocent schoolgirls might have been lost forever."

The Nigerian government and the Vatican will make no further statements out of respect for the girls and their families.

∽

THREE HOURS LATER, Elisabetta stood before a bank of microphones in the Clementine Hall in the Apostolic Palace, flanked by the Nigerian ambassadors to Italy and the Vatican. The hall was crowded with journalists who had rushed there as soon as the joint press release simultaneously dropped from Vatican City and Abuja.

Elisabetta's remarks mirrored the text of the press release. When Silvio Licheri stood to open the floor to questions, dozens of hands went up.

An Italian newspaper journalist said, "Your press release says the Nigerian government didn't pay a ransom. What about the Vatican?"

Elisabetta was prepared. "You will know that the Vatican has a longstanding policy to avoid comment on such matters," she said.

"We will continue to enforce this policy. You should not read anything whatsoever into the absence of a statement."

"But Nigeria was happy to make a denial," another journalist said.

The Nigerian ambassador to Italy leaned into his microphone. "My government has no such policy of avoiding comment. We are comfortable in our denial."

The same journalist said, "But in the past, your government asserted that ransoms were not paid when facts ultimately proved otherwise."

"Show me the proof," the ambassador said, pointing a thick finger. "Our political enemies have lied in the past about ransom payments. You must not believe everything you read in the papers, perhaps even your paper."

A reporter from the UK asked, "Would your government permit the Vatican or any other foreign state to pay ransoms to terrorists operating on Nigerian soil?"

The Nigerian ambassador to the Vatican, perhaps sensing his colleague was about to become intemperate, fielded that one. "We would certainly frown on it, even actively discourage it. However, there may be little we can do in certain circumstances."

"Was this one of these circumstances?"

"I refer you to the comment the secretary of state just made," he said.

An Italian television reporter, a well-known gadfly, said, "Madame Secretary, putting aside the matter of payments, you have made an important concession to these jihadis. You agreed to close this school permanently, a school bearing the name of the pope who made you the president of the Pontifical Commission for Sacred Archaeology and his private secretary. Don't you see your decision as a sign of weakness during this dangerous period where there is a void of leadership at the Vatican? And don't you see this as a slap in the face to the memory of Pope Celestine?"

Elisabetta caught a worried-looking Silvio Licheri from the corner of her eye. She knew what her press officer was thinking: stay calm, Madam Secretary; don't give this ass the satisfaction of losing your temper.

"These girls are between the ages of ten and eighteen," she said. "Their lives are just starting. If you believe it is weak to prevent them from being raped, if you think it is weak to prevent them from being killed, if you think it is weak to make sure they see their families again, then you are not a father or a brother or an uncle to young girls. And I wonder if you knew Pope Celestine as I knew him? He was kind and compassionate, and he would have done everything in his power to save these girls. He was a modest man who cared little about affixing his name to a building. Now, thank you. This is a busy time, and I must return to work."

∽

CARDINAL DONAHUE hastily arranged a call with the elderly cardinals on his *sede vacante* council.

"I trust everyone saw her news conference," he said.

An Italian, who in his day had been a force to be reckoned with inside the Curia, said, "It was disgusting. That fellow nailed it with his question about being weak. She gave the world a glimpse of what a woman pope would be like."

"Of course, she paid a ransom," Donahue said. "She practically admitted it to me."

A German cardinal said, "Perhaps you should contact the press, off the record, and let that be known."

"Maybe I should," Donahue said. "I wanted to get everyone together for final approval to release our press statement. I believe the Church needs our council of elders to act immediately before this woman does even more damage."

One by one, they gave their assent.

"Gentlemen, I suggest we go to the Vatican tomorrow with a select group of journalists in tow to demand that Elisabetta Celestino step aside and let us save this sinking ship of state."

∽

CAL WAS STILL WAITING.

The night before, he drove the coastal highway from Italy to France. For much of the route, a driving rain forced cars to pull over and wait out the worst of the storm. He sped on, squinting into the darkness, the wiper blades beating an urgent cadence. The hotel, Baudon de Mauny, was a listed eighteenth-century building in Montpellier's historic quarter. When he checked in at ten o'clock, he sat in his room, waiting for a Telegram message that never came. The clerk who delivered his room service meal asked if he needed anything else.

"Did I miss where the minibar's hiding?" Cal asked.

"We have none," the young man replied. "Would you like me to get you something from the bar?"

Cal pictured how a cold glass of vodka would feel in his hand and how the viscous fluid with hints of pepper and star anise would taste as it slid past his lips.

"No, I'm good," he said.

By the next morning, the storm had passed, and the south of France was bathed in warm sunshine. He walked around the city center, his hand in his pocket to feel his phone's vibration if he missed the chime. He was walking through a narrow street behind the Dominican convent when a more-familiar tone sounded. He read the text from Emilio.

> Anything yet?

He quickly replied.

> Nothing.

He had a simple lunch at a café where the locals outnumbered tourists, then toured the Musée Languedocien, a museum specializing in the region's history. He asked the young woman selling tickets about Cathar exhibits.

"Oh yes, people always ask about the Cathars," she said, circling a room on a gallery map. "We have a video installation, a few paintings, a copy of a sacred text, and some examples of Cathar crosses. However, there are no religious objects, reliquaries, or statues. The Cathars rejected all materialistic items. It was just the people and God. Nothing in between. It's what I really admire about them."

He was in this sparse gallery when his phone began blowing up with news alerts.

The Vatican had done a deal. The Nigerian schoolgirls were safe. A press conference was about to start.

He hurried back to his hotel suite and watched Elisabetta handle the barrage from the media. The question insinuating that her actions were a slap in the face to the memory of their friend, Pope Celestine, sent him into a fury. He whipped out his phone and texted her.

> Magnificent deal. Magnificent outcome. Congratulations.

To his surprise, she called an hour later.

"Thank you for your text," she said.

"I'm happy for you. It sounds like a masterpiece of diplomacy."

"I'll tell you about it one day. The important thing is that two hundred beautiful schoolgirls are back with their families. Emilio let me know you're in Montpellier. Have you been contacted?"

"Not yet. I'm wondering if something's gone wrong."

"Let's hope not," she said.

"You sound tired."

"I was going to try to take a nap when Cardinal Donahue threw a bomb."

"What did he do?"

"He sent out a press release unilaterally announcing the formation of his council of wise old men."

"Oh, God," Cal said. "He actually went there."

"They intend on showing up at my doorstep tomorrow to, quote-unquote, take control."

"What are you going to do?" he asked.

"I'll try not to think about it until tomorrow. In the meanwhile, I'll pray for the success of your mission."

"I don't even know what my mission is."

"I'm worried about you, Cal. Emilio told me you insisted on going there alone."

He liked that she was worried. About him.

He left her with this: "To be honest, I'd rather face a bunch of terrorists than Donahue and his wise old men."

CHAPTER NINETEEN

1209
Béziers, Languedoc

It had been a difficult year for Raymond VI, the Count of Toulouse. Pope Innocent III was enraged by the murder of his legate Pierre de Castelnau, who he sent to Toulouse to deal with the scourge of Catharism. At first, Raymond denied any involvement in the crime. Later, he acknowledged that his courtier had indeed killed Pierre but that the death was accidental. The pope was unmoved. He leveled threats against the noble—threats with teeth. Unless Raymond switched from protecting Cathars to acting against them, he would be charged with heresy, made to forfeit his lands and see his descendants disinherited. Raymond was pressed into service, forced to do penance by public flagellation, commit troops to the cause, and endow the salaries of theologians and canon lawyers in Toulouse. The Count breathed a sigh of relief and reluctantly agreed to turn on his Cathar subjects.

As Geralda had predicted, Innocent used Pierre's murder to launch a crusade. There would be no more negotiations, no more calls for voluntary conversions. The pope wanted King Philip II of

France to lead his holy army against the Cathars, but Philip shared Raymond's lack of enthusiasm for the bloody cause. He refused to lead the crusade and forbade his son, Prince Louis, from doing so. Instead, he lent Innocent one of his barons. Simon de Montfort, a man of unflinching Catholic orthodoxy, took the reins of this new crusade and began to foment an orgy of violence that would consume every Cathar man, woman, and child in Languedoc.

In the summer of 1209, Simon stood around a table with his fellow barons at his manor house. A map lay before them. They debated which Cathar city should be the first target in this Holy Crusade.

Most men point with a finger. Simon used his thumb and pressed it hard into the parchment.

"This one," Simon said. "We will start with Béziers."

∞

GERALDA SHUT the door to her house on Lavaur's square and took her daughter by the hand. Fabrissa was nine. She had inherited her mother's inquisitiveness and her father's pragmatism. Girls her age learned to cook and sew. Fabrissa learned these skills too, but was fascinated with the ledger book her father used to account for his wool trade. It wasn't enough for Fabrissa to hear that the squiggles were called numbers. She wanted to learn how to count and do sums. She wanted to understand why one weaver paid this amount for his wool bundle and another paid less if he promised to pay more in a few months.

"She has a head for it," Geralda told Hugh one night as he retired to his separate bed. "Teach her."

"Better a wool trader than a perfect," he said ruefully. "Are you sure you cannot lay with me, wife?"

"You know I cannot."

Geralda left Fabrissa with a neighbor woman and hurried on horseback to a farmhouse an hour away. She had received word that the farmer, Prades Escaunier, was ill and needed the services of a perfect. When she arrived at the cottage, she winced at the smell of gangrene. The farmer's wife, Sibylla, took Geralda to her husband's bedside, where the strapping fellow was lying on his side, moaning softly.

"He stumbled and fell upon his plow blade," the woman said. "His leg has become putrid. I have been applying poultices, but—"

"Let me look," Geralda said, lifting off the blanket.

One glance was all it took. The swollen leg was purple to the groin and oozing.

"It is good you called me," she said.

"I have no money to pay you," Sibylla said.

"I do not require payment. I come in the service of God. I wish your husband to have a good end."

The woman nodded and wept.

"Good sir," Geralda said, waking the man. "I am Geralda, a perfect from the village. Are you ready to receive the Consolamentum?"

Prades rolled onto his back and stared through hollow eyes. "I am."

By dint of illness and ignorance, the farmer was a passive participant in the Consolamentum. Geralda had to prompt him word-by-word in reciting the Lord's Prayer. When she finished the ritual, he rolled onto his side again and resumed moaning.

"Bless you, Mistress," his wife said.

"The time has come for his Endura," Geralda said. "It may be hard for you, but, having taken the Consolamentum, his soul will be released from the terrible cycle of reincarnation. He will be with the Lord. He may become delirious and beg for food or drink, but you must be strong. The sooner he sheds this useless worldly body, the better."

"I will miss him."

Geralda reached for her hands.

"Thank you, Mistress," Sibylla said. "Tell me. Will the pope's men come for us?"

Geralda told her the truth. "I do not know."

On her return to Lavaur, Geralda circled the square, and as she approached her house, her heart leaped with joy. Hugh's brother, Roger, was seated against her door.

"Thank God you've returned," she cried, dismounting. "Where is Hugh?"

Roger could only hang his head.

Geralda's knees weakened. "Did he receive the Consolamentum?"

~

BÉZIERS WAS a thriving city of nine thousand, the third largest in Languedoc behind Toulouse and Narbonne. It was home to a sizeable population of Cathars who lived peacefully among their Catholic, Jewish, and Muslim neighbors. Hugh's customers were of every faith, although his relations with the Cathar weavers were undoubtedly strongest. They were the ones who welcomed Hugh and his brother into their homes when he journeyed to the city to sell his product.

The weaver Bartholomew poured the brothers cups of wine, and his wife laid out a meal of turnip stew, bread, and strips of dried fish. Bartholomew asked how long they would be in the city.

"Two or three days," Hugh said.

"There have been rumors of an attack," Bartholomew said. "Did you see any signs of the pope's army on your way?"

"Not a man, not a horse," Hugh said. "What rumors are these?"

"It is hard to know what to believe," Bartholomew said. "Do you know the Cathar blacksmith—the one near the bend in the river?"

"He shoed a horse of mine my the last time I was here," Hugh said.

Bartholomew said, "He is the one who told me that someone told him that a Catholic priest received a message warning him to leave the city."

"It is a dark time when rumors fly like flocks of starlings," Hugh said. "Why would the army come here? If you want to kill Cathars in these parts, there are many more of us in Narbonne."

Hugh and Roger planned to sell their last fifteen bales of wool in

Béziers, then head home with bulging purses. But as they bedded down on that scorching July evening, the crusader army, led by Simon de Montfort's designated commander, the Abbot of Citeaux, reached the outskirts of the city and made camp by the River Orb. A few prominent Catholics received clandestine messages warning that an attack was imminent and quietly slipped out of the city. Others refused to believe the messages, and still others believed them but refused to abandon their homes.

Late at night, an emissary of Arnaud Amalric, the Abbot of Citeaux, came to the house of the Bishop of Beziers, Renaud de Montpeyroux, and informed him of the impending attack. The bishop hastily dressed, left his dwelling by the cathedral to ride through the dark streets, and crossed the stone bridge to reach the river's opposite bank.

Amalric greeted him as a brother in Christ and offered him libation which he refused.

"Tell me what you want of me, dear abbot," he said.

The abbot was fat, and his hands were greasy from pulling apart a cooked chicken.

"As you know, the Holy Father has called for two things to happen—a crusade to stamp out the heretic Cathars and an inquisition to root out any who are hiding among decent Christians. Baron Simon de Montfort is leading the righteous crusader army. I am his instrument in Béziers. As a man of this city, I want you to draw up a list of Cathar leaders so we may find them and deliver the punishment they deserve."

The bishop's mouth went dry, and he changed his mind about accepting something to drink. "By punishment, you mean what?"

"Why death, of course. Do not be squeamish, dear bishop. This is the expected outcome of heresy. But worry not. We do not plan on punishing the ordinary Cathar folk, the ones I believe they call credentes. All we will require of them is a renunciation of their bizarre sect and conversion to the one true faith. No, we want their priests."

"They have no priests," the bishop said, "at least not in the sense that we have priests. They have an elect group of prominent citizens called perfects who perform a rite they believe lets their people enter Heaven."

"Yes, perfects," the abbot yawned. "That is what I meant. I want them. How long will it take to draw a list?"

The bishop sputtered and said he would need to return to his abbey and consult with his priests. The abbot sent him on his way.

As dawn approached, Montpeyroux completed his list of some one hundred fifty men and women that he and his priests knew to be Cathar perfects. Then he rang the cathedral's bells and waited for the city's Catholics to arrive. Church bells ringing at such an hour was a sign of an emergency. Once the agitated congregation settled down, the bishop informed them of the crusader's demands and read out the roster of perfects to be surrendered. At each name, a cry of protest rang out, and by the time he was done, there was pandemonium. One prominent citizen after another decried the handover.

"These are our friends and neighbors!" one of them said.

"They do not bother us. Why should we send them to their deaths?" said another.

The most important voice was that of the Viscount of Béziers, who declared, "The Cathars are my subjects. I shall not abandon them in their hour of need."

In the end, the bishop found himself without support. He begged from the pulpit, "Then save yourselves! I will be leaving forthwith. Join me, please!"

Only a few horses and wagons followed Bishop Montpeyroux and his entourage across the river that morning. The rest of the congregation rushed to work alongside the viscount to prepare the town for a siege.

Abbot Amalric learned that the city refused to surrender the perfects. Mystified, he rallied his men to begin taking offensive siege positions. His commanders informed him it would be a week before the bombardment of the town walls could begin.

As the midday sun beat down on the crusader army, a group of armed civilians from Béziers, fortified by strong beer, made a sortie through the city gate and crossed the river bridge on foot. These were mostly young Catholic men with a few Cathar compatriots who sallied forth, waving linen banners and city flags and shouting insults at the top of their lungs on a farcical mission to scare off the heavily armed troops. It might have gone the way of pure theater had one exceedingly drunk man not gotten into a fight with a crusader. The soldier decided to meet the drunkard's bravado with brio. Blows were exchanged. A knife was pulled. The soldier fell dead.

Crusaders rushed to the support of their fallen comrade, and a wild melee broke out. Facing overwhelming numbers, the city men fell back in disarray and ran through the city gate, but the crush of crusaders chasing after them made it impossible for the wall guards to lower it.

Abbot Amalric had been watching the brawl and, sensing that there was little he could do to stop his crusaders from aborting their assault, ordered his entire army to attack. There was no time to relay orders or rules of engagement.

"This will be bloody," one of the abbot's commanders said.

"Blood is what is demanded," the abbot replied.

~

A PERFECT NAMED Andreas Bossuet rushed to the weaver Bartholomew's house to tell him that crusaders were at the edge of the city. The Catholic majority, he said, was standing with the Cathars.

"Who are your visitors?" Bossuet asked.

"My brother and I are wool merchants from Lavaur," Hugh said.

"You are a long way from home," the perfect said.

"We are," Hugh said, "and we must return as quick as we can. If they came for Béziers, they will come for Lavaur."

Hugh and Roger bade their host farewell and began to hitch their horses to their wool cart. But as they began to ride through Bartholomew's narrow lane, a crush of fleeing townspeople blocked their way.

Hugh stopped a man in his tracks. "What is happening?" he asked.

"The soldiers!" the man panted. "They are killing everyone! They are putting man, woman, and child to the sword. They are mad dogs! Run!"

Above the shouts of alarm, people heard the pealing of all the church bells of Béziers.

Hugh felt a hand grip his arm.

It was Bartholomew with his wife and sons. "Hugh, leave your wagon and come with us. We are going to seek refuge at St. Mary Magdalene. It is the closest church."

"The wool!" Roger cried.

"Leave it," Hugh said. "If we escape with our lives, we can shear more sheep."

The three Catholic churches—St. Mary Magdalene, St. Jude, and the Cathedral of Beziers filled with petrified townspeople. The priests made no effort to prevent Cathars from entering alongside Catholic parishioners. When no more could enter, the priests shut the doors and set the latches. The Church of St. Mary Magdalene comfortably held a standing fifteen hundred for High Mass. On this July day, three times as many were crammed inside so tightly that some fainted from the crush. Men held children on their shoulders so they could breathe.

Hugh and Roger found themselves pushed deeper into the church by the crush of new people, and when the doors were pulled shut, they were pressed against an iron grate in the wall behind the pulpit. At the sound of the door slamming, thousands inside fell quiet, and in that silence, they heard anguished cries of people outside being put to the sword.

A priest had managed to don his vestments and climb the pulpit steps to lead the Catholics in the Lord's Prayer. Then, the priest heard his name and looked down on a friend, the Cathar perfect Andreas Bossuet.

"Father," Bossuet cried out. "Would you allow me to give my brethren the Consolamentum?"

The priest knew of the sacred Cathar ritual and shouted to those nearby, "Let him up! For the love of God, let him up!"

Bossuet was lifted into the air and borne from hand to hand to the pulpit. He climbed up, embraced the priest, and shouted to the crowd.

"My fellow good men and good women! Receive now the Consolamentum so that you may be forever freed from this wicked material world at the time of death. Now, let us pray!"

The press of bodies prevented Hugh and Roger from kneeling. They bowed their heads and solemnly participated in the perfect's prayers of call and response.

∼

ABBOT AMALRIC ENTERED the town on muleback, protected by a phalanx of crusader knights. He watched the murdering, raping, and looting around him with profound disinterest. He dismounted outside a large limestone church and asked which one it was.

"St. Mary Magdalene," he was told.

"What would you have us do, Sire?" a knight commander asked.

"Put it to the torch," the abbot said, with the same insouciance as when he had requested a chicken for his supper the night before.

"But, Sire, this is our church," the knight said. "Surely there are Catholics inside. In pursuit of heretics, how will we spare the faithful?"

"We cannot exactly ask them one-by-one, what are you, heretic or faithful?" the abbot said. "The heretics will pretend to be faithful, and after we have left, they will resume their heresy. No, good knight, that will not do. How is your Latin?"

"My Latin, Sire? It is passable."

"Caedite eos. Novit enim Dominus qui sunt eius."

Kill them all for the Lord knoweth them that are His.

∼

Hugh raised his head at the sound of breaking glass. Pieces of stained glass rained down on the assembly, followed by flaming arrows. Some arrows stuck into flesh and extinguished. Some glanced off stonework and failed to catch. But some embedded in rafters, the pulpit, the confessionals, and the massive wooden door. And so, the blaze began.

Hugh failed to notice that his brother had his knife out and was hacking at the stones surrounding the iron grate. The tip shattered, and the skin of his palm rubbed raw from his frantic stabbing. The flames grew brighter, and the screams grew louder until the choking smoke quieted tongues.

Outside, knights began clamoring up limestone blocks and perched on sills, they kicked away jagged pieces of stained glass. It was good sport to fire down on the choking masses, and they laughed as their arrows pierced flesh and bone.

Roger cried out to Hugh, "Brother, look! I have moved the grate! The crypt is below!"

Hugh saw a run of stone stairs descending into blackness just as an arrow slammed into his skull.

~

Roger stood before Geralda's door.

He told her about the brave perfect who had delivered a mass Consolamentum to hundreds of Cathars.

He told her of Hugh's final moments.

He told her he had fallen down the stairs and woken up bleeding from the head in the crypt of St. Mary Magdalene.

He told her about escaping the smoking ruins of the church and the burning, looted city filled with thousands of slain men, women, and children.

And he told her that on his long journey home, he thought only of two things. The first was letting her know that Hugh's soul was saved. The second was that having received the Consolamentum, he would go to his farmhouse and practice the Endura.

"When I am starved to death," he said, "I will see Hugh in Heaven, and I will tell him that his good wife knows you will be waiting for her."

CHAPTER TWENTY

The night of the shooting, Gaby left her partner alone and slept on a sofa in one of the lounges. In the morning, she went upstairs and knocked on their bedroom door.

"Bouli. Let me in. Please. We need to talk."

Through the door, she heard, "Go away."

There was an adjoining bedroom. Gaby went around and slipped through the shared bathroom. Sabine was in bed, propped against the headboard, clutching a pillow, damp with tears, to her chest. The bed hadn't been slept in.

"Get out. I don't want to see you."

Gaby sat at the foot of the bed. "Please. Bouli!"

"Stop calling me that. Charles was right. It's childish."

"But I'm your Bear."

"You killed him," Sabine seethed. "You killed my brother."

"He was going to expose us. What could I do?"

"You didn't have to shoot him," Sabine sobbed.

"I had to. Do you know what number was on his phone? It was 112, for God's sake. He didn't even wait to get into his car. In ten seconds, he would have been speaking to the police."

"You shot him. He suffered."

"And I relieved his suffering. Bouli—Sabine—we have worked so hard to get here. We are so close to achieving something bigger than both of us. Something we believe in with all our hearts. I wish Charles hadn't seen the tattoo. I wish he hadn't come here. We thought of everything, but we neglected a single detail. It's my fault. You're the big thinker, the big planner. It was my job to sort out the details. I have the same tattoo, but you can hardly see it on my skin. It didn't occur to me. Remember the day we went to the tattoo parlor together?"

"He was the last one in my family," Sabine said. "I'm alone now."

Gaby reached for her knee. "Don't say that. You're not alone. I'm here. I beg you to find it in your heart to forgive me."

Sabine got up, went to the bathroom, and closed the door.

AN HOUR LATER, Sabine reappeared downstairs. Pierre Abadie saw her first and mumbled his condolences. She nodded and asked if he'd seen Gaby.

"She was heading toward the orchard," he said.

"Where is he?" she asked. "Where is Charles?"

"Gaby thought your family burial plot," he said. "We tried to make it nice. I can show you."

"Not now."

"What should we do about your professor? The men were ready to get him, but—"

"Oh, God. I forgot about him," she said. "Tonight, I think."

She found Gaby under an apple tree heavy with tender, pale green leaves.

"Hey," Sabine said, sitting beside her.

"Hey."

"You shot him, but it was me who killed him."

"Don't say that."

"It's true. I didn't anticipate what he'd do if he found out. Of course, he would have come here. I didn't want to think about what would happen to him and the company when everything came out."

"He would have done fine," Gaby said. "He was a billionaire. Now his bitch of a wife is a billionaire."

"I don't care about her, but the boys—well—" She swallowed. "She'll be looking for him. The office will be looking for him."

Gaby showed her Charles's phone. "I sent texts. He had to make an unexpected trip to Morocco. His wife is pissed at him, but she's always pissed. Charles texted Antoine to manage things at Morlet while he was gone."

"I'll have to write a letter and leave it where it will be found," Sabine said. "They'll need to know what happened to him and where he's buried. You found a good spot?"

"A beautiful spot," Gaby said. "Near your father, but not too near."

Sabine sighed. "I can almost hear them arguing from beyond the grave."

"There's room for you beside him."

"They won't put me there. Anyway, I want to be with you. I didn't tell you. It was a bit macabre."

"Tell me what?"

"I bought a plot for us in Lavaur. The two of us will be together. It's in my will."

"Bouli," Gaby said, reaching for a hand.

"Cal Donovan," Sabine said suddenly. "Last night, we forgot."

"Maybe it's for the better."

"I know you were against it."

"I still am."

"He's important to me. His lecture—"

"Yes, I know about his lecture."

"And he's the one who saw the tattoo and made the connections. It's fate, Bear."

At the utterance of her nickname, Gaby squeezed Sabine's hand.

CAL'S PHONE finally sounded with the Telegram chime. He hurriedly opened the app.

> 10 pm. Basilique Notre-Dame-des-Tables.
> Rue du Collège. Leave your phone in your room.

His feet ached from all his walking that day, but the church wasn't far, and he wanted to scope out the meeting place before nightfall.

There was a pleasant café across the street from the entrance to the basilica. He sat under an umbrella, ordered a beer, and texted Emilio.

> It's on for tonight

EMILIO HAD GROWN tired of his dinners with General Tavassi. They had exhausted their small talk, and there was nothing new to discuss operationally. He had already notified Tavassi that Cal's rendezvous was on for tonight at ten and that he would pass along updates as soon as he heard from Cal. He dined alone at his hotel. At nine o'clock, he was watching TV in his room when Tavassi called.

"What are you doing?" the general asked.

"Absolutely nothing."

"Why don't you come into the headquarters?"

"What's going on?" Emilio asked.

"Come in. I'll explain."

Emilio found a beehive of activity inside the GIS war room. Every workstation was manned. He looked for clues on the display screens, but there were only maps of Italy, France, and the Mediterranean.

Tavassi looked fresh in a pressed uniform.

"Ah, there you are," Tavassi said. "Let's talk in my office."

The general turned on his lights and asked Emilio if he wanted a drink, maybe a pod coffee.

"It's late for coffee," Emilio said.

"It's going to be a long night," Tavassi said. "Listen, my friend. I know we discussed letting Donovan contact the kidnappers on his own. And you know I agreed to honor that request for all the reasons we talked about. However, I felt obligated to inform my superior, General Commander Seghezzi. I wasn't aware of this until a short while ago, but Seghezzi alerted Maurizio Cremonesi on the theory that the head of Italy's foreign intelligence service needed to be informed. Cremonesi, in turn, felt obligated to cover his ass by alerting the French intelligence service. A big chain of ass-covering. And now we come to tonight. It seems that the French DGSE deployed a team of operatives to Montpellier to shadow Donovan."

Emilio became agitated, shook his head, and said, "No, no, no. This is terrible, Sergio. This is putting Cal at risk. It's putting the hostages at risk."

"I'm sorry. It's out of my hands," Tavassi said. "All we can do is watch the operation. We're expecting a live feed. I'm hopeful our fears won't be realized. Maybe this will work out well. Come on. Don't look so glum."

On his way back to the war room, Emilio stopped in the lavatory. When he was alone, he called Cal's mobile. It was 9:45.

Cal was at the café on Rue du Collège, sipping mineral water. His phone rang on the bedside table of his hotel room. Emilio left a message, but he knew he was too late.

Emilio folded his arms across his chest as the main screen came alive with a feed from the French. One of Tavassi's officers was in contact with a counterparty in Paris via a headset, and he provided a running commentary to the Livorno group.

"Okay, the transmission is up," he said. "This is a dashcam view from the DGSE vehicle parked on Rue du Collège in the old part of Montpellier. You can't see the entrance to the Notre Dame Basilica. It's on the right. On the left, there's a café. They say that Donovan arrived twenty minutes ago."

"Is that him?" Tavassi asked. "Blue jacket. Sitting alone next to the table with two couples?"

"That's him," Emilio said. He saw Cal lifting a glass and wondered if he was steeling himself with a vodka.

"It's a narrow street," Tavassi said. "The people in the DGSE car will be conspicuous as hell."

The officer said, "I'm told the car is empty. The operatives are somewhere nearby with direct visualization."

Not a single car or motorbike passed the DGSE vehicle for five minutes. Emilio hated the emptiness of the street.

"I wish the place were busier," he said.

"Me too," Tavassi said. "Now we wait."

Ten o'clock came and went. Another ten minutes passed, then another.

Cal fidgeted in his chair. Without his phone or a stiff drink to distract him, he was pretty left with thoughts filled with worst-case scenarios. He found himself eavesdropping on the couples at the table next to him. They looked to be in their thirties. The men drank lagers. They were fit and boisterous. The women had Camparis. They were athletic and more reserved. They were arguing about whether a film they had seen was rubbish or a hidden gem. One of the women, a brunette in a black skirt and white blouse, reminded him of someone he had briefly dated years earlier, but he struggled to remember her name. The lapse bothered him. He wasn't worried about his memory. At age fifty, he was confident his mental acuity was undiminished. He was bothered because he had lost the woman's name in the sea of dates, affairs, and one-night stands that littered his past. What had he been looking for? What hole had he been trying to fill? If he had his phone, he might have sought the answer by looking at a picture of Elisabetta. No woman had ever gotten under his skin like this nun.

She's the one, he thought. *She's the one*.

A green car slowly came into view as it passed the DGSE dash-cam. It stopped opposite the café. A passenger-side window rolled down.

Cal heard his name. A man in a windbreaker and balaclava got out of the sedan and opened the back door for him. As he rose, Cal looked at the brunette again and remembered.

The woman's name was Gretchen. She was a legal secretary. Or was she a travel agent?

"Okay," the officer with a headset announced. "Contact made. Donovan's inside the target vehicle. They're rolling and making a left turn on Rue Fabre."

The green sedan passed out of view of the static dashcam, but the camera picked up a flurry of activity. The two couples seated near Cal were on their feet, sprinting toward the DGSE vehicle.

"Hiding in plain sight," Tavassi said.

The DGSE operatives got in the car and moved through the narrow streets of the old city, before turning onto a modern road by a large shopping center. In the distance, the green sedan was barely visible on the dashcam.

On the dashcam's audio, the group in Livorno heard, "It's a late-model green Dacia Sandero. The number plate has been painted over. It's probably heading for the A9 motorway."

Two men were in the car with Cal—the driver and the guy with a windbreaker in the back with him.

"You left your phone behind?" the man asked.

Cal wondered how he knew he spoke French. "As instructed."

"You came alone?"

"Yes."

He was handed a hood.

"Is that necessary?"

"If you want to live, it's necessary."

"Then, happy to oblige."

He felt his pockets get patted down. His wristwatch and shoes were removed, and he was subjected to an intrusive search.

"That's necessary too, I suppose," Cal said.

The reply he got was a sharp jab in his thigh.

"What the hell was that?" he yelled.

"A sedative. We don't want you to remember how you got where you're going. Better for all of us."

"If I had known, I would've had a drink while I was waiting."

CAL FELT the tranquilizer kicking in. His shrouded head got heavy, and his chin bobbed on his chest. The two men were taciturn. All he heard was the hum of tires.

On the screen in Livorno, the tail lights of the green car were faint yellow dots on an empty motorway. On the audio feed, a female DGSE operative, the one who reminded Cal of an old flame, was heard saying, "We're still on the A9, passing through Raffegan. We're maintaining a distance of half a kilometer to the Dacia."

Someone in Livorno muttered that he hoped they wouldn't lose them.

"Don't worry," Tavassi said. "The DGSE are pros."

A minute later, the dashcam picked up a white SUV overtaking in the fast lane.

The DGSE driver said, "That one's driving like an idiot."

Suddenly, the SUV braked, allowing the DGSE vehicle to catch up.

"To the left! To the left!" a male DGSE agent shouted.

Cal was fading into oblivion when he heard faraway popping noises. "What do I hear?" he slurred. "Do you hear what I—"

"Shots fired!" the woman in the white blouse screamed.

The screen in Livorno showed the dashcam view of a car veering sharply to the right, scraping against a guard rail, and going airborne in a barrel roll. There were a few seconds of sickening screams before the live feed died.

THE DACIA and the white SUV pulled up to the castle's front door. Two men exited each vehicle, leaving Cal passed out in the sedan.

"Go get Gaby and Sabine," the SUV driver said. "Tell them they made the right call. The fuckers followed him."

"Are you sure you took care of them?" the Dacia driver said. "No one else was following?"

"We're good."

Gaby and Sabine came running and demanded to know what had happened.

As she listened to the details, Gaby became incensed and unleashed a profane tirade against Donovan.

"He's like all of them," she said, pulling a pistol from her waist. "He's a fucking liar."

"Stop!" Sabine shouted. "Maybe he didn't know he was being followed."

Gaby pleaded. "Bringing him here was a bad idea. We need to cut our losses."

"We'll question him when he wakes up," Sabine said. "We still need him."

Gaby slid her pistol into her waistband and went back inside. She made her way through dark rooms to the church. Inside, Henri Vaux sat in a chair, watching the sleeping cardinals.

"Hit the lights," she told the young man.

"Why?"

"Just do it, Henri."

"You don't have your mask on," he said.

"I don't care."

The cardinals woke with a start, dangled their feet off their cots, and squinted at the brightness.

"Who is the cardinal from Sudan?" Gaby asked loudly.

When no one replied, she repeated the question.

A thin voice came from the back. "Sudan does not have a cardinal."

Gaby went to him. He was an overweight, dark-skinned black man in a tracksuit that was too small for his bulky frame.

"Who are you?" she asked.

"I am Cardinal François Bol."

"Where are you from?"

"I am from Khartoum, child. I was the archbishop there."

She raged at him. "I'm not your child. Where are you a cardinal?"

"At the Vatican. I am the president of the Synod of Bishops. Are you Sudanese?" he asked.

"You're an old man," she said. "Maybe you were a priest or a bishop when I was being beaten in a Catholic orphanage in Khartoum."

"I am sorry you were abused, my child."

She whipped out her pistol and shot him in the face.

"I told you, I'm not your fucking child."

∽

WHEN CAL REGAINED CONSCIOUSNESS, he was on a bed in a dimly lit bedroom with a cotton mouth and a pounding headache.

He called out weakly. "Hello?"

He remembered everything and half-expected to find himself tied down, but he was free to move about.

"Hello?"

There was a light in the bathroom, and he stumbled in to get water from the sink. He filled a glass, drank copiously, then held onto the sink to steady himself. In the mirror, he saw a white curtain pulled around the tub. He was about to go out and look for someone when he noticed the curtain had a red smear that was impossible to ignore.

He pulled it open and fell backward, jamming his flank against the sink.

Even if he had known the man, Cardinal Bol's only recognizable features were his large brown eyes and bushy eyebrows. The rest was swollen gore.

CHAPTER TWENTY-ONE

1211
Lavaur, Languedoc

Following the massacre at Béziers, the crusaders began besieging other Cathar strongholds. A week later, the crusader army arrived in Carcassonne and cut its water supply. The town fell quickly. The residents were spared because they did not take up arms, but they were forced into exile in their undergarments. In the autumn of 1209, seven other Cathar towns fell in a frenzy of bloodletting. With each victory, Simon de Montfort grew stronger and more confident. He wrote letters to Rome detailing his barbaric methods of extermination and received effusive praise from Pope Innocent. Keep pressing on, he was told. Keep doing God's work.

And press on, he did. The following year, Simon vanquished Lastours, Bram, Minerve, Montségur, and Termes. While Simon waged war against the heretics by the sword, Arnaud Amalric, the Abbot of Citeaux waged war by other methods. Tasked with spearheading a Languedoc inquisition, the abbot and his Dominican monks swept into towns and cities subdued by Simon, determined to root out Cathar survivors.

The inquisitors invited all suspected Cathars to meet with the monks and confess their heresy. Some came voluntarily, hoping for lenience. Others were turned in by their Catholic neighbors to settle old scores or to protect themselves from charges of harboring heretics. Most Cathar credentes, fearing the consequences of denial, confessed to their beliefs and repented. If the inquisitors believed their sincerity, they were released on conditions. They were obliged to forever wear marks of their Cathar pasts so that their Catholic neighbors might readily identify and shun them. Yellow crosses, the lengths of two palms, had to be stitched onto the front and back of their outergarment. If the crosses were torn, they had to be renewed. The people of the Languedoc came to call the crosses las debanadoras, or winding reels, because the wearers could be reeled in by the inquisition at any time for questioning. A conviction for Cathar recidivism meant certain death.

Cathar perfects who found themselves appearing before a panel of inquisitors fared worse—much worse. To a man and woman, perfects refused to recant their beliefs and swear fidelity to the Catholic Church. Arnaud insisted that his inquisitors diligently seek confessions from these recalcitrant perfects. Summary executions would not suffice. There were procedures to follow. Documentary records to make. At first, the inquisitors leveled threats against members of a perfect's family. If threats did not produce confessions, relatives were hauled in and tortured in front of them. Arnaud's favorite method of torturing the perfects themselves was a method he called, the Wall. It was a prison of walled cells, permanently lacking air and light, so small that victims were unable to move. There, they languished without food or water, wallowing in their own filth until confession came, or death. Some monks preferred other methods of persuasion—hot irons, barbed whips, trusses. All instruments of torture were fair game as long as they were blessed with holy water.

Through all of 1210 and into the early months of 1211, the town of Lavaur was untouched. Geralda and its residents knew it was only a matter of time before the crusaders and inquisitors arrived. Every day of freedom was a cause of celebration. The

Cathars practiced their faith, raised their children, worked their fields, and fished the waters of the Agout.

Geralda had become accustomed to life without her beloved Hugh. Hugh's brother, Roger, kept the family sheep farm going, but income dwindled. He lacked his brother's head for commerce, and the countryside had become too dangerous to deliver wool to distant weavers. Geralda devoted herself to her two passions—the Cathar faith and motherhood. Among the perfects of Lavaur, her services were highly sought. She was regarded as a caring soul who offered good Christian advice to all and a gentle hand to the dying.

One of her champions was Aimeric de Montréal, the Lord of Lavaur who dwelled in a castle on a bluff above the River Agout. Aimeric was born and raised a Catholic and had an impressive chapel built inside the walls of his fortress. In 1199, he and his knights joined Rome's Fourth Crusade in the company of Simon de Montfort's army to liberate the Holy Lands from the Muslims. Yet, later in life, he became disillusioned with the behavior of the abbot and the monks of Lavaur, disgusted by their thievery, fornication, and familiarity with young boys. In contrast, he found his Cathar subjects possessing an enviable purity and piousness. To the horror of the bishop of Toulouse, Aimeric converted to Catharism and withdrew his support from the Roman churches of Lavaur. It was Madame Fayet, the woman who helped Geralda to become a perfect, who performed his conversion. When Aimeric's wife was stricken with childbed fever, Fayet was too elderly to come to his aid, so he summoned Geralda. Geralda gently administered the Consolamentum rite to the desperately ill woman and stayed at her bedside during the four days of her Endura, holding her limp hand till her last breath. After she passed, Aimeric wanted to give Geralda money but she refused, telling him the only payment she sought was for him to live a righteous life and do good deeds.

In the spring of 1211, Simon de Montfort decided that Lavaur would be next to fall to his crusaders. The town had long been one of his targets. It was a Cathar stronghold, it was near to Toulouse, his ultimate prize, and it was ruled by a lord, once his ally, now his enemy. However, Simon had been forced to bide his time. His earlier campaigns had sapped him of men and materials. He had taken larger towns, but Lavaur was well defended with a strong castle, eighty knights, four-hundred able-bodied men, and sturdy walls fortified by deep ditches and ramparts. It was only the arrival of a large contingent of French reinforcements from the north that changed Simon's mind.

It was Lavaur's time to feel the weight of the crusade.

In March, Simon began moving troops into position. The assembly of a large fighting force could hardly have gone undetected. From his castle tower, Aimeric had a fine view of the surrounding countryside. The people of Lavaur prepared themselves physically and spiritually as best they could.

Geralda's daughter Fabrissa was a spitting image of her mother, with high cheekbones and flowing golden hair. The twelve-year-old had never fully recovered from the loss of her father. She missed everything about him, and from time to time, she still opened his old ledger books and wistfully read the accounts of his wool trade. She was pious and diligent, and it was her fervent desire was to emulate her mother and one day, become a perfect.

The incessant hammering of the carpenters was music to Simon's ears. Every morning, he emerged from his square tent to survey their handiwork. The siege engine was taking shape, and the wooden bridge to transport it over the river was nearing completion. Aimeric began to understand the tactical nature of the coming siege. The siege tower was taking shape. At first, he thought it was going to be a trebuchet, designed to hurl boulders at the town's walls, but he changed his mind. Simon had decided that the walls were too thick to breach by catapult. No, this siege engine was a cat, a mobile tower of several levels covered by ox hides, with a large mechanical claw. It would be wheeled to the wall, allowing Simon's sappers and miners to undermine the stone structure, protected from flaming missiles, stones, and arrows falling down on them. Aimeric mobilized the townsfolk, telling them that sometimes the mice could outsmart the cat, and they set about digging tunnels.

Aimeric had no illusions that the town walls would hold indefinitely. There was room for many inside his own walled fortress, and the people of Lavaur built simple shelters in the castle bailey. He personally invited Geralda and her daughter to take a bedroom near the great hall. Geralda accepted the invitation, but worried about Hugh's brother and his family who were on their farm, cut off from the town. She was right to worry. Simon's men required food, and his raiding parties fanned out, plundering and killing. When they finished with Hugh's farm, the sheep were gone, and Hugh, his wife, and children lay slaughtered.

April arrived, a time for tilling and planting, but the people of Lavaur were divorced from the rhythms of nature. Simon declared that the siege preparations were done and commenced the campaign. The giant cat was pulled across the river on its four wheels and dragged to the ditch. The crusaders had been gathering branches from the forest for a month. Now, they filled the ditch with bundles of branches and prepared to wheel the cat over them to reach the town walls in the morning.

That night, Aimeric's mice struck. They crawled through their newly dug tunnel, and removed the branches. The cat and mouse game continued for days. The crusaders would fill the ditch by day and the defenders would empty it by night.

Finally, an engineer in the crusader camp devised a plan. Men piled grass, wood and fat outside entrance of the tunnel and lit it on fire. They layered unripe corn and grass on top of the pile to keep the smoke from rising. That night, smoke filled the tunnel making it impossible for the defenders to use it. The crusaders filled the ditch with fresh bundles, pushed the cat against the wall, and began its destruction.

Day after day, Geralda and her comrades listened to the incessant pounding of the cat's claw against the wall. Be not troubled by the sound, Geralda told her daughter. As long as we can hear it, the walls remain standing. While Geralda made her spiritual rounds inside the fortress, Fabrissa sat with Sibylla Escaunier, the wife of the farmer with gangrene whom Geralda had given the Consolamentum. Sibylla moved to town after her husband died, and Geralda and Fabrissa befriended the kindly woman.

"Do you think we will die?" the girl asked the woman one day.

"Oh, I think not, dearie. Look at all the fine knights about. And the lord's castle has been here for God knows how many years. It will take more than Simon de Montfort to topple it."

～

At the beginning of May, the town walls fell and crusaders streamed into Lavaur, burning and looting houses and shops. From the castle ramparts, Geralda watched as her house by the square went up in flames. She knew full well from Aimeric that the castle walls would crumble soon enough, so she and her fellow perfects hastened to administer the Consolamentum to the hundreds of credentes gathered in the castle bailey.

The crusaders now controlled Lavaur's main gate. Simon ordered his engineers to move his siege engine through it and set the cat against the castle walls. The cat's claw began its diabolical work and stone blocks began to shift. The weather turned and it rained for days. The waterlogged townsfolk huddled in the bailey awaiting their fate as the crusaders taunted them and blindly shot arrows over the walls. Most missed their mark—a young boy, an old man, and a horse were wounded.

On the third night of the castle assault, a weary Aimeric sought Geralda in the bedroom she now shared with women suffering from fever and exposure.

"Come, walk with me," the lord said.

He took her to his own stronghold in the keep and offered her a glass of strong beer.

"They will be upon us by the morning," he said. "There is nothing we can do to prevent the outcome."

She took the news stoically. "Will you send your knights against them?"

"I think not," Aimeric said. "My knights are brave, but there are ten of them for every one of us. We would gladly give our lives in battle, but Simon would take vengeance on everyone else within the castle."

"You think he will not do so in any event?" she said. "We know what he did in Béziers, Montségur, and other fallen cities and towns. His cruelty knows no bounds."

The lord quickly downed his beer and refilled his cup. "That is why I want to offer you a means of escape. My grandfather built a narrow tunnel under this very room. It runs to the north and ends just beyond the town wall. I want you to leave at nightfall with a group of women and children of your choosing. Take them to your family sheep farm. If your husband's brother still lives, he can offer his help. I greatly admire you, Geralda. I want you to survive. You have much to give to our fellow believers. You have raised a fine daughter. She too will have much to give."

Geralda put her cup down untouched. She wanted the clearest of heads for the hours to come. "I will do as you say, my good lord, but I will not do everything you ask. I will send out a party of women and children. I will say farewell to my daughter. But I will not leave. I will stay and face Simon de Montfort. I will affirm my faith to him. I will decry his wickedness and pray for his eternal soul. You and I have taken the Consolamentum. We will not see the darkness of this material world again. At the moment of our deaths, we will be bathed in the beautiful light of Jesus Christ. Simon and his minions will return to Earth as lowly creatures. Do not try to persuade me to change my mind. Now, show me how to reach this tunnel of yours."

※

WOMEN AND CHILDREN gathered in a dank room below the castle keep. Rush mats were pulled back to reveal a trap door and a ladder descending into darkness. The ablest adults carried flaming torches to light their way. All the women had said goodbye to their menfolk and had no more tears to shed.

Fabrissa was on the verge of weeping, but her mother took her aside and said, "You must not cry, dear child. The children will see you and they will cry too. You are the daughter of a perfect, and you will also become one of the elect when you have grown a little more. Go with Sibylla and mind her. Help with the younger children."

"But what about you, mama?"

"I will pray with our friends and neighbors until the end, and then I will go to Heaven to see your father and await your arrival many, many years from now. I want you to have this."

She gave the girl a piece of cloth, folded and tied with thread.

"What is it?" Fabrissa asked.

"It is a lock of my hair, child. It is but a small token. Everything else I have given you dwells within your heart."

∼

THOSE WHO SLEPT AT ALL, awoke at daybreak to the sound of light hammering. From the ramparts, Aimeric could see gallows rising in the town square. He looked to the brightening sky. At least the rain had stopped.

Simon's miners breached the innermost layer of the castle wall by mid-morning, and crusaders flooded into the bailey, swords drawn, ready to take on Aimeric's knights. What they found was a pile of swords and pikes with eighty knights kneeling in surrender.

Simon de Montford strode imperiously into the castle and found Aimeric dressed in his finest clothes.

"The castle is yours," Aimeric said. "The town is yours. I pray you accept our surrender with a Christian heart and spare the good men and women of Lavaur. My knights and I are resigned to our fate."

Simon puffed out his chest and said, "You, Aimeric de Montréal, are a betrayer and a heretic. To think I rode with you to Jerusalem. Let us hasten you to this fate of yours."

"Will you spare the people?"

"Their fate is in their hands," Simon said.

Aimeric and his knights were marched out of the castle to the village square where dozens of simple gallows had been erected. Simon hanged Aimeric from the highest pole, and when he ceased his thrashing, he ordered the rest of the knights to be strung up. The plan quickly went awry. Many of the poles, sunken into the boggy ground, fell over as men were strung up. Simon merely shrugged at the set-back and ordered the rest to be hacked to death.

Simon returned to the castle to address the townspeople encircled by his soldiers in the bailey.

"Those among you who call yourselves perfects, make yourself known."

Thirty men and woman stepped forward.

Simon walked among them and asked which one was Geralda of Lavaur.

Geralda raised her hand. "I am."

"I have heard of you," Simon said, lifting her chin with a finger. "You are said to be exceedingly pious and clever. Let us see how clever you are. I will spare your life if you renounce your heretic faith. Will you renounce?"

She pushed his hand away and said, "I will not."

"Will any of you perfects renounce your faith?"

One man said he would and he was led away to be examined by one of Simon's priests. The rest joined Geralda.

"And what of you who are not perfects?" Simon yelled to the other four hundred. "Who will repent?"

Only a few hands were raised.

Simon yawned and gave some orders to one of his sergeants. His carpenters began dismantling Aimeric's stables, using the lumber to build a rudimentary fence around the four hundred. Inside the fence, bales of dry hay were scattered among them. As people came to understand what was about to happen, they cried out in fear and anguish. The perfects began ducking under the fence to be with them.

When the crusaders went to stop them, Simon said, "Let them go. All except for the clever Geralda. I have something special for her."

Simon took Geralda by the arm and led her to the stone well at one end of the bailey.

"Climb up," he said. "Let me help you. I want you to have a good view of how the Holy Roman Church deals with heretics."

The four hundred began singing the *Te Deum* as the bales were lit.

Geralda stood on the well's circular wall and could not help but wail as the flames and smoke slowly extinguished the shrieks of agony.

Simon came closer and without a word, gave her a push.

She felt herself crashing against stones as she plunged into darkness. She briefly lost consciousness, but the cold, black well water revived her and she flailed her broken arms to keep her mouth and nose above the water.

Simon's head appeared against a circle of bright blue sky. "Fill the well with stones," he called out. "Small ones at first. There is no rush."

And as the stones fell, Geralda, recited the Lord's Prayer again and again.

> *But deliver us from evil. For thine is the kingdom, the power, and the glory, forever and ever.*

∼

FABRISSA, daughter of Geralda of Lavaur, lived far longer than her mother had. Like her mother, she married a good man and had children before she took the Consolamentum and became a perfect. Two sons died young. A daughter survived. Geralda had lived much of her life in peace. Fabrissa had never known it. Simon de Montfort was long dead, but others had taken his place. The inquisition raged on and the dwindling number of Cathars in the Languedoc had to go into hiding to practice their faith.

Fabrissa had been living in a village near Toulouse when a neighbor informed on her. She was taken to a monastery where priest inquisitors subjected her to deprivation and torture. Desperate to see her daughter one last time, she gave a false renunciation and was sent home with a pardon.

She took to her bed with a galloping fever and told her daughter she was beginning her Endura.

"I have something for you," Fabrissa said. "Go to the pocket of my cloak."

The cloak with yellow crosses sewn onto front and back hung on a peg.

"It is your necklace, mama," her daughter said. "Where is the rawhide?"

"They tore it off my neck. It is the amulet that is important. Take it and wear it. Remember me as I remember my mother. Catharism will never die. It will endure."

Fabrissa had commissioned the amulet many years ago from a woman who knew how to work small pieces of silver and glass into a rectangular box, the length of a thumbnail.

Inside the box, was a locket of golden hair.

CHAPTER TWENTY-TWO

The call interrupted a dreamless sleep.

Emilio apologized. "I woke you."

"It's all right," Elisabetta said. "Has something happened?"

"It's Cal."

She sat, then stood, her heart pounding.

"Is he all right?"

He was alon e in the courtyard of the GIS headquarters. The night was eerily still. "We hope so. There was a complication. It didn't go as planned. Someone on our side informed the French security services. The DGSE tried to be discreet. They sent a single team of operatives. The plan was to follow Cal after he was picked up. They wanted to find out where they took him, then devise a raid to free the cardinals."

"But they weren't discreet," she said. "Is that what you're going to tell me?"

"Cal was picked up in Montpellier. The DGSE followed the car onto a motorway. There was a second group of kidnappers who opened fire on them. All four agents perished."

"I'm sorry," she said. "What about Cal?"

"We have no idea where he is. He promised he'd come alone. I assume they'll be angry. I know it's late, but I thought you needed to be informed."

"I didn't want him to go," she said. "Now—"

Emilio waited for her to finish, but the line stayed quiet. "Are you okay?" he asked. "Will you be able to get back to sleep?"

"Sleep? I don't think so. I'll make tea. And I'll pray."

∼

CAL BANGED on his bedroom door until someone came to unlock it. The man with a windbreaker and balaclava aimed a pistol at his midsection.

"You're wanted downstairs," the man said.

The tranquilizer was still in Cal's system. He had to hold onto a polished banister as he descended the sweeping stairway into a baronial hall. He took in a detail here, a detail there. Heavy pieces of dark furniture. Ancestral oil paintings. Medieval tapestries. Silver candlesticks.

"Go through," the man said.

Cal entered a large formal sitting room decorated with antiques, ornate chandeliers, and Persian rugs. A middle-aged woman with straight blonde hair and bright blue eyes sat alone in the middle of a sofa, wearing tight blue jeans and a high-necked pullover rolled to the elbows. A second woman stood off to one side. This one was taller and far more beautiful, with high cheekbones and coal-black skin. If her hair were any shorter, she would have been bald. As he got closer, he saw a yellow cross on the white woman's forearm and an identical one, far less discernible, on the black woman.

Cal didn't give either one a chance to speak.

"Who is he?" he demanded. "The dead man in my bathtub."

"Have a seat, Professor Donovan," Sabine said.

"I asked you a question. Is it one of the cardinals?"

"Sit, goddamn you!" Gaby shouted, resting her hand on the pistol grip in her waistband.

He sat because he was woozy, not because he was ordered.

"You broke your pledge," Gaby said. "You said you would come alone. You weren't alone. You lied and people died."

"I didn't know anything about being followed," he said sharply. "They told me they wouldn't. Did you murder one of the cardinals?"

Sabine rubbed her forehead. "Gaby has a fire within her. The flame is always there, like a pilot light. But when she gets angry, it's as if a thermostat is turned up and the flame roars. She acted impulsively, in the heat of the moment. Gaby will tell you how upset I was, but it's done and can't be undone. It's Cardinal Bol from Sudan."

"Why him?" Cal said.

"Someone had to pay for your sin," Gaby said, "and I hate priests. Especially priests from Sudan."

"This sin is on you, not me," Cal said defiantly. "What about the others? Have you killed others?"

"They are well," Sabine said. "No one else needs to die."

"Why am I here?" Cal asked.

"To make sure there are no more deaths," Sabine said.

"I don't understand." His knees buckled at a wave of dizziness.

"Are you all right? Would you like something to drink?" Sabine asked.

"I'll take a vodka."

"We have none. If you want something strong, there's cognac."

"That will do."

When Gaby left to get the drink, Sabine spoke to the man in a windbreaker. "It's okay. You can go. I think Professor Donovan understands the consequences of trying to harm me."

Gaby returned and poured a cognac.

"Get some rest, Bear," Sabine said. "I'll be fine."

"You sure?"

Sabine nodded. "And you made your point. Put Cardinal Bol somewhere else so Professor Donovan can use his bathroom."

Gaby reached for the bottle.

"Leave it, Bear," Cal said, with a mocking emphasis on her nickname.

Arrows flew from Gaby's eyes. "Fuck off."

Cal put away first glass of cognac and poured another.

"Feeling better?" Sabine said. "You and Gaby have started on the wrong foot. In another setting, you would have liked her."

"The wrong foot! She killed a man!"

"I know. I deeply wished she hadn't."

"Are you going to kill me too?" he said.

"Why would you ask me that?"

"You're not hiding your faces."

"We're not going to kill you. My promises are more solid than yours."

"For the last time, I didn't know I was being followed."

"All right. I'll believe you."

"Who are you?" he asked.

"My name is Sabine Morlet."

He closed his eyes to extract a memory. "As in Morlet, the owners of the *Menelaus*?"

"It's my company."

"I'll ask again. Why am I here?"

She placidly folded her hands. "Years ago—I want to say twelve years ago—you gave a lecture in Toulouse. It was on the Cathars. Do you remember it?"

This memory was easier to retrieve. The history department at the University of Toulouse had invited him to lecture on a topic of his choosing. As Toulouse was in the heart of the Languedoc, he proposed the Cathars, a suggestion enthusiastically received by his hosts. The venue was the grand opera house within the Capitole, the city's main administrative building. He remembered standing on the stage, basking in the applause from the gilded tiers of the Théâtre du Capitole.

"I remember some of the evening. I'm sure my lecture notes are somewhere."

"I remember all of it," Sabine said. "You gave an elegant talk. I knew the history of the Cathars quite well, perhaps even better than you, but you said something that really stuck with me. You asked us to imagine what the history of Europe, indeed the history of the world, might have looked like if the Roman Church had not destroyed the Cathars. Catharism was spreading across France very quickly when the pope decided it was too big a threat. If Rome had not put its boot down, Catharism might have become dominant in France, Germany, and Iberia—maybe even Britain. Why was it so appealing? You gave the reasons. Do you remember? It lacked a corrupt class of priests and bishops. The faithful had direct contact with Jesus Christ, unclouded by rituals and churches. It was humane. The killing of people and animals was not allowed. And it was egalitarian. Women were the same as men. Imagine that! In the heart of medieval Europe, a religion that treated women equally."

"It was, undeniably, a remarkable movement," Cal said.

"You said that if Catharism had replaced Roman Catholicism, there would have been no Martin Luther railing against the corruption and pomposity of the Church. There would have been no Reformation, no Protestantism. The religious wars of Europe would not have happened. Catholic missionaries, who spread tyranny, corruption, and death to the New World, Asia, and Africa, would not have existed. Women would have taken their place at civilization's table a thousand years earlier. But instead, we were destroyed."

Cal's eyes narrowed. "We?"

"Oh yes, we," she said. "Cathar blood courses through our veins. Flesh could be defeated, but not a beautiful idea."

"Are you claiming to be a Cathar?"

Sabine held her head high and said, "I am a Cathar woman. Not the kind who does reenactments for the tourist bureaus of the Languedoc. We are real Cathars, thoroughly immersed in our religion and culture. I describe myself as a modern Cathar perfect. There aren't many of us, but we are dedicated. We are determined. We are resolute."

Cal put his cognac down. He had consumed enough to take the edge off. Any more, and he'd be at a disadvantage at the verbal sparring he imagined was coming.

"You haven't mentioned revenge," he said. "Is bringing the

Vatican to its knees revenge for a crusade that happened eight hundred years ago?"

"Yes, this is about revenge, but it's also about reform. For sure, I'm interested in righting a historical wrong," she said. "But we have larger goals."

"The ones in your video," he said.

"Look," she said. "I have no illusion about history repeating itself. This is the twenty-first century. Catharism will not spread in the Languedoc or elsewhere as it did in the twelfth century. Catholicism is the dominant Christian religion in the world we live in. It has deep roots. I attended a Catholic primary school. Most of my friends, neighbors, and business associates are Catholic. Despite our best efforts, a Cathar revival would only be a minor religion. As we thought about—how I hate the royal we—as *I* thought about it—it seemed the intelligent approach was to use Cathar ideals as the basis for improving Catholicism. For years, I worked quietly, using my money to promote feminism within the Church. I supported nuns who wanted a greater say in how they lived their lives and conducted their work. I funded international efforts that encouraged the ordination of women. I was heartened by the action of Pope Celestine, appointing a nun as his private secretary. I was overjoyed when Pope John made Sister Elisabetta his secretary of state. And then, it all came crashing down when he made his famous declaration on female ordination. Do you remember it?"

At the time, Cal had been surprised by the stridency of his friend's tone. The pope was heading to Mexico to attend the World Youth Congress. In a press gaggle at the back of the plane, he was asked about his position on female ordination. The appointment of Elisabetta Celestino was still fresh, and there was speculation he was signaling a shift in policy. Yet, behind the scenes, there was so much blowback to making her secretary of state that John felt a need to placate the conservatives.

"He reaffirmed the Church's long-standing opposition to the ordination of women," Cal said. "He described the declaration, *Inter Insigniores*, issued in 1976 by Pope Paul VI, and Pope John Paul II's

1994 apostolic letter, *Ordinatio Sacerdotalis*, as settling the matter permanently."

Sabine spat out the word. "Permanently."

"And this was your justification for poisoning him?" Cal said.

"He disappointed me, but I didn't hate him. As popes go, he wasn't that bad. No, his death was a necessary first step."

"I thought Cathars abhorred killing."

"I do abhor it. I found it painful but necessary. We needed a conclave. I didn't want to wait, God knows how many years, for his natural death. It would have been easier to kill the two cardinals who couldn't climb down a ladder, but I said no. We risked taking the time to bind them. I abhor what my friend did to Cardinal Bol. It was unnecessary. I don't want to kill the hostages. Their deaths would be unnecessary. But they are preventable."

"Depending on how they vote in your manufactured conclave," Cal said.

"If there is a two-thirds majority for Sister Elisabetta, she will be pope," Sabine said. "There is nothing in canon law stipulating where the conclave must be held. There is nothing in conclave law about coercion. If they vote for her to be pope, she will be pope, and the Church will have turned to the light."

"How's the conclave going?" Cal asked derisively. "I'm guessing you haven't seen white smoke."

"That's one of the reasons you're here," she said. "They've been defiant. For three days, they've abstained. I want you to persuade them to do the right thing. I want you to persuade them to save their lives."

His urges got the better of him, and he uncorked the cognac. "You want me to persuade them."

"Yes."

"You seem like a highly intelligent person," he said.

"I won't accept your compliment until I know where you're going with it," she said.

He swigged a small mouthful. He was tired as hell and had an image of his life ending in this drafty castle somewhere in the

French countryside. "Where am I going?" he said. "A great deal of planning went into this. This wasn't a spur-of-the-moment plot."

"I began to think about it the day Pope John broke my heart."

"So, you spent two years pulling this off. You needed people and a lot of money."

"Money was not a problem. I have enough for a hundred lifetimes of luxury. Joaquín Guzmán—el Chapo—paid an engineer one million dollars to make a tunnel to get him out of prison. I paid that engineer fifty million dollars. I found capable men who make fifty-thousand euros a year, if they're lucky, and paid them five million for a year's work. I rented houses and warehouses for huge premiums, paid the neighbors on Viale Vaticano a fortune not to complain about noise, bought a giant helicopter, for God's sake!"

"And here you are," Cal said. "You've pulled off a crime for the ages. You stole a conclave. If you were a chess player, I'd say you played a brilliant opening and middle game. But your end-game strategy is going to fall apart. The college of cardinals is a principled lot. They have spent their lives serving an institution they believe in, heart and soul. They won't vote under duress to change the fundamental tenets of the Church. You won't be able to persuade them, and neither can I. I suspect they'd rather go to their deaths as martyrs. Then where will you be? You'll be known forever as a rich madwoman who became a mass murderer. The memory of Catharism as an enlightened movement will be permanently stained with blood."

Sabine smiled. Cal realized she had hardly moved the whole time they'd been talking. Her hands remained folded on her lap, her back proudly erect.

"Don't you want to see a woman as pope?" she asked. "Celestine and John were your friends. You must know Elisabetta Celestino. Don't you think she would make an excellent pope?"

Elisabetta's image flashed through his mind. "I think she would be excellent in any job she wanted. I very much doubt she wants to be pope."

"I think she'll surprise you," Sabine said. "She will understand that when she utters, I accept, she will wipe away two thousand years of injustice. She will rise to the majesty of the occasion. Use your powers of persuasion with the cardinals. Give Elisabetta the chance to change history."

Cal poured another cognac. "I'll speak to them, but I know what they're going to say."

"You're drinking like a man who expects to be killed," she said. "I told you I wasn't going to harm you. I need you alive."

He almost told her he was perfectly capable of drinking heavily for no apparent reason. "Why?"

She got up and opened a desk drawer.

"I want you to publish this manifesto. It's called *Modern Catharism—A Pathway for Reforming the Catholic Church*. Do you remember the Unabomber's manifesto? He was a mathematician. I studied literature. Mine is shorter and better-written. His was the work of a loon. Mine is reasoned and rational. I'll be gone, but I want my manifesto to be read and debated. I hope people will be inspired to examine the faith and embrace it. At the least, I hope that Cathar principles of respect for human life, animal life, and the equality of women will find a home within the Catholic Church."

"You say you'll be gone," Cal said.

"My friends and I are good Cathars. We have taken the Consolamentum. We are content to shed our mortal bodies. We will be gone, but I pray you will publish this manifesto and tell the world about us. I want to give you a gift for your time and traumas."

She opened the door of a glass-fronted case, took down three leather-bound books, and put them on a table.

"Have a look."

They were handwritten parchment manuscripts he recognized as the three sacred texts of Catharism, *The Gospel of the Secret Supper*, *The Ascension of Isaiah*, and *The Book of the Two Principles*.

"These are museum pieces," he said. "They're priceless."

"I told you I was rich." He saw her fingering something at her neck, under her pullover. "Will you take them?" she said. "I won't be needing them any longer."

CHAPTER TWENTY-THREE

Sabine Morlet came home in tears, yet again. Children from her school rode the bus or their parents picked them up. Sabine was had a chauffeur. When she was dropped at the door to her parent's castle in Pézenas, her mother was told by a housekeeper that the girl was in a state. Madame Morlet rushed to her bedroom.

"What now, my love?"

Sabine was picking at her blonde hair to undo a braid.

"What now?" the girl shrieked. "I hate them. I hate them all."

Her mother sat on the bed and had her daughter back up so she could fix her hair.

"Tell me all about it, sweetheart."

"Sister Angelique yelled at me for being idle because I was looking out the window. I finished the assignment before the others. It was pathetically easy. What did she want me to do? Pretend it was hard?"

"Did you raise your voice to her?"

"I gave her a piece of my mind."

"I expect you did. Was there anything else?"

"On the playing field, the girls ganged up on me. They called me names and made fun of where I live."

Her mother began brushing her hair. "I see. Were they at least creative?"

"They called me Marie Antoinette. They said I'm from Versailles."

Madame Morlet tutted. "Well, then, Marie, would you like some cake?"

Sabine giggled and hugged her mother. "I love you, mama."

"And I love you. So, I have news I think you'll like. I've finally gotten your father to agree. He was resistant. When he was a boy, he went to your school."

"Sister Angelique was probably his teacher too."

"Possibly. She is quite ancient," her mother said. "Next term, you're going to attend a new school."

"Really?" Sabine screeched.

"Yes. It's a wonderful private school in Toulouse. It's very progressive, and they say it's perfect for very clever children like you. And best of all, there are no nuns and no priests."

"Can I start tomorrow?"

"You must wait until after Christmas."

"But Toulouse is far. I'll be in a car all the time."

"It's a boarding school. You'll make new friends. You'll love it there. Now go and play with Charles. He's bored and making a fuss. Jean is in a mood and refuses to entertain him."

On a cold January morning, a crust of frost on the castle grounds, Sabine waited in her mother's sewing room to start her new life. Madame Morlet left her to get something from her jewelry box, and Sabine was excited, hoping for one of her mother's baubles.

"Here's what I have for you," her mother said, opening her palm. "It's very old and very special."

It was a necklace charm on a silver chain, a rectangular glass box a centimeter long with silver edges. Inside the box was a tangle of yellow hair.

Sabine took the amulet and held it up to her face. "What is it?"

"My mother gave it to me. She told me it holds a lock of hair from a very distant relative who died almost eight-hundred years ago. Her name was Geralda of Lavaur. She was a brave Cathar woman."

"What are Cathars?" the girl asked, gazing at the amulet.

"Here. I have a book for you. I got it when I was a girl. I'll tuck it in your suitcase. This amulet will give you good luck and protection, just as it has given me. I was wearing it the day I met your father. Mothers have passed it to daughters for generations. When they had no girls, they passed it to sons to give to their daughters. One day, you will pass it along. Now, there's our car. Let's go to Toulouse so you can start your new life."

Sabine put the necklace on, looked at herself in the mirror, and took her mother's hand.

FOLLOWING A LONG-STANDING TRADITION, the school headmaster placed the newest girl with the second-newest girl. The dormitory matron showed Sabine to her room and left her to make her own introductions. A willowy, pretty girl with coal-black skin was reading on one of the beds.

"Hello," Sabine said shyly. "I'm—"

The girl put down her book and flashed a bright smile. "You're Sabine Morlet. I've been expecting you. My name is Gaby Cerf. That's your bed, your dresser, and your desk. We share the closet. What do you like better—books or sports?"

"Books," Sabine said.

"Splendid," Gaby said. "We're going to get along fine."

It took little time for Sabine to learn Gaby's history. She was Sudanese, orphaned at an early age, and raised at a Catholic mission school in the slums of Khartoum. According to her account, she was smarter than the nuns and was vocal and opinionated. Two priests, a head teacher and his assistant, ran the school, and took turns meting out punishment to the headstrong girl. A rod of thin, woven twigs was their favorite instrument. Gaby stripped down to show her scars to her new roommate.

"I think they got off on it," Gaby said.

"What do you mean?"

Gaby pointed to Sabine's crotch.

"Oh."

"The nuns knew," Gaby said. "They did nothing."

Sabine recoiled at the raised lines on her thighs and buttocks. "How horrible."

"It was bad," Gaby said, "but I escaped."

"How?" Sabine asked, wide-eyed.

"Monsieur and Madam Cerf," Gaby said. "They adopted me and took me to France. My father was working in Khartoum. He drills for oil. My mother found me at the orphanage."

"They rescued you," Sabine said. "How wonderful."

"Not before the priests had one last go at me."

"What did they do?"

"The older one held me down and the younger one—well, use your imagination. They told me if I said anything, they'd stop the adoption. I never told anyone before. You're the first."

"Why me?"

Gaby grinned. "I've got a good feeling about you."

Sabine beamed at the compliment and reached for something to say. What emerged was the awkward question, "Are your parents black, like you?"

Gaby was unperturbed. "They are as white as these walls. They don't mind what I look like, and I don't mind what they look like. This school is much better than my last one. I was so happy when I heard they didn't have priests and we didn't have to go to church. What's your story? You look rich."

"How can you tell?"

"Look at your clothes. Look at those shoes and your fancy suitcase. Don't worry. I won't hold it against you. My new parents are rich too. It is much, much better than being poor."

Sabine unpacked her case under Gaby's watchful eye and stacked her few books on her desk.

"I know those. I don't know this one," Gaby said, pouncing on a worn paperback, *The Remarkable Story of the Cathars*.

"My mother gave it to me," Sabine said. "I'm the relative of a famous Cathar woman."

"Cool," Gaby said, leafing through the book. "I have no idea who they are. You can read it to me tonight."

∼

WHEN THEY WERE OLDER, both would say that their boarding-school years were the happiest in their lives. That is when they fell in love. They were inseparable, even after the dormitory matron, worried about their proclivities, assigned them to different rooms. During school breaks, Gaby stayed with Sabine. Her adoptive parents soon had their own child and became less interested in the black girl. The girls roamed the vast grounds at Pézenas and found infinite nooks and crannies inside the castle to cozy into. They especially liked the old, deconsecrated church—how it was cool on a hot summer day, and how their singing voices sounded within its echoey walls. Sabine's father, Claude, the third-generation owner of Morlet, SARL, the shipping company in Montpellier, never warmed to the African girl, as he called her, and couldn't understand why his daughter didn't want to be around the children from her riding academy. But, Sabine's mother was open and inviting, even after she came to understand the girls' relationship. Sabine's brothers left them alone. The youngest, Charles, was a sports maniac who paid no attention to the bookish girls. Michel, the oldest sibling, rarely emerged from his room. When he did, he was a surly and sour presence.

"What's the matter with him?" Gaby asked Sabine the first time she met him.

"I don't know," Sabine said. "No one speaks about it."

"Was he always like this?"

"When I was little, he was devoted to me. He would play the guitar and I would dance and sing. He was the sweetest brother. I loved him so much. I still do, but he changed."

In their free time, they immersed themselves in Cathar lore, embracing the David versus Goliath elements of the story. They thought Catholic rituals were pompous and incomprehensible. Gaby, especially, had good reasons for despising clergymen. Yet, they both believed in God, and on its own, they liked the Christ story very much. Christ and the Gospels, presented the Cathar way, appealed to them. They thought that the way Cathars worshipped Jesus, unfiltered by Catholic rigmarole, was dignified. And of utmost importance, they cherished the way that women were front and center in the Cathar ethos.

They would run through the castle's fields and meadows, waving real medieval swords pilfered from Claude Morlet's collection. Sabine would shout, "I am Geralda of Lavaur, defender of the faith." And Gaby would yell, "And I am Aimeric de Montréal, Lord of Lavaur, and defender of Geralda."

They went on to attend the University of Toulouse, where Sabine studied literature and Gaby studied mathematics and computer science. Sabine could easily afford the spacious apartment, envied by their impecunious classmates, that became a center for feminist activities on campus. Sabine and Gaby happily threw themselves into their studies and their deepening relationship.

One Saturday, they were shopping by the River Garonne when they passed a tattoo parlor with colorful templates in the window.

They pointed at the same time.

"Look!" Sabine said. "The Cathar cross. Should we?"

Gaby pinched Sabine's bottom. "I think we should."

They were at their apartment, nursing sore arms, when Sabine's mother called.

"My love, you need to come home. It's Michel."

They went shopping again, this time for black dresses and headed to Pézenas for several terrible days. It was Claude Morlet who found his son hanging in the stables and cut him down with his own hands. After the private funeral service and interment at the family plot, Claude closeted himself away, and Sabine didn't see him for the rest of her time there. That night, she sat with her mother and finally learned the truth about her brother's moods. When he was a young altar boy, a priest had abused him for over a year. Eventually, the boy's mother coaxed it from him. She told his father, who confronted the priest in the confessional booth.

"I know what you did. If you touch my son again, I will expose you."

The shaken priest never had the chance to touch Michel again, but there were rumors that other altar boys were not so lucky. Rumors but no actions. The priest remained at the church for his entire career. Eventually, he retired to a comfortable clerical home in Burgundy and died of old age.

"Make no mistake," Sabine's mother told her. "This wasn't suicide. That bastard killed my son."

Gaby was waiting for her, when Sabine finally came to bed.

"You look awful, Bouli. Were you with your mother the whole time?"

"She told me everything."

"Do you want to talk about it?"

Sabine started undressing. "Later. All I can say is, the Catholic Church can go to Hell."

∼

Sabine and Charles were always going to join the family company. A literature degree was poor preparation for a career in shipping, but Sabine was highly intelligent and learned the business quickly. She started in the customer relations department, and cycled through personnel, logistics, finance, and operations roles. Charles had been more classically trained for commerce. When his time came, he joined the company's accounting and finance department.

Gaby and Sabine had a house in Montpellier, a short drive from the company. After graduation, Gaby hopped from job to job, usually getting fired for her temper or quitting in a fit of rage. Since her schoolgirl days, she had never suffered fools. According to her, most of her employers idiotic. Eventually, she managed to land a trainee job at IBM in Toulouse, where she finally found managers she could respect. On weekends, she took the train to Montpellier to be with Sabine.

After a few years at Morlet, Sabine was made assistant manager for operations, and she concluded that the company's logistics were a mess. Who better to fix them, she thought, than a computer expert? Her father didn't care what she did within the bowels of the company, but Charles objected to hiring Gaby.

"It's nepotism," he said.

"Are you out of your mind?" Sabine told him. "This entire company is built on nepotism. Do you think we'd have our jobs if our last names weren't Morlet?"

"What would you say if I wanted to hire my wife?" he asked.

"If she were as qualified as Gaby, I'd say—good idea. If a position opens up for a professional shopper, let's bring Marie in for an interview."

So, Gaby Cerf became Morlet's new computer analyst, her first step to founding the company's information technology department.

∽

ONE NIGHT, years later, Sabine and Gaby were reading in bed, when an article on DNA and genealogy piqued Gaby's interest. They had been spending more and more of their spare time immersing themselves in the region's Cathar past, making trips around the Languedoc to famous Cathar sites and castles. One summer holiday, they trekked the Cathar Way, a two-hundred-sixty-kilometer trail from Port la Nouvelle on the Mediterranean to Foix, tracing the history of the Cathars through the Eastern foothills of the Pyrenees.

"Look at this," Gaby said. "It used to be impossible to get DNA from a hair sample. There's a lab in Austria that's figured out how to do it."

"So?" Sabine asked.

Gaby put her hand on the amulet around Sabine's neck.

"I'd be scared to know the truth," Sabine said. "What if the story's a myth?"

"If it's a myth, it's still lovely," Gaby said. "But if it proves your heritage—well then."

In the end, Gaby persuaded her. A jeweler opened the glass box.

They sent a hair sample to Austria with a swab of Sabine's cheek and a generous check to support the lab. Two months later, they received the report. There was a significant match. If the hair was indeed Geralda's, then Sabine was her distant relative.

When Sabine called her mother with the news, she said, "I didn't need scientific proof, Sabine. In my heart, I always knew we carried Geralda's blood."

The DNA match seemed to change Sabine. Her confidence grew. She developed a swagger. She stood straighter, spoke more confidently, had more fire in her belly. She had always taken her mother's tale with a pinch of salt. Now, she knew. She was part of an unbroken chain leading to a heroine. Her Cathar hobby became an obsession.

A short while later, Sabine was touring the *Menelaus*, one of the ships in their fleet. When she went to shake hands with the master, Pierre Abadie, a compact, bandy-legged man twenty years her senior, she immediately noticed a tattoo on his bulging upper arm.

The yellow cross.

She pulled up her sleeve to show hers.

The master's demeanor changed instantly, from a suspicious employee saddled with a home-office inspection to a voluble comrade.

When they were alone on the bridge, he told her, "I started a group with men from my town, mostly ex-navy and reservists. We call ourselves Men of the Languedoc. We do Cathar reenactments. The men joke that I should become a perfect one day."

"Don't forget the women of the Languedoc," Sabine said.

"Yes, of course," he agreed. "We embrace equality of the sexes, as the Cathars did. Well, it's a little hard for some of the fellows, but I think we are getting there."

"You must come to my house," Sabine said excitedly. "I was expecting a routine ship tour today. I never expected to find a fellow Cathar. I am walking on air."

DURING THE YEARS his children were getting their corporate sea legs, Claude kept tight reins on the company. In time, his health declined to the point he felt he had to make a move. Sabine was thirty-five, Morlet's Vice President for Global Operations, when he called her into his office.

"I can't do this any longer," he said with a leaden heaviness. "It's time for me to move aside."

Sabine was unprepared for the conversation. "You're fine, papa. You've got years left."

He dismissed her with a wave. "I had to choose between you and Charles—"

"I agree," she said, cutting him off. "It should be Charles. I'll support him totally."

"God, will the women in this family ever let me finish a sentence! Charles is good with numbers, but he drives me crazy. He argues about everything. I'll admit he's a better manager than I thought he'd ever be. When he was younger, he was always so unserious. But numbers don't grow Morlet. Relationships grow Morlet. Fundamentally, shipping is a people business. I've seen how you are with customers. You charm them. You flatter them. You persuade them to give us their business. You will be my successor, and Charles will support you. I wish you weren't the way you are in your personal life. I wish you would have children. You are who you are, and you're my daughter. We'll have to leave the bloodline to Charles, I suppose. Enough. I'm tired, and I'm going home. Make me proud."

~

WHEN CLAUDE MORLET's body gave out, he was buried in the family plot. His wife developed cancer and soon joined him under the shade of a beech tree. Sabine inherited the castle in Pézenas and moved there with Gaby. Under Sabine's influence, Pierre Abadie's group became the Good Christians of the Languedoc, and came to the castle every month to study Cathar texts. With the group's encouragement, Sabine and Pierre took the Consolamentum and became perfects. Pierre was divorced and had no girlfriend, and he had no problem accepting celibacy. Gaby was less than pleased with Sabine's decision.

"The purpose of celibacy is to avoid procreation and the reincarnation of souls," Gaby complained. "Last time I looked, neither of us had a penis."

"It demonstrates my spiritual commitment," Sabine said. "We'll continue to share our bed and share our lives. But no, I'll be done with sex."

Sabine and Gaby were watching the evening news in the comfy lounge by the kitchen, the night Pope John's airplane interview aired throwing ice-cold water on the ordination of women. Sabine sprang from the sofa, highly agitated.

"I can't believe what I heard," she vented. "We thought he was headed in the right direction. He names a nun to the top job—a cardinal's job—and then he throws all hope of progress into the garbage. What the hell happened?"

"What happened is that he's a son-of-a-bitch like the rest of those cock suckers," Gaby said. "Who are you calling?"

"Pierre," Sabine said. "We need to do something."

"Like what?"

"Something to force them to start acting like us Good Christians."

Sabine finished the call, opened her laptop, and began furiously typing.

Gaby asked what she was doing.

"I need to put all our thoughts into writing," Sabine said. "I'm writing a manifesto."

∽

THE DAY they took possession of the house on Viale Vaticano, Sabine, and Gaby poured champagne for the eight men crowding the sitting room. All of them were from their group, Good Christians of the Languedoc. They were strong, proud men who worked with their hands. They had military training; some were still active members of the reserves. To a man, they believed in Cathar ideology and distrusted the Church. But they had families and weren't about to sacrifice everything in the name of Sabine's mission. She secured their services for more money than they could ever imagine and promised them their identities would never be known. With partial payment in hand, they quit their jobs and signed on to a year of heavy labor in Rome. For over a year, Pierre Abadie carried the diagnosis of advanced prostate cancer. He was in remission and was able to work, but unlike the other men, he didn't intend to keep living when this was over. Sabine had made him very happy with a five-million-euro trust fund for his children. There was a foreigner in their midst, a bespectacled Colombian engineer with a briefcase stuffed with old maps of Roman necropoli. His French was limited to the basics, but Gaby knew schoolgirl Spanish and translated as needed.

"Today, we begin something truly historic," Sabine said, "actions that will force the Church to make amends for how they crushed our beautiful Cathar culture. We will not destroy the Catholic Church. It is too big and entrenched. Instead, we will force it to become a better Church, and by doing this, we will show the world the face of our magnificent Cathar religion. We hope that Catharism will grow alongside the Church of Rome. Perhaps one day, they will be smaller, and we will be bigger. Our equipment arrives tomorrow. Gaby has taken a leave of absence from Morlet and she will be in charge in Rome. So, tonight, let's drink. And tomorrow, let's dig." She raised her glass. "To us! To the Cathars!"

Gaby added a coda. "And fuck the Church!"

CHAPTER TWENTY-FOUR

Cal parted the bedroom curtains and got his first good look at the castle grounds. The morning haze was burning away, and sun-splashed meadows extended to a line of dark trees in the distance. A solitary figure, a man with a rifle slung over his shoulder and smoking a cigarette, patrolled the gravel drive. Cal tested the door. It was still locked. Cardinal Bol's body had been removed, but the stained curtain was a reminder of the atrocity as if Cal needed one. He couldn't bring himself to use the shower.

He got dressed and pounded on the door for attention. A masked guard responded and ushered Cal to the kitchen, where Gaby was pouring a coffee.

"Sabine will be here soon," she said. "Do you want some?"

He accepted a cup and said, "This isn't going to end well for you. You know that, right?"

"Sabine tells me you're a very intelligent man, but you're wrong. This will end brilliantly."

"You're happy about dying, aren't you? You've taken the Consolamentum. No more reincarnations. You and Sabine floating off to a heavenly plain. Leaving behind a very un-Cathar-like trail of death."

She gave him a dose of side-eye. "Trying to get in my head, Professor?"

Sabine breezed in, asking how he slept. He wasn't in the frame of mind for politeness.

"I want to see them," he said.

"That's why you're here."

She took him through a series of reception rooms into a long hall lined with old, dull-colored oils.

"My ancestors were Cathars at heart, but Catholic," Sabine said, waving her hand. "It's a very strange legacy. Neither fish nor fowl. Through there, you'll see I grew up with my very own church. We used to play inside. It finally has a better purpose—hosting a conclave to choose a female pope."

It took Cal several moments to process the scene. A cavernous, medieval church of yellow limestone, with row after row of camping cots. Over a hundred old men were lying and sitting on the mattresses or standing in small conversational knots. Most wore identical tracksuits, but a few clung to their soiled ecclesiastical robes.

Some noticed him right away. The rest looked toward the door when Sabine clapped for their attention. They murmured in surprise at the presence of an unmasked man and woman.

"Is that their ringleader?"

"It's got to be."

"He's not wearing a mask either. Who is he?"

"Must be one of the guards."

"Don't you recognize him? That's Cal Donovan. What in God's name is he doing here?"

Sabine said, "For those of you who don't know who him, this is Professor Calvin Donovan. I invited him here as an honest broker to help resolve our impasse. The professor is an expert in your world and an expert in mine. He knows a great deal about the history of the Cathars. Tomorrow afternoon is your deadline. You will cast four ballots today and four tomorrow. Vote for Elisabetta Celestino and go home. Continue your obstinance and mark your papers, *I refuse*, and perish. It's that simple. Professor Donovan, see if you can save their lives."

The moment she left, Cal was mobbed. Cardinal Archer pushed his way forward and shook Cal's hand.

"Well, you're a sight for sore eyes, Cal," he said. "She asked me about you the other day—the Boston connection and all that—but I never imagined you'd show up."

"Eminence, how are you?"

"You'd better call me Reggie, or you're going to be in even bigger trouble," the cardinal said with a wink. "I'm fine. All of us are fine except for our dear colleague, François Bol."

Macy also barreled through. "Cal!" he exclaimed. "Aren't you a sight for sore eyes? How'd they get you here?"

"I was in Rome reporting on the conclave. After you were taken, I stuck around. I noticed that this woman, Sabine Morlet, had a tattoo of a Cathar cross. I let the authorities know what it meant. The media found out, and my name got splashed around. Morlet saw me lecture on the Cathars years ago, contacted me, and here I am. I'm worried as hell about you. I want to help in any way I can."

Cardinal Fischer said, "It's wonderful of you to put yourself into the lion's mouth, Professor, but I'm troubled that two of the principles, the woman who shot François and this Sabine woman, have both shown their faces. Now, she has a name. Doesn't this bode poorly for us?"

"Not necessarily," Cal said. "Sabine Morlet and the other woman —I only know her as Gaby—are fanatics. They don't expect to survive this. They see themselves as modern Cathars who'll wind up in Heaven, liberated from a cycle of reincarnation. I think there's one other man, the captain of the ship you were on, who's in the same camp. The others—the men who dug the tunnel and are guarding you —they're mercenaries. They intend to finish their job and melt away."

Cardinal Mertens was short in stature. He stood on his cot to speak over the heads of others. "How do you see your role here, Professor Donovan?"

"She called me an honest broker," Cal said, "but I don't think that's the case. I'm not here to represent her position. I only want to find a way to get you out of here."

"Do the authorities know you are here?" Cardinal Bizimana said.

"They tried to follow me," Cal said. "I believe they failed. We can't count on a rescue."

Cardinal Navarro waddled around the rear of the huddle to get closer. Cal got a whiff of him before he talked. He had been seasick onboard the *Menelaus*, and his robe was stained with vomit.

"Professor Donovan," he said, "I agree that you are not an honest broker, but dare I say it—perhaps you are a dishonest one. You are famously known as a supporter of Elisabetta Celestino, the woman who seems to be the reason we are here."

Cal disliked Navarro. He was disappointed when Pope John didn't purge him for being one of Elisabetta's plotters early in his pontificate.

Cal turned to face him. "It's true that I am one of her supporters, Eminence. I believe she's done a fantastic job at the Secretariat during John's time and during this *sede vacante*. But do I think she should be a pope? I do not. And I know for a fact that she doesn't want this either."

A craggy voice from the crowd asked, "What is your position on the ordination of women?"

Cal saw it was coming from one of the papabiles, Cardinal Colpo.

"I'll give you my honest answer. I don't know. It's a complicated subject. I'm happy to discuss it with you."

Another voice rang out. It was Cardinal Sauseda. "Gentlemen, I know we have much to talk about. I believe we should first celebrate morning Mass. We can think of it as a Mass of thanksgiving for Professor Donovan. His presence can only be a good thing for us. We decided that today's honor would go to Cardinal Santagati. Roberto, would you like to proceed?"

As the cardinals returned to their places to stand by their cots, Cal approached the Italian.

"Cardinal Santagati," he said. "They found your crucifix. I thought you'd like to know that."

"Ah, that is wonderful to hear! I would dearly like to wear it again."

∿

Sabine was inspecting the food stock in the pantry when Gaby found her there.

"We're running out of everything," Sabine said.

"It's only today and tomorrow," Gaby said. "Most of them could stand to miss a few meals anyway."

"I don't want to be cruel to them."

Gaby scoffed at her. "You've treated them better than they deserve. Besides, if they keep up their bullshit, they'll be in a mass grave tomorrow night. Unless—"

"Unless what?" Sabine asked.

"Unless you lose your nerve and your mind."

"I'm hopeful Donovan will persuade them," Sabine said. "I'm trying to be optimistic."

"If they vote for Celestino, the thing persuading them was what I did to Bol."

"Oh, Gaby," Sabine said sadly. "It was an act of great barbarism. I still can't believe you did it."

Gaby let out a deep breath and said, "I am what they made me."

∿

The war room in Livorno had been running nonstop since the failed DGSE operation in Montpellier. Emilio and Tavassi pulled all-nighters and looked the worse for wear. No amount of coffee could brighten their sunken eyes.

They were putting all their money on their only solid bets—the kidnappers' cars. By analyzing the body style of the green Dacia sedan, analysts narrowed down the model years to 2019 and 2020.

The DGSE discovered nineteen-thousand green Dacias of those vintages registered in France. The white SUV that flashed by the dashcam was harder to identify, but the consensus was that it was probably a second-generation Renault Koleos. The body style hadn't changed since its introduction in 2016. There were over eighty-thousand white ones registered in the country. Emilio's suggested that they cross-reference the ownership of the two pools of cars with the hope that a single common owner would pop out.

French data analysts worked through the night but failed to come up with a point of intersection.

"So, people," Tavassi hoarsely called out mid-morning, "where are we?"

No one looked up from their workstations.

"We're nowhere," Emilio groaned.

It was a strange Mass, a Mass in captivity without any accouterments of the ritual. But Cal found it the most moving Mass he had ever attended. When it was over, he tried to figure out how best to lead the men in a group discussion. Many older and more infirm clerics had returned to their cots for a rest.

The doctor approached Cal, his necktie still tightly knotted.

"Doctor Bellisario, it's good to meet you," Cal said.

"You know my name!"

"Of course I do. The entire world knows your name. I'm sorry you were taken, but it's good you're here for the men."

"I'm doing what I can, but all I can do is listen," the doctor said, showing his frustration. "Many need medicines, but the kidnappers are ignoring my requests. Please, when you speak to the woman again, tell her she must get me the insulin I need for Cardinal Sauseda. He took his last dose this morning."

"I promise I will. I need to get them to gather around."

"Let them sit. Some are quite weak."

Cal spotted a chair near the door, occupied by one of the masked guards. He asked if he could borrow it to address the group.

"Yes, take it, please," Henri said agreeably. "I hope you can make them see the light. Most of them are nice old gentlemen."

Cal put the chair in the center of the church, climbed up, and lifted his voice.

"As I understand it, you're due to vote twice before lunch. I'm not here to tell you what to do. All I want to say is that no one—not a single person at the Vatican, not a single Catholic among the billion and a half faithful, not a single rational person on the planet—wants to see you martyr yourselves. I think you need to take these people at their word. I saw what they did to Cardinal Bol. They are capable of committing an atrocity."

Cardinal Rowekamp of Chicago spoke up. "What are you suggesting we do?"

Cal had been thinking about nothing but this question. "I'm not making this suggestion lightly," he said. "I fully understand the implications. I think you should vote to make Elisabetta Celestino pope—"

The outcry stopped him from finishing the sentence.

He shouted over it, "—and then you should recant the minute you're released. People will understand you were forced into it. Make the vote unanimous so there's no finger-pointing and scapegoating. I'll be your loudest supporter. I'll explain that it was my idea to vote and recant. I'll tell the world that you reluctantly agreed for the good of the Church. Let's go back to Rome together. Let's go today. Tomorrow, you can return to the Sistine Chapel, resume your authentic conclave, and choose one among you to be the next pope."

∽

Pilgrims standing vigil in St. Peter's Square noticed the men as soon as they entered Vatican City. It would be hard to imagine a more conspicuous group during the present moment: seven cardinals, marching in lockstep, surrounded by a pool of photographers and videographers.

Pilgrims began flocking, excitedly asking whether the hostages had been freed. Cardinal Donahue, walking at the head of the contingent, called back, "We are not the cardinal electors. Our brethren remain in captivity. We are the elders of the Church."

They climbed the stone stairs to the Portone di Bronzo, the grand bronze door at the main entrance to the Apostolic Palace. Two Swiss Guards in full blue and gold Renaissance regalia stood between massive marble pillars on the landing.

"We are here to see the secretary of state," Donahue said.

A guard looked quizzically at him. "Do you have an appointment, Eminence?"

"We do not."

"Then, I am sorry. We cannot permit you to enter."

He was not about to accept no as an answer. "Please inform Elisabetta Celestino that Cardinal Donahue and his fellow cardinals are here for an audience. We will wait."

The guard called on his radio, and a few minutes later, Elisabetta's private secretary emerged through the bronze door and frowned at the presence of the videographers. He politely listened to Donahue's demand and informed the group that Secretary Celestino was in meetings and couldn't be disturbed. He added that if the eminences desired a meeting, they could call the office to find a mutually agreeable date and time.

Donahue turned to face the press and said, "There you have it. The secretary of state is refusing to meet with her senior clergy. During this unprecedented crisis, a *sede vacante* like no other, the secretary of state acts as if she is conducting business as usual. We seven cardinals have over three-hundred years of collective experience as ordained servants of this Church. We have offered our services as a council of advisors to fill the void of our missing cardinal electors. Our offer has been rebuffed for reasons only known to the secretary of state. We will respond prayerfully. We will go now to pray within the basilica and remain there fasting until Elisabetta Celestino comes to her senses."

Elisabetta was at her desk reading dispatches from her nuncios when her secretary asked if she wanted to take a call from her sister.

"I can think of no one I'd rather talk to," she said.

Micaela launched right in. "Did you see those assholes?" she said. "Since when did you start recruiting circus clowns to run your Church?"

Elisabetta laughed for the first time in days. "I wish you'd tell me what you really think."

"I think you should let them starve themselves to death. No, wait. Most of them are so fat it would take weeks to die. Maybe pipe disco music into the basilica until they leave screaming."

"You do have the best ideas."

Turning serious, Micaela said, "Any word on Cal?"

"Nothing. Emilio hasn't heard a thing. I'm worried."

"He'll be fine," her sister said. "He's a very resourceful man. He's got a lot to live for."

"Yes, he does," Elisabetta said. "He's in the prime of his life."

"You're such an idiot," Micaela said. "I'm talking about you."

∼

Henri Vaux and Felix Bain finished their shift and passed the baton to two other guards to watch the cardinals during supper and into the night. They removed their balaclavas and went outdoors for a smoke.

Like the other men, Henri was in the operational reserves of the French military, serving several weeks of active duty per year. His cousin, Rene Chaput, had recruited him to Pierre Abadie's original group, Men of the Languedoc. Dressing up in medieval gear and reenacting battles had been a lark, but in time, the teenager began taking a shine to Catharism. Growing up, he had never been much for church-going, so it wasn't as if he had to abandon one set of beliefs and practices for another. He believed in a deity and was happy to pray directly to God without Catholic rituals, and since childhood, he had been attracted instinctively to the idea of reincarnation. The other men had all been active military, most serving under Pierre Abadie in the navy. Henri joined them in the reserves to add some spice to his life and supplement his car-mechanic wages with a bit more cash. Pierre always got a kick out of Henri's sunny disposition and kidded him about being the baby of the group. He was in his late twenties now but still the youngest—five years younger than his cousin Rene.

Pierre had recruited Henri for Sabine's mission over a beer at a working men's bar in Narbonne.

"You're a good lad. I like you," Pierre had said. "Sabine likes you too. You've got a good head on your shoulders. I've got a proposition for you."

"Oh yeah?"

"How would you like to earn so much money that you'd never have to work another day?"

Henri had snorted. "Who'd I have to kill?"

"This isn't a joke, son. And you wouldn't have to kill anyone. You'd have to work your butt off for Sabine for a year. One year only of hard labor. There would be some danger, but she and Gaby are smart women who've thought through everything."

"How much are you talking about?"

"Five million euros."

"You're joking."

"I'm not."

"Then I'm in."

"Without hearing more?"

"I heard everything I need."

Rene lit Henri's cigarette, and both inhaled deeply. It was a fine afternoon, full of fresh, breezy air and birdsong. It had rained earlier, but the sky was pale blue now, the color of a robin's egg. They began a circuit around the castle, leaving footprints on the lawn.

"One more day," Rene said. "One fucking day."

"There's only one way I want it to end," Henri said.

"Either way, we get our money," Rene said. "I'm going to Thailand. You decided where you're going?"

"Haven't thought about it."

"You look like your dog died. What's the matter with you?"

"Do you think Sabine's going to kill them?"

"She's a serious woman. I believe what she says."

"I'm hoping she's bluffing."

"Gaby shot that guy in the face. Did that look like a bluff to you?"

"It wasn't planned. She was pissed," Henri said. "I haven't slept since she did it."

"First person, you ever saw killed?"

Henri nodded. "You?"

"I saw a guy get crushed to death on a ship. It was an accident."

Henri flicked ash that scattered in the wind. "They're nice old men," he said.

"The red hats?"

"Yeah. I don't have a beef with them. They've behaved well. Even courageously. A couple of them remind me of my grandfather. I don't want to shoot them."

"They won't make you pull the trigger, cousin."

"Even if I'm not the one to shoot, I won't be able to live with myself," Henri said. "Despite the money."

Felix gave him a motivational punch in the shoulder. "Let's just hope the American professor persuades them, and we all go away happy. Let's get some food, okay?"

"I need a word with Sabine. The doctor's making me crazy about the insulin."

∽

SABINE CAME DOWNSTAIRS when she heard Cal was in the lounge. The bottle of cognac was where he had left it the previous night, and while waiting, he helped himself to a glass.

"Is that a celebration drink or one for drowning your sorrows?" she asked.

"The latter."

She sat across him on an opposing armchair. The cushions were firm, and she winced in discomfort before taking her phone from her back pocket and putting it on the small table between them. "I see. Tell me what happened."

"They listened to me," Cal said. "We had a reasoned discussion. They believe their assembly represents a valid papal conclave despite the forced circumstances. They feel they have a moral duty to behave as such and exercise their responsibility to God and the institution of the Church to vote their conscience. They cannot vote in good conscience to agree to your demands. They will not agree to ordain women. They will not vote for Elisabetta Celestino. I watched them solemnly and deliberately cast four ballots today. All were marked, *I refuse*."

She sighed heavily. Cal thought her lower lip might quiver, but she was only setting it in stone. "Tomorrow is their last chance," she said.

"I'm—"

He stopped at the sight of the young man at the door to the kitchen. He had pulled the balaclava over his head again.

"What is it?" Sabine asked.

"Could I have a word?" Henri asked.

"Will you excuse me?" she told Cal.

Cal stared at her phone. "No problem. Mind if I use the toilet?"

"First door on the right," she said.

He locked the door and tried hard to conjure up the number, but he could only remember Emilio's last several digits. There wasn't time to call 112 and explain the situation to an operator. That's when Eli's number flashed through his head.

He opened Sabine's message app and sent a text.

Trace this location. Do not reply. Cal

Then he deleted the text, flushed the toilet, and hurried to his chair.

Sabine returned and looked absently at her phone.

"Dr. Bellisario has been relentless about Cardinal Sauseda's insulin," she said.

"He asked me to talk with you, too," Cal said. "Are you going to get it?"

"He can last one more day. Either he'll be released with the others and get his medicine tomorrow night in Rome, or he won't need it. It's all up to you, Professor. Persuade them tomorrow."

"They're prepared to die," Cal said.

She picked up her phone and stood. "Then they'll die."

CHAPTER TWENTY-FIVE

Emilio felt the burn from head to toe as if every cell in his body was on fire.

Elisabetta's call came out of the blue, like a bolt of lightning on a clear day. It sent him running from his hotel to GIS headquarters. It was early evening, and he wasn't sure if Tavassi had gone home. He found the general, briefcase in hand, about to leave.

"We've got him!" Emilio shouted.

"Got who?"

"Cal. He just texted my sister from his location on a mobile phone. I've got the number."

Tavassi was cool in a crisis. He did an about-face toward the war room and said, "Let's get to work."

In a matter of minutes, the GIS analysts geolocated the cell phone from its tower pings and pinpointed its location on a map—a small red dot with a pink circle of probability surrounding it.

"Let's see a satellite view," Tavassi said.

The dot lay over a sprawling yellow building surrounded by parkland and forest.

"What is it?" Emilio asked.

An analyst quickly came up with the answer. "It's a private residence, Colonel, a medieval castle called Château de Morlet."

Normally, Emilio would have been embarrassed by his outburst. But given the circumstances, his "Fucking hell!" seemed appropriate.

"The *Menelaus*," Tavassi said. "It's been there right under our noses. Find out who the number belongs to."

A call to their DGSE liaison officer in Paris was all it took. They quickly found the name assigned to the mobile account—Sabine Morlet.

"Did you have your money on her brother?" Tavassi asked Emilio.

"I'm sorry to say that I didn't have suspicions about either of them," Emilio said. "The phone is hers, but we can't be sure he's not involved too. We'll sort that out later." He called out, "Someone tell me the distance to Pézenas."

"About seven-hundred-fifty kilometers," the analyst said.

"I need a jet," Emilio said.

"I'll have one scrambled," Tavassi said. "Let me call General Bayssas in Marseilles. We're going to need his Scorpion group mobilized." He shouted to the room, "People, get me everything there is to know about Sabine and Charles Morlet and Château de Morlet. I want it ten minutes ago."

~

MORNING CREPT IN, almost unannounced. The cloud cover was so heavy over Pézenas that the transition from night to day was muted. Pézenas was a small town of only eight thousand surrounded by agricultural land. Overnight, Lieutenant Gautier, the commander of Force Scorpion, had studied the maps, trying to find a staging area that wouldn't give away their presence. Emilio spotted a possibility.

"How about there?" he said, pointing to a rural spot about three kilometers from the château. "It looks like a Church property."

The Chapelle st. Siméon was an abandoned seventeenth-century hermitage, sitting on two acres of groomed land maintained as an historical site by the local Catholic diocese. One call to the archbishop of Montpellier secured its use. Gautier moved his troops from Marseilles by helicopter to keep them fresh and had the assault vehicles driven three hours to Pézenas. Six Bastion ACMAT armored personnel carriers, each capable of transporting six fully-armed men, left Marseilles at midnight.

The hermitage grounds were set back from the road, allowing the Scorpions to get ready away from prying eyes. General Bayssas brought the municipal police at Pézenas and the Montpellier Gendarmerie into the mix to assist the operation and prevent accidental interference.

At ten in the morning, Gautier huddled on the hermitage lawn with Emilio, the local police chief, and a Gendarmerie colonel, studying a map of the Château de Morlet obtained from the Pézenas planning department.

"I don't like it," Gautier said. "They could be anywhere on the property. Here, in these barns and stables. Here, in the old church. Here, in the cellars. Here, in the main house, distributed among reception rooms on the ground floor or bedrooms on the second and third floors. There are thirty rooms. More than six-thousand square meters of space. It's the size of an office building. If we go in blind, there could be many casualties. The Élysée Palace won't accept this outcome."

"What about drone surveillance?" the Gendarmerie officer said.

Gautier surveyed the slate-gray sky and said, "The ceiling is too low. A drone flying two hundred meters over the château will be heard. The weather is going to be horrible all day. Besides, it won't tell us what's going on inside."

"What about thermal imaging?" the police chief asked.

"Through a slate roof and limestone walls?" Gautier said. "Impossible."

After a fruitless discussion, Emilio said, "I think our best chance is direct surveillance. There's only one road leading to the château.

If we position unmarked vehicles by the side of the road here and here, if we're lucky, we'll catch someone leaving the property going either direction."

"Then what?" the police chief asked.

Gautier liked the idea. "Then, we do our magic and make them talk."

∼

CAL WAS UP EARLY, but the guard outside his room wouldn't let him out until nine. When he was brought down to the kitchen, he saw a few men pushing carts of breakfast food toward the church. Sabine was finishing a meal with Gaby and Pierre.

"Don't look so glum," Gaby said. "It's not their last supper. That will be their lunch."

"You know you're not being amusing, don't you?" Cal said.

"Take a coffee, Professor," Sabine said. "Let's talk. Just the two of us."

In the lounge, Sabine asked him what he planned to say to get them to capitulate.

"I'm convinced whatever I say won't make a difference," he said.

"You mustn't fail. Whatever the outcome, today will be my last day," she said with an eerie serenity. "I can see how uncomfortable I'm making you, Professor. By the end of the day, church bells will toll in sorrow or in thanksgiving. I pray the cardinals make the right decision so I can leave the world with the sounds of thanksgiving in my ears."

Cal put his cup down and said, "I'm going to morning Mass."

"Who is officiating?"

"Cardinal Colpo."

"A hardliner," she said. "Not a good omen."

∼

COLPO DELIVERED THE AGNUS DEI, and the cardinals began lining up to receive Communion of scraps of bread. Suddenly, there was a commotion mid-line, and Dr. Bellisario was summoned. Cardinal Sauseda had fallen to his knees, vomiting.

"Help me get him to his bed," the doctor said.

Cal ran over, and he and Cardinal Macy lifted the Spaniard onto his cot. The doctor did a cursory exam of the delirious patient using the only tools available—his hands and his senses. He got a whiff of fruitiness on his patient's breath and stood up, furious.

"He has been skimping on his insulin doses," he shouted. "He ran out and had none this morning. He has ketoacidosis from dangerously high blood sugar. He'll be dead in a few hours without insulin. You promised me you would get it."

Henri and Felix withdrew to a corner.

"What did Sabine say when you spoke with you her yesterday?" Felix asked.

"She said he'd get insulin tonight if he's released. Otherwise, it didn't matter."

"Well, there's the answer."

Henri was on the verge of tears. "But the poor fellow is suffering," he said. "That's not right."

"There's nothing we can do," Felix said. "If you want to take a break, I'll tell the doctor."

"I don't care what she says," Henri whispered. "I'm going to get him his medicine."

"How?"

"I'll take one of the cars. The keys are in the office. I'll run into town and go to a pharmacy."

"Gaby will kill you when she finds out. Besides, you need a doctor's prescription. A French doctor."

"No, you don't. My grandfather has diabetes. He can get his insulin without a prescription. I'll be back in no time. Cover for me, okay?"

"Even if Gaby doesn't skin you alive, you won't get paid."

"I can't let him suffer."

When the Mass concluded, Cardinal Sanz addressed the group.

"Let us pray for Hilario. The young guard told the doctor he would get insulin. God willing, he will be in time. Today is the last day of this conclave in captivity. I suggest we take the first ballot. This afternoon, we will learn our fate. The Holy Spirit is among us. We are not in the hands of the kidnappers. We are in His hands."

Cal tried one more time. "I beg you," he called out. "Please reconsider your position. Please vote to live."

The chamber was silent until Cardinal Colpo shrieked, "I refuse!"

One of the men patrolling outside the castle came in, yelling for Gaby. She ran from the kitchen and met him in the front hall.

"One of our cars—the Dacia—just took off down the drive," he said.

"Who's at the wheel?"

"I didn't get a look."

She sprinted to the office to check the security monitors and began winding back the feed. Soon, she had her man, and she went tearing through the castle for the church.

She barged in as cardinals were casting their ballots and pulled out Felix.

"What the hell is Henri doing?" she demanded.

"He went to get insulin. Cardinal Sauseda is in bad shape. Henri lost in."

"Why the fuck didn't you stop him or tell me so I could stop him?"

Felix's balaclava concealed his fear. "He wouldn't listen to me, and I didn't want to get him into trouble. He said he'd be back within the hour."

"I'll deal with you later," she said. "Get your ass back in there."

Emilio saw the château's electronic gate swing open and a green car make a right turn onto the road. He had borrowed the police chief's personal vehicle and left it well off the road on a grassy verge opposite the castle. Anyone driving by would think someone had parked to go hiking in the forest or foraging for mushrooms. He slunk low in the driver's seat and got on the radio.

"Green Dacia, probably the one that picked up Donovan, just passed heading east toward the town. Single male driver."

Gautier responded. "Received. Will intercept."

At the intersection of the D13 and Rte de Caux, units of the municipal police and Marseilles Gendarmerie stopped the Dacia and pulled Henri Vaux out without incident. Emilio heard the traffic stop on his radio and sped back to the hermitage.

One of Gautier's men took custody of Henri and hauled him by his handcuffs to the back of one of the Bastions.

A policeman showed Gautier the contents of his pockets—a loaded Sig Sauer semiautomatic pistol and a black balaclava. The lieutenant motioned for Emilio, and they climbed into the personnel carrier, a low-ceilinged vehicle with two opposing benches. Henri sat on one, shivering with fear.

Gautier was a muscular and imposing man who used his size to intimidate.

"I'm not a policeman," he said. "I'm a soldier. Have you ever heard of the Scorpions?"

Henri seemed too scared to answer. He shook his head.

"We're the meanest motherfuckers in the French army. We don't take names. We take heads. We don't have rules like my friend here with the Italian carabinieri. We only answer to the highest levels of the French government, and those levels don't give a shit how I get the information I need. Say yes if you understand me."

A dry yes tumbled out of Henri's throat.

"What's your name?"

"Henri Vaux."

"How old are you, Henri Vaux?"

"Twenty-eight."

"You're young enough that you'll spend fifty years in prison before you die of old age. Cooperate with me, and you'll get less time. Are you going to cooperate?"

"Yes."

"Where are the cardinals?"

"In the castle."

Gautier smiled. "Good start, Henri. Are they all alive?"

"All but one."

Emilio worked the inside of his cheek and tasted blood. "Who is dead?" he asked.

"Cardinal Bol. He was shot."

"Who shot him?" Emilio asked.

"Gaby."

"Gaby, who?"

"Cerf. Gaby Cerf."

"Who is she, and why did she shoot him?" Emilio asked.

"She's Sabine's friend. Her lover. Gaby was angry because the American professor was followed."

"Is the professor okay?"

Henri started to bawl and snot like a child. "He's okay, but Cardinal Sauseda is sick. "He needs insulin. I was going into town to get it. Please let me get it and take it back to him. Dr. Bellisario says he'll die in a couple of hours if he doesn't have it."

"What about the other cardinals?" Emilio asked. "Today is supposed to be the deadline. What's happening with the voting?"

Henri got control of himself. "They keep marking their papers, *I refuse.*"

"Are they going to be killed?"

The question set him off again, and his chest shuddered. "I won't do it. They say they will shoot them this afternoon after the last ballot. I hope they don't."

"Is Sabine Morlet the one in charge?" Emilio asked.

"Yes."

"What about Pierre Abadie?"

"He's there."

"And Charles Morlet?"

"He's dead. Gaby shot him. He was going to go to the police. Please let me get the insulin," he sobbed. "Let me go back."

"It's okay, Henri," Gautier said. "You seem like a good guy, but you're not going back. That's not going to happen. This is what's going to happen. We're going to bring you a map of the interior of the castle. You're going to show us where the cardinals are being held. You're going to tell us how many armed men there are, where they're stationed, what weapons they have, what kind of training they possess, and the location of security cameras. If you talk fast, we'll be able to get the cardinal the help he needs before it's too late."

***

THE THREE MODERN Cathars met for lunch in the formal dining room. Sabine led Gaby and Pierre in a simple prayer of thanks, and they passed around the salad bowl and a loaf of crusty bread.

Sabine caught Gaby constantly glancing at the wall clock and said, "Checking the time isn't going to bring Henri back sooner."

"It's two hours. Two fucking hours!" Gaby said. "He ran away, or he went to the police. Take your pick."

Pierre grunted. "He's a good boy. He wouldn't have done either. Maybe he had an accident. I should take a car and go looking for him."

"We need you here," Sabine said.

"We need to double the number of men on the grounds," Gaby said. "If they come at us, I want to know as soon as possible. And please, Bouli, don't pay Henri his share. And give Felix a haircut for failing to turn him in."

"I'll take your first suggestion but not the second two," Sabine said. "I made wire transfers to the men's accounts this morning. Also, to your trust fund, Pierre."

"Thank you," he said, raising his glass of wine.

"Did we send another man to the church to take Henri's place?" Sabine asked.

"I shifted Marcel from kitchen duty," Gaby said.

"So, another disappointment this morning," Pierre said. "Two more no votes. The game is over if your professor can't get them to change their minds this afternoon. I've discussed it with the men. Only two of us will do the shooting. Me and Andre. Everyone else will have clean hands. Next to me, Andre's the oldest. He's killed before."

"Where?" Gaby asked.

"Mali. Six years ago. Operation Barkhane. He shot a bunch of Islamists."

"I'll do it too," Gaby said. "You forget I've killed before too. The blood is still on my shirt."

Sabine pushed away from the table and got to her feet. "No one is doing any shooting," she said. "Whichever way they vote, I'm freeing them. I can't kill them. I already called for the helicopter to pick them up at five o'clock. The men can scatter as soon as they're gone."

"No!" Gaby exclaimed. "You can't be serious. Why in hell did we go through all of this just to let them go?"

"We've made our point," Sabine said. "The world will know who we are, what we did, why we did it. Professor Donovan will go on TV and the lecture circuit, spreading our manifesto to millions. People will see the beauty, equality, and open-mindedness of Catharism and the ugliness, inequality, and close-mindedness of Catholicism. If we kill the cardinals, we'll be labeled as villains and crackpots, and Catharism will be dead forever."

Gaby was on her feet too. "Was this your plan all along? To pull the wool over everyone's eyes? The cardinals? Our men? Pierre? Me?"

Sabine looked weary and small. "I can't remember when I made up my mind."

"Then why keep up the stupid charade?" Gaby said. "Go to the church and tell the fuckers they're off the hook. Give your precious professor a bottle of cognac and let him spend the afternoon drinking."

"Because I still have hope they'll break down and vote for the nun," Sabine said. "I would like to die knowing we beat them and finally avenged Geralda and all the fallen Cathars. I don't measure revenge by the number we slay. I measure it by change. It doesn't matter whether the change is voluntary or by force. Once they vote for equality, there's no going back."

∽

CAL HAD a bread-and-cheese lunch with the cardinals. He sat with the American delegation, trading stories about Pope John, the first American pope.

"I hope you're going to be able to get out of here," Palmer said to him at one point.

"Sabine said she's cutting me loose," Cal said. "She hopes I'm going to be the Johnny Appleseed of Catharism."

"It sounds like it was an interesting sect," Deetz said. "If we survive this, I'd like to do some reading."

"There's a book in this," Macy teased. "Another Cal Donovan bestseller."

"Hopefully, you'll write the forward," Cal said.

"From your lips to God's ear," Macy said.

Before they started the final rounds of voting, Cal stopped by Sauseda's cot. Dr. Bellisario was looking funereal.

"He is almost past the point of no return," the doctor said. "There's nothing I can do without insulin and fluids. I suppose it is fortunate that many here can administer last rights."

∽

AS THE SCORPIONS began loading into the Bastions, Gautier noticed Emilio checking the magazine of his Glock.

"What do you think you're doing?" he asked.

"I'm wishing I had another clip," Emilio said.

"You're not going with us."

"You're not going to stop me. They're my cardinals. They're my responsibility. I'll walk if I have to, but I'd prefer a ride."

Gautier pulled a magazine from his tactical vest. "We use Glock 17s too. Let's get you a vest, then have you find a seat with my guys."

Under a blanket of charcoal clouds, the convoy of Bastions rumbled out of the hermitage onto a single-lane road leading toward the castle. On the way, they encountered a farmer on a tractor who stubbornly refused to give way until Gautier climbed out of the lead armored personnel carrier and pointed a gun at the old fellow with a roll-up dangling from his lips. The farmer dropped his cigarette and pulled onto the grass.

Gautier's plan was simple. The castle sat roughly in the middle of two-hundred acres of land. They knew from Henri that the hostages were in the church at the rear of the castle. Two Bastions would approach the front gate, holding back and out of sight until four Bastions were in position off the road to the rear of the property. There was no high ground for snipers, and given the weather, drones were still out. Two dozen troops would deploy on foot from the rear, creep up on the church, and hold fifty meters out. When they were in position, Gautier would storm the gate with two Bastions, drawing fire from the front and engaging hostiles. During the firefight, the Scorpions at the rear would enter, secure the church, and protect the hostages until the threat was neutralized.

∼

When Gaby stormed in, Sabine was in the bedroom, making the bed and tidying her things.

"Don't," Sabine said.

"Don't what?"

"Don't be angry at me. Not on our last day."

Gaby sank to the rug, pulling her knees to her chest. "You're right," she said. "It's Sabine's world and Sabine's money, and I'm just along for the ride."

"We're a team," Sabine said. "We've always been a team. But I can't agree with you. I won't kill them."

"You've never been as angry as me," Gaby said. "They didn't hurt you the same way."

"Let's not have a competition about who was more damaged, Bear. Let's just say goodbye to this wicked world feeling good about what we accomplished. Let's—"

They startled at the sound of gunfire and ran to the windows. Two olive-green armored vehicles were barreling through the meadows, muzzle flashes coming from gun ports. The Bastions stopped a hundred meters from the house, and soldiers spilled out of the backs, firing.

Sabine saw one of her men collapsing by the front door, clutching his throat.

She screamed, "No!" at the sight of Pierre Abadie running toward the soldiers, firing his rifle, before he was cut down.

She yelled, "Come back!" and heard Gaby shouting back from the hall, "Stay there. I'm going to the church."

The cardinals heard wild gunfire and froze in fear. Cal was thirty years from his army training, but the muscle memory was still there.

"Everyone, get down!" he screamed. "Pull the cots over you!"

The gunfire got closer. Outside the church, men were shouting and screaming.

The door to the courtyard was open to let air in, and their guards, Felix and Marcel, rushed to close it. They were near the threshold when two soldiers and Emilio Celestino burst through, firing rounds point-blank into their chests.

Cal was at the center of the church and was about to hail Emilio when Gaby appeared at the hallway door, letting out a bloodcurdling scream. Cal saw Cardinal Bizimana getting up to see what was happening, and he threw himself over the African as Gaby pulled the trigger of her AK-47. He heard a long burst of automatic fire as bullets struck stone and flesh and felt blood splashing against his face.

Cardinal Macy was a couple of meters from Gaby. He, too, had ingrained youthful memories of diving for a loose ball on the basketball court. He pushed Cardinal Colpo out of harm's way and launched his big body into the air. Gaby saw him coming and swiveled her hips to redirect her fire, but his arms found her knees. She yelped as she landed hard on the stone floor. Macy worked his hands to the barrel of her rifle and grabbed it. It was hot as a stovetop. He screamed in pain but kept a purchase on it with one hand while delivering a punch to the side of her head with the other. That loosened her grip enough for him to get control of the firearm.

"Go ahead, shoot me!" she screamed, picking herself off the floor.

"I'm not going to do that," Macy said, "but I want you to leave."

Cal was on his feet in time to see Gaby fleeing into the hall and Macy holding her rifle.

Just then, the rest of the Scorpions barreled through the courtyard door.

Cal heard men groaning and praying out loud.

He heard Dr. Bellisario calling for medics and first-aid kits.

He saw soldiers fanning out to form a protective perimeter around the survivors.

He wiped the blood away from one of his eyes—someone else's blood, and looked around, not understanding why he couldn't see Emilio.

He found him lying on his back by the courtyard door, staring at the church's vaulted ceiling. Blood was gushing from a hole in his trousers from a torn artery.

Cal clamped his hand on his thigh and pushed down as hard as he could.

Emilio turned his head. "Cal," he said. "Tell Eli—"

And then he slipped away.

Gaby ran up a rear staircase to avoid the gunfire coming from the front hall. She found Sabine sitting placidly on the bed as if all hell wasn't breaking loose around her. A pistol rested on her lap.

"You're safe, Bear," she said. "I was afraid—"

"I'm here, Bouli," Gaby answered, sitting beside her.

"It's going to be very short Endura," Sabine said.

"Followed by an eternity in Heaven," Gaby replied.

Sabine fingered the amulet around her neck and said, "I am Geralda of Lavaur, defender of the faith."

Gaby took her hand. "And I am Aimeric de Montréal, Lord of Lavaur, defender of Geralda."

Lieutenant Gautier reached the top of the stairs. From down the hall, he heard two gunshots.

CHAPTER TWENTY-SIX

MICAELA AND ELISABETTA WANTED EMILIO'S FUNERAL TO BE AT THE family church, Santa Maria in Trastevere. Carlo Celestino refused to participate in the decision-making. He told them he never wanted his son to be a policeman, withdrew to his bedroom, and refused to come out. His daughters smelled his pipe smoke creeping under the door but left him alone.

Of the thousands of condolences Elisabetta received, the first was hand-delivered by Cardinal William Donahue. His meaning was clear enough—please don't ask the next pope to remove me from my position at Santa Maria Maggiore. Elisabetta asked her secretary to throw it away.

It soon became apparent that their church could not accommodate the number of people who wished to come. The venue was changed to St. Peter's Basilica, with the family priest from Santa Maria officiating. The attendance was as large as Pope John's funeral. Most of the Vatican Gendarmerie and Swiss Guards were there, with many members of the Curia, the Italian government, and dozens of cardinals. Sergio Tavassi, Cal Donovan, Dr. Massimiliano Bellisario, and the president of Italy were among the pallbearers. At the service, Micaela and Elisabetta flanked their father, linking arms. A family friend remarked that no one had ever seen Micaela wearing black.

The College of Cardinals resumed the conclave a week after returning to Rome to give three lightly-wounded cardinals a chance to participate. Five cardinals died at Château de Morlet. Samuel Bol was the first casualty. Gaby's final volley killed Jaime Mamami of Peru, Mark Palmer of San Diego, and Samuel Laguerre of Haiti. Hilario Sauseda died of a diabetic coma before he could be evacuated.

The other casualties at Pézenas—Pierre Abadie and his men—were buried in private family ceremonies. Sabine Morlet's wishes were granted. She and Gaby Cerf were interred, side-by-side, at a cemetery in Lavaur. Their headstone bore a yellow cross.

CNN asked Cal to resume his on-air commentary during the conclave, but he turned them down. In deference to those who lost their lives, he held off on releasing Sabine's manifesto to the media. There would be a time and a place, but he was in no mood to think about the Cathars.

On the afternoon the cardinal electors returned to the Sistine Chapel, Elisabetta invited Cal to her office to await the result of the first ballot. There was a sense that this would not be a lengthy conclave, which proved true. At six o'clock in the evening, white smoke wafted into a perfectly blue sky.

Cal and Elisabetta leaned out her open window at the Apostolic Palace, their eyes, and the eyes of the masses of pilgrims, on the loggia of St. Peter's Basilica.

The protodeacon was the first to appear on the loggia. A step behind him was a tall man in white.

"We were right," Elisabetta said.

Cal resisted the urge to touch her hand. "Yes, we were."

Victor Macy, Cardinal of New York, took the name Pope John XXV, telling the crowd that his predecessor had been taken too soon.

Cal whispered, "Good man," and let tears streak his cheeks.

CAL HAD BEEN AWAY from Cambridge for too long. The day before his departure, he accepted an invitation to a farewell dinner at Carlo Celestino's apartment. When he arrived, only Micaela and Carlo were there.

"She called from work," Micaela said, pouring Cal a vodka. "She'll be here soon."

Emilio's absence was so palpable it was hard to make conversation. Carlo sat in his chair, looking forlorn, his unlit pipe in his mouth.

Micaela was back in her usual rainbow colors. She said, "Oh, the hell with it. You're smoking all the time when we're not here. Go ahead and light it, papa."

Carlo brightened a little and began puffing away.

Cal noticed some crumpled papers on Carlo's side table near a pad filled with equations.

"Are you back to work on Goldbach?" he asked.

It was Carlo's lifelong quest: to solve the unsolvable Goldbach Conjecture, the problem in theoretical mathematics that kept the old man going.

"I've had a new idea," Carlo said, a cloud of Cavendish smoke enveloping him.

"Good. Keep at it," Micaela said. "Don't stop till you've beaten it. We all need a Goldbach. What's yours, Cal?"

Before he could answer, his personal Goldbach came through the front door. Elisabetta glanced at the clothes tree in the hall where Emilio would hang his suit jacket and holster and swept into the living room in her habit and veil.

"I'm sorry I'm late," she said.

"Are you going to change?" her sister asked.

"Give me a minute." She smiled at Cal and made a remark about the lit pipe.

"I should lose my medical license," Micaela said.

Elisabetta looked exhausted, but to Cal, she was as lovely as ever. He stared at her a little too long to capture an image in his mind to take back to Cambridge.

"What kept you?" Micaela asked.

"The pope wanted to see me."

"Good," Micaela said. "Who's he picking as your successor?"

Elisabetta poured herself a glass of wine, sipped it, and said, "He asked me to stay on as secretary of state."

Cal watched her face as he listened to Micaela and Carlo doing the verbal equivalent of spitting into the gutter.

For his part, he said, "It's the right decision."

"What did you tell him?" Micaela asked.

Elisabetta normally nursed her wine, but this time, she finished it in two more swallows.

"I told him no."

Carlo said, "Hallelujah. That calls for another beer."

"I'll get it," Cal said, moving toward the kitchen. He wanted a minute to collect his thoughts, and was surprised that she followed him. He took a beer from the fridge and turned to her.

"What do you think Emilio wanted to tell me?" she asked.

"I don't know," he said, "but I'm sure it was loving."

"I'm sure you're right," she said. She had her arms stiffly by her side, as if she didn't know what to do with her hands. "Even before he died, I was doing a lot of thinking."

He let her speak.

"All the battles, all the hatred—it takes a toll."

He took an expectant breath.

"I've made another decision. I'd like to go to Cambridge with you."

Suddenly, the beer felt awkward in his hand. He put it down and watched her remove her veil.

The only thing he thought to say was, "Can I kiss you?"

And she said, "Yes."

THE END

ABOUT THE AUTHOR

Glenn Cooper is an internationally published thriller writer with over eight million copies sold in thirty translations. Many of his twenty novels have been top-ten bestsellers. Cooper has a degree in archaeology from Harvard College and a medical degree from Tufts University School of Medicine. He practiced internal medicine and infectious diseases before becoming a biomedical researcher and biotech CEO. He has also written numerous screenplays and produced three feature films. He draws on his experiences and studies to create fast-paced thrillers with historical, philosophical, religious, and scientific themes.

For more information visit his website:
glenncooperbooks.com

- facebook.com/GlennCooperUSA
- amazon.com/stores/author/B002L10BFU
- bookbub.com/authors/glenn-cooper
- goodreads.com/glenn_cooper

ALSO BY GLENN COOPER

The Will Piper Trilogy:
Library of the Dead
Book of Souls
The Keepers of the Library

The Down Trilogy:
Down: Portal
Down: Floodgate
Down: Pinhole

The Cal Donovan Series:
Sign of the Cross
Three Marys
The Debt
The Showstone
The Fourth Prophecy
The Lost Pope

Others:
The Cosmos Keys
The Tenth Chamber
Near Death
The Resurrection Maker
The Devil Will Come
The Cure
The Taken Girls

Printed in Great Britain
by Amazon